MIXED

MIXED

A NOVEL

BEKA J. PEREZ

THE PAPER HOUSE
PUBLISHING

Copyright © 2024 by Beka J. Perez

All rights reserved.

No part of this publication may be reproduced, distributed, or transmitted in any form or by any means, including photocopying, recording, or other electronic or mechanical methods, without the prior written permission of the author, except in the case of brief quotations used in critical reviews or scholarly articles. Any unauthorized reproduction, storage, or transmission of this work, or any part thereof, is strictly prohibited by law and may result in legal action.

Published by The Paper House

www.thepaperhousebooks.com

Published in 2024

Printed in the United States of America

For permissions, requests for excerpts, or inquiries regarding the use of this material, please contact the publisher or author directly through the official website.

To the women who have opened their hearts to me, you've been my collective muse over the years. I'm in awe of your ability to love without conditions, forgive the unforgivable and find the strength to start over, again and again.

To my Enigma—thank you for loving me in spite of myself. You're my constant reminder that there is still good in this world.

I'll always be your girl.

To Kai—Thank you for all of the light and joy you've poured into this dark and twisty world. Your love and friendship changed the course of my life.

To my boys–being your Mama has been my favorite thing of all and I will love you forever and always.

To all of my readers out there who are thriving somewhere in the middle, riding the fence and swimming in the grey of uncertainty, I see you. It is a rare and precious gift, in this polarized world, to have the strength to admit that you don't have all the answers and to continue to love those who demand you pick a side. Empathy and compassion will always keep you somewhere in the middle. Be happy, there.

To my Father—even when the doubt creeps in, I will never stop seeking your light. Thank you for loving me, with no conditions.

Thank you to my editor, Emily, for tolerating my inexperience and pulling more out of me than I ever thought I had to give.

CONTENTS

1. June 2023 — 1
2. February 2022 — 11
3. February 2022 — 19
4. February 2022 — 29
5. March 2022 — 35
6. 1971-1983 — 49
7. March 2022 — 55
8. March 2022 — 63
9. March 2022 — 71
10. March 2022 — 77
11. March 2022 — 85
12. 1983-1993 — 95
13. March 2022 — 99
14. March 2022 — 111
15. March 2022 — 119
16. April 2022 — 123
17. 1993-2003 — 131
18. April 2022 — 143
19. December 2001 — 153
20. April 2022 — 159
21. April 2022 — 167
22. April 2022 — 175
23. April 2022 — 185
24. 2002-2019 — 193
25. May 2022 — 203
26. May 2022 — 209
27. May 2022 — 225
28. May 2022 — 233
29. May 2022 — 241
30. May 2022 — 249
31. May 2022 — 257
32. May 2022 — 269
33. May 2022 — 279
34. May 2022 — 287

35. May 2022	297
36. May 2022	307
37. May 2022	315
38. May 2022	323
39. May 2022	331
40. June 2022	339
41. June 2022	351
42. 2020	361
43. June 2023	369
44. June 2023	375
45. June 2023	387
About the Author	397

ONE
JUNE 2023

I ONCE SAW A PICTURE ON SOCIAL MEDIA THAT STAYED WITH ME. My friend, who was grieving the loss of her mother, posted a photo of two hands. One hand was younger, glowing from a recent trip to Bahli, nails perfectly manicured and painted a pale pink like the color you see riding the edge of a cloud across a sunrise. It held another hand, which was grey and bloated from the lack of oxygen. There was a space between the nail polish and cuticle that told me it had been about six weeks since a loved one sat at her bedside, talking to her while painting her nails for the last time. There were no words to the post, just the picture that said so much. It articulated the last hours, minutes, the last breath, the final exit, the essence of a beloved mother that vanished like the dew on a summer morning.

My own mother moved to Florida when I was in college. It was always her dream to return to Tampa Bay, but it wasn't long after her move that she was diagnosed with breast cancer. She fought the good fight, had a double mastectomy, radiation, and chemotherapy and yet thirty years later, the monster returned. By the time they caught it, it was in her bones and lymph nodes, so she decided to forego treatment and move forward with end-of-life care. I flew down to Tampa and made all of the arrangements to have her moved into a hospice facility on the intercoastal. I rented a little vacation bungalow on the water and became fast friends with the owner, Jake, as I flew back and forth to visit my mother as much as I could. I was back at home, in Middle Tennessee, having breakfast with my husband, Gabe, when I received the call from her hospice team. She was transitioning into the active-dying phase. I should come quickly, they said.

Fueled by caffeine, I took the redeye from Nashville to the Tampa International Airport and rented a car. It was early in the day as I crossed the Courtney Campbell Causeway and continued on SR 60 towards the intercoastal. I was running on two hours of intermittent sleep and in desperate need of more coffee. I pulled off the road at the next coffee shop and sat in the ridiculously long drive-through line. As I inched forward, I thought about that social media post again and I imagined my friend as she sat by her dying mother, her heart full of love and gratitude, the memories of playing at the beach, picking out a wedding gown, fawning over the first grandbaby, all of the closeness they experienced through the decades flowing between those two hands. I knew the experience I was about to have with my own mother would be quite different.

As the cashier reached through the window to pass the coffee to me, she smiled and said, "Have a blessed day."

"I'm going to visit my dying mother," I snapped. "How's that for blessed?"

"Uh...I'm so sorry," she mumbled. And then she froze, unable to move or speak which made the drive-through window look oddly like a picture frame.

"Will you just give me my muffin so I can get out of here, please?" I was crabby and tired and out of patience. I didn't want to be there, in the stifling, humid heat, on my way to a hospice center on the water to see my dying mother. I wanted to be back home with my husband and dogs, waking up to have breakfast together again on the deck in the cool mountain air.

I snatched the bag out of her hand and hit the gas. As I waited for a break in the traffic to turn right onto SR 60, a seagull landed on my rental car. He just sat there, on my hood, judging me with his beady little eyes.

"I know, I know," I said aloud to the bird. "I'm tired and cranky. I can't help it."

I thought once I started moving, the bird would fly away, but he didn't. The lazy bastard hitched a ride all the way across the bridge. I sat at a red light, thinking surely he would look up and see a friend soaring in the sky and take off to follow him, but again, he didn't. He held on as I turned onto the roundabout, his feathers trembling in the wind. He continued to stare at me as I pulled into the parking lot of the Crystal Waters Hospice Center. I wasn't in any hurry to go inside. I sat in my car with the air conditioning on full blast and finished my muffin and coffee trying not to think about the next few days when the essence of my own mother would vanish into the ocean breeze. As I opened the car door, my hitchhiker took a giant leap, spread his wings, and bummed another ride as the wind carried him to wherever he was going.

I walked into the building clutching my purse like I expected someone to jump out of the bushes and try to steal it. My whole body was tense, my shoulders were up around my neck. The dread of what was about to happen weighed heavily on my heart and body. I was an only child, and it was my duty, my responsibility. There was no one else. She has nieces but I didn't really know them. I imagine that she made some friends in the retirement community, but I had no idea who they were.

Gabe wanted to come with me, but I didn't know how long it would take, so I said no, not yet. I told him to wait until I saw her and had a chance to talk with the staff. They would know. They always knew. They were experts in death. They knew everything about the end of life—what it looked like, how it sounded, how much longer it would take.

I stood in the lobby and looked around at the place that had become my second home over the last five months. Palm printed sofas lined up against the wall of windows, framing the ocean view. In the middle of the room, there was a table with pamphlets arranged by topics such as "End of Life" and "Grief Counseling for Families." The ceiling was high, the air was cool and very quiet. An elderly woman, who I didn't recognize, stood up from the front desk and walked towards me.

"Hello, I'm Patricia," she said. "How can I be of service to you, today?"

She took off her oversized cat-eye tortoise glasses and put them on top of her head, tucking them into the tufts of her bright, white hair. Her voice was warm and kind. It was as if she could see the stormy clouds of sorrow all around, trying to suffocate me. To be honest, I just wanted to fall into her arms. I wanted her to hold me and tell me everything would be ok.

"Are you alright?" I heard her say.

I shook my head to bring myself back to the present. "I'm sorry… um..yes…my name is Farrah Acosta. I'm uh…I'm here to see my mother," my voice quivered as I said her name. "Mercedes Langford. She's in room eight," I cleared my throat, hoping it would help steady my voice and keep my knees from buckling.

"Hi, Farrah. Would you mind if I walked you back? Would that be ok with you?"

I knew that she could see my fragile state and so I nodded in agreement and followed her footsteps, counting the black and white floor tiles as we walked past each door. I was afraid to look up or to the sides. Every time I visited, a previously occupied bed was empty, or a previously empty bed had a new occupant who wouldn't be staying for very long. I lost count of all the moans, the cries, and the sound of stretchers moving down the hallway. It took a few weeks, but I learned not to look.

It took an eternity to reach my mother's room and yet, as Patricia opened the door, I still wasn't ready to go inside. I needed time, so much more time.

Patricia held the door open as I crossed the threshold, once again, into my mother's last and temporary home. I found her sleeping with pillows behind her head and underneath each of her arms. She looked peaceful and comfortable. I immediately looked at her fingernails. They were still the same warm apricot color I had painted them on my last visit. They looked pretty against the golden, deep beige tone of her skin. Patricia patted me on the shoulder and left me alone with my mother.

I stood at her bedside and took inventory of her body as I had done on every visit. I looked for changes that could tell me about the future. Her hair was combed, her lips were dry, her skin was thin and crepey, and her body was small and frail. I laid my hand gently on top of hers and thought about that photo, once more.

Though I loved my mother, I never understood her. To be honest, she was the reason I decided that motherhood would never be a part of my own journey. I saw how unhappy it made her and I wanted nothing to do with it. And yet, there I was, grieving the impending loss of my mother and also grieving the relationship I always wanted with her but never had. It was too late now. There would be no reconciliation, no change of heart. I would never get an apology from her, and I would never be able to say, "It's ok, Mom. I know you did the best you could."

I backed away from the side of her bed and sat on the sofa against the wall. I leaned my head back and closed my eyes. The exhaustion set in immediately. My body ached from the constant tension, and my head hurt from inadequate sleep and too much caffeine. My mind wouldn't settle down. I rubbed my hand across the sofa cushion, wondering how many others had sat in the same place, waiting for a loved one to die. It was a morbid thought and yet everything about that building, the room and sofa was all about impending mortality.

For those that were admitted here, there was no going home. This was the end.

My mind began darting in and out of other thoughts, lists of things to do and other things not nearly as important as the room I was sitting in and the reason why I was sitting there.

"Would you like a pillow and a blanket?" His voice startled me, and I jumped as I turned my head towards the door. It was Seth, my favorite nurse. He was a tall, muscular, middle-aged black man who wore white scrubs that highlighted the flecks in his goatee. The light that was floating in from the window across the room reflected on the side of his bald head. His eyes were gentle, and his smile was genuine. For people who believe in angels, Seth was one of them.

"I apologize for startling you," he continued in a deep, quiet voice. "I heard that you were traveling all night and I thought you might like to rest for a bit."

He put the pillow and blanket on the sofa cushion beside me. "Can I get you anything else? Some water or a snack?"

I thought about asking for a time machine, a rocket ship, or an escape hatch. "Some water would be nice. Thank you," I mumbled.

"I'll be right back," he said as he slipped quietly back into the hallway.

I just wanted to rest my eyes for a moment, until Seth returned with my water. I leaned over and let my head sink into the pillow. I took a deep breath, and my body immediately surrendered as my tired mind faded into unconsciousness.

"Farrah!" She shouted from somewhere in the distance.

"Mom?" I shot up too fast and had to give myself a moment to allow my blood pressure to catch up. I stood slowly and walked the three steps from the sofa to the bed. She was still sleeping, peacefully, in the same position. Did she really call my name? Did I dream it?

I returned to the couch and looked at my watch. It was almost noon, which meant I slept for three hours. I grabbed the bottle of water that Seth had quietly left in the room during my nap and then opened the French doors onto the small back patio to sit for a few moments. The humid air hung thick and heavy in the breeze and carried a slight scent of seaweed and fish. It made me nauseous, but I needed the sunlight.

It took only fifteen minutes before the heat became overwhelming, so I decided to go back inside. As I opened the door, the cool blast hit me and as my eyes adjusted to the dimly lit room, I saw that Seth was sitting beside my mother.

"Hi Farrah," he tilted his head to the side. "Did you get some sleep?"

"Hi, Seth. Yes, I did." I gave him a half of a smile. It was the best I could do.

"Would you like to sit down with me and talk for a bit?" He asked, almost in a whisper.

I had a feeling I knew why he wanted to talk to me. "Sure," I hesitantly agreed.

We sat down together on the sofa, one on each end, facing each other.

Seth extended his hand, barely touching my arm as he said, "You know she is reaching the end of her time with us, right?"

"Yes. I mean, that's what they said when they called me. It would help if someone could be more exact about how much time she has left. Can you do that?"

"Farrah, your mother is actively dying. We use that term to describe the last two or three days of someone's life. We can't know exactly when she will pass, but we do know it will be soon."

"Can you tell me exactly what is going on with her that tells you she is at that point?" I needed details to understand it and was hoping that the brutal facts would help me to accept it.

"Her blood pressure has dropped significantly, her breathing pattern has slowed and has become irregular. She hasn't been conscious for the last twenty-four hours."

JUNE 2023

"What am I supposed to do now? Is there anything I can do for her?" I looked back at my mother, so quiet and still, slipping further away from me as each minute passed.

He turned towards her as he patiently explained what would happen next. "She doesn't need much at this point. Her body is doing what it's designed to do. She doesn't need food or water or the things you and I need. We will manage her pain, comfort, and hygiene until she leaves us. The most important thing she needs right now is to know that she is loved and not alone."

Kind of like what I needed from her as a child? I thought to myself.

Are you aware she requested another visit from her priest?" His eyebrows were raised, creating lines in his forehead and it felt like he was asking me a question to which he already knew the answer.

"She has a priest? No, I was not aware of that," I was embarrassed and looked away, hoping to hide the fact that I was a terrible daughter.

"A priest has visited her several times during her stay, here. She made it clear that when she enters the actively dying stage, she wants additional prayers at that time."

I shook my head in disbelief. I had never known my mother to be spiritual. The only times I remembered her going to church were for weddings or funerals and for Christmas Eve Mass when my Aunt Maria visited occasionally.

"No, I had no idea. So do I need to call the priest?" I could feel the heat of shame rising in my face, giving me away.

"We already contacted him. He'll be arriving later this afternoon." He reached over and patted the top of my hand.

"Ok," was all I could muster as I looked down, around and up at the ceiling.

"Have you had lunch?" He asked.

"No, I'm not that hungry."

"You should try to eat a little something."

"I know. What I really need is a shower and a change of clothes." The dried sweat and embarrassment felt sticky on my skin, and I wanted to scrub every bit it off my body and out of my mind.

"You are welcome to shower, here," He stood up and gestured towards the bathroom.

"I'd rather not. Do you think I have time to go to the rental house where I'm staying? I should only be about an hour or so."

"I think that would be fine. We have your number in case we need you. Go take care of yourself." He gently demanded.

"Thank you, Seth. I'll be back as soon as I can."

I didn't waste any time. I grabbed my purse and headed down the hallway as quickly as I could, keeping my head down until I saw the tile floor transition to wood planks that signaled the safety of the lobby. I waived to Patricia and headed out the door into an explosion of heat no one should have to endure. It was offensive to my skin and lungs and sweat began to pour off of my body. I opened the car door and was met with a rush of heat that almost made the outside air feel cool. "Who would choose to live on this hellfire island?" I shouted to no one specifically.

I turned the car on, put the air conditioning on full blast and then stepped out to stand under the shade of the trees until the interior of the car reached an acceptable temperature. I checked my email on my mobile to see if Jake had sent me the entry code for the bungalow. He was on it, as usual, and said it was no problem if I checked in early.

As soon as it was safe to re-enter the vehicle, I drove the four blocks to the bungalow, grabbed my suitcase and went inside. Jake had placed a large fruit basket on the kitchen island with a card that said, "Take good care of yourself." His kindness made me cry as I tore open the plastic wrapping. I took a seat on a barstool, unpeeled a banana and ate it with the salt of my tears sneaking in with each bite. I laughed at myself, and how silly it was that even with all of the sorrow in my life and the unfairness in the world, it was the simple acts of kindness that always brought me to tears. After pulling myself together, I guzzled a bottle of water and headed to the bathroom to wash the airport and seaweed odors out of my hair.

JUNE 2023

I turned the shower on cool and stepped in, lifted my head towards the faucet and let the water pour over my hair and face. I was shivering, but I didn't care. It was invigorating and felt so much better than the ridiculousness that was going on outside. After finishing my shower, I drowned my skin in my favorite sesame oil and wrapped my body and hair with the big fluffy white guests towels Jake so generously provided. I went to the bedroom and picked out a maxi sundress and sandals and returned to the bathroom to blow-dry my hair. After applying a little bit of waterproof mascara and a dab of lip color, I stepped back and gazed at the woman in the mirror. I was twenty years younger and about two inches taller, but my face was my mother's. The warm beige skin, wavy chocolate hair, even the auburn flecks that danced around the pupils of my big brown eyes, it was all from her. The evidence was all there, she was definitely my mother, but the chasm had always been there too, denying us the closeness I had always envied when observing other mother and daughter relationships. I hung my head, not wanting to see my mother's face looking back at me in my own reflection. The disapproval, the judgement, it was too much for today. Ready or not, I was about to become a motherless daughter. I grabbed another bottle of water and headed out the door, not entirely ready to brave the inevitable discomfort that was sure to come.

TWO
FEBRUARY 2022

I WOKE UP A DIFFERENT PERSON THAN WHO I WAS YESTERDAY. SOUNDS weird and dramatic, I know, but it's true. True in the sense that I was grieving the end of what had been a significant chapter of my life but hopeful that it may also be the beginning of a new adventure. Yesterday marked the last day of my corporate career. When I opened my eyes this morning, I had no direction or agenda, no calendar ladened with meetings, no alarm clock, no projects, and no back-to-back conference calls late in the evening to accommodate clients across the globe. At first, it felt wildly liberating to be able to just go wherever the day took me. I had one goal, and that was to find my real passion and a way to make a living doing something that I loved.

My career, as an analyst, took off right after college. Like young graduates sometimes do, I bounced around large corporations for a number of years before landing a sweet job with a consulting start-up, collecting, and analyzing data for small to mid-size companies. The organization was headed by a group of young, ambitious, entrepreneurial boys who quickly realized, much to their benefit, that they needed some diversity on their team. Not to brag, but I was good at my job and had a knack for office politics. Eventually we built our process into groundbreaking software and were courting Fortune 500 companies. An executive at the age of thirty-eight, C-suite by forty-five, it seemed as if the universe just continued to propel me forward. But all along, while success continued to level me up, I always felt as if I didn't belong there. It wasn't that I hated my job. In fact, there were parts of it that I actually loved. But I was a spectator, watching the years of my life just fly by. So, I quit.

That makes it sound like the decision was easy. But daring to imagine a different life, especially one that didn't include my lucrative salary, was terrifying. Since my husband, Gabe, spent his career in civil service, I was the primary bread winner. There were so many things to consider, and this would be a life-altering change for both of us. We met with our financial advisor to create a plan forward and once the plan was in place, I submitted my resignation. The executive team and the board did everything they could think of to retain me, but I stuck to my guns. I was done.

I started the first day of my new life out on the deck with my two Australian Shepards, Ouiser and Truvy. Ouiser, a two-year-old blue merle was my shadow and no matter where I was, she was always touching or leaning into me. Truvy, my three-year-old black and white, was more independent. She always stayed close but liked her own space. I sat down on the outdoor sofa with a hot cinnamon tea, a yogurt biscuit drizzled with honey and some introspection, while the dogs found their spots at my feet and immediately fell asleep.

It was late February, and the air was crisp and cool on the bluff. The sun was shining, and the occasional clouds would float by and hug the mountain tops in the distance. It was a good day to be unemployed and yet my brain had not caught up to the reality that I no longer had to think about work. Occasionally, a project that I had been sponsoring would pop up in my head and I had to remind myself that I no longer had to entertain those thoughts. That part of my life was over.

In the months leading up to my resignation, I waffled hourly, sometimes even daily, trying to navigate between those intense feelings of restlessness and guilt for not being content with the life I had been so graciously afforded. This morning was no different. The initial euphoria was immediately followed by a non-specific feeling of anxiety that invaded my thoughts. Had I made a mistake? Who did I think I was to turn my back on a career that had been so kind and generous to me? Had I lost my mind?

At some point, when I was a child, I learned that worrying served me well. It became a mode of preparation of sorts to help me avoid unwanted surprises, so much so that my daddy always called me his "little worry wort." I never knew, in my younger years, that the relentless brain chatter was not normal. It was just a part of my life, a constant companion that was always around. Eventually, I gave it a name—Eris, the Greek goddess of strife and discord. She was a constant fusspot and very meticulous, which sometimes played out well in my career. Because of her, my foresight was excellent, and I was able to avoid major pitfalls in new projects and implementations. My team often teased that I was psychic because I had already thought of anything and everything that could go wrong and created a plan to work around it.

In real life, though, Eris was a total bitch. She liked to play out horrific scenarios. She was an expert on my fears and insecurities and liked to remind me of them on a regular basis. The graphics in my presentations could have been better, I could have picked a nicer suit to wear for the board meeting, no one would take me seriously because I was so short and on and on she went. She reminded me constantly that if I wasn't the best, I wasn't good enough.

She was also extremely adept at acting out the many ways one could die. Spider bites, car accidents, train derailments, plane crashes, and falling down a flight of stairs were her areas of expertise. She had my funeral planned to the last detail, including the location, flowers and music. It wouldn't be a celebration of life. There would be a lot of crying and wailing by the only two guests that loved me enough to attend, my husband and my best friend, Corrina.

As I grew older, I learned that I didn't have to let her go on and on. When she showed up, I would tell her to shut up and most of the time that seemed to work. Other times though, she wouldn't be quiet no matter what I did. But there was no way I was going to allow her to ruin my first day of freedom.

Determined to find a new purpose for my life, I grabbed my mobile and used the notepad application to make a list of all the many hobbies I had dabbled in and parts of my former career that brought me true joy. The list was ridiculously long. I guess somehow, I always knew that I wasn't in the right place. Otherwise maybe I wouldn't have been searching for the next thing that had the potential to lead me to that illusive state of contentment.

I was always envious of those people who seemed predestined to serve the world in a certain, narrow, and intentional capacity. Like the universe had decided before they were born that they would be a professional athlete or concert pianist or a world renown pediatric cardiologist. They had these large glaring gifts that were impossible to ignore. They were put on this earth to make it better in a very exact and purposeful way. Their paths were certain. Their futures were crystal clear. There was no questioning for them, no pondering, no agonizing. Just a straight line forward to their destiny. You know the kind of people I'm talking about. Not all of them are famous. I've been jealous of my dentist, my friend that transports organ donor parts all over the country, even my hair stylist when she's in the back room working magic with tubes of hair color like a sorceress. And there I was, on the deck with my dogs after three cups of tea, trying to find a new career that could justify the reason for my existence.

Yes, it felt silly, but I kept going. Looking through the list again, I deleted all of the hobbies that, at some point, I had abandoned. I started many of them simply because it was something new, something I didn't know how to do. Things like gardening, crocheting, and repurposing old furniture, they were challenging me to achieve, while also daring me to fail. Some challenges I mastered, some I quit because of boredom and others I failed to achieve because Eris convinced me that it was ridiculous. And let's be honest, I wasn't going to make a living making multicolored beanies or selling my little cherry tomatoes that I grew in the same pots that I bought from a parking lot outside my local hardware store.

Eventually, I narrowed it down to four possibilities. What these four things had in common is they relentlessly kept calling me back, again and again. *Executive coach, painter, writer, and photographer.* I know what you're thinking, that one of those doesn't belong. And I agree. I knew that no matter how much I loved coaching and developing others, it would require me to get back into the corporate world and my appetite for that was gone.

With three options left, I wasn't sure what to focus on first. I didn't learn how to paint until I was in my thirties. It started out as one of those things I knew nothing about. The most artistic thing I could claim were the doodles on my notepad during a boring conference call. But the challenge was calling out to me, urging me to try. So, I bought books and I worked at it.

At first, I was into realism, painting animals, faces and landscapes. I spent months learning about shading, but if my painting didn't look exactly like the photo, I threw it away with disgust. Gabe, the sweet guy that he is, used to run behind me to the trashcan and collect my discarded works of art. I discovered he had been doing that when I was cleaning out the garage. I found a big box with a bunch of rolled up canvases, my failed attempts at finding my life's purpose. Then one weekend, I took an abstract art class, and I fell in love with the freedom to express whatever I wanted in any way that I felt like. No rules, no boundaries, just my imagination and a paintbrush. And while I've never stopped painting, I've also never had the confidence to put a price tag on a single finished piece of art.

My love for photography has been around as long as I can remember. I used to sit in a dark room with my dad, watching him develop prints. He was an amazing photographer and had an eye for capturing moments that spoke to the heart. I'd like to think he passed that gift on to me, but I had no desire to make a career out of it. It was something that I loved doing for me and, on occasion, for those that I love.

And then there was writing. In college, writing papers came easy to me and I thoroughly enjoyed it. Two of my professors talked to me about my career path, wondering why I was majoring in business when I clearly had been blessed with the gift of writing. One of them even made a life-long standing offer to edit my book, should I ever write one. She was old then, so I'm sure she is no longer with us. Probably a spider bite.

I'm sure you're wondering if I took all those career and vocation tests that are out there on the internet. Yes, I did that too, even before I resigned. Nothing appealed to me. Nothing grabbed me. Nothing even reached out, daring me to fail, like I did before when I tried to crochet monogrammed beanie hats for Corrina's daughters, and they turned out four sizes too big. Or when I tried to grow a little vegetable garden in the backyard and all the deer had a feast before I could harvest one single tomato or pepper.

I read one article that said I should think back to when I was a kid and what I wanted to be when I grew up. The author went on to explain that whatever I thought about when I was a child, before life jaded me, was my original purpose and I should follow that path. So, I took it seriously and thought back to the original hopes and dreams of my youth.

In the late seventies and early eighties, I was obsessed with Quincy, M.E., a popular television show about a medical examiner who investigated causes of deaths using clues from the bodies of the deceased. At the age of nine, I had married myself to the idea that I was going to become a forensic pathologist and solve hideous gruesome murders with my intelligence and witty sarcasm. But then one day in high school, a girl projectile vomited on me. I had hot tomato chunks all over my sweater, stuck in my hair and smeared all over my shoes. I gagged, involuntarily, for days on end and decided that I could not tolerate working with anything that had to do with the inside of the human body. My senses were not built for appalling sights and smells. My hopes and dreams were crushed, and I believed that author to be full of shit.

So, I decided to stick with my list and choose that one thing I could wake up every morning excited about doing and it felt like I had made substantial progress. I was proud of myself but realized I could probably use some help deciding on which of the three I should tackle first. Gabe was no help at all. He was either too kind to be honest or he truly believed I would be successful at anything I set my mind to doing. So I decided to call a friend and get her opinion on my ideas. She was my truth sayer, the one that loved me enough to show me my blind spots, even when I didn't want to see them.

What I didn't know was that call would change the course of everything. My future was about to unfold and at an extremely fast pace.

THREE
FEBRUARY 2022

Corrina Lane Bannerman, my closest friend for most of my adult life, lives in Kentucky with her husband, Judge, and their two girls, Vassy and Lauren who are both college students. Corrina's house is about a three-hour drive north of where my husband and I just built our dream home in Middle Tennessee.

Life is always busy, but we've tried to stay in touch as much as possible. Once a month, Corrina and I meet halfway at a little café that sits on Shanty Hollow Lake in Southern Kentucky. Corrina is my anti-Eris, and I couldn't wait to bend her ear and get her advice. Although it was not our regularly scheduled date, I texted her to see if she could meet me for an impromptu lunch. She texted back immediately.

"You or laundry? I'll take you."

I texted back, "I feel so loved. Don't be late, as usual."

I met Corrina right out of college. I had taken a job as an analyst at the big county hospital where she worked as a labor and delivery nurse. I was in front of her in line at the local deli, when I heard a guy making inappropriate comments about how her ass looked in her scrubs. The more she ignored him, the more adamant he became to get her attention. After the third or fourth remark, I had enough and turned around and asked her if she wanted to trade places.

"I'll buy your lunch every day this week if you do that for me," she said with a relieved sigh.

So, we traded places and he just kept on going. He moved to the left to get a look at her again and I moved to block his view. He moved to the right and well, you can see where that was going. We made our way through the food line and started over to the cashier. That guy was relentless, making those disgusting grunting noises, staring. It was so pitiful, so gross. I just had to help him out.

"Hey, guy. You are lying to yourself if you think you have *any* chance of ever getting with that woman. She is a goddess. You're a short, premature balding prick with bad skin and a striped sweater vest. You're creepy. Go away. Don't come back."

I made Corrina keep her promise to buy my lunch every day that week, and she's been my closest friend ever since.

It was a beautiful day for a drive to the cafe. Horse and cattle farms dotted the back winding roads that were outlined by black fences. In the spring and summer, the fields were usually full of wild purple coneflowers offering their nectar to the drunken bees and fluttering butterflies. If the sun was shining, my Jeep would go topless. It was a little too chilly for that today, but I enjoyed the drive, nonetheless.

I arrived about fifteen minutes early and grabbed my camera out of the back seat. The backdrop never got old, and I loved seeing how the landscape changed as the earth moved around the sun. I found a place to sit on the big rock that hugged the edge of the lake and began shooting the sun-kissed diamonds that were floating on the water. Winter had undressed the enormous red maples and basswoods for the season, and they made the perfect frame.

"Farrah, I'm here," Corrina said as she sat down on the rock beside me while leaning her head on my shoulder. I leaned back into her and rested my hand on her knee. If I was ever lost, I only had to see my friend and I was home again.

I took a deep breath and immediately felt the tears stinging my eyes, the kind that just show up like an uninvited guest. Since I received the gift of perimenopause, tears seemed to accompany every little emotion, and the ever cool, calm and collected Corrina was not about to give me any grace.

"Are you crying *again*?"

"Yes. I'm happy to see you. Or at least I was about thirty seconds ago."

"Seriously, Farrah. You're *crying* because you're *happy* to see me?" She was *laughing* at my emotional suffering.

"Well, I *was*. *Now* I'm crying because *you* just hurt my feelings."

"You're a mess," she shook her head and continue laughing at me.

"You have no idea. But you're about to find out how big of a mess I really am, my friend."

She pulled away, lifted my chin, and wiped my cheeks with the sleeve of her sweater. "I'm famished and very thirsty. Can we remedy that, please?"

We went inside to the bar, ordered a couple of boozy sweet teas, some turkey and avocado sandwiches, a mixed greens salad and French fries with a side of ranch and then moved our little party onto the back patio of the café. We laid all of the food on the table like a mini-buffet and shared our lunch with each other like we had for the last three decades.

"So, Farrah Langford-Acosta, tell me *all* the things dirty and scandalous and I promise to hold it against you," she smirked as she folded her hands under her chin.

"I quit my job." I opened my mouth wide, anticipating her surprise.

"Say again?" She lowered her sunglasses and her chin while raising her eyebrows, clearly questioning my sanity. Unlike other friendships, Corrina and I talked openly about most things, even money, and she knew what I had given up.

"Yep. My last day was yesterday."

"And I'm just finding out about this now because…."

"Because up until the last day, I wasn't sure if I would have the courage to actually do it. But here I am, all void of ambition and very unemployed. Besides being incredibly lost and confused, I need *you* to help me figure out who *I* am because I really have no idea."

"Well, I'm quite sure that's *your* job, not mine. I do find it interesting though, that because you aren't working, you've seemed to have lost your identity. I mean, you're a person outside of your career. So, what's with the angst?"

"This isn't a new thing for me. It's not a mid-life crisis. I've felt this way since I finished school, like I took a wrong turn somewhere." I admitted.

"Really?! Why didn't you ever say anything?" Corrina asked, completely shocked.

"I'm not sure. It's been this dormant thing that has popped up every once in a while. Most of my life has been focused on work, my marriage, and my friends, but in the moments when I've been alone, and my mind wasn't preoccupied with other things, I would just daydream about a different life. I guess that is why I've never mentioned it. For many years, I just chalked it up to a kind of fantasy," I sighed. "But over the past few months, I started thinking about the parts of my life that I have really enjoyed and the things that felt most natural to me. And I came to the realization that while I've been successful in my career, I'm tired of feeling like an imposter and it is time to do something else. I made a list this morning. Here, look," I handed my phone over to her and waited as she read my list.

"Painter. Writer. Photographer." She lifted her head and looked me dead in the eyes, "Farrah, you're not that good of a painter, girl," she grinned in that perfect way she always does when she insults me.

"But that isn't the point, now, is it?" I remarked, snatching my phone back. "And besides, I could be, asshole, if I had been putting all those lost, corporate years into it."

"Maybe," she shrugged. "What do they say? It takes thousands of hours of practice to turn someone into a master of a craft? So, if you put in eight hours a day into painting, starting today, we could schedule an art show in, oh, about three and a half years. I mean, Grandma Moses didn't start painting until her seventies. You have a couple of decades on her, at least."

"Your sarcasm is not my favorite thing about you," I retorted. But she had a point. I was fifty years old. Who was I to be so whimsical at this age? And just then, Eris showed up to remind me that I had something to fear, to be insecure about.

"Oh shit, Corrina. This is stupid, isn't it?! What am I doing? What have I done?" I put my hands over my face. I was embarrassed about my decision to give up on my career. I had agonized over it for months and now I felt so ridiculous.

She reached over and put her hand on my shoulder. "Don't go diving in the drama dumpster, Farrah. You're navigating through a major life change. It isn't supposed to feel cozy. We don't get neon signs about what direction to take. We're all just trying to feel our way around in the dark, here."

We sat quietly as we took in the scenery while finishing our lunch. The breeze coming off the lake was cool, but the sun was warm on our faces. Corrina slid down in her chair, leaned back and closed her eyes. "You know, Farrah, maybe any direction in life is ok as long as you're being a decent human being along the way. Do you know how many people have been born on planet earth?"

"Like, since the beginning of time?"

"Yes, take a guess."

"No. I will not."

"C'mon"

"Nope."

"Just try. I wanna see if you're even in the ballpark."

I was done with her reindeer games, so I ignored her last plea.

"Fine," she said as she sat up, opening her eyes. "I don't know the *exact* number. But I know it's a lot. Like a hundred billion or something like that. The sad fact is that most of us will not make an indelible mark on the world. We'll live, we'll die, and we'll soon be forgotten after we're gone. I think my point is that we each do something, however small, to leave this place in better condition than how we found it. Give yourself a break and maybe try not to take it so seriously. What if your sole purpose in life was just to be here? Would that be enough for you? Life isn't all smiles and unending joy but even with all the grief and sorrow, I'm still glad I get to be here. With you." And then she closed her eyes again and leaned back to soak in some more sunshine.

"Yeah, I am pretty amazing."

She opened her eyes just to roll them at me and then closed them again with a smile. "So, take your time. Meditate. Clear your mind. You'll figure it out, I'm sure of it."

"I hope you're right."

And then she went silent again. After a few minutes, she lifted her head and continued looking at me. "While we're here, I have something to tell you, too," She swallowed hard and then said, "I think he found me, Farrah."

I just stared back at her for a moment. Then it finally clicked, and I shot straight up in my chair. "Why have you been holding out on me? You let me go on and on about my own little crisis and didn't say anything?! How?! When did this happen?!"

I got a call while I was on shift yesterday and then I heard the voicemail late last night. It just said, "Hi. This is August Collins. Please call me back at your earliest convenience."

"August, huh? How do you know it was him?"

"His voice was husky, velvety, just like his father's. And then, I snooped on his social media. He has my hazel eyes, Farrah. And my dimples."

"I'm still stuck on his name. Why do you think she named him August? He was born in July."

"Yeah, but the first of August is when she took custody of him. That must be the reason, don't you think?" Her voice was wistful. Her finger lingering across her mouth was her signature tell that she was feeling things she was not ready to say. I just sat there with her in silence, waiting for her to continue when she was ready.

"Here's this thing that I've been waiting for, the last thirty-two years, and now it's arrived. I don't know if I'm ready. And I don't know if I'm ready for everyone else to know. I haven't even told the girls. They know nothing about him. *And Mom*. I'm certainly not ready to deal with all of *that*."

"Yeah, Charlotte is extra, Corr. Gotta love her."

"Yes, yes we do," she quipped with a smile.

"Your life could be a book, Corr. You should write it all down, one day. Maybe they'll turn it into a limited series. The amount of crazy stuff that has happened in your life, it's extraordinary. Makes mine seem so boring."

"Are you saying that my shitty life could be someone else's entertainment?"

"Yeah, for sure. That or a lesson in resilience. Few people would survive everything you've been through, much less be thriving as you are. You have a story to tell."

"Well, you don't have anything to do. Why don't you write it?" We both threw our heads back and laughed... until we didn't. *Painter. Writer. Photographer.*

We sat there and looked at each other for a minute. I gazed at the phenomenon that was my closest friend. This tall, graceful gazelle, with her wildly curly hair, the sprinkle of freckles across her nose, her big, soulful hazel eyes, and her warm, amber skin. She was a stunner with an easy laugh and a brain that would intimidate most people. I'd known her since we were both twenty-two years old. I knew her wins, her losses. I knew her dark and twisty side. I knew her better than anyone.

I didn't know what to think. She just threw it out there in the wind. "Is that a joke? Are you joking with me?"

She took a second to answer. "Hmm...I don't think I am. Let's think this through, out loud, for a second," she leaned back in her chair, hand to her chin. "One," she held up a finger, "a writing project will keep you busy, so you don't turn into a lazy, good-for-nothin'-fifty-somethin' without any plans for the future."

"That's true. A lazy, good-for nothing-fifty-something is *clearly* not my goal."

"Two," she held up a second finger, "becoming a writer was on your list. And personally, I think you have a better shot at it than making a career out of those paintings that don't make any sense at all."

"You are unkind, Corrina Lane. So unkind." I shook my head in mock disappointment, but she was right. Though I loved my abstract paintings, they didn't make a lick of sense to anyone else. Kind of like quitting my job.

"And three," a third finger joined the other two, "it would be a clever way to get you into motion, so you don't stay paralyzed by fear, like I imagine you would." She gave me that sassy look that I loved and hated so much.

"No respect. Do you not love me at all? Even a little?"

"To be anything, you must start with *something*. To be a writer, you *must start writing*. Anything. Newton's 1st Law of Motion, right?" She kept nodding, trying to convince me that she was right.

I sat and thought for a moment and started to consider the possibility. "On second thought, I don't think your life is that interesting after all. I might have to find a more captivating subject to write about." I shrugged and took another sip of my drink.

"Liar. You've always been obsessed with my sad story, and you know it!"

"That's true but only because I had what most people would consider to be a normal, boring childhood. If it weren't for the gifts of travel and media, I would probably still think all humans grew up like I did. Think about all the people who never move, Corrina. They live and die in the same town as they were born. They never travel, never see the world outside of their little bubble. Their perspectives and belief systems are handed down through generations. The differences in our backgrounds are only one of the many reasons I'm obsessed with you. Speaking of motion, what is your next move with August?"

"I'm going to call him back, but I have to talk to Judge first. He was already sleeping when I listened to the voicemail last night. Not sure how this reality will hit him." She was quiet for a moment, staring at her food, before returning to the world. "I mean, he's known since before we were married but the idea of August becoming part of our lives, I just don't know." Her voice trailed off and her eyes drifted over to the lake.

"That man adores you and will do anything you need him to do, Corr," I said in hopes of reassuring her.

"I know. I just don't know if it is fair to upend the lives of the people I love, who count on me."

"Look. You don't know what August wants from you. He may just want to make the connection, see you, talk with you. Maybe it is a type of closure that he needs. *Or*… or *maybe* he wants a relationship with you. Point is, you don't know what he wants. When you're ready, just call him and find out. Then you can figure out what to do next."

We walked back to the parking lot, arm in arm and gave each other a long, lingering hug. I breathed in her hair that smelled of lavender and vanilla, not wanting to let her go. We walked backwards from each other towards our cars and waved obnoxiously as we said our goodbyes.

"Bye, my beautiful bitch," I shouted. "Thanks for the talk. You're the absolute best and I'll miss you!"

She stopped and took a dramatic bow, "I know, but it will be ok. Try to keep it together on the way home, ya big crybaby! I'll miss you more!" And then she blew me a kiss.

I hopped back in the Jeep to head home. The sun was heading west while I was driving south. I kept turning our conversation over in my mind. My thoughts bounced from Corrina and how her life was about to change, to my own life and the changes I wanted to make. The seed of writing a book had been planted and my mind went to work. The history and angles, conflicts, tragedy and sorrow, it was all there in Corrina's story. But I had a recurring thought that I couldn't escape. As I pulled up to my house, I sat in the driveway and called her. "Hey, are you home yet?"

"No. I stopped for takeout on the way. What's up?"

"I was thinking about our conversation and a thought kept creeping into my mind. Your story is incredible, but it goes back for generations. Nothing makes sense about your life unless one knows how it all came to be. Do you think your mothers would talk to me?" There was silence on the other end. Never one to simply react, she was thinking before she answered.

"Oh Farrah. Lovedy and Charlotte adore you, obviously. And while Clara hasn't met you, I've told her all about you and I'm sure she would love you too. I'm sure all of them would be happy to spend time with you. But there is a lot of unsavory history there, on both sides. Whatever you do with this, you would have to keep their anonymity. It is one thing to gab about these things over lunch but to write them down is another thing. *An enormous thing.*"

"I know, I know. But I have to admit, I'm getting excited about this idea."

She was quiet for a moment, then said, "I do have one question for you. I have two mothers and a grandmother that was like a mother to me. Where in the world will you begin?"

"That's the easy part. I'll start at the same place you did."

She laughed and then said, "Ok. You and Lovedy have fun. I'm sure she'll call me, but I want your take on it too. Keep me posted. Vassy and Lauren are coming home for dinner tonight. Gotta run."

FOUR
FEBRUARY 2022

I SAT IN THE DRIVEWAY FOR A MOMENT, ADMIRING OUR SPRAWLING, beautiful home, nestled among the treetops at the edge of the bluff. I felt so lucky to be able to live this life with a man that I adored and yet I also grappled with feelings of guilt for having so much when others had so little. I whispered "thank you" into the void and headed inside.

Gabe met me at the door, bent down and kissed me on the forehead. "Hola, mi chica hermosa," he said, as he grabbed the camera bag from my hands and took it into the kitchen. He had the idea that a woman should never carry anything if a man was around. Seems antiquated, I know, but somehow, it works for us.

Gabe was a huge, Hispanic guy. And by huge, I mean six feet, four inches, two hundred and thirty pounds of man. He had just retired from a thirty-year career in law enforcement and yet still woke up every morning with purpose and an amazing amount of self-discipline. He made the bed every morning, worked out three times per week and had a list of things to accomplish every day. He was two years older than me, and except for a little salt sprinkled in his hair, he really hadn't aged that much. Honestly, I found it a bit annoying.

"How was your lunch with Corrina?" he asked. "How's she doing?"

"She's good. There's a twist that I need to bring you up to speed on, but I'll tell you over dinner. I do have a question for you, though."

"Shoot."

"Do you ever feel guilty for having all of this?" I waved my arms around our enormous kitchen, with its lofty ceilings, cedar beams and state-of-the-art appliances.

"What? Farrah, we've worked our asses off for everything we have. It wasn't *given* to us. We both paid our way through college and have been working ever since. Why would I feel guilty because we are enjoying the fruits of our labor?"

"Yeah, I know. It's just that sometimes, when I think about the world, I feel like I won a lottery of some kind. I mean, our parents were never rich, but we weren't born into abject poverty either. Why not? Why not us? It just doesn't seem fair. Sometimes I feel guilty about it. Like, how much extra are we allowed to enjoy when three million children die of starvation every year? There must be some type of universal law that we are breaking here."

He walked over, wrapped his arms around my waist and looked down at me. Almost in a whisper, he said, "This guilt and anxiety you're always carrying around, it has to be so heavy. I do think you should talk to a therapist about it one day," he tapped his finger on the bridge of my nose. "But for now, I think this is too deep of a conversation for your first day as a lady of leisure. And to add to your guilt, I'm putting steaks and veggies on the grill for dinner."

"Seriously, Gabe." I playfully pushed him away. "You don't ever think about it?"

"Ok," he admitted with a defeated sigh. "I do. I do think about it. What I will say is that after thirty years of seeing the things that I have seen, I'm sure of one thing. Life isn't even close to being fair. It isn't just about the lack of nutrition or starvation either. There is disease, traffic fatalities, natural disasters, abuse, neglect, homicide, rape, mental illness. I could go on, but my point is that you're right, Farrah. It isn't fair. None of it is fair. And without knowing the logistics, I think we could *actually solve* world hunger and some of the other problems that plague our globe. The problem is that humanity is a greedy, selfish fellow and he would never follow through because he only cares about himself. Which I think makes it worse." He looked down at the floor and shook his head. "Ugh, this conversation is depressing."

"Yeah. We're all going to hell."

"I thought you didn't believe in hell."

"I don't, but I strongly believe in your grilling abilities," I grinned.

While Gabe was outside cooking dinner on the grill, I sat down on the loveseat with the dogs and began creating an outline for Corrina's story. *Every object moves in a straight line unless acted upon by force. Write something. Anything.* Corrina's words propelled me into forward motion. The entire story started with Lovedy.

Lovedy was Corrina's biological mother, or her "birth mom" as Corrina describes her. Lovedy had Corrina at a young age. She was seventeen years old when she brought a baby girl into the world. I'll never forget meeting her for the first time at Corrina and Judge's engagement party. I knew she was invited, and I couldn't wait to meet the woman who had given life to my favorite person. I also knew who she was the moment she walked into the room. A white, tall, lanky, woman with a warm confidence, a sleek, salt-and-pepper bob and an incredible sense of style, it would be impossible for her to blend in anywhere or go unnoticed.

Corrina called me over so she could introduce us. Lovedy ignored my outstretched hand and wrapped her arms around me. Stepping back, she held onto my arms, and with the kind of eyes that look into your soul, said, "Well, aren't you a beautiful, itty-bitty thing! Corrina, you didn't tell me she was this short or this pretty. My, my, girl. You really are a pretty one."

"Thank you, Mrs. Lachlan. It is such a pleasure to meet you."

"You can call me Lovedy. Now where is the bar? Mama's thirsty."

I put my hand on her back to guide her in the direction of the bar, at the same time looking back at Corrina with my mouth wide open. Meeting Lovedy was an epiphany. I always wondered where Corrina got her bold, brazen confidence. I made a mental note that we needed to have a nature-versus-nurture conversation. Based on my first impression, Corrina was more like her "birth mom" than her "earth mom," Charlotte.

Through Corrina's wedding planning and life events, I grew to know Lovedy better over time. Not that she would have given me a choice, but she became like a second mother to me. She was a force of nature, an oak and one of the strongest women I had ever known. The strength she exuded was not a front to hide some vulnerability or insecurity. She was made of steel, strengthened by fire, and I only knew the half of it.

I brought Gabe up to speed during dinner and told him of my plans to take a stab at writing a novel. He was supportive, as always, and just laughed when I told him I was going to start by talking with Lovedy. Rubbing his hands together, he said, "This is going to be *muey bueno.*"

Like that steak. Damn, that steak was good.

I spent the next week writing all I knew about Lovedy Barclay-Lachlan. I had learned quite a bit through Corrina, but Lovedy was a great storyteller. Funny, animated, she could hold an audience with ease, and I was more than happy to sit in rapture on many occasions over the years. Her southern drawl made every story more interesting and entertaining. But it would be the fool's notion to sum up this southern woman using any bias or assumptions. That lady was intelligent, educated and very perceptive. And to her family's chagrin, she was a raging democrat. I knew I would have to be up front with her about my intentions.

All it took was a phone call. I wrapped up the small talk quickly and then laid all my cards on the table. And there it was...that familiar silence I knew all too well. I waited, letting her think it through until she said, "Well, young lady. I would love to see you. Why don't you come out to the house this weekend and plan on spendin' a couple of days with me? We'll see where it goes."

"Ok if I arrive on Saturday, around noon?"

"That works for me, darlin'. See you then."

I spent the next two days packing and planning. My initial idea was to take notes during our conversations, but I did not want to miss something important; nor did I want to interrupt her in the middle of a story to ask her to repeat herself. I decided that I would record the conversations with her consent, which would allow me to be fully present during the time I had with her.

Though Gabe was supportive of my new quest, he wasn't exactly overjoyed that I was taking off for the weekend by myself. He wanted us to spend the weekend together to celebrate my early retirement and newfound freedom. But he could see that I was inspired to give writing a try, so he didn't push back too much and agreed to stay back and care for the dogs and the house while I was gone. I assured him I wouldn't be gone for more than a few days and that I would stay in touch as much as I could.

It seemed like this was really going to happen, which was exciting. And yet, the same nervous energy continued to plague me. The worrying, the constant mind chatter, Eris trying to ensure that I didn't make any mistakes...why wouldn't she just let me enjoy this new chapter in my life?

FIVE
MARCH 2022

Saturday came quickly, and I was pulling out of the driveway just after the sun came up. I had my podcasts and playlists ready to keep me company during the drive to western North Carolina. Typically, I enjoy road trips and the solitude it offers. Catching up on the latest true crime series or blasting my favorite tunes are not only things I truly enjoy but that render me a temporary sense of control over my life. And yet on this particular drive, I was feeling nervous. Eris continued to remind me that I had never drafted a novel before and that I had absolutely no idea what I was doing.

I arrived a few minutes early and was still feeling jittery. I was trembling a bit as I got out of the Jeep, so I paused a moment, took a deep breath, and looked around, trying to calm myself before I approached the house.

The sun was out and the light snowfall from the previous night was dripping off the rooftops. A moment later, Lovedy came out to meet me with her two boxers, Abbey and Costello, and instantly put me at ease.

"It is so good to have you here, darlin'. Leave your bags in the car. David will bring them in for you." She gave me one of her famous hugs and we headed inside, her arm still around my shoulder. It reminded me of a conversation we had years ago. She said, "Hugs are like handshakes. You're either a giver or a taker. If you decide to engage, always be a giver. Wimpy handshakes and hugs are simply weird, and nobody wants 'em."

It was my first time visiting her home. It was a modest ranch on a sprawling piece of land that sat across the street from a horse farm. She gave me a quick tour. The house was light and airy with zero clutter of any kind in any room. The furniture was traditional but high quality and built for comfort. There was a large free-standing garage out back that was bigger than her house. She caught me staring at it through the kitchen window. "I know, I know. There are *six* cars in that damn garage and *one* of them belongs to me."

"Don't get that woman started!" David walked in smiling, carrying my bags. He sat them down for a minute to give me a quick hug. I always liked David. I didn't see him as often or know him as well as Lovedy, but he was always so warm and welcoming when I was around him. With kind eyes, a ready smile, and a quiet way, he was simply easy to be around.

"Oh hush," Lovedy scolded as she started to shove him out of the kitchen. "He's leavin' for his first car show in about an hour. It is his first since the quarantine ended. He'll be out of our hair so it will be a girls' weekend!" When he was out of sight, she pointed to a large paper sack that was labeled "Whino Warehouse" and then did a funky dance across the kitchen floor.

When she was sure he was out of earshot, she filled me in. "He's been off the sauce for over twenty years, so I try not to drink around him. That would kinda make me a shitty wife. But when we go to social gatherin's, I like to have a beverage or two, and that's where he cuts me off. He says my mouth becomes a slippery slide at three drinks and one never knows what will glide out of it. So, I bought four bottles, three for me and one for you," she snickered. "We'll try to make 'em last all weekend."

After David left, Lovedy and I sat down to eat lunch. She had prepared chicken salad with grapes and apples, spinach leaves with mandarins, dried cranberries and creamy goat cheese, and a bottle of chilled, tart Pinot Grigio. We caught up on recent events, Covid, mostly. I was interested in her professional opinions about vaccinations and potential treatments. Lovedy is a recently retired nurse practitioner and was deeply knowledgeable about how the virus was managed in the United States and even in other countries. We caught up on the family too, mainly Corrina and her kids.

When we were full, I helped her clear the table and then we moved to the den and collapsed on her deep, cozy couch with our glasses and the remainder of the bottle from lunch. We sat close to each other with our feet up on the ottoman, sharing an oversized throw blanket. The dogs were snoring by the fireplace. We were full and relaxed and it felt like a suitable time to lay the groundwork.

"Lovedy, I want to tell you how much I appreciate you inviting me into your home and your willingness to spend some time with me. Since I decided to leave my career behind, this project gives me hope that I can still contribute, create, and give something back to the world. I don't know what will become of it, if anything, but I'm certainly willing to put my all into it. However it turns out, I just wanted to say thank you for opening your heart and sharing your story with me."

She looked at me with a sly smile and asked, "So, is this a biography? Or fiction? What is the genre you're after?"

"That's a good question. Corrina mentioned that anonymity would be critical. So, after a bit of research and planning, I've decided to collect all the stories and characters, put them in a proverbial blender and change the names to protect the identities of those involved. I also want you to know that I will approach these conversations with zero judgment. I'll probably ask you many questions, but you have total control over what you wish to share with me and what you prefer to keep to yourself."

"Well then! If no one knows it's me, I don't mind sharin' all the dirt with you. I am a bit curious to know though, who else is gonna be a part of this project?"

"Well, I'm obviously going to include Corrina. We've spent endless hours talking about our childhoods and the events that occurred before we met each other. But I'm sure I'll have questions for her after I speak with you and others. Then there is Charlotte."

"Of course, she raised our girl. Can't leave her out! Anyone else?"

"Yes, one more. I'm not sure how you will feel about this, but I want to include Clara Carter?"

She turned her head towards the fireplace and went silent for a moment. "Was that a question, a statement, or are you just wantin' to know how I feel about it?"

"I want to know how you feel about it."

"I have no issues with it at all. Clara has been a rock in my life and a huge influence in Corrina's."

"Good, good. So, one other thing. Are you ok if I record our conversations? I'll just put my phone somewhere nearby. No video, just audio and you won't even know it is there. Would that be ok with you?"

"Sure, I'm ok with that. If the slippery slide shows up, I may have to retract a statement or two," she said with a wink.

"Of course. As I said before, your identity will be completely protected, but you have the right to keep anything you want to yourself."

"Top me off and let's get this show started."

I filled both of our glasses. It was kind of strange how calm I felt inside and yet excited. No stress, no anxiety, no Eris. Just two women about to share their hearts with each other. "Ok, then let's start at the beginning. Can you tell me about your childhood?"

"I was born in 1954 and grew up next door," Lovedy began as she stood up and pointed outside through the window. "Well, the actual house isn't there anymore, but all of us were raised right over there on that lot where that new house is bein' built."

She returned to the couch and continued, "God and farmin' were the reason our town existed. My parents, Marshall and Caroline, ran a dairy farm that had been passed down through the family for generations. Daddy was a tall, strong, and handsome man and worked hard to provide for his family. We didn't have a lot of what we wanted but he saw to it that we had everything we needed. He always wanted a boy, but God saw fit to bless him with four girls. Faith is the oldest. Five years later, I was born. Hope came two years after me and then Patience, we call her Baby, came along two years after Hope. Mama had a miscarriage somewhere in there between Faith and me. She always said that lost baby was Daddy's boy."

"Did you feel closer to one parent more than the other?" *Certainly, I wasn't the only one.* I thought to myself.

"While Mama and I couldn't agree on anything, I was the apple of my Daddy's eye. My sisters did things that most people back then would consider normal for a girl, like playin' with dolls, takin' piano lessons or sewin' their frilly dresses, but I was different. I loved being outside, helpin' daddy tend to the cattle, playin' ball, climbin' trees, or fishin' in the creek. Barefoot in nature was my favorite place to be. I guess that's why Daddy and I were so close when I was little, we spoke the same language. He wasn't perfect, though. He had his secrets, one of which eventually tore us apart. But I'll get to that part later."

I wanted to follow up on that God thing, so I interrupted. "Quick question. You said religion was a big part of your childhood. Can you expand on that?"

"I could talk about that all day. I have some strong feelin's about it. Like most families in our town, we were a church-goin' family. Every Sunday mornin', Sunday night and Wednesday night, we were sittin' on those hard wooden pews, listenin' to the pastor tryin' to convince us to repent and ultimately avoid the lake of fire that was waitin' for us all. After Sunday morning sermons, the church ladies would lay out their Sunday dishes and everyone would eat together in the church hall. Because Baptists don't drink or dance or do anything that is considered worldly, eatin' was the center of every social event. Those food tables were covered with every kind of casserole you can imagine, vats of sweet tea, and a dessert table that was responsible for half those people havin' diabetes."

"It doesn't sound like you really enjoyed those church services. Am I wrong about that?" I asked, hoping my question didn't offend her.

"I didn't *hate* it, but we were kids, and it was hard to sit up straight and pay attention, service after service. I do remember reading "The Song of Solomon" over and over during church. Mama thought I was just following along with the pastor's readin' when really I was obsessed with King Solomon and how much he adored his first wife. They were passionately in love, and it intrigued me how he described her… it was quiet sultry," She lifted her eyebrows, making me laugh.

"How did he describe her?"

"He talked about her beautiful feet, described her legs as jewels and her navel like a round goblet that never lacked wine. He said her waist was like a mound of wheat encircled by lilies."

"Seriously? That's a little overkill."

"Wait, there's more. He talked about her eyes, her nose and said her hair was like royal tapestry and he was held captive by her tresses," she gestured to her own eyes, nose and hair as she described his writings.

"I've *got* to read this book…"

"He said her body was like a palm tree and her breasts were like clusters of fruit," she held her hands out in front of her chest like she was holding coconuts with a raised brow and a smirk.

"You *lie*, that is *not* in the Bible, Lovedy."

"I'm still not finished. Then he said he wanted to climb the palm tree and take hold of its fruit," to which she made grabby hands, groping the air.

"C'mon, you're kidding me, right?"

"I'm *not* kidding you," she raised her hand, swearing her truth. "Read it, you'll see why I was obsessed as a kid."

"Were your sisters obsessed with it too?"

"How do you think I learned about it?" She threw her head back and laughed, then continued. "Mama wanted us to present ourselves as a well-mannered, Christian family but my sisters and I were always gettin' into some kind of trouble at church. Baby had this thing about fartin'. She was always doin' a drive-by with the older ladies. They would be in a huddle gossipin' about someone and Baby would walk by, drop one and watch them scatter like roaches. I remember one time the preacher was doin' an alter call and…"

I had no idea what that meant, so I asked, "What is an alter call?"

"At the end of every service, the preacher would do an altar-call. That's when he would invite the same people that attended the same services, week after week, to come forward and surrender their life to Jesus. *Again.* Anyway, everyone had their heads bowed and their eyes closed, and Baby just lifted her cheek and let one go. It bounced right off that hard wooden pew and reverberated against the church walls. We knew if we laughed out loud during any service, we'd get an ass-beatin' when we got home. So, we all held it in as best we could.

Our faces were all red, void of oxygen, pew just a shakin' until Mama couldn't stand it anymore. She stood right up, waved her hands at the pastor and shook her head 'no' to let him know she wasn't re-surrenderin'. Then she pointed at Baby and directed her to the back of the church. She took Baby into one of the Sunday School classrooms and let her have it. Baby came back into the sanctuary just as they were givin' closin' announcements. As she scooted past us girls to get to the end of the pew, her tear-stained cheeks turned up into a big grin. She was totally satisfied with herself. The funniest part is that Baby knew very well what would happen, but the punishment was worth the crime just to get her sisters laughin' and piss off the old ladies in the congregation."

We both laughed for a while at that story and then I asked her, "Did you ever have those tent revivals I've seen on TV with the miracle healings and such?"

"Well, sort of. Every year, a revival tent would get set up in the pasture across from the church. Folks would come in from all the neighborin' towns to get yelled at by those preachers and put their precious few dollars into those gold plates with the red-felt bottoms. Those weren't the kind of revivals you've seen on TV, though. There weren't any miracles, snakes, or people passin' out. Those were good ol' Baptist revivals and they were always preachin' about the rapture and the book of Revelations or about how rock and roll music would be the vehicle that would carry many folks straight to hell.

Now, don't get it twisted. I loved those people in that congregation, but I was never able to reconcile the things they preached from behind that pulpit with how they treated people in our own community. We'll get to more about that later."

"Was religion practiced in your home, too? Or was it mainly a church thing?"

"Back at home, we always gave thanks before meals, and I would see Mama readin' her bible early in the mornin's. Mama and Daddy were always helpin' our neighbors. Daddy was great at fixin' farm equipment and findin' lost cows. He could always be counted on to go across the street to help the Widow Ruth fix a broken window or a leaky faucet. Mama was always visitin' sick people in the hospital or feedin' the elderly. They always told us that you get back what you give out and that helpin' others was the best way to make God happy. That part always made sense to me, and I still believe it to this day. Other than that, Mama and Daddy sometimes did stuff that the church would view as sinful."

"Oh yeah? Like what?" I leaned forward, curious about that part.

"She would turn over in her grave if she heard me tell you," she looked left and right like the woman herself rose from the dead and was standing over her shoulder, "but Mama would swear like a sailor when she was mad. I remember one time when I didn't get home before dark, she was mad as a hornet. She was screamin', 'Lovedy Barclay, you get up to your room and say your fuckin' prayers 'cause I'm comin' up there with the belt to beat your ass!'"

I laughed at the paradox in her mother's words but was very curious about the belt. "Sounds like physical punishment was a frequent thing in your house, huh?"

"I think it was a frequent thing in most homes in the sixties, especially in the bible belt. 'Spare the rod, spoil the child' was practiced in the literal sense. It was considered ungodly not to discipline your children and a sure way to push them towards the ways of a sinful world."

I was even more intrigued. "Interesting. What other things did they do that wouldn't have been condoned by the church?"

"Compared to other families in our town, our parents were considered fairly liberal. They would let us watch TV programs and even listen to secular music on the radio. In the sixties, the pastor was always preachin' against the women's movement, how it would destroy the Christian home. They believed women were created to serve men," she waved her hand in a dismissive way.

"They never liked women in the congregation to wear pants, work outside the home, or do salacious, ungodly things like wear shorts or wear a bathing suit in public. Dancin' or swimmin' with men would get you labeled as a Jezebel, being that you caused men to sin in their hearts. But my folks never cared about stuff like that. I remember one time, on a rainy day, us girls were playin' hide-and-go-seek in the house and Faith hid in Mama's closet. She found a romance novel hidden in the back corner behind her shoes. The pages were all worn like she had read the book a thousand times. Some pages were even dog-eared. Come to think of it, that's how my sisters and I learned about sex."

"Your parents never talked with you or your sisters about sex?"

"Well, yes, but not intentionally or directly. But we'll get to that part later, too."

I smiled and nodded in agreement, but my mind couldn't wait to get to those "later parts." "That sounds good" I nodded. "Didn't you meet Isaac as a child?"

"Yes," she smiled. "I did."

"How did you meet him?"

"Well, Daddy had a few workers that he brought in to help on the farm, but Jeremiah Carter was his best friend and his right hand. Daddy always said Jeremiah was the only man in town that he trusted. Jeremiah was strong, a lot like Daddy, a man of few words. You could tell he was always watchin' people. He was kind but guarded and fiercely loyal to Daddy. He worked on that farm like it was his own.

Jeremiah and his wife, Clara, had a son named Isaac. Durin' the summers, Isaac would often come to the farm with Jeremiah. After I finished my mornin' chores, I would pack lunch and run down to the barn just waitin' for him to get there. I would beg Daddy and Jeremiah to let him play with me. We just loved explorin' our little world together and we would stay outside all day until someone started screamin' our names.

Isaac was a year older than me. He was extremely smart and funny and a fast runner. Those summers would get unbearably hot so we would eat our picnic lunch and drink lemonade under the shade of those big oak trees. We swam almost every summer in that big creek out back and we were *obsessed* with collectin' bugs. We'd catch and glue them to a piece of barn wood and then scratch the names of each bug under their little bodies. As the years went by, Isaac and I became inseparable. And as we grew, our conversations evolved. I remember one time we climbed our massive Magnolia and spent all afternoon talkin' and dreamin' about the future. I wanted to be a nurse or a teacher. Isaac wanted to be a lawyer. Those were good days. Happy days.

Then, the summer after I turned fourteen years old, Isaac stopped comin' to the farm with his Daddy. I kept pesterin' Mr. Jeremiah, askin' where he was and why he wasn't comin' over. Jeremiah just said he had chores to do at home. Eventually, Daddy told me I needed to quit askin', and I cried every day for the rest of that summer. I missed my friend so much. About two weeks later,

Jeremiah stopped workin' at the farm too. Daddy said he got a job workin' at the hardware store, because it was closer to his home.

Another year went by, and the next summer, a bowlin' alley opened in the town next to us. One Saturday afternoon, Faith talked Daddy into lettin' her take all of us girls to go see it. We were so excited. We didn't have much money, so we couldn't bowl, but we all still wanted to go. We packed sandwiches and crab apples into a paper grocery bag, then piled into the wagon to start our little adventure.

Before we started our drive, we snuck over to Widow Ruth's place to steal some muscadine grapes off her vine that grew over the picnic table behind her house. We played rock-paper-scissors to see who had to make the heist. Baby lost. She always lost because we all knew she would always choose paper. But that girl could sure run fast. She took off and ran around just inside of the wood's edge, snuck up to the picnic table, and grabbed all the grapes she could, packin' them in her shirt that she rolled up from the bottom.

Widow Ruth came barrelin' out of her back door. 'Patience Barclay! I see you stealin' my grapes, girl. Wait 'til I tell your mama!'

Baby just kept on runnin'. With her arms holdin' the grapes, she kept pumpin' those skinny bruised knees so high in the air. At the same time, she was yellin' back at Ruth, 'And I'm gonna tell my mama you were flirtin' with Daddy again at the church brunch!' We were rootin' for her the whole way, 'Go, Baby, Go!' Faith hopped out and opened the tailgate of the wagon and Baby never even slowed down. She just threw her body, headfirst, into the wagon. Faith slammed it shut, hopped in the driver's seat and we took off, leavin' a cloud of cow patty dust behind us.

About twenty minutes later, we arrived at the bowlin' alley. We sauntered in like we owned the place not even aware that we looked and smelled like farm girls. Baby's shirt had turned purple on the front, and she smelled like Baptist communion and cow shit.

And then just like that, I saw the back of him, and I knew it was him. He was pushin' one of those dry mops across the floor. He wasn't a boy anymore. His muscles flexed as he moved the mop back and forth. He was tall. *So tall*. I just stood there in silence, not even aware that my sisters had walked away and sat at a table by the side entrance. I said his name out loud, more to myself than to him. 'Isaac?'

He immediately looked up and met my face with the same surprise. 'Love?' He looked me up and down in a way that made my body feel alive. I had grown up too and I think he noticed. I wanted to hug him. I wanted to punch him. How could he just disappear like that?

'It's me,' I said coldly and then I intentionally stuck my nose up in the air to let him know I wasn't happy. He walked up to me, now about six inches from my face and said, 'It's good to see you. How have you been?' He sounded so grown up. Manly. His voice had changed. It was like velvet caressing my ears. I pretended not to notice and snapped, 'I'm fine. Isaac, *where* have you been? Where did you go? I thought we were friends.'

And then his expression changed when he said, 'We were. I mean, we *are* friends. But Pops said we were gettin' too old to hang out together like we had been. He said your Daddy didn't like it much either and that he told Pops that I couldn't come to the farm anymore. I didn't have a choice. I've thought about you a lot, though. I've missed you, Love.'

And then I felt bad for being so snippy. I apologized for Daddy's behavior and told him he was just protective over us girls. Isaac understood and said he'd probably be the same way with his daughters one day. I invited him to go over with me and say hello to my sisters, but he had to get back to work."

"Wow. So, what were you feeling at that moment? Do you remember?"

Lovedy paused for a moment, then thoughtfully said, "I was feeling all kinds of things I didn't really understand. Excitement over findin' a long-lost friend, mad as a snake at my Daddy, havin' this attraction to someone I had loved since I was a small child and thoughts of not wantin' to lose him again. It was a lot for my young mind to process.

Eventually, I found my way back to the table with my sisters, but it wasn't even a question in my mind. I knew I would be comin' back. And the next time, I would brush my stringy blonde hair and steal a bit of Faith's lip gloss. Did I mention that Jeremiah, Clara and Isaac were a black family?"

I smiled. "No, but I already kind of knew that."

She smiled back. "You ready to take a break? I could use the restroom and I need to let the dogs out."

"Yeah sure. That sounds good to me."

She got up from the couch then turned around and winked at me. "The *later parts* are comin' up soon so you won't have to wait much longer."

"Oh thank the gods. Hurry back!"

There was enough wine for us both to have a smidge more. It was late in the afternoon at that point, and I wondered how much more she was going to share with me that day. I didn't want to push but I knew there was more ground to cover.

SIX
1971-1983

My childhood was vastly different than Lovedy's. To explain, I guess I have to start with my own parents. My mother's family was from Cuba. My grandparents moved to Tampa, Florida when my mother, Mercedes, and her older sister, Maria, were young children. They lived in the projects near Ybor City where my grandparents both worked in the cigar factories for many years.

My father, Thomas Langford, was of English descent. His family had settled in the United States generations ago. He met my mother while he was in Florida, attending college there. He frequented a Cuban cafe that was well known for its coffee and pork sandwiches. My mother was waitressing there and one day, he asked her out on a date. As soon as he finished school, they married and moved to Lexington Kentucky, where my father started selling insurance. One year after they were married, on July 2nd, 1971, I was born.

Unlike Lovedy, I was an only child and my house was noticeably quiet most of the time, except when my mother could be heard speaking Spanish on the phone to my Aunt Maria. When Mom was talking to her sister, she would come alive, chatting in a very animated sort of way, very unlike the mother that I knew. Other than phones calls she made to her family and her bouts of unhappiness, my mother almost never spoke Spanish in our home.

Actually, both of my parents had a quiet way about them, but for different reasons.

My father was a gentle, sweet man. There was a calmness, a quietness that seemed to come from his core. I never heard him raise his voice to my mother, to me, or to anyone, for that matter. He loved his work, his whiskey, his photography, his wife and I always knew that he loved me.

My mother's quietness seemed to come from a different place, an angry place, which was derived from a deep dissatisfaction with her life in general. She never liked living in Lexington and made sure to mention it every time we were in the car, driving around the city. She didn't hide her resentment towards my father for taking her away from Tampa and her family. She would always say that she didn't belong there, that she was "un pez fuera del agua."

Daddy did the best he could to make her happy. He worked hard to provide her with the things he thought she wanted. When I was six, they bought a modest tri-level three bedroom, two bath house in the suburbs of Lexington. On the weekends, he always took us to the mall, so she could shop for a new dress, hat, or purse. He doted on her, walking on eggshells most of the time to avoid the silent treatments that would inevitably occur when he said or did something wrong.

At an early age, I developed a keen sense of my surroundings and became an expert on the many moods of my mother. If she was humming to music while fixing breakfast in the mornings, I knew it was safe to go downstairs. If I didn't hear humming from my upstairs bedroom, I wouldn't go down to the kitchen until I knew Daddy was already in there. He was my buffer, my safeguard and we braved the very unsteady presence of my mother, together.

Despite being lonely, my childhood wasn't all bad. My father, sensing that I needed companionship outside of school, enrolled me in all kinds of extracurricular activities like gymnastics, dance classes and piano lessons. I loved competing and made it my mission to be better than all of the other kids. The only problem was that right before a competition or recital, I would be so nervous, I would throw up. It got to the point where I simply could not go on stage or on the mat unless I had vomited, first. I grew to count on it. It became my way of purging my anxiety and fear. The only thing I loved more than competing, was winning. Winning a trophy or ribbon always made my mother smile and clap and that was far better than any award they gave to me.

Mom would always remind me how much money they spent on those *frivolous* activities and demanded excellence in return. Mistakes were not tolerated in recitals or meets and could be avoided by trying harder and practicing longer. Every evening, while she was making dinner, I was required to practice on the piano for thirty minutes. Every mistake I made earned me an additional five minutes of practice until I got it right or it was time to eat.

There was no physical punishment in my home. Daddy would always sit and talk with me when I did something wrong. He believed in reasoning with children and providing guidance while also allowing children to learn from their mistakes. My mother yelled at me once and only once.

It was a Saturday morning, which was the day of the week that I would help her with household chores. I wasn't allowed to go outside and play with my neighborhood friends until my room was clean and I had completed whatever chores she had assigned to me. Once I was done, I would let her know so she could inspect my work before releasing me outside to play.

That morning, she noticed I had a shirt folded over the back of a white wicker chair that sat in the corner of my room. She began yelling at me, close to my face, bouncing in and out of English and Spanish as she walked towards me, forcing me to take steps backwards. She demanded to know why I left the shirt on the chair instead of hanging it up or putting it in the wash. Did I really expect her to believe that I had done my best work when I couldn't even bother to hang up my shirt? Though my mother had never laid a hand on me, there was something about her anger that made it hard for me to breathe and I would tremble in the face of her obvious disappointment.

My father was downstairs and heard the commotion. As soon as I heard him bounding up the stairs, I found my breath again. My shield, my protector had arrived to save the day. "Mercedes," he said in a quiet and even tone, "can I have a word with you please?"

My mother followed him outside in the hallway, closed my bedroom door behind her and then I heard their bedroom door close. I heard the muted tones of their conversation but couldn't make out the words. Then next thing I knew, Daddy opened my door and said, "Your chores are done, Sunshine. Go outside and enjoy this beautiful day with your friends." But I was too afraid that going outside would make her even angrier, so I just laid in my room, listening to mixed tapes on my cassette player.

But that was it. The remainder of my years at home, my mother never yelled at me again. She communicated her anger with silence or mumbling Spanish under her breath, both of which were louder and scarier than the one occasion in which she raised her voice to me.

Her tolerance for mistakes wore thinner as I grew older. "You should know better, you're old enough to know better!" was her favorite phrase to use when chastising me.

One weekend, we were getting ready to attend a wedding for one of my dad's work colleagues. I was in seventh grade and hadn't quite mastered the unruly waves in my hair. We were about to leave the house when Mom saw that I had knots in the back of my head. "Farrah," she said quietly. "Please go into the bathroom with me so I can fix your hair, properly." I followed her to the bathroom and stood quietly as she angrily ran the wire brush through the back of my hair, my head jerking back with every pull. "You should know better than to leave the house with this mess in the back of your head. You're old enough to know better, Farrah. Are you trying to embarrass me in front of your father's coworkers? They will think I don't know how to raise a daughter!"

"I'm sorry, Mom. I'll try harder to take care of my hair," I mumbled as I stood there, waiting for her to finish.

"Vamos, vamos a llegar tarde," she said under her breath.

But I didn't care. I didn't care if we were late. I only cared that I had disappointed my mother once again and I knew that my father and I would pay the consequences of my actions for the rest of the evening. And I was right.

Mom didn't say a single word in the car on the way to the wedding. Once the ceremony was over, she sat at our table in the corner of the reception hall, drinking her wine and not saying a word to anyone. She glared as my Daddy swept me up from my chair into his arms and danced the night away with me.

That was the same night I got my first period. I was embarrassed and ashamed. It felt like I had done something wrong. I didn't tell my mother, but I did tell my father.

SEVEN
MARCH 2022

Lovedy returned about ten minutes later and we resumed our positions on the couch with our feet on the ottoman, glasses in hand.

"Now, where were we?" Lovedy said.

I couldn't hide my anticipation. "You were at the bowling alley, mad at your Daddy and plotting your return!"

"Oh, yes. And my return was not the only thing I was plottin'. I kept lookin' around for Isaac but didn't see him again that day. When we got home, Mama got after us for stealin' grapes from Widow Ruth's vine. She sent us to our rooms and said we could stay there for the rest of the night and think about how we would make it up to Ruth, which was perfectly fine with me. I didn't want to see Daddy anyway.

It wasn't long after that when Faith moved out. She was twenty years old by then, had a job at the bank and found a roommate to share housin'. It was weird being one girl down. The dynamics in the house had changed. I started to think about my future when she left. None of my family had ever attended college, and it became a goal of mine. School was always easy for me, and I knew I could make somethin' of my life if I put my mind to it. I started babysittin' to earn my own money. I spent very little of it and hid the rest in a rain boot at the back of my closet." The similarity didn't escape me, so I asked Lovedy, "Because closets are for hiding things, right?"

"Yes. Yes, they are," she said. "Romance novels, money and other things, apparently." She had a frown on her face that made it seem like she knew more about hiding things in closets than what she had told me so far. And then she continued with, "Well, I might as well tell you this part. I would probably leave it out if I didn't think it mattered that much. But it mattered. It still matters."

Here we go, I thought to myself.

"Somethin' weird started going on at home with Daddy. He became a deacon at the church and just got stricter about some things. I knew he was always protective of us girls, but he started makin' new rules. Weird ones. One of them was that we were not allowed to sit next to any of the black boys on the school bus. He told us that if we broke that rule, we would be in big trouble. Well, the next day, Baby got on the bus and headed straight for the first empty seat next to a black boy that she could find. We were sittin' behind her, and she kept turnin' around and smilin' at us in defiance. Hope and I told her that she had to do dinner dishes for a week, or we were gonna tell Daddy what she'd done. Baby did the dishes every night that week, even when Mama told her it wasn't her turn. Mama's wrath was one thing, but Daddy's was a whole different ballgame.

She started shaking her head as she continued the story, "That new bus rule confused me a lot. I mean, Daddy's best friend was Jeremiah. Why did that suddenly become a rule? Why was race suddenly an issue for him? It made me think about Isaac and the real reason that Daddy wouldn't let him come to the farm anymore.

So, one day, I made up my mind that I was gonna ask him outright. He was workin' in the barn, so I headed down there and sat down on a bench just inside the barn doors. I tried to make small talk and slowly work my way into the conversation. Finally, I asked him if I could talk to him about somethin' important. He said, 'Sure thing. I noticed it's been a while since you wanted to talk to me about anything.'

I told him I was just a little confused about some things. Like, the new rule about us not being able to sit next to black boys on the school bus. Then I asked him if he had the same rule for Faith when she was my age. He didn't look at me, just kept hosin' down the floor and then said, 'Yep. I sure did.' Then I asked him the reason for the rule. He just said, 'Well Love, when girls reach a certain age, boys want other things from them than just friendship. And it is my job as a father to protect you and make sure you don't get into any trouble.' I knew what he was talkin' about, and he knew that I knew what he was talkin' about, so I just asked him outright why that rule was only about black boys. Didn't white boys want the same thing from girls too? He just said, 'I'm sure they do, Love. I'm sure they do.' Then I asked him why I was allowed to sit next to white boys on the bus. Wasn't he scared of white boy trouble too? He just sighed heavily and told me it was gettin' late, and he needed to finish cleanin' up before dinner.

I didn't like his answers or the way he was shovin' off the conversation. On the one hand, I could see where that conversation was goin', what it meant. But I just didn't want to believe it. I saw how the landscape was changin' in our country. I saw the marches and the riots and the social unrest on the evenin' news. By that time, Kennedy had been shot and MLK had been murdered. In the late sixties, they were bulldozin' black neighborhoods in cities like Charlotte and black families were moving to the north and west to find a place to live. And in response, white students were enrollin' in private schools by the thousands to avoid desegregation. But as progress continued to happen, white folks continued to push back. Picketing, bomb threats, it was awful. The schools around our town had been desegregated since I was in the fifth or sixth grade. But it was *never* a topic of conversation in our house. Almost like it wasn't really happenin'. I was almost sixteen at that point. Still young, but old enough to know when somethin' wasn't right. I saw what was happening in our own home and I wasn't about to let it slide or be swept under a rug. I was gonna keep at him until he said out loud what I already knew in my heart was true.

It was about two weeks after that barn conversation when I was helping Mama do some cleanin'. We were puttin' away our winter clothes in the attic, and she asked me to run out to the barn and get some moth balls in the supply closet. And that's when I saw it.

I wasn't snoopin', I was just lookin' for the box of moth balls. I just happened to look up on the top shelf and saw something shiny and red sticking out of a box. It was shimmering and caught the light just right. Whatever it was, it looked out of place in a barn. My curiosity got the best of me, so I got a ladder and climbed up there. I reached my hand into the box and grabbed what felt like a bed sheet and started pulling on the material. It just kept coming and coming, until it got stuck. So I yanked at it and the whole box came down on top of me. I lost my footing and crashed to the ground, hitting my head on the way down. There I was, on the floor with that big white sheet on top of me and a big knot on the side of my head. I just laid there, staring at the box that was resting on its side next to me. Its contents had spilled out, which included a matching mask with eye holes and pointy hat, a bright red cape and a pair of shiny boots that looked like they had just been polished. I wasn't sure which hurt more, my head or my heart."

Lovedy's demeanor had changed. She looked sad; her eyes were misty. I asked if she wanted to take a break, but she said no, that she was anxious to get past that part.

"I put everything back in the box and returned it to the shelf. My head was pounding, and I was so full of rage. I didn't know what to do. I grabbed the moth balls and headed back to the house.

Mama had changed clothes and was puttin' on lipstick. I asked her where she was goin'. She said, 'Oh, your Daddy and I are goin' out on a date when he gets back from helpin' Ruth out with her fence.'

And before I knew it, the words just flew out of my mouth.

'You've *got* to be kiddin' me. So, he's going to pull it out of her and then come home and stick it in you and you're gettin' dressed up for it?"

Mama was stunned. She got up close to my face and hissed, 'Lovedy Barclay!! What in the world, girl? Why would you say such a thing?'

My rage kept me from backin' down, so I hissed back, 'Oh, c'mon, Mama! You can't even pretend to stand here and act like you don't know Daddy has been layin' down with that woman for God knows how long.' But she denied it. Said she didn't know anything of the sort and then started to defend him, going on about what a good husband and provider he was and then shamed me for disrespecting him in his home, of all places.

But I saw it in her eyes. She was lying to me. I knew that she knew. And she knew that I knew she was lying. I started to back off and said, 'Well, Mama. I'm sorry if my words hurt you. They hurt me too, among other things.' I sat down on the bed next to her. After a couple of minutes, I whispered, 'I don't want to be here. Can I call Faith and have her come and pick me up? Can I stay the weekend at her place?'

Her shoulders were slumped. She looked defeated just sitting on the bed next to me, lipstick still in her hand. All she said was 'Sure, Love. That's probably a good idea.'

Faith came by and picked me up. I didn't even give her a chance to come inside. I had packed a small bag and was waitin' by the window. I ran out the door as soon as I saw her car pullin' up the dirt road to our house. It was a quiet car ride except for the radio and the wind from the open windows.

Faith was smokin' a cigarette. I watched her as she would take slow drags and then flick the ashes out of the window. The smoke kind of smelled good to me and I made a mental note to try it one day. She looked really cool with her red lips and nails. She had on big sunglasses and a colorful scarf tied around her head with her long blonde hair hanging loose. Finally, she asked me what was wrong. I had never spoken to any of my sisters about it but I trusted Faith and really looked up to her. So, I just said it.

'How long have you known that Daddy has been ballin' Widow Ruth?' Turns out, she had known since Baby was a baby. She had gone over to Ruth's house with Daddy once and saw them kissin' in the kitchen. Then she wanted to know how long I'd known.

I told her exactly when I found out, 'Remember when Baby stole those grapes on the way to the bowling alley? And Mama made us rake her front yard that whole fall season? Daddy had come over one time to burn the leaves. I went in the back door to use the bathroom and he came in at some point after me. They didn't know I was in there and I heard them talkin'. She was mad at him about somethin'. They were arguing like lovers do, not like neighbors. She was cryin' and I heard her tell him she loved him, and she was tired of waitin' for him to love her back. I waited in the bathroom until I heard them go back outside.'

Then I told Faith about the fight I had with Mama and explained that's the whole reason I asked her to pick me up. I felt bad about leavin' Hope and Baby there, but I just didn't want to be there when Daddy got home. Faith flicked her cigarette out of the window, reached over to touch the side of my face and said, 'Everything will be ok, Love. Mama will forgive him, like she always does. And they will go on pretendin' nothin' ever happened.' I knew she was right.

I figured while I was on a roll, I might as well ask her about the robe and hood. She didn't believe me. Said she never heard Daddy say a hateful thing about anyone in her whole life. And then she asked me if the robe and hood could possibly be someone else's. She thought maybe one of the men who worked for Daddy put it up there, or maybe it belonged to one of our uncles. I told her I wanted to believe that but if the costume had been up there for a long time, it would have had some dust or dirt on it, and it looked perfectly clean, even the boots. She still couldn't believe it. But I told her some things were true whether you want to believe them or not.

Then I asked her about the bus rule and why she thought it was only about black boys. And she said, 'I always thought it was because of Madeline Hendrix getting pregnant by that basketball player. That shook up our whole town. That girl disappeared pregnant and came back without a baby. Madeline was kicked out of the church and her whole family was shunned. They had to move! I think the bus rule was Daddy's way of makin' sure that didn't happen to any of us.'

I thought her answer was bullshit, so I shot back with 'Oh! And white boys can't get us pregnant? Sure, they can! I think that rule is about race and that having a baby that was anything but white would bring shame on the family. Look at Yvonne and Daniel! They were both white and she was very pregnant in her senior year, and they got *married*. They *still* go to our church! I'm right and you know it!'

Then she started talking about how our ancestors were slave owners and how those warped ideas that folks had about race, they not only ran down the bloodlines, but they bled out at dinner parties and church functions. She said people did stupid stuff because that's what they've been taught, and they accepted those ideas as truth without challengin' them. She said all it would take to change things is a new generation that stood up for what is right. She seemed to think changes were happenin' and that it would just take some time until all people were considered equal. Faith was the first person to ever talk to me openly about what was going on in our country. I could tell she was part of that new generation. And I wanted to be part of it too.

Then I asked her to do me a big favor. I wanted her to take me by the bowling alley so I could see Isaac again. She made me promise not to do anything that would get me into trouble. I told her that I just wanted to see my friend, that was all. And then I brushed my hair and put on some of her lip gloss."

EIGHT
MARCH 2022

As the sun began to set, Lovedy and I went into the kitchen to make a veggie pizza together. We sat on barstools, side by side, at her kitchen island and carefully placed the marinara, cheeses, onions, peppers, olives and tomatoes on top of the round crust while she continued her story.

"It was early evening, and the bowling alley wasn't busy yet. Faith dropped me off and told me she would be back in thirty minutes. I found Isaac almost immediately. He greeted me with that same dimpled smile that made me blush and I asked him if he could take a break and talk for a bit. He got two sodas, and we went out the side door, behind the building, to the back of the property. We sat down on the grass and started talkin' about old times.

The conversation was effortless, the laughs came easy. We caught up on the last couple of years. Isaac was doing well in school and was on the track team. Jeremiah was workin' at the hardware store and Clara was keepin' books for a business in the city. I asked Isaac if he ever came through my town anymore. He shook his head. 'Your town is a sundown town, Love. I don't go through there at all, not even when the sun is up. It isn't safe for guys like me.'

I was embarrassed for my town and heartbroken for him. I laid my hand on top of his and just said, 'I'm sorry.' Then he flipped his hand upside down and there we were, behind the bowlin' alley, holdin' hands.

I asked him if it would be ok if I came to see him again soon. He said that would be fine with him. I left the bowlin' alley and jumped in Faith's car with a smile and some determination to not lose my friend ever again.

As soon as I turned sixteen, I got my driver's license. I kept my babysittin' jobs during the week, and I would study after the kids went down in the evenings. I also got a weekend job at the new skatin' rink they had opened in the city. Daddy let me borrow the station wagon to get back and forth. I just kept workin', studyin' and piling money in that rainboot. And about once a week or so, I would sneak a visit to the bowlin' alley to see Isaac. By that time, I knew when his break was, and it became a regular thing. I didn't even have to go inside. I would just pull around back and he would be there waiting for me with a soda and that beautiful, dimpled smile.

We would sit on the grass, hold hands, and just talk, and laugh. It was all so innocent, just two lifelong friends enjoying each other's company."

"What did you talk about?"

"We talked a lot about music and TV shows. He would talk about civil rights and books he had been readin'. I would tell him about that latest critter I had dissected in science class. We talked about the war...we talked about everything, really."

Lovedy stood up to put our veggie creation into the oven. She turned around to look at me and sighed, "To be honest with you, if it weren't for me always pushin' things, there probably wouldn't be much of a story to tell. There wouldn't be a Corrina and you and I wouldn't even know each other."

"What do you mean by *pushing* things?" I asked.

"Well, one Saturday evening, the rink was slow because of a parade or somethin', so my boss let me off early. I called the house and told my folks that I had to work late. I swung by the bowlin' alley and ran inside to see what time Isaac was gettin' off work. I asked him if he wanted to hang out and told him I would give him a ride home. He called his dad to tell him that he had to work late too, which meant we had about three hours to spend together.

I waited for him in the parking lot, and he came out with burgers, fries and sodas, and we took off in the wagon. I drove out to a big field outside the city and parked under a line of huge oak trees. We laid down the back door of the wagon and sat on top of it, eatin' our dinner. We watched the sun take its final dip into the night as the sky exploded in beautiful watercolor hues of pink and red. I turned up the radio and we had a little dance party under those trees that were highlighted by the fading rays of the sun. But at some point, Gladys Knight and the Pips started singing "If I Were Your Woman" and the whole mood changed.

I took a step towards him. Then another step. I wanted him to take me in his arms and slow-dance with me. But he just stood there, lookin' at me with a serious look on his face. I quietly said, 'Its ok,' and then I stepped in even closer and put his arms around my waist. I slid my hands up the sides of his arms and let them rest around the back of his neck. My face was barely touching his, like a whisper of the skin. We just started swayin' back and forth in each other's arms. You might think what happened that night was just two young kids lettin' their hormones get away with them. Or you might think it was rebellion on my part. But it wasn't either of those things. As our bodies explored each other, it felt like the most natural thing in the world. I've heard people describe their "first time" as something clumsy, horrendous, and short lived, but this wasn't anything like that. It started out slow and hesitant, but then it turned into a primal desire that came from a place where the physical meets the emotional and it just consumed us. We both surrendered to what was happenin and let it take us away. Away from our homes, our parents, our worries and fears. It felt transcendent, otherworldly. We were just feelin', not even thinkin'. Not thinkin' about the past, or the future or the consequences. And we were certainly not thinkin' about birth control."

My hand flew over my mouth, and I gasped, "Don't tell me you got pregnant your first time, Lovedy!"

"Well, it's possible. Isaac and I kept seeing each other but after a couple of months, I noticed something goin' on with my body. I was over Faith's one day and told her I wasn't feelin' well. I was always tired, my boobs were sore, and I kept vomiting out of nowhere. She asked me if I was pregnant and then laughed. But I wasn't laughin' at all.

She said, 'Lovedy, why are you starin' at me with your mouth open like I just said something that was not a joke? When was your last period?' And at that moment, my world came crashin' down. So, I came clean with her and told her the whole story. She laid into me hard, ranted about irresponsibility and how a pregnancy would impact me, our family, Isaac, and his family. I begged her not to say anything. I needed time. I wanted to tell Isaac and I wanted to have time to think before I told my parents. I knew it was goin' to be a shitstorm.

So I waited. And then I waited some more. I was thin and had a bulge early on, but I kept wearing baggy shirts, tryin' to hide it. Eventually, I started feelin' butterflies and I knew I had to get it over with at some point.

When I told him, we were at the bowlin' alley, sitting in the parking lot, holding on to each other tightly. We sat in silence, just listenin' to the radio for a while. We agreed that we would both tell our parents that night. And at that moment, we knew we wouldn't be seeing each other again for a long time. He told me that he loved me and wanted to marry me. I just closed my eyes and pretended that we were older and wiser, living in another time where that dream could actually become a reality."

Lovedy took our pizza out of the oven and poured us each another glass of wine. We sat on the barstools, ate and drank together as she continued tell me about her pregnancy…

"Faith agreed to meet me at home and support me when I told my folks. I fully expected them to start yellin' and screamin', but Mama just sat down on the sofa, lookin' defeated again and Daddy put his hands over his face and started rubbin' his eyes as if they had betrayed him instead of his ears. Then he leaned forward and stared at the floor for what seemed like an eternity.

Finally, he looked up at me, his jaw sticking out. There was no doubt he was enraged. 'Get in the truck, Love,' he demanded as he stood up and headed for the door. I was scared and asked him where we were goin'. He turned around and very quietly said it again. 'Get in the truck, Love. Do it *now*.'

We got in the truck, and everything was poundin'. My head, my heart. I just wanted to jump out and run away. He didn't say a word, not a single word, all the way to the Carter's house. He hadn't even turned off the headlights before Jeremiah bounded out of the front door, down the steps and towards the truck. He had his hand up and was yellin', 'Stop, Marshall! Take a breath! We can work this out, now. Don't do anything rash!'

About that time, Clara came out and invited us inside. 'Y'all come into the house, now. We'll figure this out together. C'mon, Marshall. C'mon, Jeremiah. Y'all come inside. We don't need the whole neighborhood in our business, now. Just come inside. We'll work it out.'

Daddy told me to stay in the truck and I waited for what seemed like an eternity before he came back out. He slid behind the wheel and as he was closing the door, he said, 'You will *never* see that boy again.'

I don't know what came over me. I flung the door open and started runnin' to the front door. I was screamin', 'Isaac! Isaac! *Please*, Isaac!' I ran up the stairs and put my hand on the doorknob, but it was locked. I just kept screamin' his name and poundin' on the door. Daddy was comin' up behind me fast and I was panickin'. I just wanted to see his face. But they wouldn't open the door.

Then I heard Isaac's voice from the other side, 'Love, just go home. Do what he tells you. Go home, Love!' I just slumped down right there on the front porch, cryin' with my head leanin' against the front door. I was devastated and exhausted. Daddy literally scooped me up and carried me back to the truck. He put me in the back seat, and I laid down, cryin' the whole way back.

When we arrived at home, Daddy told me that I wouldn't be going back to school for a couple of days while they figured out how they were going to handle my "situation." I just went to my room and except for trips to the toilet and to take a shower, I didn't leave. Baby and Hope would bring food to the room and every once in a while, they would drop by just to give me a hug and rub my back.

Three days later, Mama and Daddy came into my room. 'This is what's gonna happen. We've contacted a mission in Georgia. It is a group home for pregnant girls. You're goin' to go stay there until they find a suitable family to adopt your baby.'

I freaked out, 'Daddy No! Please! Please don't do that to me!' He said he didn't see any other choice. He said I would have my own room, they would feed me, provide me with maternity clothes and I would get free checkups. When the group home found a family to adopt my baby, I would go live with them until it was time to deliver. And that is exactly what happened.

I packed my bag that night with the few clothes that still fit me. I emptied my rain boot and hid the money in a pair of socks. I took two packs of cigarettes that I stole from Faith the last time I was at her house and hid them in another pair of socks and we left the very next day."

Lovedy seemed to drift off somewhere else for a few moments and then said, "And that's where I'm going to leave it for tonight. I'm ready to turn in."

Her face told me she was done for the night, too. "Of course, Lovedy. Of course."

"But tomorrow morning," Lovedy said, "I want to take a walk with you after breakfast. I have somethin' to show you."

We cleaned the kitchen together, then she turned off the gas fireplace and the lamps that were glowing nearby. She double-checked the doors and then made a clicking sound with her mouth. The dogs popped up out of their sleepy stupors and followed her to the back of the house.

I found the guest room where David had placed my luggage. I was too tired to do anything with the hours of audio I had, so I took a long hot shower and climbed under the covers. I called Gabe to say goodnight and then drifted off into a deep sleep.

NINE
MARCH 2022

I woke up to the aromas of coffee and warm cinnamon bread swirling their way into my room. I got up and opened the blinds. There wasn't a cloud in the sky. I got ready for the day and put on an oversized sweatshirt, some leggings and sneakers and went out to say good morning to Lovedy. She was sitting at the table, with a steaming cup of coffee in her hand, looking out the window. "It's going to be a gorgeous mornin'. Grab yourself some coffee and breakfast and let's go sit out on the deck."

We sat down and started picking at the warm bread and a fruit salad. "Did you sleep well?" She asked.

"Mmmm...slept like a baby. How about you?"

"Me too. Usually, I have a hard time sleepin' without David. I don't know if it was the wine or all that talkin' but I was out like a light."

I looked out at the landscape which was farmland almost as far as my eyes could see. But if I squinted, I could see what looked like a housing development in the distance. "You said this land has been in your family for generations. Do you and your sisters still own it?"

"No, it's been split up and sold off little by little over the decades.

None of us wanted the farmin' life, so we sold the last of it to help pay for Mama and Daddy's care as they were aging. Everything you see behind our three little acres has been sold to developers. Let's go take our walk and I'll show you before the clouds start rollin' in. You ready?"

I grabbed my phone and Lovedy picked up a backpack and a warm blanket. We headed out from the back of the house and walked across the empty field and rolling hills. The sun was bright, but the breeze was still a bit chilly. The grass was brown, dormant, and crunching beneath our shoes.

Finally, we came up to a massive Southern Magnolia tree. I had never seen a Magnolia so enormous. There was a wooden bench sitting at the base, just outside of where the tree limbs finished stretching towards the sunlight. She laid the blanket on the bench and put the backpack on top of it.

"Come with me," she said.

We walked up closer to the tree, and she pointed upwards. "See up there? That's where Isaac and I would climb and have our talks durin' the summer months. Just sittin' up on that big branch with the rich perfume of those magnolia flowers all around us, bare feet dangling, laughin' with my best friend, and imagining what life might look like when we became grown-ups."

"That is precious, Lovedy."

"Yes, and it still is one of the sweetest memories of my life. That's why I put the bench out here. Sometimes trauma can make you forget who you are, sendin' you down another path that wasn't intended for you. I put this bench out here, so I'll always have a place to remind me of who I was in the raw, in the innocence, before the world tried to change me. I hope the developers don't bulldoze it. That would be tragic. It really is a beautiful spot," she gazed up at the tree for a moment more before turning to me, gesturing towards the bench. "Anyway, let's sit and chat a while."

I turned on my recorder and she began telling me about the trip to the group home. She stayed there almost three months and never spoke to her family, not even once. Her bedroom had cement walls and floors. The furniture consisted of a twin bed, a nightstand with a small lamp, a wooden chair and a wardrobe in the corner. There were no mirrors, no magazines, no posters, no pictures and only one book in the drawer of the nightstand. She said it felt like a prison cell. She had to rise at seven o'clock every morning for prayer service, then breakfast. They had mandatory classes she attended, most of which were religious. They also had classes to prepare some of the young girls for motherhood, but she wasn't invited to those because she wouldn't be needing them after giving birth.

Every minute of her day was scheduled, including daily chores of kitchen duty, cleaning bathrooms, and working in the laundry facility. Even nap time was scheduled. Visitors were not permitted; calls and letters were not allowed. She didn't really make any friends because they kept everyone so busy. Sundays were reserved for rest. By that, they meant Sunday morning service and an evening service with quiet time in between for meals and personal devotion time.

There was a doctor who visited the home once a month to examine the girls and make sure their pregnancies were moving along as expected. She was early in her third trimester when a front office worker knocked on her door one morning and said she needed to pack up her things and go to the administrator's office. Lovedy told me that she knew what was about to happen and she didn't really care. She just wanted to get out of that miserable place. She was tired of hearing about sin and repentance and the constant reminders of how much she had disappointed God and her family.

I could tell the memory irritated her as she continued, "I walked into the office, and I met Phillip and Charlotte Walsh, the couple who were going to be the parents of my child. My first observation was that they were short and then I noticed they had an adorable little girl with them. My next thought was about who had made this decision for me, for my baby. No one consulted me. I hadn't spoken with my parents in months, but I kept my mouth shut and just played along. I figured it was a sure way out of there and if I found their home to be horrifying, I would just run away.

After the paperwork was finished, I followed them out to their car. Phillip carried my bag for me, which I thought was nice, and I sat in the back seat. It was *so hot* and there was no air conditioning. The windows were down, and a quartet was singing gospel songs on the radio. I remember a wooden cross was dangling from the rear-view mirror. The little girl was sittin' in the back seat with me. She must have been about two or three years old, with jet black hair, fair skin and the biggest green eyes. I wondered where she came from, if she was their biological child or if they had adopted her too. She seemed shy but smiled a lot at me. I wondered if she was happy. I wondered if she was loved.

I didn't even pay attention to where we were going. After a few hours of being in the car, we stopped for gas. Charlotte got out and went into the trunk and brought back a large metal lunchbox. She had packed some peanut butter sandwiches, so we sat in the filling station parking lot and ate in silence with the windows down. Occasionally, a car would pull in to fill up. There were single men, single women, old people, young people, families. I tried to imagine who they were, where they were going and if they would offer me a ride if I tried to escape. Charlotte interrupted my daydreams and offered me some water from a thermos. I guzzled it down and asked for more.

The little one had to go to the bathroom, so I offered to take her and refill the thermos. I grabbed her hand, and we went to the side of the building. I took her in and let her do her business. There was a dim, dirty mirror over the sink and I caught my reflection for the first time in over three months. My face was full, my belly was huge, and my hair was an absolute mess. I bent my knee and lifted the little one up on it and helped her wash her hands. She was looking at me in the mirror and I was looking back at her. I put her down so I could refill the thermos. I *had* to ask her, while I had the chance, so I did. 'Are your parents nice to you?' She smiled and nodded yes. 'Do you love your mommy and daddy?' Again, she nodded yes. 'Do you have toys at home?' Yes. 'Do you have our own bed?' Yes, again.

As we were leaving the restroom, I saw a group of women coming from behind the building. I knew why they were back there and not in the same restroom as me and the little one.

They were all dressed up in brightly colored dresses and matching hats. It looked like they were goin' somewhere fancy. They were talkin' and laughin' as they walked back to the front. They seemed happy. Happier than I was, that's for sure.

Little One and I returned to the back seat, and we returned to the highway, the hot breeze making the knots in my hair even worse. I kept thinking about those women at the fillin' station. It made me think of Isaac and how easily we laughed together. I wondered how he was doin' and if he was still smilin' and laughin' or miserable like me. I missed him so much, my heart literally ached. I leaned my head back on the seat and tried my best to stifle the tears. I didn't want them to see that my heart was breaking, because I had no desire to be comforted by strangers. But then, a little, chubby hand patted my arm. I looked down to see that she was smiling at me. Yes, a toddler was comforting me, but I didn't care. She was the only friend that I had. So, I put her hand in mine and held on for dear life before I drifted off to sleep."

TEN
MARCH 2022

As we sat beside the massive magnolia, the clouds were gathering, casting a grey tone all around us. Lovedy spread the blanket over our laps and continued telling me about her trip to Phil and Charlotte's house.

"Someone was tapping me on my shoulder. When I opened my eyes, Little One was standing up on the back seat with her face directly in mine, saying, "Home!" I turned my head to look out the window. I don't know what I expected to see but the house was kind of cute. A 1940's one story red brick cape with a rounded entryway and a big porch, it looked like something out of a story book. The yard had a massive oak tree in the front, a bed of daffodils, and I could smell the honeysuckle flowers in the breeze. For a moment, I was encouraged. It didn't look like a terrible place to be, for myself or my baby.

Charlotte took me inside and showed me to my room. It was a small bedroom at the back of the house. There was a double bed, a dresser and a closet, handmade curtains and a quilt with those little yarn strings growing out of the squares. There wasn't any air conditioning but there was a small fan that sat on the dresser. It was definitely more welcoming than the room I had at the group home.

Little One's bedroom was across the hall with Phil and Charlotte's bedroom next to hers. There was only one bathroom, but it was close, which I really appreciated because I had to pee every fifteen minutes!

There was a living room, kitchen, dining room and a laundry room. There were pictures of family on the fireplace mantel and a large painting of flowers in a wicker basket above the couch. The hardwoods were dotted with gold and green shag rugs. The furniture looked a bit worn but the house looked and smelled clean. The backyard was a decent size for kids and there were several trees with a swing set off to the side. There was a free-standing garage, as well, behind the house that backed up to an alley. It didn't have a car in it, but it looked full of stuff. I made a mental note to snoop later. It had been my experience that everyone hides something.

After an extraordinarily long prayer, we ate left-over pot roast for dinner. Then Phil held what he called "family devotion" for about thirty minutes while we were all still at the table. Both Little One and I were noddin' off and the only thing that kept me awake were the smells of the meat and vegetables growing cold. It was startin' to make me nauseous.

Finally, the post-dinner sermon was over, and I helped clean up the kitchen. Charlotte gave Little One a bath and put her in pajamas. She came runnin' out to me in the livin' room and jumped on the sofa beside me. Her hair smelled sweet like baby shampoo as she snuggled up to me, gently patting my belly. She looked up to me and said, 'Baby?' I nodded and said, 'Yes, baby.' Then she handed me a book and I read the story to her all the while wanting to tell her that life is anything but a fairy tale.

Phil was readin' the newspaper, but on several occasions, I would look up from the story book and catch him lookin' over the paper at me, watching me interact with Little One. I understood it. I was a stranger to them, as they were to me. I would have been protective over Little One, too. After the second time reading the story,

Charlotte took my little friend in her arms and put her down for the night.

When she returned, she quietly sat down on the sofa beside me with a cup of tea. It felt like she was waitin' for somethin', but she just kept lookin' at Phil and then back at me. I could tell a conversation was about to happen. And then Phil put his paper down and started speakin' slowly, measurin' his words, like he had practiced them.

'Lovedy, Charlotte and I want to thank you for givin' us this incredible gift. We'd like to assure you that we will love the child and do our best to be good parents. You haven't been here long, but I'm sure you can see that Little One is a happy, thriving toddler. We adopted her through the same mission that connected us to you, and we've been waiting to add another blessing to our family. Do you want to ask any questions about us?'

The sofa cushion was pilling, and I kept twirlin' the little fabric balls between my fingertips. The baby started kickin' and rearrangin' itself and I wondered what questions the baby would ask if she could.

I'd thought I'd start with the most important ones. My first question was why they didn't have a television. His answer made me feel like I was back in my hometown, sittin' on a wooden pew. 'Because,' he said, 'God's word tells us that we are to be separate from the world. And the programs on television portray lifestyles that do not give glory to God but give glory to humanistic views. In many homes, the television turns into an idol. Many families worship that electronic device instead of focusing on their relationships with each other. We listen to some shows on the radio but would rather keep the television set out of our house.'

I just nodded and said, 'Ok... um... I have another question. Is it possible for me to use your telephone on occasion and call my family? I have money and I can pay you for the long-distance charges.'

His response was a punch in the gut when he said, 'We were

advised that permitting you to use the telephone would not be a wise choice in case you were tempted to contact folks that are not part of your immediate family. We think it is best that you don't use it at all.'

After that response, I was just plain pissed. So, then I said, 'Ok, just one more for now. Are you aware that my baby's father is black and very tall, and my baby will look nothin' like any of you?'

Charlotte choked on her hot tea, and it dribbled down her chin. 'Yes', Phillip replied with a very calm and measured tone. 'We are aware that the baby's father is black, and we have been counseled on the best ways to handle this situation.' I could only imagine what he meant by that, but my eyes were getting heavy, like my heart, and I just wanted to go to bed and sleep forever.

I said goodnight and got ready for bed. I slipped under the covers and tried to go to sleep but the baby had hiccups, and sleep wouldn't come. For the first time in a very long time, I prayed. It was a simple prayer, one that I'm sure many people of all ages have uttered when they are terrified and alone, 'God, please help me.'

The days and weeks dragged on and on and my stomach kept gettin' bigger and bigger.

I went to church with them on Sundays and Wednesdays, just like at home. The church was bigger than mine, but the sermons, hymns and altar calls were the same. The people were cordial, but I was sure they knew who I was and why I was there. There was a large group of teenagers that always sat together during the service, laughin' and whisperin'. I may have been paranoid, but it always felt like they were starin' at me.

During the announcements, they would always mention upcomin' activities for the youth group, but I was never invited. Just as well, I thought, because I wouldn't be there much longer. My baby would be born in a month or so.

I spent most of my days playin' with Little One. I grew to love that little girl. She seemed to have such a sweet spirit about her, which was good because she would be my baby's older sister. Phil and Charlotte would sometimes leave her at home with me while they went to visit sick people in the hospital. It was good that they felt comfortable enough to leave me alone with her but that wouldn't have been the case if they knew what I was doin' after Little One went to sleep.

I took full advantage of their absence. I snooped in their rooms and searched through their closets but never found anything interestin'. I thought they must be the most boring people on the planet. One night while they were away, I grabbed a cigarette out of the sock, checked on Little One to make sure she was still sleepin' and snuck out the back door. I'm not sure why I felt the need, it had been months since I had smoked. It didn't even taste good. So, after a couple of drags, I put it out and buried it under a pile of leaves in the alley. And that's when I remembered seeing all that stuff in the garage. I was worried about the time but thought I would just take a quick peek and I could come back later to look some more.

I walked around to the front and went inside. I turned on the light and saw a big machine sittin' in the middle of the floor. It was an old printin' press. There were boxes stacked up around it and I started openin' them. They were full of booklets that had cartoon drawings of the devil, demons, hell, and the lake of fire. The kind of stuff that would give you nightmares. The light was too dim to read the words, but the pictures scared me. I knew Phil and Charlotte would be coming back soon, so I took one of the booklets and headed back inside.

My stomach was hurting, so I poured myself a glass of milk and went to my bedroom to lay down. I read the booklet, and instead of scaring me, it made me sad. I remembered having nightmares as a kid about the lake of fire and "the rapture." No kid should have nightmares about burning in hell or bein' left behind without their parents. I didn't want my baby growin' up, having the same type of terrifying dreams.

At that moment, I just wanted to take my $302.64 and run away somewhere. I thought maybe Isaac and I could go to New York or California, get married and raise our baby by ourselves, but I knew that would never work. I was stuck, stuck in that house, stuck in that bed with the ugly quilt and its stupid red little yarn strings, and my big, uncomfortable belly and a devil booklet. I missed Isaac. I missed Faith. And even though my due date was approaching, it seemed like the nightmare I was living in would never end.

But it did end, the very next day. I woke up in the early hours of the morning in terrible pain. Phil took me to the hospital. Charlotte stayed back with Little One and planned on getting a ride later in the day from a friend. I was admitted and labored alone in my room, except for the occasional nurse that would come in to check on me. Ten hours later, my beautiful baby girl was in my arms.

She was nine pounds, three ounces, and my body had been ripped from bow to stern. They cleaned her up while the doctor was stitchin' me up. Wanda, my favorite nurse, brought her back to me and laid her on my chest. She bent over and put her hand on my head and then whispered softly in my ear, 'You have about five minutes with her then I'm going to have to take her. But don't worry. I promise you; everything is going to be ok. She's going to be ok.'

She was swaddled in a blanket, but I wanted to see all of her. Her fingers, her toes, her tummy, everything. I unwrapped her, determined not to cry because I had important things to say with little time to say it.

I kissed her forehead over and over and wrapped her little fingers around my finger. 'No matter what name they give you,' I whispered, 'you'll always be Breanna Audrey Carter to me. It means, *"strength."* I know your life will probably not be easy, but you're going to grow into a beautiful, strong woman. No matter what they tell you, God is good. He is kind. And no matter what you do in your life, or where you go or who you love, God will love you, and I will love you and nothin' will ever change that. One day, if you can forgive me, I hope you find me. Until then, I will pray for you every day, and I will miss you more than you will ever understand. Oh, and here's a kiss from your daddy.'

I kissed her again on her pudgy little cheek, and then Wanda very gently ripped her from my arms and tore a hole in my broken heart."

ELEVEN
MARCH 2022

MENOPAUSE BE DAMNED, I COULDN'T HOLD BACK THE TEARS WHEN Lovedy described the moment Corrina was taken from her arms. I sat there on the bench, next to her, unable to imagine the enormity of her pain but seeing hints of it leaking from the corners of her eyes as she kept going.

"They kept me for two days at the hospital. The hours just crept by with no visitors or phone calls. The nurses would stop by every few hours and help me to the bathroom. Finally, they discharged me, but I was in no shape to travel. I needed a few days to heal before making the trip home. I wanted to stay with Phil and Charlotte, but they didn't think it was a good idea for me to be around the baby and form an unhealthy attachment. They arranged for me to stay at the home of their friends, Donna and John. Donna was sweet and took good care of me, doting on me as if I were her own daughter. She brought me ice cream with raw cookie dough mixed into it and let me watch whatever I wanted on TV.

On the fourth day I was there, she came into the family room and said she wanted to talk to me. I sat up on the couch, wincing at the constant reminder that I had just given birth. She spoke very softly,

MARCH 2022

'Lovedy, I don't know if it matters to you, but I wanted to tell you that I think you are very brave. You've been through a lot and have had to make a difficult decision. Unfortunately, there is more that needs to be done to make that decision binding in this state. You're going to need to meet with a family lawyer to sign adoption papers so that the baby legally belongs to Phil and Charlotte. Do you understand what I'm saying?'

I nodded yes and waited for the rest. 'Your parents will be in town tomorrow and I'll take you to the lawyer's office to meet them there, ok?'

Again, I nodded yes, but I wasn't sure how I felt about seeing them again. What I was excited about was the possibility of seein' my baby girl again at the lawyer's office.

'One more thing,' she said. 'This is a private adoption, so you may see Phil and Charlotte there.'

I didn't care about them. I just wanted to see my Breanna. 'So, should I pack my bags tonight? Am I going home with my parents after we sign the papers?' It was her turn to nod yes.

The next morning, Donna helped me load my bags into the car and we headed towards the lawyer's office. It was autumn, and the trees along the backroads were swayin' back and forth, showing off their brightly painted leaves. "Creedence Clearwater Revival" was playing on the radio. They were singing about trouble being on the way and I felt every word of it in my gut.

When we arrived at the lawyer's office, Donna told me to head on inside. She was goin' to wait in the car to say goodbye when we were finished. I walked inside, slow as a turtle, partly because I was still very sore, and partly because I wasn't in a hurry to get in there. Mama came up immediately and gave me a big hug and started cryin'. Daddy just stood back and said, 'Hey, Love.' I said, 'Hey, Daddy' and then found a seat in the little lobby. The chairs were hard and uncomfortable, much like the situation at hand.

Phil and Charlotte came inside a few minutes later. I was hoping I wouldn't see them. They shook hands with my parents and said hello to me. Little One wasn't there and neither was my Breanna. The realization that I may never see her again came crashin' down on me, just like that box in the barn. My chest felt tight, and I couldn't breathe. Tears started spillin' out of my eyes and I excused myself to ask the receptionist if I could use the restroom. I walked in as fast as I could and slammed the door. I sat on the toilet with my clothes on and just kept repeating Wanda's promise. *'Everything is going to be ok. She's going to be ok.'*

It wasn't long before we went into the lawyer's office. I tried to listen, to understand what he was saying but much of it went over my head. I was a teenager after all, and I just wanted it to end so I could get out of there. I didn't really want to go back home, but anywhere had to be better than where I was at that moment. I kept thinking about Breanna and her little fingers, her curly hair, and heart-shaped lips.

We had to sign a bunch of papers and that's when I saw her name. *Corrina Lane Walsh. Father-Phillip William Walsh. Mother-Charlotte Mae Walsh.* It felt like I had nothin' to do with bringin' that little girl into the world. And what kind of name was "Corrina?" I had never heard of it before and wondered where it came from and what it meant.

The lawyer kept readin' a language I didn't understand until he got to one part that got my attention. I wasn't sure that I heard it correctly, so I asked him to repeat it. *Revocation of adoption. One year waiting period before adoption is finalized.* My mind started racin' and I started doin' the math. I would turn eighteen before the one-year period was up. Isaac and I could come back and get our baby. All I had to do was be patient and wait.

Once everything was signed, my parents shook hands with Phil and Charlotte like they just sold them a car. It made me sick, and I walked out of the room without sayin' a word. I went back to the lobby and waited by the door. Lookin' out of the window, I noticed it had turned gloomy and it was sprinklin'. That's when I noticed Donna sittin' in her car. She was holdin' a baby. *Was that My baby?*

I flung the door open and started walkin' to the car as fast as my broken body would let me. I walked up to the window and pleaded, 'Donna, *please* open the door!'

But she just shifted the baby up on her shoulder so I couldn't see her and said, 'I'm sorry, Lovedy. I can't.'

The rain was comin' down faster as I tried to open the door, but it was locked, and Mama and Daddy were walkin' quickly towards me. 'Please Donna, I only want to give her one last kiss. *Please, Donna, please*!'

But she wouldn't let me see her, hold her, touch her, nothin'. Daddy gently grabbed me by the arms and tried to turn me around. 'C'mon, Love. We have to go now.'

But I wrangled myself free and in the pourin' rain, I kissed my fingertips and then pressed them to the window and said, 'Everything will be ok. You will be ok.'

It was the longest five-hour car ride ever. Mama and Daddy made small talk the whole way. They talked about the farm, Baby's science project, the fall festival, the upcoming holidays, and the weather. No one asked how I was doin', how I was feelin' or the ordeal I just went through by myself for the past six months, which was fine with me, because I had a plan. And it didn't include either one of them.

I asked them to stop every hour so I could use the restroom and eventually it started to annoy Daddy. He tried to make a joke by askin' me if I had a bladder the size of an acorn. I wasn't in the mood, so I shot back, 'I'm not sure if you noticed, but I just had a baby, left it in another state and I'm bleedin' like a stuck pig from my vagina. If you want blood-stained seats in your truck, then just keep on drivin'. If that doesn't seem like a good idea, then you probably need to stop so I can use the restroom. It's up to you and makes no difference to me.' Daddy didn't say a word, he just shot me some eye daggers from the rearview mirror. Mama turned her head towards the passenger window and put her hand over her mouth to cover a smile, but I saw it and for the first time in a long time, I smiled too.

When we pulled up to the house, Hope and Baby came runnin' out and almost knocked me over. Mama started warmin' up the dinner she had prepared the night before and I went upstairs to take a shower. When I returned to my room, Hope and Baby were sittin' on my bed, waitin' for me. They wanted to know everything. *Was it a boy or a girl? What did she look like? Did I give her a name? Does this mean they are aunties? Will they ever get to meet her? What are her new parents like?* I was touched that they gave a shit. It was more than I could say for Mama and Daddy. I answered as many questions as I could before Mama called us down for dinner. She had made my favorite meal and put out the nice dishes. I ate my roasted chicken, mashed sweet potatoes with butter and cinnamon and string beans she had canned from the garden, in total silence. If Mama and Daddy were not going to acknowledge the absolute hell I had been through, then I wasn't going to acknowledge their pitiful attempts at welcoming me back home.

After dinner, I helped clear the table and then I waited for Mama and Daddy to go into the den to watch their nightly TV programs. I quietly pulled the phone from the cradle, unwound the cord and dialed Faith's number. I went out the kitchen door and sat down on the back porch as far away from the door as the cord would allow, to talk to her in private. She said she was sorry for not being there when I arrived and told me she was not invited. She didn't even know I was comin' home. I filled her in on the highlights of my time away but what I really wanted to know is if I could come and stay with her over the weekend. We made plans for her to pick me up on Friday evenin' after she finished work.

The mood of the house was weird for the rest of the week. I was still moving slowly, and it was more comfortable to lie down than to sit on anything, so I mostly stayed in bed. When Mama and Daddy weren't around, I would sprawl out on the couch and watch TV. I would hear the girls leave in the mornin's for school and return in the afternoons. Wednesday night came around and they never asked me to go to church with them. Fine by me. My answer would have been a definite no.

Friday evening finally arrived, and I was startin' to feel more like myself. Faith came over and had dinner with all of us. At one point, I heard her on the back porch, arguing with Daddy but I couldn't hear what they were sayin'. We cleaned the kitchen, played some cards with Hope and Baby, and then I left with Faith for the weekend.

Once I was in the car, I was talkin' a mile a minute. I gave her all the details about Phil and Charlotte and Little One. But I spent most of my time talkin' about my beautiful Breanna. I told Faith about my plans of getting my baby back after I turned eighteen, and about my dreams of marryin' Isaac and movin' to California and raisin' our family together. She didn't say much on the way to her house, she just listened, for the most part. I wondered if her argument with Daddy was botherin' her. I asked her about it, and she said that Daddy was just bein' Daddy.

We went to bed not long after we arrived at her duplex. My mind was whirlin', and my body was restless. Faith began twirling my hair like she's done for as long as I could remember. It always helped me fall asleep. I was just about to doze off when she said, 'Lovedy, I need to tell you somethin.' And then her voice trailed off. I braced myself and just waited quietly for her to finish. 'I thought when you asked to spend the weekend with me that you might want to see Isaac. That's what Daddy and I were arguing about on the back porch tonight. He wanted to make sure that wasn't going to happen when you were in my care.'

Her care? I wasn't a baby! I was almost eighteen years old and just had a baby of my own! I sat up in bed. I was so tired, emotionally, physically, and mentally. I was tired of worryin' about what other people thought I should do, where I should go and who I should love. 'Well, I do want to see him,' I cried, 'I *need* to see him. I just don't know where he is or what he's doin'. I don't know if he's still workin' at the bowlin' alley or maybe he went to college after he graduated high school. I have no idea.'

She sat up beside me and put her arm around me, pullin' me in close. 'Love, I saw Mrs. Carter a few weeks ago in town. There is no easy way to say this, but Isaac enlisted after he graduated. He's been deployed to Vietnam. He isn't here.'

I was stunned. I couldn't believe what she was telling me. In all the conversations we had about the war, he never once mentioned voluntarily joining the military. In fact, I remember him talking about how the government was drafting young black men to serve and protect a nation that hated them and how it didn't make any sense to him. I dropped my head back onto the pillow and said, 'I wish there was some way I could talk to him.'

And then Faith gave me the best news I had heard in a long time. 'I thought of that. I asked Mrs. Carter if she could give my address to him the next time she wrote him a letter. I told her I would love to hear from him and that maybe I could send a package with some cookies and candy or some nuts and ground coffee. She just smiled at me and then asked me about you. It seemed like she genuinely cared about you and the baby. And I was thinking, maybe…that you might want to see her this weekend?'

I didn't know what to say. I always thought that his parents would hate me. That they would think I was a Jezebel who ruined their son's life. So, the idea of Mrs. Carter caring about me made my heart feel a little bit lighter. 'Yes, I want to go see her," I said with a little nervous excitement. Then Faith started twirling my hair again and I fell fast asleep next to the only person I could count on."

Lovedy and I talked for a couple of hours. When our butts would get sore from sitting on the bench, we would take a short walk and then return to the warmth of the wool blanket. The time just flew by. But I had questions so I asked if she could fill in some of the blanks for me.

She laughed and said, "Sure, I'll fill in what I can. But I'm going to need some juice." She unzipped the backpack and pulled out a bottle of Pinot Noir and two tumblers.

"One thing I've been very curious about, is how a seventeen-year-old navigated through all of this by herself. Moving to a group home, staying with strangers, an intense labor and then surrendering a baby. *That* is *a lot.*"

She thought for a moment and then said, "Looking back, I think I was just trying to survive. I was young and immature, but I did the best that I could. I didn't have any control over what was happenin', and I think that was the hardest part for me. It was very frustrating. I was incredibly angry at my parents, at Phil and Charlotte and I was angry at myself."

"Why were you angry at yourself?"

"Aside from the shame that I felt from my parents and my church, I knew that I should have made better choices. I had a plan. I was studying hard, working and saving my money for college. I was goin' somewhere. When I found out I was pregnant, I thought my dreams were no longer a possibility. And I was angry at myself for lettin' things like love and emotions get in the way of that. I was angry at myself because I was in such a hurry. I wanted what I wanted and no one and nothing else mattered. I just didn't think it all the way through. But then again, I was seventeen."

"That is a heavy load for a teenager to carry around. When did you go back to school?"

"About four weeks after I had the baby, I started my senior year. It wasn't easy. Everyone knew what happened and they all treated me differently, but I tried not to let it bother me. I just went right back to studyin'. I caught up on everything I had missed in my classes and went back to babysittin' in the evenings and on weekends to earn more money for my rain boot."

"What about your parents? Did they ever talk to you about your time away, the adoption or anything having to do with Corrina?"

"Not one single word. Not ever. It just wasn't talked about. It was like it never happened. There was no doubt that my relationship with my parents had changed. I'm sure part of that was because of the pregnancy, but I also think it was because I was almost an adult, and I was seeing more of who they were as people, and I think they knew that. They handled me with kid gloves, from then on. I think they knew when I graduated, I was movin' out immediately."

"And did you? Move out?"

"Yes," she nodded, "I did."

I sat on the bench, sipping my wine and thought about myself when I was seventeen. I couldn't imagine going through the trauma that Lovedy experienced. I would have crumbled into myself and given up. I wondered how she had so much fight inside of her. How did she stand up to her parents at that age? I still had a problem doing it now.

TWELVE
1983-1993

THE TEENAGE YEARS ARE HARD. IT IS SUCH A *WEIRD* TIME TO BE A HUMAN being. You're not really a child anymore but not yet an adult, either. It definitely was not an easy time for me, especially when it came to developing friendships.

I never saw my mother cultivate close friendships with women. She never invited any friends over to our house. Aside from my Aunt Maria visiting, the only time we had guests was when my father would invite a work colleague and his spouse over for dinner. Even then, my mother was not the most gracious host. She would cook an incredible meal and clean the house from top to bottom but, at the dinner table, she would barely say a word.

In my earlier years, there were six other kids on my street and all of them were boys. On the weekends, and during the summers, I spent all of my time with them, playing football, riding bikes, digging in the dirt and climbing trees. I was always small for my age, but I was tough, and could hold my own.

I had girlfriends at school, at dance class and gymnastics but those friendships were different. Once, in middle school, I was given an invitation to a slumber party for a classmate's birthday. When I showed it to my mother, she seemed happy about it and even took me to the mall to pick out a birthday present. She helped me pack an overnight bag and drove me to my friend's house the night of the slumber party. I remember as I got out of the car, I looked back at my mother to say goodbye and was shocked to see that she was smiling.

That night, I watched as my friend's mother hung out with all of us in her pajamas. She made us s'mores and popcorn and we all watched a funny movie. She laid across the sleeping bags in the living room and told ghost stories. When everyone else was asleep, I watched intently as she bent over and gave her daughter a kiss on the forehead. I heard her whisper, "Goodnight birthday girl, sweet dreams" as she gently brushed her sleeping daughter's hair to the side. I remember how foreign that exchange seemed to me and how emotional I felt as I grabbed my pillow a little tighter and quietly cried myself to sleep.

The next morning, my friend's mother made a big pancake breakfast for all of the girls and we celebrated outside, swimming in their pool and eating birthday cake on her deck that was decorated with balloons and streamers. Her mother had made a big sign that said, "Happy 13th!" that was strung along the back fence. When gift time came, her mother rolled out a beautiful new bicycle. It was a pale yellow with flowers painted on the side, white wall tires and a basket that hung off the front bar. My friend screamed, jumped up and down and clapped her hands when she saw it. It was exactly the one she wanted, and she actually cried because she was *so happy*.

I was jealous, but not about the bike. I was jealous of how much her mother adored her. I decided they must be a really weird family and that other girls must need more attention than I did. That was when I also decided that I would rather be friends with boys. I understood them better. They didn't seem to be as emotionally needy. They didn't cry as much, and they seemed to have two moods-happy and angry. I was an expert on the moods of others and handling two was a breeze.

In high school, my love for dance recitals and piano lessons was replaced with a passion for writing and taking photos for the school newspaper. I went to all of the sporting events, the debates, the club meetings. I learned that by holding the camera, I had special powers. *Everyone* wanted their picture in the newspaper, especially the girls, and I found that to be very annoying. I didn't care about the same things as most of the other girls. They were always fawning over boys and giggling about things that weren't really that funny. If they weren't giggling or gossiping, they were crying. Most girls belonged to a friend group and the smallest things, usually related to boys, would get you kicked out. I wanted nothing to do with it so I stayed as far away from that nonsense as I could.

To be honest, I really wasn't invited into the female friend groups. My high school friend group consisted of mostly boys, which pissed off a lot of the girls and labeled me as an undesirable candidate. But again, I didn't care. Boys were easy and I understood them.

I graduated high school in 1990 and immediately went to college at the University of Kentucky. I helped out with their school newspaper, drafting articles and doing some photography. I lived at home while I was in school to save money and got a job waitressing at a sports bar. I stayed busy, which meant I wasn't home much, so I never saw it coming.

One night after work, I walked in the front door of our home and saw my dad sitting on the couch. His elbows were on his knees and his hands were covering his face.

"Dad? Are you ok?"

He looked up with puffy, red eyes. I was rattled because I had never seen my dad cry.

"Dad! Please tell me…what's wrong?" I persisted.

"Hey, Sunshine…can you sit down and talk with me for a few minutes?"

"Uh, sure." I laid my purse and keys on the coffee table and sat next to him. "What is it, Daddy? Tell me…"

"It's your mother. She's gone."

"What do you mean, she's gone? Gone where?"

"She left me, she went back to Tampa."

Mom never made it a secret that she wasn't happy. I could think of a myriad of reasons why she would have left, but I still wanted to hear the specifics.

"Why? Did she say?"

He hung his head, "She said we didn't need her anymore and that she wanted to go back home to her family. She's moving in with her parents so she can help care for them."

"Are you getting a divorce?"

He shook his head. "She didn't say anything about a divorce. I just think she wanted to get out of Lexington," He put his hand on top of mine, "I tried, Sunshine. I tried so hard to make her happy."

"You don't have to defend yourself to me, Daddy. I lived here."

THIRTEEN
MARCH 2022

The clouds were gathering, and the temperature was dropping, so Lovedy and I decided to walk back to the house. We ate a bit of leftovers for lunch, then she suggested we go for a drive. We grabbed our coats and walked to her garage. When she opened the door, she looked back at me and said, "You should prepare yourself."

I don't know much about cars, but I knew enough to know that what I was looking at was quite the hidden museum. It was a collection of American made metal that would make any car enthusiast drool with envy. Every single car was meticulously restored with not even a scratch, a dot of rust or speck of dust in sight. Even the floors of the garage were spotless. Every tool was in its place.

"Wow," was all I could utter.

"Yeah, wow. That is exactly what you would say if you were to see my utility bills," she mumbled as she rolled her eyes. "He has this whole garage climate controlled. The temperature is maintained at fifty-five degrees and the humidity never exceeds fifty-five percent." She held up her hand and said, "Don't ask me why, because I have no idea. I would give you a detailed tour, but I don't want to steal his thunder. That man has been *obsessed* with cars since before he could crawl, and he just *loves* to show them off. That one over there with the flying lady ornament, I call that one "Mistress" because there was a time in our marriage when I was jealous of her. The time he spent with her, the way his eyes would sparkle when he talked about her, it drove me nuts. He still can't mention her without smiling." She shook her head with an amused smile of her own.

I laughed as we hopped in her car. She backed out of the garage, and as we headed to the edge of town, Lovedy told me she was going to stop at The Doghouse.

"The doghouse? What is the doghouse?" I asked.

"*The Doghouse* is a florist and chocolate shop owned by my very good friend, Rita Anne Jensen. She recently put some couches and tables in there and added a coffee bar. She does pretty well with it. We've been friends since we were kids, but I need to warn you about her."

"Uh oh. Why? What's wrong with her?"

"Nothin' is wrong with her, really. She's just a handful."

"What do you mean?"

"Well, for one thing, she's one of those people that is irritatingly confident about everything. She's confident that the extra fifty pounds she is carryin' around is in exactly all the right places. She's sure her son, Jake, is gonna be the next president of the United States, even though he's thirty-five years old and works down at the manufacturin' plant. She's sure that all men secretly love her."

"She sounds like a lot of fun," I giggled.

"Oh, she's a laugh a minute. Some people just don't know how to take her."

We walked into The Doghouse, and I met Rita about a second later.

"Lovedy, git your boney ass 'round this counter and give me a hug! You gonna buy somethin' today or not? I've started chargin' the sniffin'-only customers, you know, and I'm not gonna make an exception for you. Skinny people still take up chair space too! Now sit down right there and let me help you *expand* your girly features."

"I just spent an hour on the weight machine this morning tryin' to firm up my girly features," Lovedy declared, "I'm perfectly satisfied to sit here and fantasize. Or better yet, I'll just live vicariously through you. C'mon Rita Anne," she fired back as she lifted her brows, "tell me, was it the mousse or that three-layer chocolate transgression over there that you had for breakfast?"

"Jealousy is not a sexy look on you, Lovedy."

"Rita Anne, stop insultin' me and meet my friend, Farrah Acosta. She's Corrina's closest friend."

"Well, hello darlin'," she said with her hands defiantly on her hips, "Don't you listen to a word this lady says about me. I'm a nice person. I just say what everyone else wishes they had the balls to say. That's all."

"Hi, Rita Anne. It is so nice to meet you." I waved to her from the front side of the counter.

"First timers always get a free sample of my tantalizin' sweets." she said as she placed three beautifully wrapped chocolates on the countertop.

"I'm not afraid of chocolate" I said, as I immediately began opening the first one.

Rita smiled, "I just met you and I already know that you're my people, Farrah. Do you know why?"

Lovedy interjected, "You don't have to answer her. She's gonna tell you anyway."

"Yes, I am," Rita said. "Because you get it, Farrah. God created chocolate for women, and you are smart not to deny yourself its mystical powers. It's a natural anti-depressant. It makes us roll our eyes back in our heads. Women forget themselves when they visit my little shop. Why do you think all of the men hang out in here? I can tell you they are not here for the chocolate lattes and comfortable chairs."

Lovedy sighed loudly, "Are you done, Rita? We just stopped by to get some flowers. I need four arrangements today, please. Make it the usual."

"Comin' right up, Love."

Rita moved over behind the floral counter and pulled fresh flowers out of tall blue buckets that were lined up on the floor. In no time, she had created four beautiful bouquets for Lovedy.

"I'll put it on your tab that you never pay," Rita Anne said with a laugh.

Lovedy put cash on top of the countertop, winked at Rita Anne and said, "Give that hunky husband of yours a hug for me," as she started walking towards the door, motioning me to follow her.

"He doesn't like skinny girls!" Rita yelled out across the café, leaning over the counter with a smirk on her face.

"Is that what's he's been tellin' you all of these years?" Lovedy shouted over her shoulder as she headed for the door.

"Don't you have any other friends?" Rita yelled back.

"Yes, but they all hang out at the gym! You wouldn't like 'em!" Lovedy shouted. "I'll see ya on Tuesday!" Then after getting the last word in, Lovedy let the front door slam behind her and we laughed all the way to the car.

I helped Lovedy put the arrangements carefully on the backseat. I asked her what they were for, and she said we were going to visit some loved ones. As Lovedy drove down the road, The Bee Gees were playing "Too Much Heaven." She pulled up to a sprawling cemetery and it felt like one of those moments you might describe as serendipitous.

As she drove around the paved road, I looked at the rows and rows of headstones. Some were big, and some were very small. Some had flowers, and others had little flags that were fluttering in the breeze. One didn't have a headstone but still had a mound of dirt on the top with a tent standing over it. I thought about those who had recently stood under that tent, ladened with fresh grief, just trying to get through the day without their loved one. I wondered if they were children, siblings or spouses. Friends or lovers. Or even parents.

She pulled the car over to the side and took two of the flower arrangements out of the back. We started walking and came to a stop in front of a companion plot. She squatted down and brushed off some leaves that had gathered around the headstones. She carefully placed an arrangement on each one and then took a step back as I read the epitaphs aloud.

Marshall Grant Barclay
Beloved Father
May 13, 1930-June 20, 2012

Caroline Jane Barclay
Beloved Mother
January 31, 1931-November 12, 2012

"In case you're wonderin,'" Lovedy said in a low, lingering voice, "I did eventually make amends with my parents. And I'm sorry to say, it was a long journey to forgiveness for all of us."

We stood there for a few more minutes. I heard her sniffling but didn't want to interrupt her moment of sorrow. I wanted to comfort her but didn't know what to say. So, I just put my arm around her waist and stood there quietly with her, hoping it would help in some small way.

"For Pete's sake, I'm not cryin', Farrah. I'm allergic to baby's breath. We've got more places to go. C'mon." And then she turned around and started walking back to the car.

She drove slowly on the narrow, winding road to the other side of the cemetery. I started noticing the fresh flowers, the evidence of the grieving who had recently visited, and the graves that looked abandoned. I wondered how long they had been resting there before people no longer cared that they were gone.

"We're here. Let's go," she said as she grabbed the other two arrangements from the back seat. We walked to the end of the row, and I saw the first grave with a name that I recognized.

Jeremiah Eugene Carter
Born-September 30, 1932
Resting with Jesus-June 14, 1992

"That's Isaac's Dad"? I asked.

"Yes, massive heart attack. Such a kind soul and a good friend to everyone who knew him." She knelt down on her knees, brushed away the dead leaves that rested there too, and laid the vibrant flowers in their place. "These are from Ms. Clara," she said quietly. "She's doin' well. Still bossin' everyone around. She misses you. We all miss you." She kissed her fingertips and touched the headstone, then she stood up and moved over to the next one. My stomach flipped when I read the name of the body that was resting there.

Isaac Eugene Carter
Born-March 18, 1953
Resting with Jesus-December 21, 1975

She did the same thing as the other graves, placing a bouquet of flowers on the headstone after brushing away the sticks and leaves that had fallen from the towering oaks. Their long limbs stretched out so far, hovering above the endless rows of plots. I imagined what it would look like in the spring and summer when those giants would bloom and generously provide shade for all those who were sleeping there.

I knew that Isaac was deceased, but Corrina and I had never spoken about the specifics, and it had been a long time since we spoke about it at all. I was shocked that he had passed away so early, in the prime of his life.

"Yes, he was very young," she said, reading my mind. "So very young."

Again, I wasn't sure what to say. It had been forty-four years since Isaac was laid to rest, but I had no idea if time had healed anything for her. There was just no way of knowing.

"I'm so sorry, Lovedy," I whispered and waited for her to say something, but she didn't. Still kneeling, she just continued to stare at the headstone. Finally, I asked her, "Was he killed in Vietnam?"

Her words were thick with emotion. "No, he survived Vietnam. He just didn't survive coming back home."

I was confused but didn't want to press too hard. "Are you ok talking about this?"

"Yes, it's ok, Farrah. I'm ok," she took a deep breath in and let it out before she spoke, "What happened to Isaac was all over the local news and in the papers. I think what I might do is give you some newspaper clippings when we get back to the house. That will give you some time to read and get caught up before we have dinner," she pried her eyes from the stone and looked at me. "Sound good?"

"Whatever you want to do, Lovedy, is fine with me." And I meant it. I was conflicted about the whole thing. Bringing up all these memories and watching her there, kneeling by the grave with her runny nose, the guilt of what I was doing to her rested heavy on my heart.

"Alright then, let's get back to the house. It's gettin' chilly out here."

We returned to Lovedy's house, and she immediately went up into the attic. She came down with a large, wooden, floral box and laid it on the dining room table.

"Everything you need to know about Isaac's death is in there. I'm going to walk the dogs and then lay down for a bit. I'm sure you're going to have questions. We can talk about it over dinner." And then she disappeared outside.

Even though she gave me permission to look in the box, it still felt like I was snooping. It was an odd feeling, being out in the open part of the house, so I grabbed the box and my phone and retreated to the guest room. I put the box on the bed and called Gabe. I told him about the walk to the magnolia tree, the museum garage, and the drive to the cemetery.

"How are you feeling about it so far?" He asked.

"I'm not sure how I feel about it. It's hard to remain objective and not get caught up in the emotions of it all. Lovedy is like family to me, and I care about her. I wonder if this is worth dragging her through all of this again."

"Well, I'm sure she relives it occasionally without you there. Who knows, it could be therapeutic for her."

"I don't know about that," I said, feeling uneasy.

I couldn't shake the feeling that our dinner conversation would be difficult for Lovedy. I didn't want to press her too much but to fully appreciate everything she had overcome in her lifetime, I couldn't ignore the depths of her suffering.

Gabe and I said our goodbyes and I thought about taking a nap, myself, but I didn't want to waste time. I needed to be fully versed on the contents of the box so that I was prepared for our conversation at dinner.

I opened the box and found a large manila envelope full of newspaper clippings laying on top of what looked to be at least a hundred or more letters, each one clipped to an envelope of its own. I didn't know where to start but remembered that she mentioned newspaper clippings, so I started with the large envelope.

Over the next two hours, I read every single article while frantically taking notes and writing down any questions that popped into my mind. The articles were arranged by their publication date, so I had to rearrange them to make sense of what happened and how it happened. Once I had them all laid out in order of events, I wrote the highlights down in my journal:

Isaac Eugene Carter. Black male. Twenty-two years of age. Veteran, served in Vietnam. No prior record. Intoxicated in public. The Perpetrator was not cooperative. Resisted arrest. Officer Riley did not follow standard procedure and discharged the firearm unintentionally. Attempted to resuscitate. County paid settlement of five thousand dollars to victim's family. Officer convicted of manslaughter and sentenced to serve three years.

The smells of dinner wafted through the house as I watched the sun sinking down into the western sky outside of the bedroom window. Shades of orange and yellow were cast along the room making it look like I was inside of a piece of gold. I heard Lovedy out in the kitchen and decided to go help her. Knowing what I knew now, I wasn't even sure what to say.

"How was your nap?" was all I could think of at the moment.

"Good. Restful. Naps are good for the body and the mind. I try to lay down at least twenty minutes every day," she replied.

I set the table and listened to her talk about afternoon naps and how they help your cardiovascular system and improve your cognitive function. I hadn't taken a nap since I was a toddler and made a mental note to schedule naps into my new routine.

She brought the dishes over to the table while I opened the bottle of wine and poured us each a glass.

"I prepared some comfort food for us," she said with a wink.

I looked at the spread in front of me. It was her favorite meal.

Roasted chicken, fresh green beans, sweet potatoes with cinnamon and an artisan bread loaf made with garlic and rosemary.

Then she raised her glass and gave a toast, "To good food, cozy blankets, afternoon naps and sharing a bottle of wine with a friend. To all the good things that help us get through the day. Cheers."

"Cheers, Lovedy. And thank you for this beautiful meal."

As we broke bread together and drank the wine, I eased into the conversation as gently as I could. "Did you ever go to see Mrs. Carter that weekend you stayed with Faith?"

"We did. And she was so loving and gracious to us. When we arrived, she ran outside and wrapped her arms around me and just held on. There was something so powerful about that simple embrace. She saw me and knew that I had a need. For the first time in so long, I felt accepted, understood, and comforted. She was an emotional giver and she's the reason I love a good hug so much.

We spent the whole afternoon with her. She asked me about Corrina. I wished I had photographs to share with her, but I described every inch of her the best that I could. We talked about Isaac, and I asked her why he enlisted. She said that foolishness came about because of an argument that Isaac and Jeremiah had after Isaac graduated from high school. He enlisted, went to boot camp, and was in Vietnam a couple of months later. It was all to spite his Daddy. She gave me the address so I could write to him, and I promised that I would visit her again soon."

I had to ask, "Those letters in the box, are those letters between you and Isaac?"

"Yes, they are. We wrote to each other for over two years, until he finished his duty and came home. By that time, I was in nursing school and living with Faith and her new husband."

"So what happened when he came home?"

"We had a little party at Clara's house to celebrate his return. Faith and I went over early to hang streamers and balloons. We made a big "Welcome Home" sign to put in the front yard. His extended family, as well as some friends from high school, came to celebrate. I remember him walkin' in the door, so tall, strong, and handsome. He hugged his Mama first and I remember her yellin' 'Thank you, Lord, for bringing my baby home!' Then he walked over and hugged me so hard I thought he was going to break me in half. He kissed me right there, in front of everyone and held my hand through the entire party. I felt genuinely happy, like everything was comin' together in my life."

"Did you guys talk about getting Corrina back? Or was it too late by then?"

"Yes, and yes. Back when I found out that Isaac enlisted, I tried to figure out how I could do it by myself. I had a few hundred dollars saved and I was still living at the farm until I graduated. At that point, Corrina was eight months old. I knew my folks wouldn't help me, so I didn't even bother to ask. I didn't even want them to know that I was thinking about getting her back. Isaac and I wrote back and forth about it, trying to figure it out. I knew my parents wouldn't help me. I talked with Faith about it, but she didn't have enough money to help me pay for my own lawyer and the court fees and I didn't have anywhere else to turn. Before I knew it, the one-year waiting period was over and it felt like I had failed her all over again."

FOURTEEN
MARCH 2022

We took a break and cleaned up the kitchen. My plan was to leave early in the morning to return home but I knew there was still so much ground to cover. We took our wine and went back into the den. The fireplace was roaring, and the dogs were snoozing on their oversized dog beds. This time, Lovedy sat across from me, curled up at the end of the love seat. As she continued with her story, she avoided eye contact with me and focused on rubbing the stem of her wine glass.

"Things were good for about six months," Lovedy continued, still not making eye contact. "Isaac stayed at his parents' house to save money. He started attending community college and was working full time at the tire shop. Between our jobs and school, we didn't have a lot of time to spend together. He started to get angry about it and would accuse me of runnin' around on him. He just wasn't himself. He started drinking with friends from work. We would agree on a time to meet so we could hang out, but he would either be late or not show up at all. I spoke with Clara about it because I was really worried about him. She said he had been having nightmares and she would hear him crying in his room. They tried to talk to him, to help him but he would just shut down. She even suggested he talk to their pastor, but he refused.

And then, one night, just over a year after he returned home, he was at a bar with some friends. They left but he stayed behind. He decided, for whatever reason, to walk home. He was yelling at people as they were driving by and one of them called the sheriff's department and told them an intoxicated man was walking in the middle of the street, swearin' at people and actin' crazy. And well, you know the rest."

"How did you find out about it? Where were you when it happened?"

"I was at Faith's. It was late, probably midnight by the time we got the call. It was Daddy who called us."

"Your dad?" I was surprised at this piece of information.

"I know. Shocking, right?" She scoffed a bit at the irony. I hadn't really spoken to him since I graduated. Once I moved out, I left that little town and all of its bullshit behind me. I didn't even go home for Thanksgiving or Christmas. I would just make excuses that I had to work or study. I would see Hope and Baby when they would come over to visit though.

I knew Mama and Daddy would never approve of my relationship with Isaac. Remember the barn box? I *knew* who they really were, so I made my choice. As far as I was concerned, they were dead to me."

"How did he find out so quickly?"

"Jeremiah called him. I didn't really understand it at all. I was hysterical and in shock. After Daddy called, Faith drove me directly over to the Carter's house. There were cars along the entire street on both sides. The sheriff was there with several deputies and two men in suits, the extended family was there… it seemed like half the town was there. It was pretty chaotic. And then there was my Daddy, standing in the middle of all of it."

"Why? Why was he there?"

"Part of me thinks it was because he loved Jeremiah and Jeremiah loved him. The other part of me thinks it was because Jeremiah was a very smart man. He could see what was about to happen and he needed someone to help him deal with the police. He knew Daddy was friends with the sheriff, that they went way back. It was his only chance to get to the truth.

I remember the house being really crowded and everyone was cryin'. Some people were prayin' with Clara. I had to get some air, so I went out the back door and sat down on the steps. And then I heard Daddy talkin' to the sheriff. It sounded like they were around the corner of the house. I quietly walked to the edge but stayed on the back side of the house and hid in the shadows so they wouldn't know I was there. I heard the sheriff tell my dad that the deputy was new on the job and didn't follow the proper procedure. I heard him say it was a bad shot and he just wasn't sure what to do about it.

That's when I stepped out of the dark and into their view. I could only see their silhouettes in the brightness of the streetlight, but somethin' in me exploded and I started rushin' them. I got up in the sheriff's face, 'Your deputy shot an *unarmed* man. And while you may not be sure what to do about it, I'm telling you right here, right now, you *will* do the right thing by Isaac.' Then I took a step back and said, 'I *heard* the conversation. I *know* what happened. And I won't let you get away with lying about it!'

Daddy grabbed me by the arms to settle me down. 'Love, I know you're upset, but you don't know the whole story. These are complicated matters you are just too young to understand. Now go on back inside and let the sheriff and I talk this out. I'll take care of this, *I promise*. Now go, Love. Go on.'

I ran back into the house and immediately started searching for a quiet place to hide. I had never been in Isaac's room but the moment I opened the door, I felt him there. I laid down on his bed, brought his pillow to my face and screamed. I couldn't believe he was gone. I cried for Isaac, I cried for his Mama, I cried for me, and I cried for his baby girl that would never have the chance to see his beautiful smile.

I cried about the cruelty of the world. I cried about the loss of my first love. I cried until I couldn't breathe.

After a while, I opened my swollen eyes and looked around his room. His work uniform was hangin' on the door of his closet, waiting for him to come home and put it on in the morning. On his nightstand, there was a lamp and a mason jar full of coins that sat next to his Bible. There was another book there called "The Angry Ones" that had a bookmark in it.

I got off the bed and walked over to his dresser. On one side, there was a stack of clean, folded shirts and a small dish that cradled an old watch and his class ring. On the other side there was a record player with a vinyl sitting on the platter. I dropped the needle and sat on the bed, listening to the same song and remembering the dance we shared under that oak tree on that chilly night.

And then I started thinking about what else I could have done to help him, to keep all of this from happening. *I was responsible,* I told myself. I didn't pull the trigger, but I made so many decisions that started the events that led up to this one. If only I hadn't kept pushing him. If I hadn't held his hand or made him slow dance with me. If I hadn't kissed him or climbed into the back of the wagon with him. If I hadn't gotten pregnant or left home for six months. If I would have loved him better or spent more time with him when he got home. If I would have tried to get him more help. There were so many things I could have, and should have, done differently. But now he was gone. Forever."

As I listened to Lovedy sharing her memories about the end of Isaac's life, I had a feeling that we should end our conversation. She had been revisiting a lot of painful and grief-filled moments during the last two days and I had more than enough to get started on my work. On the other hand, I knew her story didn't end there. I was so curious to learn about her life after the baby, after Isaac. But I thanked her profusely that evening for her generosity, for hosting me in her home and for trusting me with her story that was so profoundly and deeply personal. The rest would have to wait for another time. For now, it was enough.

We relaxed there for a little while longer, enjoying one another's company. We got on the floor, played tug with the dogs, and had another glass of wine together. David came home and gave me a tour of his beloved garage. Lovedy was so right about the sparkle in his eyes. That man was head over heels in love with his mistress.

I woke up early the next morning, eager to hit the road and get home so I could start writing. I showered, packed my bag, and left a thank you note on the nightstand. Thinking Lovedy and David might still be sleeping, I quietly stepped out to the kitchen to grab some fruit and water for the road.

"Mornin', Sunshine!" Lovedy shouted, obviously intending to startle me. "You tryin' to sneak out of here without sayin' goodbye?"

I laughed at her little prank and said, "Your daughter likes to scare me all the time. Must be in the genes. By the way, do you guys always get up this early?"

"Not quite but close to it. The dogs usually wake us up. But I knew you would be wantin' to leave early, and I wanted to catch you before you left. I know we didn't plan on this, but I thought you might want to meet Clara on your way home. She's about an hour west of here, right off the highway that you're takin'."

"Oh wow! That would be great! I had planned on meeting her through Corrina, but this would work just as well. Are you sure you wouldn't mind making that drive?"

"Not at all. I usually go over there at least once a month and it has been three weeks or so since I've seen her. She loves havin' company and would be so tickled to meet you. Just give me a few minutes to get my things together and we can leave."

David carried my bags out to the Jeep and gave me a hug. I watched him walk over to the garage. As Lovedy was backing out, she stopped and put the window down. He leaned in, put his hand on the side of her face, and kissed her lips. I smiled, so happy that she had found someone to love her in a way that was so caring and obvious.

I followed Lovedy to the assisted living facility where Clara had lived for the past three years. It was a gorgeous building on a large property with mountains in the backdrop, a variety of trees, and lush landscaping. Lovedy stopped me outside of the home before we went in so we could talk.

"Clara is eighty-nine years old," Lovedy said, almost in a whisper. "I just want you to be aware that her sight is failin' her, however, her mind is fully intact, and her ears are bionic. Don't say anything that you don't want her to hear."

I smiled at her description. "Corrina has spoken so much about her over the years. I'm just so excited to finally meet her. I can hardly stand it."

We walked into the lobby and checked in with the front desk. I followed Lovedy down the hall to Clara's apartment and she knocked on the door. An attendant showed us in and took us to where Clara was seated in a large recliner that seemed to swallow her tiny body. Her apartment was small, a one bedroom with a kitchen, bathroom and a small living area with a small dinette, a sofa, recliner and coffee table. Clara stood up to greet us and I was struck by how petite she was, especially standing next to Lovedy.

"Hi, Clara!" Lovedy bent over and gave her a kiss on the cheek. "I brought a visitor with me today who has been wanting to meet you for a long time. Her name is Farrah. She's Corrina's friend."

"Oh my Lord! Corrina has told me so much about you," she said with a big smile, reaching out to hug me. I embraced her, thinking about the story Lovedy told me about the mystical powers of a Clara hug. And she was right. She held onto me for a few moments, and I felt the love and compassion flowing from this woman who I had met only moments ago.

She sat back down in her chair, and we began to talk as if we were old friends. She told me about her move to the facility and how much she missed living at home. She told me about the people she had met in her new community that she had grown to love so much. Then she asked me, "Did Lovedy tell you I was blind?"

I wasn't sure how to answer that question, so I turned to look at Lovedy, who was sitting on the love seat beside me. I was hoping she would give me some sign of how to answer. But before I could get any direction from her, Clara piped in and said, "Obviously, she has spoken mistruths. I just saw you whip your little head around to see how you were supposed to answer that question. I can see you, I just can't make you out very well. My macular degeneration is closin' in on me. Pretty soon, you'll look like a little pinprick but until then, don't believe a word she says. I can see just fine." She had a low, slow giggle that was so contagious.

As we sat and visited with Clara, I observed the repartee between these two women. It was a familiar exchange, forged by years gone by and time well spent together. They knew each other by heart. And then, Lovedy graciously opened a door for me.

"Farrah started writin' a book, Clara. It's fiction but is inspired by Corrina's life. Farrah just spent the weekend with me, learnin' about the beginnin' of Corrina's life and how all of that came to be. And I thought you would have some history and insights to share with her, as well. What do you think about that? Are you open to spendin' time with Farrah and talkin' to her?"

Clara didn't hesitate to welcome me into her life, into her memory. "Well, I don't have much else to do these days, that's for sure, and I would love some company. But I'm an old woman with a good memory. Which means, this could take a while and we should probably do it quickly. Jesus could call me home any minute now," she smiled as if she had somewhere to go and was looking forward to it.

We talked about the logistics of how I could get time with Clara, being that I lived four hours away. We put together a tentative schedule that included in-person visits and phone calls. My original plan was to go home and start writing, using the notes and audio I had from my visit with Lovedy. Then my next step was to spend time with Charlotte, then Clara. But I knew I had to be flexible. The schedule of a woman approaching ninety years old who was a little too eager to meet Jesus should most certainly take priority.

We sat with her a little while longer until the attendant came in to help Clara get down to the dining hall for lunch. We said our goodbyes and I promised to call her very soon.

Lovedy and I signed out in the lobby then went out to our cars. She gave me a hug and I thanked her repeatedly for everything. She invited me to come back out to her house whenever I traveled to meet with Clara again, and I was so glad because I knew there was more to talk about with Lovedy too. I took off in the Jeep with a feeling of peace, like everything was coming together.

FIFTEEN
MARCH 2022

I spent the evening with Gabe and the pups. We had dinner and then lounged around, watching TV, and catching up on the rest of my visit with Lovedy and Clara. We went to bed early and did what lovers do. We fell fast asleep in each other's arms with one of my legs kicked out from underneath the covers. But that still didn't keep my body from reacting to the furnace that was my husband. That man generated so much heat and it didn't work well with the changes that were going on with my body. Once I awoke, it was impossible to go back to sleep. My mind was spinning, thinking about Lovedy, Isaac, and Clara. I got up, took a quick shower, and put on one of his gigantic white undershirts that came down to my knees. Then, I slipped out to the den with my phone, laptop, and earbuds, and started listening to the conversations with Lovedy. Almost immediately, I was so thankful for the audio. I could never have remembered all the details and nuances that were part of her story, and I had it all there to refer to anytime I needed.

I just started typing and before I knew it, the faintest hint of a sunrise started peeking through the open blinds. Had I really been working for three hours? The time just flew by.

Gabe was up a couple of hours later. We had breakfast together and he headed off to the gym and to run some errands. I grabbed another cup of hot tea and went right back to my laptop. Writing furiously, another four hours passed by.

I took a break to eat and then decided to walk the dogs. I could feel a slight warmth in the air signaling spring was just around the corner and tiny buds would soon appear on the neighborhood landscapes. I took another trip around the block before heading back to the house to throw a load of laundry into the washing machine. And then I went right back to the laptop.

I had somehow tapped into an internal drive that I didn't know I had. No one was making demands on me. There was no project deadline or client expectations to be met. I wasn't working to please anyone. It felt just like breathing..easy, necessary, and yet instinctive.

Gabe came home, and I was still in his white shirt, typing away. He suggested we get out of the house for dinner, so I slipped on some jeans and a light sweater, put my hair up in a messy bun and swiped on some lip gloss.

There was a spot where we loved to eat that became a regular place for us not long after moving to Tennessee. It sat on the side of the mountain with gorgeous views of the valley and river. Family owned, the food was fabulous and mostly farm to table. They had the best soy-ginger pan seared salmon I had ever tasted, and their vegetables were fresh year-round. It was the kind of place you would never think twice about when driving by it, but once you had the culinary experience, you knew you'd found someplace special.

As we were finishing up the last of our wine, Gabe said he had an idea he wanted to share with me. "While you were away, I started thinking about the conversation we had about the house and our lifestyle. You know what I'm talking about…the guilt conversation?" I nodded yes and he continued. "I'm fully retired and you're sort of retired, so I was thinking about ways that we could give back, pay it forward. I think you're right that there is a limit to the amount of excess that should be allowed. So, I did a bit of research and found there are many ways to give to others. There are monetary contributions, of course, but there's also things like time, effort, and expertise. And I thought maybe we could come up with something that we could do together, a joint effort if you will."

"That's an interesting idea. I love the thought of us working on something together. Did you come up with any specific things we could do?"

"I'm working on it," he said with a grin, "and I can tell just by watching you for the last twenty-four hours that you're going to be really immersed in writing this book. You keep working on that, I'll keep working on this, and we'll keep checking in with each other. By the time you're finished with the book, we should have some solid plans in place. And if you keep up this pace, I don't think it will be very long."

I had a general plan laid out, but I had no idea how long it would take. Eris showed up and started to remind me about some issues Gabe and I had during our marriage. In my former career, any time there was a job or big project to do, I tended to become fixated and, if I'm being honest, neglected my marriage. My thoughts were getting louder, and I began to worry about how I would balance the time I needed to work on the book with the demands of a husband who had a lot of free time on his hands. Truth is, *I wanted to get lost* in Corrina's story. I wanted to forget about everything and everyone around me, put my head down and do what I loved to do.

You're a selfish bitch and you're going to trade in your marriage for a pipe dream, Eris scolded me.

As we stood up to leave and he was helping me put my coat on, it suddenly became very warm. The pounding in my chest started, then the shortness of breath, and the tingling in my fingertips. I just wanted to get outside and get some fresh air. When he opened the door, the cool blast hit me, and I found my breath again. Once I got into the car and laid my head back, my heart rate started to slow down.

I knew that he noticed, and I was embarrassed when he asked

"You ok? Can I do anything?"

"No, nothing. It's going away. I'll be ok in a second." I was hoping he would let it go but it wasn't like Gabe to let anything go unresolved.

"I've said it before, and I'll say it again. I don't think it would be a bad idea for you to see a therapist about this and figure out where it is coming from. It can't hurt."

"I'm aware," I snapped. "I've just tried to imagine how those conversations would go. I've had good friends my whole life, a support system, a successful career, and a husband who loves me. What is there to be anxious about? I'd just feel foolish."

"Well, if I see it ramping up, I'm not going to give you a choice. I'll make an appointment and drive you there myself if it comes to that."

I surrendered, with a sigh. "Fair enough. But I feel normal now. Sometimes it just takes a few minutes."

"For thirty years, I solved problems for a living. It frustrates me that I can't solve this for you. I'm just asking you to please consider talking to someone. For yourself, but also for me. It hurts me to see you go through these episodes, mi amor." The look on his face, it pained me.

"I know…I know. I'm sorry, Gabe. I promise I'll think about it, seriously."

"Thanks. That's all I'm asking. For now." Then he started the car and pulled out with a frown on his face. I grabbed his hand just to let him know that I heard him.

The moon was full and lit up the mountain tops as we headed home. I started thinking about how I used to draw it on construction paper when I was a kid. I never considered the entire egg-shaped rock that hangs so effortlessly in the night sky. My drawings were always flat and crescent shaped, as if the parts that were not exposed by the sun didn't really exist. It made me think about people, even about myself, and how we can so easily ignore things that we know are there but cannot see with our eyes.

SIXTEEN
APRIL 2022

Over the next four weeks I devoured the audio recordings from my visit with Lovedy. I relived all the conversations we shared in her living room, kitchen, sitting by that magnificent magnolia and walking among the stones that bore witness to the lives of those no longer with us. I created a chart so that I could keep the fictitious names straight and protect the hearts that were so generously sharing their joys and sorrows with me.

Just as spring showed up and the foliage came back to life, I traveled back to North Carolina to stay another weekend with Lovedy and have my first official visit with Clara. As I pulled up the driveway, Abby and Costello came out to meet me just like before. But that time, I brought my new friends a bag of crunchy bacon.

"Don't spoil my dogs, Farrah!" Lovedy shouted as she bounded down the steps of her sprawling front porch. She grabbed one of my bags as we headed inside, the dogs glued to my heels.

"How's the writing goin'?" She asked as she put out salads made with Brussels sprouts, bacon, toasted almonds and drizzled with a warm apple cider dressing.

"I'm really enjoying the work. You were so generous with the details. It made it easy to capture the authenticity of your story. Thank you for that, Lovedy."

"I can't help it. My mind works with all five senses in overdrive. Memories aren't just visions to me. Touch, sound, taste, even smells of the past are all still there, stored away in my brain. Couldn't get rid of them if I tried. It drives David crazy. He can't remember what he had for lunch yesterday," she laughed as she poured us some sparkling water and we sat down at the table.

We started with small talk but honestly, I couldn't wait to get the conversation going again. I turned on my recorder and said, "Forgive me for diving right in, Lovedy. After listening to the audio, I was just wondering how, after all the trauma you went through, you found a path forward?"

She smiled at my eagerness and then her face turned serious. "It wasn't easy. For a while, I was just goin' through the motions. I continued goin' to my classes and focused on studyin' and I visited Clara and Jeremiah as much as I could. I know that sounds selfish, bein' that they were dealing with so much grief of their own, but spending time with them felt a little like being with Isaac.

For months, I kept having the most vivid dreams about him. We would be climbin' that magnolia, playin' in the creek or chasin' each other through the cow pastures, playin' hide-and-go-seek. I would wake up and feel like I just spent hours with him. The dreams were so comforting that I couldn't wait to fall asleep just so I could see him again. But, dear God, the daytime was different. Grief can be a crushin' monster and it would visit anytime it wanted. It would overcome me while I was doing everyday things like takin' a shower or eatin' breakfast or sittin' in class, takin' a test. Faith was my everything during those days. She didn't try to fix anything for me. She just told me that when grief was bangin' on my door, I should invite it in. She told me to surrender to it, to feel all of it. So that's what I did.

Eventually, life moved on. And the grief became a little less crushin' and more like somethin' I carried around with me all the time. I was finishin' up school and doin' all the things I should have been doin' but my heart was always heavy. I felt guilty for being alive. I couldn't laugh or smile without feelin' like I was betrayin' Isaac in some way. It was a conversation with Clara that profoundly changed my course. I shared my feelings of guilt with her one night over dinner. Her reaction was not exactly one of compassion or sympathy. It was the first time I had seen even a speck of anger in her eyes. She pounded her fist on the table and said, 'He is *gone. Isaac is gone.* Whether you choose to live your life tormented with guilt or decide to embrace every breath and sunrise that the good Lord gives to you, it doesn't change what happened to Isaac. But it will change what happens to you. So, make your choice, but make it for you.'

I graduated nursing school not long after that and started workin' at the hospital. I wasn't ready to live on my own, so I decided to stay at Faith's. I helped them with rent and bought my first car. I started laughin' again. I started lookin' forward to wakin' up in the mornings. I loved my patients and my job but what I loved most was feeling like I had a purpose. I started to feel like myself.

I still visited with Isaac almost every Sunday. I would take him fresh flowers and talk about my week. Even in death, he was still my friend and I never stopped lovin' him.

And then one day, a patient who had been in a car accident was brought up to my floor. He was a mess. Concussion, broken leg, cracked ribs, lacerations, and contusions everywhere. Even with the pain he was in, he was a hopeless flirt. His name was Shane, and he was very handsome with his cleft chin and his bright blue eyes. When he was bein' released, he asked me out on a date. I said no and explained that I didn't date patients. He just smiled and said, 'ok' and left in his wheelchair. About eight weeks later, a bouquet of flowers arrived at work with a card that said, *'Not a patient anymore. Fifth Ave Coffee Shop on Saturday at 1:00?'*

I didn't go because I had to work, and I had no way to call him. But the next week, another bouquet arrived with, '*Fifth Ave Coffee Shop on Sunday at 1:00?*' But I already had plans to go to the lake with friends from work. Then a *third* bouquet arrived, but this time he was holding it, leaning on the nurses' station counter with his head cocked to one side and a big ol' grin on his face, and I couldn't resist.

It was a whirlwind romance. We fell hard and fast, and before I knew it, we were at the courthouse, and I had a ring on my finger. We bought a house and started to build a life together. He was teachin' history and coachin' football at the local high school, and I continued with my nursin' at the hospital.

Then one day, I talked to Shane about continuing my education. His response was totally unexpected. He told me that he wanted us to start a family, and he didn't understand how that could happen if I was workin' *and* goin' to school. Up until that point, I hadn't really thought about havin' more kids, but I kind of liked the idea of having children with him. We started tryin' to get pregnant immediately, but month after month I would get more and more disappointed when it didn't happen.

He started gettin' frustrated too. One night, about six months after tryin' and failin', he asked me if I was even able to have a baby and suggested that I go to see a doctor. And that's when I told him about Corrina. He freaked out and started throwin' and breakin' things. He got up in my face and accused me of being a liar and a whore. I was stunned but I was not one to back down. I wasn't thinkin', just reactin' when I hauled off and slapped him in the face."

"You *slapped* him?" I questioned, jaw open with shock.

"Regrettably, I did. He took a step back and laughed in a wicked sort of way, and then he hauled off and slapped me so hard that I fell back onto the couch. I swear, I saw stars and my ears were ringin'. But I jumped back up, told him to go to hell and that I never wanted to see him again. I ran into our room and packed a bag. He followed me and kept apologizin' over and over but I ignored him, got in my car, and went to Clara's."

"Clara's?"

"Yes. I would have gone to Faith's, but I knew that was the first place he would look for me. He didn't know Isaac's family so I knew that I could hide there."

"How did Clara handle it?"

"Like she always does, with love and compassion. I didn't even call ahead. I just showed up and knocked on the door. When she saw my face, she pulled me into her arms and just let me cry. She didn't push, didn't ask me any questions. She put an ice bag on the side of my face, kissed me on the top of my head and told me I could stay as long as I needed. I had a couple of days off work but when I returned, there was a bouquet of flowers waitin' for me that said, *'I'm so sorry. Fifth Ave Coffee Shop on Saturday at 1:00?'*

I jumped in immediately to protest, "Tell me you didn't go!"

"Wish I could, but that wouldn't be honest. I did meet him at the café with all of my defenses on full display, but he was his usual, charmin' self, and I felt responsible for the whole thing. I thought if I had just been honest with him all along or if I hadn't hit him first, then we wouldn't even be in that position. We forgave each other and made promises to love each other better. I went to Clara's, picked up my things and went back to the house that night. Six weeks later, I found out I was pregnant."

"Woah…" was all I could say. I had *no idea* she had another child. In all the years I had known her, she never talked about it, Corrina never mentioned it, there weren't any pictures of her children in her house. My mind was racing to get ahead of what she was about to say. What was I missing?

"Yes. We were so happy. He doted on me like never before. We painted the guest room a pale yellow and bought a crib and a rocking chair. The girls at work threw me a baby shower. We didn't know the sex of the baby, so everything was yellow and green. The pregnancy was going flawlessly, and I had never seen Shane so happy. He was so excited to have that baby that he would put an X on our wall calendar, marking one less day until he would be a father. Then one evenin', about two weeks from my delivery date, I was takin' a shower. I don't know how to describe what happened next other than to tell you what it felt like."

My heart was up in my throat as I waited for her to finish.

"I literally felt my baby's spirit leave my body. It was like an ethereal whoosh feeling followed by a sense of emptiness, stillness. My belly was still big, my baby's body was still inside of me, but I just knew. My baby was gone.

I screamed for Shane, and he ran into the bathroom and found me in hysterics. He dried me off and dressed me, then we went to the hospital. There was no heartbeat, so they induced me. After they cleaned her up, they put that sweet, swaddled bundle in my arms. I had about thirty minutes with my sweet Clara Jean. She was a beautiful baby girl and she looked so at peace. I remember everything about her. Her little fingers, her smell, the softness of her skin, the blonde wisps of hair. She looked like an angel sleeping in my arms."

"My God, Lovedy. I am so deeply sorry." My heart was in my stomach. Her grief was thick and palpable as we sat at that dining room table together. I had no words of comfort or wisdom to give her, so I just reached over and took her hand in mine as she continued.

"If you're wondering why there wasn't a grave for her at the cemetery, it is because we had her cremated. I wanted her with me, all the time. I couldn't stand the thought of her bein' in a cemetery all by herself." And then from the rock, flowed a river of tears. I cried with her and held her hand and then stepped away to get a box of tissues.

When she was ready, she continued. "My relationship with Shane didn't survive the death of our daughter. He wanted to try for another baby soon after we lost Clara Jean, and I just didn't have it in me. I made the decision, for myself, that I would never have any more children. He knew I was firm in my choice and we both knew that he really wanted to have a family. So, we filed for divorce soon after and I moved back in with Faith. There was no fightin', no screamin', no nasty words to each other. It was just two people who couldn't find a way forward and quietly surrendered to the inevitable end of their story together."

SEVENTEEN
1993-2003

AFTER MOM LEFT, I SWORE I WOULD NEVER GET MARRIED. I KNEW, FROM growing up in my own home, that love and marriage were nothing like what I read in books or saw on television or the movies. Love and life weren't anything like the fairytales I was obsessed with as a young child and, as an act of self-preservation, I decided that I would spare myself the inevitable heartbreak.

As an only child, I became an expert at managing loneliness. I didn't necessarily like it, but I knew how to do it and I didn't see the point of changing that as an adult. Besides, if it was just me, then I had complete control of my destiny. I could make my own decisions without having to think about the impact to someone else. My plan worked, at least for a little while.

After graduating from college, and starting my first job at the hospital, I was still living at home. I liked the idea of not having to pay rent and I wasn't quite ready to leave Daddy by himself. But that all changed after I met Corrina that day in the café.

After having lunch together five days in a row, Corrina told me that she was looking for a roommate. She lived in a two-bedroom duplex and her roommate had moved out. Her place was so close to the hospital that she walked to work on most days. I was intrigued.

Even in my twenties, most of my friends were guys. But Corrina was different than most of the girls I knew. She wasn't moody and wasn't always chasing her emotions. She didn't gossip about people and, like me, she couldn't stand watching soap operas. She was direct in her communication, and secure in her own skin. She was sure and steady. She took her time when making major decisions and weighed things thoughtfully and carefully. I trusted her.

I told her I would think about it and that week I talked it over with Daddy. He encouraged me to get out on my own and made me promise to keep a weekly dinner date with him so he could get his regular dose of sunshine.

Two weeks later, I bought a new bedroom set with some of the money I had saved and had it delivered to the duplex. I left everything from my childhood in my room at Daddy's house and took only what I needed to start my new life as an independent adult.

Adulting in the nineties was *fun*. Corrina and I did all the things together that twenty-somethings love to do: bars, clubs, beach vacations, and road trips to the mountains. But our favorite thing to do was attend concerts. We went to so many: Ice Cube, U2, Oasis, Whitney Houston, The Wallflowers, just to name a few and in 1996, we even took a road trip to see Tupac in Cleveland. But that's where Corrina met Judge and brought our good times as single twenty-something adults, to a screeching halt.

He lived in Cleveland, so their relationship was long distance which meant either she was gone on the weekends, or he was staying at the duplex, and I became the dreaded third wheel.

I didn't like him at first and didn't think he was the right guy for Corrina. Sure, he was tall and handsome, a former marine and a college graduate but he was a gym rat and had a solemn way about him. He bogarted conversations with grown-up topics like politics, economics, and the environment. He was a strong black man, physically, emotionally and mentally. I found him to be rather boring. But there was no doubt, Corrina was smitten.

I, on the other hand was the queen of casual dating. I would hang out with a guy until he confessed his feelings for me, then I would give him the boot, saying we were just meant to be friends. Corrina didn't understand my behavior and told me so on a regular basis.

In 1998, at the age of twenty-seven, I met a guy named Julio. He treated me like a princess. He opened doors for me, took me out to fancy dinners and plays and spoiled me with luxurious perfumes and jewelry. He was three years older than me and had a solid career in computer software development. He didn't suffocate me with emotional junk, and he gave me space when I needed it.

One morning, after he stayed over, he made breakfast for all of us, then left to go home. I was cleaning the kitchen and noticed Judge and Corrina were staring at me in silence.

"Don't start with me, Corrina," I snapped as I continue to wipe the counters.

"I haven't said a word," she snapped back with a smile on her face.

"Yes, he's nice. I enjoy his company. That's where it ends," I explained to both of their questioning faces.

"Why does it end there?" Judge piped in.

"Because that's where I *want* it to end. And not that I even want a long-term relationship but he's too short for me. I can't wear my stilettos around him and that's a deal breaker."

"Really, Farrah? It comes down to the height of your heels? That's what love is all about for you?" Corrina quipped.

"Who said anything about love?" I hissed. "There are no rules about relationships. I'm not a princess holed up in her castle waiting for some handsome prince to rescue me and whisk me away to my happy ever after, Corrina. I'm not interested in that."

"I'm not either, Farrah" she glowered. "I'm not talking about children's books, I'm talking about adulthood, companionship and opening your heart to the possibility of sharing your life with someone. It's not a rule, no one says you have to get married and have kids, but it can be something that enhances your life. I get that being vulnerable isn't an easy thing, but it has its perks," she turned her head and smiled at Judge. And then I saw him wink at her, which struck me as sexy for a moment, but then made me want to vomit.

"Is that what you and Judge are doing? Sharing your life together?" I demanded to know.

Judge looked at Corrina but seemed to be talking to me when he gushed, "I asked Corrina to marry me, and she said yes."

My mouth dropped open and I could feel the heat gathering in my face.

"Really, Corrina? When were you going to tell me?" I fumed as I threw my hands in the air.

She looked back at Judge and asked him to give us a minute. He excused himself and went outside as Corrina walked over to the kitchen and sat on the barstool, her elbows on the counter.

"This is how it's going to go, Farrah. I love Judge. I respect him and I want to spend my future building a life with him. You're going to put aside all of your bullshit notions about love and marriage and you're going to be happy for me. You'll stand up with me at our wedding and you'll be the godmother of our children. You may not want marriage and children for yourself, but you will relish in my happiness because you're my friend, my best friend, and that's what you're supposed to do. Are we *clear* on this matter?"

"God, you're so bossy." I sneered. "Yeah, I get it. *Loud and clear.*" And then I went to my room to watch a movie and ponder the many ways my comfortable life was about to change.

Judge and Corrina were married in September of 2000. He moved to Lexington, and they bought a four-bedroom house in the suburbs, leaving me to fend for myself in the city. I didn't want another roommate, so I moved out of the duplex, bought some living room furniture and a dinette set and settled into a one-bedroom apartment in downtown Lexington. It was closer to my new job, a start-up with a bunch of young guys at the head of the table. I saw enormous potential in what they were trying to create in the data analysis field, and I was having fun helping them to realize their dreams.

Corrina and I still saw each other on a fairly regular basis. She continued to work at the hospital on the labor and delivery floor while Judge decided to use his business degree to fulfill his dream of opening a gym. Life was good. It wasn't what it used to be, but I already knew that nothing stays the same forever.

In 2001, Judge and Corrina were vacationing in Cabo for their anniversary. The morning after they left, I was driving across town to meet with a client while listening to the local morning talk show on the radio. The DJ broke his regular programming with news that an airplane had hit the World Trade Center. I went into my client's building at 9:00am and didn't finish our meeting until two hours later. By the time I returned to my car, three more planes had crashed and almost three thousand people had died.

I was trembling as I drove through the city. I wasn't sure where to go. Should I go back to my office? Should I drive straight home?

I didn't want to be alone, so I drove to the office. I ran from my car to the front of the building and bounded the steps, two by two, to the second floor. I flung open the door and ran down the hallway. All of the offices were empty except one. I found Rajeesh, one of the executives, sitting at his desk. The lights were off, and he was staring at a small TV in the corner of his office.

"Rajeesh? Are you ok?"

"I'm ok," he murmured, not taking his eyes off of the television. "I sent everyone home for the day. You should go home too."

"Um...ok. Are you sure? Are you staying or leaving?"

"I'll be leaving in a few minutes."

"Ok, then. I'll see you tomorrow?"

"Yeah, sounds good, Farrah. Thanks for checking in."

He never once looked at me, never asked about the client meeting, but I understood. The menial things in life just didn't matter as they had the day before.

I got back into my car and headed home. I turned on the radio and heard the terror being replayed over and over. As soon as I got inside my apartment, I turned on the television and saw it with my eyes for the first time. Over and over, they replayed the video, as witnesses told of the dreadfulness they had experienced. I kicked off my shoes and backed into the sofa, sinking down without taking my own eyes off of the television. It was surreal, like a horror movie that I couldn't stop watching.

I called Daddy, and we stayed on the phone with each other, watching the news together. He invited me to go over and stay at his house, but I didn't want to get back in the car and I didn't want him driving either.

I was too afraid to go to sleep that night. So much was unknown. Was it over? Would it happen again? Was it safe to go outside? To the market? To a restaurant?

I wondered about Corrina and Judge. They were in Mexico and all planes had been grounded over the North American airspace. Were they ok? How would they get home? I needed them to come home.

I turned down the volume on the TV, clutching my pillow tightly, and continued to watch the images flashing on the screen in silence. And for the first time in my adult life, I yearned for companionship, for someone to care for me, to mourn with me, to hold me until my heartbeat returned to normal.

Turns out, being alone was not all that I had cracked it up to be.

Just nine days after 09/11, President George W. Bush addressed Congress and the nation, declaring war on Al Queda. That was the same day that Corrina and Judge returned home from Mexico. We were all frazzled and adjusting to the new normal. And while there was a new sense of unity among many Americans and patriotism was at an all time high, Muslims and people of Middle Eastern, South Asian, and Arab descent became targets of racial profiling. Skin tones, turbans and long beards struck fear in the hearts of every day citizens.

Most of my coworkers were from India and two of them were Sikhs who wore turbans and beards in devotion to their faith. I saw the fear in their eyes as people stared at them, spoke disrespectfully towards them, calling them terrorists and towel-heads. They were afraid to leave their homes. When the evening news was particularly frightening, I knew I would go into an empty office the next day.

On one of those lonely days at the office, I left to go visit a client. I was stressed, like everyone else, and not paying attention to the speed limit. I heard the chirp of the siren and saw the berries and cherries light up in my rearview mirror. My heart started pounding and beads of sweat starting dripping on my forehead and down my chest. A flood of curse words tumbled out of my mouth as I pulled over and rolled the window down with shaky hands. I was careful to place my hands back on the wheel as my Daddy always taught me to do.

"License, registration, and proof of insurance, please ma'am."

He was absolutely delicious. An obviously hispanic male in his early thirties, tall, broad shouldered, with narrow hips, dark amber skin, thick brown hair that had been kissed by the sun and aviator sunglasses like you see in the movies. I immediately wanted to stick my wrists out of the window and tell him how sorry I was for breaking the law and beg him to forgive me as he placed on the handcuffs.

"Ma'am, I need your license, registration and proof of insurance, please."

"Oh, I'm sorry," I shook my head to bring myself back to the present. "I'm going to reach over and get it out of the glovebox, ok?"

"Yes, thank you."

I leaned over and fumbled around until I found the current

registration and insurance card and then pulled my license out of my wallet, handing them both to him with my best flirtatious grin.

"Do you know why I pulled you over?" He asked politely.

I don't really care. You're a god, I thought. "Was I speeding? I was probably speeding," I confessed. "I tend to do that when I'm stressed." *Shut up, Farrah, shut up,* I scolded myself.

"Yes, you were speeding. I'll be right back," he warned as he turned and walked back towards his patrol car, showing off his perfectly toned butt that was framed between the baton and the semi-automatic that was clipped on each hip.

I kept watching through my rearview and side mirrors but thought that I should make better use of my time until he returned. Using my own weapons that I had at my disposal, I rifled through my purse, whipped out my brush and lipstick, fluffed my hair, swiped on a little color, and shamelessly unbuttoned the top two buttons of my silk, collared blouse. I used everything I had in my arsenal to get out of that ticket.

But it had no effect on him. He sauntered back in all his glory, this time wearing one of those goofy hats, promptly handed me a traffic ticket and explained that all of my options were listed on the back of the document. Then he asked me to sign it.

"Do I *have* to sign it?"

"Your signature is not an admission of guilt, it is only acknowledging that you have been issued a traffic ticket."

He isn't so cute anymore, I thought as I snatched the ticket out of his hand and scribbled an illegible signature on the dotted line. I gave it back to him at which point he generously ripped out a copy and handed it to me. I tossed it on the passenger seat without breaking eye contact and then asked snidely, "Am I free to go?"

"Yes ma'am. Drive safely now," he smiled with his perfectly straight teeth.

I pursed my lips in retaliation and mumbled "You too," as I put my car in drive and took off.

I pulled over in the next parking lot and immediately called my dad.

"Hi Sunshine, how are you?" I could hear his smile through the phone.

"Daddy, I just got a speeding ticket," I cried angrily.

"Oh honey, don't you worry about that. You have some options. Have you read the back of the document?"

"No, it just happened. Do you know what they are?"

"If I remember correctly, you can just pay the ticket and be done with it. But there will be points put on your license, which could cause your insurance rate to increase. You can get those points removed by taking a safety driving course, or you can bet on the deputy not showing up to court."

"Why, what will happen if he doesn't show up?"

"If the deputy's reason for not showing up isn't justified, then the judge will probably dismiss the case. If there is a valid reason, the judge may reschedule the court date."

"Hmm…I think I'll just pay it and try to get the points removed. I'm not wasting any more time on it and I don't want to give that guy the satisfaction of beating me in court. He's the type that would definitely show up."

"You do what you think is best, but don't spend any time worrying about it. It happens to most people at one time or another. Most importantly, I need my girl to drive safely. Ok?"

"I will. I promise."

About three months after the unfortunate speeding incident, I went out for dinner with several guys from work. We were sitting at a round table that was next to the bar, and that's when I saw the most handsome guy sitting at a bar top with two other guys. I excused myself to go to the restroom so I could get a closer look. As I passed his table, I heard them talking about their day. Their haircuts, broad shoulders and conversation gave me no doubt they worked for the sheriff's office. I made eye contact with him as I continued walking towards the restroom. It was his smile that gave him away.

Oh, it's you, without your stupid smokey hat, I thought. The instinctive smile that I gave in return faded into a frown and I continued marching towards the restroom, pretending not to recognize him. No way was I going to give him the satisfaction of thinking he made any impression on me. I stayed in the restroom for a couple of minutes, freshened up my lipstick and ran a brush through my hair. If I was going to ignore him again, I was going to look pretty doing it.

"Ms. Langford," he said as I passed his table. *What? How does he remember my name?* I pretended not to hear him and kept walking.

"Farrah!"

Seriously? He remembers my first name too? What a jackass.

I turned around ever so slowly with my best glare on display.

"Yes?" I hissed. "Can I help you?"

"I just wanted to say hello. It is good to see you again."

"Well, you're alone in that sentiment. Enjoy your dinner." I sauntered away, with an extra sway in my hips.

I went back to the table and enjoyed my own dinner with the guys, making sure to smile and laugh at every joke like I was having the best time ever despite the palpitations in my heart. I kept waiting for him to leave, but he just kept hanging out at that bar top, telling stories and laughing with his buddies like he had nowhere else to go.

I was nervous and had too much wine to drink, so after getting tired of waiting for him to go, I called a cab to take me home. As I was waiting outside, I heard him say my name again.

"Ms. Farrah Langford."

I whipped around, "Why do you continue to say my name? You want me to know that you have a good memory? Well, you do. So there, you happy?"

"Very happy. Happy to see you again. And I don't have a great memory but your name, Farrah, it is unusual, pretty, and hard to forget. It is a fitting name for you." He stuck out his hand and introduced himself, "I'm Gabe. Gabe Acosta."

I knew I would never forget his name either and then my lips betrayed me as they curled into a smile.

He asked me out and I said yes, but it wasn't anything like a fairytale.

EIGHTEEN
APRIL 2022

I left after lunch at Lovedy's to head to Clara's. As I sat behind the wheel and cruised down the highway, my mind was reeling, and my heart was heavy. It wasn't my story. It wasn't my grief. I still felt the weight of it, nonetheless. I called Corrina and when she didn't pick up, I left her a message, telling her that I was on my way to Clara's, and would try to get a hold of her on my way back to Lovedy's that evening. It had been a while since we spoke and there was so much to talk about.

I arrived at the care facility right on time, checked in at the front desk and walked back to Clara's apartment. This time she greeted me at the door, all smiles, and warm hugs. She sat down in her recliner next to the window, and I sat across from her on the loveseat. There were lemon cookies, a pot of tea on the coffee table and a variety of magazines stacked underneath an old black bible with faded gold ink on the cover.

As I sat my phone down on the coffee table, I asked, "Ms. Clara, would it be alright with you if I recorded our conversations? I'm afraid my memory isn't as good as yours and I may forget some important parts of your story."

"That would be just fine with me," she said as she waved her hand at me.

"So, why don't we start with where you were born and what life was like for you growing up?"

"Oh my goodness, girl. You're goin' way back!" She chuckled and thought for a moment. "Let's see now, I was born in nineteen and thirty-three, just after Franklin Roosevelt was elected to office. Those were the depression years, and it was a tough time for our country. It was especially hard for Black communities. So many families had migrated up north, hopin' to find work, but my parents stayed here, in North Carolina. My sister, Evelyn, was born two years after me. My parents went through challenging times, especially havin' two little mouths to feed but we somehow survived it.

We had a small two-bedroom house on the east end of town. In the thirties, before integration and urban renewal, that area of town was primarily African American families. Everyone helped each other out durin' those years. It was just the way of life for us. Our church had programs to help get food and other essentials for people who needed it. We had a grocery store and a barber shop, a good school and other black-owned businesses that provided goods and services to our people. Even though most folks were livin' in poverty, our community still thrived in the ways that mattered most. I have good memories of growin' up in that neighborhood with Mama and Pops and my sister.

Mama had it set in her mind that my sister and I would be teachers. Back in their day, they learned to read at their church, and she knew even back then that education held the keys to success. She was so strict about our studies and didn't have much tolerance for foolin' around. Thank the sweet Lord we both loved to read!"

"You mentioned church earlier. Was faith a big part of your family life?" I asked.

"Part?" She chuckled and went on, "It was the *center* of our family and our community. Our hope for better days was rooted in the belief that God was good, that He saw our needs and heard our prayers.

God was the reason, that amid financial ruin, our east end community didn't fall apart. He took care of us by reminding us, in the scriptures, to take care of each other. So many people in this world want all their prayers answered but they don't want to be *the answer* to someone else's prayer. Makes no sense to me," she shook her head in resignation.

I poured us both a cup of tea and waited for her to continue, but she stopped for a moment and then asked me a question I wasn't expecting.

"Was faith a part of your family life, Farrah?"

I paused, thinking how I should answer that question and just landed on telling her the truth. "I would say no, especially in a theological way. My mother was Catholic, but we didn't go to church much or pray. My parents did believe in being a good person though, helping others, serving your community. Things like that."

"Ah, I see. So, you don't really believe in God. Is that right?" She was staring at me intensely, waiting for my answer.

I was taken aback by her candor. It was a question I would never ask anyone unless they brought it up first. But knowing what I knew about Clara, I figured she wouldn't throw me out if I told her the truth again, but I couldn't escape the feeling that I was about to disappoint her. "Can't say that I really do. Sometimes I've wondered about it, but there are so many things I can't reconcile, that don't make sense to me. I've decided that not knowing for sure is ok with me."

"Well, we're not that far apart, then. Neither of us know for sure, right? The only difference is I choose to believe anyway, and you don't," She turned to look out the window as she continued. "Looking back, I don't know how I would have made it through without my faith. It has given me hope when there was no reason to have any. It held me up during the bad times and gave me someone to thank for all the joy and good times I've had. And there have been a lot of both, that's for sure."

While I appreciated the role that faith played in Clara's life, I felt the need to keep the conversation moving, so I changed the subject. "Where did you meet Jeremiah? Did he live in your town?"

"We grew up together. He was a year older than me. Our families were friends, so I suppose we knew each other since we were babies. I can't remember a time when I didn't know him. He was sweet on me early on but my parents wouldn't allow any of that nonsense until we were teenagers. His daddy was the pastor of our church, and he was really strict on Jeremiah too. We married young and lived with my parents for a couple of years until we got our own place. Jeremiah made a livin' fixin' machinery. He was a whiz at that stuff. I did some domestic work for a while, cleanin' houses, doin' laundry, things like that.

We had always talked about having a big family. My sister and her husband were havin' babies left and right, but it took us a while to get pregnant. It wasn't for a lack of tryin' if you know what I mean," she said with a laugh and a pointed look, making sure that I knew what she meant. "That man was always on me. It was a wonder why I wasn't havin' a baby every year! Then in August of nineteen and fifty-two, I found out I was pregnant with Isaac. Jeremiah was beside himself with joy, and it was one of the happiest times of my life. I used to read to Isaac when he was in my belly. And I would sing to him all the time."

And then in that sweet, faint voice, she started singing a song about God being real.

"Is that an old gospel song?" I asked.

"Yes, it sure is. Was written by Kenneth Morris back in nineteen and forty-four, I believe. If you've never listened to black gospel, you've never heard real music."

"Can't say that I have, Ms. Clara. Besides Kenneth Morris, who else would you recommend that I listen to?"

"There are so many Black gospel artists that are the root of a lot of music created over the decades. You have that Google thing, look it up. But make sure you don't miss out on Mahalia Jackson. You know she sang at MLK Jr.'s funeral? She's gonna sing at mine too." And she smiled again like she was going on vacation, soon.

I'm usually having an anxiety attack when Eris plans my funeral, I thought, *and here she is grinning like she knows she's got the winning lottery numbers.*

I wrote a reminder to myself to research the history of black gospel music and quickly moved on from the funeral talk.

"Did your pregnancy go ok?"

"It went beautifully. Some women have such a tough time with the nausea and the backaches and all that. I didn't have any of it. I loved being pregnant so much, I didn't want it to end. But then on March eighteenth of nineteen and fifty-three, my sweet Isaac was born. Do you know what the name Isaac means?"

I shook my head. "No, I sure don't."

"The Hebrew name Isaac means 'he will rejoice'. And I tell you what, that boy was smilin' at everything at two-months old and never stopped until Lovedy went away. He was such an easy baby and a very happy child."

"Did you try to have more children after Isaac was born?"

"Like I said, Jeremiah was always tryin' to have another baby. He was always chasin' me 'round the house. Even after I went through the change, that man was still tryin' to get me pregnant. Couldn't keep his hands to himself, all the way up until the day he passed."

She started with that low, slow, contagious giggle again and I couldn't help but join in with her. The more she giggled, the more I laughed, and it took us a few minutes to get back to the story.

"After Isaac was born, Jeremiah continued with his machinery business, but it became more of a side thing. He wanted more steady work and Marshall was lookin' for someone to help run the dairy farm. I suppose you know that's how Lovedy and Isaac met. He would only see her in the summers, but that boy loved goin' to work with his Pops. He would come home covered in mud and dirt and smellin' like a barn," She crinkled her nose, remembering the sight and smells of her beloved baby boy. "I always made him take a bath before dinner because I couldn't stand the smell of him at the supper table. He would go on and on about his little friend and how she wasn't like other girls. He never talked about her sisters, only Lovedy."

"Do you remember Lovedy as a child?"

"Oh, yes. Jeremiah and I shared a car, so I would drive them to the farm on days I had to work or needed the car to go to the market. Most days, she would be outside the barn waiting for our car to pull up. I remember she was a skinny little thing. She was long and lanky and always had scratches and bruises on her legs. Even though Isaac was a year older, she was as tall as him, and she had this light blonde, wispy hair that was always knotted and flyin' around in the wind. Always covered in mud and dirt, just like Isaac. What I remember most is how she had this serious, intense look on her face. While Isaac was always smilin', she was always scowlin'. They were quite the pair."

"Do you remember when Jeremiah stopped working at the farm?"

"Oh yes. Remember, there was so much racial tension goin' on in those days and we lived in the south, and it was the sixties. Marshall and Jeremiah were loyal friends and alike in a lot of ways. They were both extremely hard working, quiet men. Both were good with machinery, family men, believers and led simple lives. But along the way, Marshall got mixed up with some bad people and Jeremiah started hearin' things about him and some other men, including the sheriff."

"What kind of things?"

"That they were part of the Klu Klux Klan. And that Marshall was the treasurer of the local chapter."

"Did Jeremiah ever try to talk to Marshall about it?"

"Oh yes. After Marshall told Jeremiah that Isaac was too old to be comin' to the farm, Jeremiah started suspecting that maybe the rumors were true. He would talk about it often, especially at night when we were in bed. He knew the truth but just couldn't believe it. He couldn't reconcile the friend that he knew with the man he was hearin' all those things about. I tried to tell him to leave it alone and to let things be, but he wasn't havin' it. One day, he asked Marshall outright if he belonged to that group. "

"What did Marshall say?"

"He told him yes, he belonged to the KKK but that it wasn't because he hated black folks. He told Jeremiah that he loved all God's children but there was a lot of pressure in the town to keep things separated. He said black folks should live among black folks and the same for the whites. He didn't believe in all the desegregation efforts that were going on. Didn't think it was right to force people to integrate if that's not what they wanted to do. And that's when Jeremiah told him that he couldn't work for him anymore."

"How did Marshall respond?"

"Marshall went into the house and told Jeremiah to wait in the barn. When Marshall returned, he handed Jeremiah the wages he had earned for the week and even gave him an extra week's pay. Marshall even apologized and asked Jeremiah to try and understand the pressure he was under in that town. Jeremiah said he just kept goin' on and on, trying to defend the indefensible. Marshall extended his hand, but Jeremiah couldn't stomach it. He just looked Marshall in the eye and said, 'That's enough' and then he turned around and left."

"Did Isaac know about Marshall being in the KKK?"

"We never told him directly, but I think he knew. Isaac came from a different generation. Those young people were fighters. He and his friends from high school used to sit around in our livin' room, watchin' the TV, and talkin' about civil rights, how they wanted to join the movement and make a difference. We knew what was happenin' to young folks across the country, especially in the south, and we were worried about Isaac gettin' hurt. Jeremiah and Isaac used to argue about it a lot. Jeremiah wanted Isaac to fight by taking full advantage of the opportunities we didn't have when we were his age. Going to college, becomin' successful and providin' his own family with a better future was Jeremiah's way of fightin' back. Success was the best revenge, he would always say. But Isaac and his friends weren't about generational changes. They wanted what was fair and right at that very moment. I loved what he stood for, but it scared me to death, all the same."

"Did you ever believe that he was in danger in your own town?"

"In our town, not so much. But in the surrounding towns, yes. We heard stories of kids gettin' beat up or arrested when they were drivin' through other towns after dark. It was a very scary time. Jeremiah kept telling Isaac to keep his head down, stay low, graduate, and get out of there. Sometimes I felt like Jeremiah was being unfair to Isaac, making him live a smaller life, dimming his light, so to speak. But I know Jeremiah's intentions were good. He was just tryin' to keep his son alive. He wanted him to have a chance at a life that was better than his own."

Chills ran up my spine as I continued to listen.

"Progress was painfully slow and it felt like for every step forward, we were pushed two steps back. Brown versus the Board of Education happened in nineteen and fifty-four. And then Emmitt Till was brutally murdered in fifty-five. I'll never forget seein' his poor, young, bloated body in that newspaper or the look on his mother's face. Most of the Jim Crow laws were overturned in nineteen and sixty-four and sixty-five and yet it was still an uphill battle."

"That was just a couple of years before the time Isaac stopped going to the farm, right?"

"Yes, that's right."

"Did you and Jeremiah know that Isaac and Lovedy had reconnected?"

"Yes, we knew. When he saw her again for the first time at the bowling alley, he told us all about it. He was all smiles. Told us how much she had grown up and how she was mad at him because he stopped going to the farm, but we never heard another word about her until he told us she was pregnant."

"And how did that go?"

"Like you would imagine. He was young and naïve. He told us he loved her and that he wanted to marry her. Jeremiah exploded and responded with some harsh words, which I won't repeat. When he asked Isaac if Lovedy's parents knew, Isaac told him that she was tellin' her parents that night too. Jeremiah ran into the bedroom, brought out his shotgun and put it by the front door. He sat down and waited for Marshall to arrive. When he heard the truck, he stood up and grabbed his gun, but I told him to leave it. I knew Marshall would be angry, but I didn't believe for a second that he would try to hurt anyone. Maybe I was just being naïve too."

"When Jeremiah went flyin' out to the front yard, I knew I had to get them back into the house. No good would have come from those two grown men yellin' at each other in my front yard. They finally came in and you should have seen the look that Marshall gave Isaac when he came into my house. He looked like he wanted to kill him. But Isaac did what he should have done. He apologized to Marshall and told him he loved his daughter, that he had always loved her, that he wanted to marry her and take care of her."

"How did Marshall respond?"

"He did what most fathers would have done. He got up in Isaac's face and cussed him. Told him that he had ruined Lovedy's life and that he better not ever come near his daughter again. He was so red in the face, veins were bulging out everywhere. I was nervous, worried that Isaac would get mouthy or disrespectful. But he didn't. He stood there and looked Marshall square in the eye. Eventually, Jeremiah stood up, walked over and put his hand on Marshall's shoulder. He just said, "That's enough, now." Then, he turned to me and asked me to take Isaac to the back bedroom so he could speak with Marshall alone."

"Do you know what they said to each other?"

"No, sure don't. But trust and believe, Isaac and I had our ears pinned to the door. They were talkin' so low; we couldn't hear anything. Then I heard the door slam and figured Marshall was leavin', so we came out of the bedroom. The next thing I knew, there was a loud bangin' at the door. I could hear Lovedy cryin', just sobbin' away and screamin' Isaac's name. Isaac started headin' for the door, but Jeremiah grabbed his arm. He said, 'Boy, don't you open that door. Let her go home to her family. They got to figure this out.' And that's what Isaac did. He told her to go home, but you should have seen the tears just pourin' out of his eyes. It broke my heart to see those two young ones torn up like that. When I look back, though, I think about all the ways that night could have gone. As scary as it was, I guess we were lucky it stayed as calm as it did."

The time with Clara went by in a blink and I needed to leave as Lovedy was expecting me for dinner. So, I bent over and wrapped my arms around her tiny frame as she sat on the edge of that giant chair. "Thank you so much for spending time with me today. I'll be back to see you in the morning, Ms. Clara."

"I'm lookin' forward to it," she said as she patted my back. "I think I'm going to go take a nap before dinner. You drive safely, now."

NINETEEN
DECEMBER 2001

When Gabe and I met, I had just turned thirty years old. I was stubborn and set in my ways. I had my own apartment, my own routine, and my own remote control. And so did he.

We started out like most couples during the first few months of a new relationship, putting the best versions of ourselves on display. We were agreeable even when we didn't agree, were always kind and polite, and took an interest in each other's hobbies to build more mutual ground and fabricate additional reasons why we should continue seeing each other.

Our schedules were a challenge. He was on patrol and worked two days on, two days off then three days on and another two days off. Workdays were twelve hours for him, in the heat, the rain, and the snow. Most days, when he finished working, he was physically exhausted and only wanted to stay home. On his off days, he ran errands, went to the gym and was always ready to spend time with me. He loved to meet me for lunch, talk on the phone when I had time between meetings and make dinner for us in the evenings. I didn't see much of him on the days he was working but on his off days, he was *always* around.

DECEMBER 2001

About six months into our relationship, the company I worked for experienced a growth spurt and began acquiring new clients across the nation, which meant I was traveling often. My schedule was getting busier and finding time for lunches, midday phone calls and evenings together with Gabe became more difficult. And after a full day of conference calls and facilitating sales meetings, I didn't really want to talk all that much. That's when the problems started.

"Is something wrong?" He asked one evening over dinner.

"No, why do you ask?"

"You're just really quiet, mi amor"

"Sometimes I like the quiet, Gabe. Especially after talking all day at work."

"But I haven't seen you in two days. I don't understand why talking with me over dinner is a problem for you," he put his fork down and folded his hands together, his elbows on the table.

"It isn't about *you*. I said I'm tired from talking all day *at work*," I repeated myself, my frustration growing.

"But after not seeing me for two days, shouldn't it be about us right now? Having time together, talking and enjoying one another's company? Do you not want to make our relationship a priority?"

Here we go, I thought to myself, *the beginning of the end is now approaching*.

"Gabe, can we talk about this some other time? I'm not really feeling up to it." I pleaded as I continued to pick at my salad.

"*No*, we need to talk about it now. Do you know why? Because it is important. It is more important than being tired or frustrated. I don't like the way this conversation is going either but you're more important to me and I want to fix this problem."

"Problem? *What* problem?" I demanded and as I stood up from my chair. "What problem do we have, Gabe? The fact that I don't feel like talking every second of the day? That I would like to enjoy my dinner in silence, for once? This is a problem for you?"

"Yes, mi amor. It is a problem for me."

"Well, the fact that it is a problem for you, is a problem for me! So there, now we both have a problem."

"Estas siendo dificil! Tu corazón no está abierto! No estás escuchando con tu corazón y no quieres acercarte más a mí."

I stood up to clear the table. "Speak in English or don't speak at all," I muttered under my breath.

He sighed and looked down at his half-eaten dinner, wiped his hands with a napkin and stood to his feet. "You are not listening to me with your heart. It seems that you do not want to grow closer to me. I feel you pushing me away. Am I wrong?"

I didn't know how to answer that question. Yes, pushing men away is what I had always done. Was I already doing that to Gabe? Did I *want* to do that with Gabe? Suddenly, I realized that I wasn't ready to let him go and yet, I knew that I didn't want a long-term relationship.

I started feeling weird, my heart started racing and my palms began to sweat. I needed to sit back down but I didn't want my body language to tell him I was giving in.

"I don't know, Gabe. I didn't think I was pushing you away intentionally but that wouldn't be an unusual thing for me to do."

"And why is that mí amor?"

"Because…I don't want a serious relationship. I don't want marriage. I don't want to have a family. I don't want any of that."

He stood there looking at me, dumbfounded. "Then what are we doing, here, Farrah? If we're not growing into something or towards anything, what is the point?"

"To enjoy each other's company? Is that not enough for you?"

"No, it isn't. If you're not open to what life has to offer you, including love, then this is not the relationship for me. You are not the right girl for me."

"Then I don't know what else to say." I looked away from him, out the window, at the ceiling, anywhere but his beautiful face.

"Tell me this," he started taking a step closer towards me, "we've been together for more than six months now. Do you have feelings for me, Farrah?"

I turned my eyes towards him and saw that he was searching for something I could not give to him.

"What kind of feelings are you talking about, Gabe?"

"Love, Farrah. I am talking about love…something you obviously are not interested in finding with me." And then, "I think I should go, yes?"

"Yes, that's probably a good idea."

Two weeks later, I was sitting at home, flipping through the channels trying to find a distraction from my loneliness. My phone buzzed; it was a text from him.

'*I miss you,*' was all that it said.

'*Come over,*' was all that I texted back.

Ten minutes later, he was at my doorstep.

As I opened the door, he took one step inside and swept me up in his arms, my feet dangling in the air.

"I love you, Farrah," he said as he carried me to the couch. He set me down gently and knelt down on the floor in front of me, putting his hands on top of mine.

"I love you," he said again, "and I don't believe you. I don't think you want to live your life alone, going from one empty relationship to the next. I think you're scared. I think you're scared because so many people can't make it work. But we can make it work, Farrah. I want you in my life forever. I want to spend the rest of my life making you smile. I'll do everything and anything it takes. *Just believe*. Can you do that? Can you just try to believe with me?"

My answer didn't come from a logical place. It didn't come from the decision that I made the day my mother left my father. My answer came from my heart. I did love him, and I wanted to believe.

"Yes, I will try."

With my pounding heart and sweaty palms, I tackled him onto the floor and told him that I loved him too.

As we laid beside each other on the floor of my apartment, all the alarms were going off inside my head and body that were meant to guard my heart and preserve my wellbeing. But I ignored them, and less than one year later, we promised forever to each other.

TWENTY
APRIL 2022

I called Corrina as I climbed into the Jeep and headed out on the highway towards Lovedy's. She picked up immediately.

"Oh my God, Farrah. I'm dying over here. How has it been going? Tell me everything!"

"Girl, I don't even really know where to start but I have to say that both Lovedy and Clara are truly exceptional human beings. I've loved every moment I've spent with them. Even with this crazy, messed up story, I kind of love that you've had these beautiful, charismatic, strong women in your life to love and support you. It explains a lot."

"Explains a lot about what?"

I laughed at her charming and very fake naivety. "About you, dummy. I always wondered about you and whether it was your genes or environment that had the biggest impact on you. And while I haven't spent time with Charlotte yet, I'm seeing so much of you in your mother and grandmother. It's a little unnerving."

"Don't get ahead of yourself. You'll understand more when you meet with Charlotte."

"Yeah, speaking of that. How is that going to go down? I don't

APRIL 2022

really know her all that well. When I'm ready to meet with her, do you think you could come with me? Maybe we could do a girl's trip?"

Sometimes her silence was annoying. For once, I wanted her to not think but just say yes.

"I suppose I could do that. It's not a cruise to the Caribbean but a week with you would be fun anywhere we go!"

"Ok, good. Now, tell me about August. And I want to know *everything*. Don't leave *anything* out."

"I haven't called him back. I will. I just haven't yet. I did talk to Judge, though. We both agreed that we wouldn't talk to the girls about it until we knew more about where it was going. I think I need to navigate through this myself before I share it with the family."

"Oh my god. You *chickened* out."

"No! I did not! I just need some more time, that's all."

"Time? Time, for what? It's been weeks. You don't need any more time, Corr. What you need is some balls. If you want to talk to him, then just call him back. Don't make that boy wait anymore."

"Oh, yes. I'm sorry. You're right. I forgot who I was talking to, Mrs. Farrah Langford-Acosta, the authority on all things regarding children and adoption."

"Is that sarcasm I hear? Are you being a smartass?"

"Yes, but you deserve it. I don't need your advice. I just need you to listen."

"Fine. I'm listening."

She told me about her fears, why she was afraid to take a step forward. And then I talked her ear off all the way back to Lovedy's house and filled her in on all the things I learned while visiting with Lovedy and Clara. We promised to keep our lunch date when I returned and then said our goodbyes as I pulled into Lovedy's driveway.

David answered the door with, "I hope you're hungry. She's made a meal big enough to feed our whole town."

I sat down at the table and looked at the generous spread of pot roast, carrots glazed with parsley and molasses, mashed potatoes drizzled with garlic-olive oil and sour cream fan rolls. Lovedy was proving to be quite accomplished in the kitchen. Every meal she had made for me was simply delicious and I made sure to tell her so.

"You should open a restaurant or write a cookbook or something, Lovedy! Every meal you've fixed for me has been *heavenly*."

"Oh, thank you darlin'. I do love to cook. And cooking for people that I love makes it all the more fun. I think I got it from my mama, except I don't use all the butter and bacon grease that she did. Do you like to cook?"

"God, no. I'm a *terrible* cook. Never really had any interest. It's usually going out or take-out for us. If we're eating at home, it's because Gabe will throw some meat and veggies on the grill. I guess if I had to, I could follow instructions and make a meal but I'm not one of those people who can just throw something together. I've always been a little jealous of people like you."

She laughed, "It isn't hard. Just takes some practice. Speaking of good cooks, how is Clara doing today?"

"She seemed like she was doing well. We had an enjoyable conversation this afternoon. She was a bit tired when I left, so she was going to lay down and take a nap. I'm going back to spend more time with her tomorrow morning."

"She loves having visitors. Did she offer you some hot tea?"

"Oh yes. It was on the coffee table when I arrived. Why, is that a regular thing that she does?"

"Yep. Clara believes that drinking black tea helps you live longer. I always thought she was full of it but then I read a medical publication a couple of years ago and sure enough, it seems she may be correct. Not a surprise, she's usually right about most things."

"She did start asking me some questions. I think maybe she was trying to flip it around and interview me."

Lovedy laughed at that one. "That sounds just like her. She is a very caring and compassionate person but sometimes she's nosy as hell. She doesn't mind gettin' personal either. What was she asking you about?"

"Well, she had mentioned the role of church in her community during the depression. So, I asked her to tell me more about that part of her life. She answered my question but then she turned it around and asked me the same question."

"Did you answer her?"

"Yes, I sure did. She wasn't pushy about it or anything. She accepted my answer and we moved on from it."

"Well, I promise that will come back to haunt you. She stayed on me about that stuff for years until I finally relented."

"What do you mean? You told me before that you believe in God. Was there a time that you didn't?"

"Oh yes. I started questioning my faith after Isaac passed away. And then when I lost Clara Jean, that kind of did it for me. I just didn't want anything to do with a cruel God who could allow those kinds of things to happen. I started thinkin' about wars and famine and natural disasters and all the horrible things that happen in the world. It just didn't make sense to me anymore. Besides, I was a student of science. Things just didn't add up."

"Then what changed your mind?"

"I don't think my mind has changed at all. I still can't make logical sense of it. I would describe it more like a change of heart."

I helped Lovedy clean up after dinner, then we sat outside and watched the sun go to sleep over the horizon as I listened to her talk more about the years after she lost little Clara Jean.

"I continued working at the hospital and decided to devote myself to continuing my education. I didn't make time for much of anything else. I wasn't interested in relationships beyond those that I already had in my life. I started to develop a deep association between love and loss and creating meaningful attachments to people became difficult for me. In the late seventies and early eighties, a lot was changing with my family. Faith and her husband had two kids, Hope got married and moved to South Carolina and had a son and Baby ended up having three babies…with her black husband. Now, go on and ask me how Daddy felt about that because I know you want to know."

"Yes, of course I want to know!"

"Wesley and Baby started datin' during their senior year of high school. It was nineteen seventy-six, I think. He was the star of the basketball and debate teams, and she was a cheerleader. They were both great students and extremely popular. The thing is, they never tried to hide their relationship. They put it up front and center for all to see. People whispered and sneered but Baby and Wes just went on about their business. She would invite him over to the house to study and not even tell Mama and Daddy that he was comin' over. She would put an extra plate at the table, daring them to say a word about it. They never did."

"Why do you think they had such a different reaction to Wes, then they had to Isaac?"

"Baby lived her truth out in the wide open. I think Daddy thought Wes was just a phase and he wasn't willin' to lose another daughter over somethin' he thought was just about Baby's rebellion. But the relationship continued beyond high school. They both went to college and then right after graduation, Wes asked Mama and Daddy for Baby's hand in marriage."

"And?"

"And Daddy said, 'hell no' but Mama told him to shut up and then told Wes she would be happy if he became part of our family. It was a small ceremony under a pavilion at a park. Mama went to the wedding and walked Baby down the grassy aisle, but Daddy stayed home.

Then Wes and Baby started havin' babies right away. They had a boy and then twin girls and Baby kept taking those little ones over to Mama and Daddy's house. Daddy had no idea, but the whole time Baby was just whittling away at the calluses on his heart. I have to say, when I completely turned my back on him, she never gave up. It was a lesson for me. People can change and sometimes all they need is someone who believes in the goodness that is there, buried deep inside where you can't see it."

"Is that what prompted the reconciliation with him?"

"No, I think it laid the groundwork, but the rest didn't happen for a number of years later."

"Why didn't you ever confront him about the box you found in the barn closet?"

"What I found in that box destroyed the idea of who my father was in my mind. I thought he was lovin', kind, and generous. I thought he was a believer, a man of faith. I trusted him. What I found in that box was so egregious, I didn't have any motivation to talk to him about it because I felt like I didn't even know him. And to be honest I really didn't want to know him anymore."

We continued sitting at the table after dinner, munching on oatmeal-raisin cake and sipping coffee.

"What year did you reconnect with Corrina?" I asked.

"It was...nineteen eighty-seven, I believe," Lovedy was looking up at the ceiling trying to recall the year. "I got a phone call from Phil and Charlotte telling me that Corrina wanted to meet me. She was sixteen at the time. I tell you, my heart just jumped out of my chest. Of course, I agreed. Corrina and I wrote letters back and forth for a few months. I thought it was best to ease into it. She was young and I didn't want to scare her or turn her life upside down. I also didn't know my role, which is a weird thing to say because *I'm* her mother but I'm not *her* mother. You hear what I'm sayin'?"

I nodded, "Yes, I get it."

"Anyway, one weekend, I drove down to see her. I was nervous the whole way. She had sent me pictures of her at various ages, but I was about to meet my daughter and I missed her whole life up until this point. I didn't really know her, and I didn't really know how much I should tell her about how her life started, about her daddy and my family. There was so much I didn't *want* to tell her. So, I made the decision to give her the basics and then answer whatever questions she had for me."

"How did it feel when you first saw her?"

"I remember walking up to the house as she was standing on the porch. It felt like time slowed down and the sidewalk suddenly became longer, making it further and further until I could reach her. My mind and heart were flooded with so many thoughts and emotions. Will she like me? Does she hate me for giving her away? She's *so* tall. Oh my god, she looks just like her daddy. Look at those long legs. She's skinny, just like me. And then she smiled, and I saw Isaac's dimples. I saw her in my arms in the hospital. I saw her little head in the car when I kissed the window and promised she would be ok. Was she ok? Had her life been ok? Did I feed her to the wolves? Or was she loved and cherished? But then she started walking down the steps with her arms outstretched, her curly hair bouncing with her graceful, leggy stride. I quickened my step until she was in my arms and then I just held her and decided I would just keep holding her until she decided it was time to let go."

"Did you spend the whole weekend together?"

"We sure did. I got a room at a hotel and Phil and Charlotte graciously let her spend the night with me that Saturday. We talked and talked and talked some more. She had a lot of questions, which I answered carefully. I took her out for a bite to eat and I watched her every gesture, memorized the way she spoke and moved. We talked about boys and plans for college. She told me she wanted to be a nurse, which tickled me. She asked me about her daddy. I brought some pictures for her. I didn't give her all the details or the story leading up to it, but I told her in very general terms what happened to him. Then the next morning, I drove her to church to meet her parents for Sunday service."

"How was that?"

"Honestly? It was awkward. I saw some of the same people that were there when I was pregnant and livin' with Phil and Charlotte. They were all staring but I didn't really care. I was simply happy to be there, to be with her. I tried hard to be present and take it all in. Being there with her after missin' her for sixteen years…it felt surreal. I had imagined it a million times over the years but never honestly believed the day would ever come. It felt like a dream."

"Did you see Little One? Was she still living at home with them?"

"Yes, she was there. Still had the same dark hair and green eyes. She was so petite, Corrina just towered over her. They couldn't have looked any more different. When we were in church, Corrina and Little One got to gigglin' about something. It reminded me so much of sittin' in the same kind of pews with my own sisters. I felt grateful that Corrina had Little One to grow up with through the years. I could tell they were close and had their own language, the way sisters so often do. And with Little One also being adopted from another family, she could understand Corrina's feelings, her experiences. They didn't come from the same place, and they didn't look anything alike, but it didn't take a genius to figure out they were of one heart."

TWENTY-ONE
APRIL 2022

AFTER LOVEDY AND DAVID TURNED IN FOR THE NIGHT, I STAYED UP FOR A while. Lost in my thoughts and the conversations I had with Clara and Lovedy, I decided not to wait, and I grabbed my laptop to start writing. When I got to the part about Lovedy's feelings when she first saw Corrina again, I sent a text to Corrina and asked her if she had ever spoken with Lovedy about how she felt that day.

She responded, *'No, why?'*

'If I were in your shoes, I would want to know.'

'Hmm. Sounds interesting. I will soon. Night.'

I called Gabe and chatted with him for a while after. Still not tired, I took a shower and began writing again. I fell asleep and dreamed of magnolia trees, fields of grass dotted with Jonquils and wintery night skies filled with many moons of all shapes and sizes.

Morning came quickly. After getting dressed, I ate a small breakfast with Lovedy and David and then headed out to see Clara again. When I arrived and checked in, an attendant met me at the front desk and told me that Clara was feeling a bit under the weather. She was in bed but still wanted to see me. So, he led me down the hall and into Clara's apartment.

She looked so small lying in that queen-sized bed. She was still in her nightgown, covered with layers of blankets. Her hair was uncombed, but her face lit up with that beautiful smile as soon as I walked in.

"Hi Ms. Clara. I heard you aren't feeling very well today," I bent down and gave her a kiss on the cheek.

She waved her hand at me and said, "Don't fuss over me. I'm just a little tired this mornin'. Didn't really feel like gettin' up today. So, you just sit there in that chair, and we can talk just like we planned."

I was quite sure she was bossing me, but I wasn't about to argue with her or do anything other than what she said. So, I pulled the chair up a little closer to the bed and turned on my recorder.

"So, where were we when I left yesterday?" I asked, as I obediently sat down.

Not missing a beat, she said, "Marshall and Lovedy had just left our house after Jeremiah told us she was pregnant."

"Oh, yes. That's right. See? I told you my memory wasn't as good as yours."

"Well, Marshall and Caroline sent that poor girl away and Isaac was just a mess. He was angry all the time and he let his grades drop at school. Jeremiah and I tried talking to him so many times, but if he wasn't at work or school, he just wanted to stay in his room and listen to his records and read his books. We thought he just needed some time to come around. Eventually, Jeremiah started getting frustrated with him and they began arguin' again. After Isaac graduated high school, he was rarely at home. I don't know what he was doin' with all his time. I know he was still workin' at the bowlin' alley and hangin' out with his friends, but he was still angry. Angry about what happened with Lovedy and the baby, angry at his daddy and especially angry at the ways of an unfair world. He was stuck in a dangerous place. While I felt all his anger was justified, it hurt me to see my boy so twisted up.

Then one evenin' over dinner, Jeremiah told him he needed to grow up and become a man, which started another argument. Isaac rarely came home for dinner anymore and it seemed that every time he did, Jeremiah would pick a fight with him. They went back and forth over the same things they had been arguing about, and then Jeremiah said that the military could make a man out of him. I held my breath, waitin' for Isaac to say something he would regret, but he didn't. He just gave his daddy a dead stare and said, 'Ok. I'll join.' I was so mad, I made Jeremiah sleep on the couch that night and many nights afterward. And I prayed hard. I prayed to the sweet Lord Jesus to help me not kill my husband."

"How did you guys adjust to Isaac being gone?"

"Well, it was just the two of us. The house was so quiet. I had started working an administrative job in the local school office and Jeremiah was still at the hardware store. That was our life, just work, church and occasional visits with our extended families. Then one day, I got a letter from Isaac saying that he was goin' to Vietnam. I just dropped to my knees and gave it all to Jesus. We prayed for him every mornin', at every meal and every night before we went to bed. I don't know if it was because he was so far away from home, but he started writin' more often. We used to read his letters, over and over again. I still have every single one in a box in that bottom drawer there," she pointed to the bottom drawer of the nightstand. "Some of them have faded, some have coffee stains on them and there are some that have smudges where Isaac's ink and his daddy's tears blended together on the paper. But I tell you what, those letters have kept us goin' through the years. On days I was missin' him so much that I could barely breathe, I'd pull out that box and read every one. It was like spendin' time with my boy again.

Then one day, I was at the market, and I ran into Faith. She asked me about Isaac. When I told her that he was in Vietnam, she asked me for his address. I knew she really wanted it for Lovedy, but I didn't care. I just thought about how happy he would be to hear from her again."

"Do you know Lovedy kept all his letters too?" I asked. "She keeps them in a beautiful wooden box that has flowers painted all over it."

"Oh yes. She brought them over one day about six months after he passed. We just sat at the table and read them all together. Did she let you read them?"

"She gave me the box, but I haven't read them yet. I don't know if I will. It just feels too intrusive. I feel like those letters are a very personal conversation between Isaac and Lovedy and I don't know that I need to read them to tell this story. Does that make sense?"

"No. That doesn't make sense to me at all. I'm sure Lovedy explained the relationship to you from her point of view, but aren't there two sides to every story? Don't you want to hear my boy's voice and hear what he had to say?"

I think she was bossing me again.

"Ok, Ms. Clara. I'll think about it. I promise. But who has the letters that Lovedy wrote to Isaac? Does she have them, or do you have them?"

"I do. She can have them when I'm dead." Her smile was sweet but sly at the same time and I laughed again at her candor.

"Can you tell me about when Isaac came home?" I asked.

She smiled again and then asked me to hand her an envelope that was on the dresser. She opened it and handed me a stack of photos. I gasped. They were all there. Jeremiah, Clara, Isaac, Faith and Lovedy. There were balloons and streamers. Her home was full of family and friends and food. I saw Isaac's smile, his dimples. His arms around his little Mama. Her face buried in his chest. I saw it all.

"That was a sweet, sweet day," Clara said wistfully. "He was alive. He was safe. My boy was finally home. He had been gifted another chance to start his life all over again. As I watched Isaac and Lovedy together at that welcome-home party, I remember thinkin' about how long they had loved each other and how much they had been through together. But to be honest, I had conflicted emotions about the whole thing."

"What were you conflicted about?"

"As a mother, I just wanted my son to be happy and fulfilled. If Lovedy was meant to be a part of that for him, I would have been fine with it. I loved that girl, and she was already like family to me."

"But?" I pressed, eagerly waiting for the opposing angle.

"But there was a part of me that wanted him to find a nice black girl at our church to marry." She paused and let those words hang in the air between us. It felt thick and uncomfortable, and I was confused about this new revelation.

"Ms. Clara," I blinked as I tried to process what she dropped in front of me, "I'm going to need your help on this one."

She just laughed at me. "I figured as much. You're probably sittin' there askin' yourself how my view was any different than Marshall's. Am I right?"

I nodded, "Basically, yes."

"Well, you have to see it from my point of view. Before the Civil War, interracial marriage wasn't that uncommon. Then along came Abraham Lincoln. And while he opposed slavery, he still believed that white folks were superior to other races. He didn't want black folks holdin' office, votin', being jurors or marryin' the whites. In the twentieth century, most of those opposin' interracial marriage were white evangelicals. Can you believe that mess? They thought that because God put different races on different continents, it was a sin to marry outside your race because it would mess up His original design. It was just in 2000 that the state of Alabama finally struck down their anti-interracial marriage law, so you can imagine what it was like back in the seventies. Marshall's opinion was based on the idea that the white race is superior to other races and should not be watered down by the likes of us."

"Is that in the bible? The interracial marriage is wrong?" I asked.

"Heavens, no. Says nothin' of the sort. It says marriage between family members isn't good, but I think we can all agree on that."

"Then why would they say interracial marriage was a sin if it wasn't?"

"Oh, honey," she said, laying her hand on mine. "Mankind has grossly misrepresented God for its own advancement. I imagine there will be many church leaders held accountable for that one day in the hereafter. Imagine how many have turned their backs to the idea of God because the church used God as a political pawn to serve their own agendas. It runs shivers up my spine just thinkin' about it."

"So, what was *your* reason for preferring that Isaac marry a black woman?"

"I didn't think the world was ready for what Isaac and Lovedy represented. They were just two young adults who were crazy about each other but that's not what the world would see. The world wouldn't see the love they shared, their experiences, and everything they would build together. It would only see what made them different. And I was scared what that would mean for them."

"Why were you afraid? Did you think someone would hurt them?"

"I've seen a lot in my eighty-nine years. And one thing I've learned is that most people aren't comfortable with what is different from them, and folks don't like to be uncomfortable. So, they either try to get rid of the source of discomfort or they try to ignore it, treat it like it doesn't exist. I didn't want either of those reactions towards my boy and the woman he loved. I worried about people harassing Isaac and Lovedy. Even worse, I worried that they would be forced to live smaller lives because others didn't want to be a part of something that didn't look like them.

The idea I had of Isaac marrying a black woman was about wanting his life *to be easier*. But in the end, what I really wanted for my boy was something that transcended race and antiquated ideas. I wanted him to experience the fullness of love, the kind that comes from two hearts upliftin' and encouragin' one another. A field of unconditional love is where we grow to be our best selves, and I wanted that for him."

I sat there and looked at this petite woman with the kind smile, infectious giggle and warm heart lying in her bed, freely imparting her wisdom and experience to a woman she hardly knew. And then I wondered what it would have been like to grow up with a mother like her. Would I be a different person now? My thoughts ran away from the conversation and Eris took over. She circled around a collection of memories that I had long since filed away. Suddenly, I was very warm, nauseous, my heart was pounding, and I was starting to sweat. I needed to get out of there.

"Farrah, are you alright?" I heard her say it, but it sounded faint, like it was coming from somewhere distant.

"I'm fine, Ms. Clara. I'm just having a hot flash and need to get some fresh air," I lied.

"Just go stick your head in the freezer. Grab some ice and put it on the back of your neck."

I could hardly breathe. "Ok, can I get you anything while I'm up?"

"No, I'm good. You go on, now."

I hated that this was happening. Why now? I did what I was told and stuck my head in the freezer. Then I grabbed some ice cubes, wrapped them in a hand towel and sat down on the love seat. I leaned forward, resting my head on my knees and put the towel on the back of my neck. I heard a little voice coming from the bedroom that said, "Deep breaths. In…hold…out." I followed instructions and found my breath, once more.

TWENTY-TWO
APRIL 2022

AFTER I PULLED MYSELF TOGETHER, I WENT BACK TO CLARA'S BEDROOM. She told me there were some finger sandwiches in the refrigerator and suggested I put on a pot of tea. I was relieved to have a few more moments to sharpen my senses and feel more like myself. I put the sandwiches and teacups on a tray while waiting for the teapot to whistle at me. I saw a small vase of flowers on the kitchen counter and moved it to the center of the tray before taking it into the bedroom. But when I returned, Clara's eyes were closed, and a book was lying on her chest. I put the tray down on the dresser and walked over closer to the bed. All her talk about seeing Jesus soon just made me want to see her chest moving up and down. When I was satisfied that she was still breathing, I took the tray out into the living area and sat down on the love seat.

As I ate lunch and sipped the tea, I decided to do some research on therapists that lived near my home. I couldn't dodge this any longer. It was intruding on my life and my ability to do things that I wouldn't even consider to be stressful. I had always considered myself to be one who was in control of my mental and emotional health. Even with Eris and the constant chatter, I felt like it was manageable. But now, the anxiety had begun manifesting itself in a physical way and it was visible to others. It made me feel vulnerable and weak and I decided that I finally had enough of it. I bookmarked a few web pages of therapists that looked interesting to me and had great reviews. Then I put my phone down and leaned my head back and drifted off.

It was a loud knock on the door that startled me back to consciousness. It was the attendant, wanting to check on Clara. I waited on the couch until she was finished and then I heard Clara calling me back to the bedroom. The tea was cold, so I took her some water and sandwiches then sat back down on the chair. "How are you feeling? Did you have a nice nap?"

"Yes, I'm feeling better. Are you?"

"I do feel better, thank you. I took a little nap out there myself."

"Short naps are good for the body, you know."

"That's what I've been hearing lately. Lovedy has been telling me the same thing."

"I know she's a nurse and all, but she got that from me. Don't let her fool you," she waved a finger as if she was scolding me.

I laughed and asked if she felt up to talking more. Part of me thought she may have had enough for that day. Her response surprised me.

"I've been thinking a lot about what is coming up next. You know, we're at the part where we lost Isaac," she said quietly.

"Yes," I nodded slowly. "I figured we would get there soon."

"I could tell you what happened and how it happened, or you could read about it *as it was happening*."

"Lovedy already gave me the newspaper clippings, which I've read. Is that what you're talking about?" I asked, not really understanding what she meant.

She shook her head no and pointed to her closet. "There's a box at the bottom of the closet. It has all my journals in it. Go on and take them with you."

"Are you sure about that, Clara?" I asked uncertainly.

"I wouldn't say it if I wasn't sure," staying firm in her stance.

I had to think about it for a few moments. Looking through Lovedy's wooden box felt weird and intrusive, but this was *beyond* weird. Clara's thoughts, her emotions, written in her own words, you couldn't get any more personal than that. If my book were to ever be published, I wasn't sure she would want it all out there for the world to see.

"Ms. Clara," I said, "is there anything in those journals you don't want me to share?"

"You told me that no one would know it is me. That is still the case, isn't it?"

"Yes, of course."

"Then go on and take 'em. I have nothin' to hide from you. Only thing I ask is that you don't include my cuss words."

"Cuss words?"

"Yes. As you can imagine, I was rather angry there for a while." She looked down, twisting her ring that she still wore on her left hand.

"Well, if no one will know that it's you, why are you worried about swear words being included in the book?"

"I don't want to set a bad example. Cuss words are for people who don't have an adequate vocabulary to describe their emotions. And truth is, I didn't have the words at the time to describe the many stages of my grief. But I don't want to encourage others to use that kind of language."

"Oh. I see." *I wish you could hear your granddaughter when you're not around. Your ears would bleed out,* I thought. "I can work around that. It won't be a problem," I smiled assuringly.

Clara said she was ready to get out of the bed, so I helped her to the living area. I put on another pot of tea, and we gabbed a bit. I did have one question that was lingering but I wasn't sure how to ask.

"Ms. Clara, I have a follow-up question for you, but I'm having trouble finding the right words."

"Just try your best. We'll figure it out."

"Back when you were talking about Isaac and wanting his life to be easier..." I paused, not knowing how to say the next part.

"Go on, honey," she said, encouraging me to continue.

"Well, when you were talking about the history, I was just thinking that if I were in your shoes, I would probably wince at the thought of my son marrying a white woman. But maybe for a different reason."

"I'm listenin'..."

"I just think I wouldn't want to give anything more of myself or my family to the white community, especially when so much had already been taken away. Am I making sense?"

"You're dancin' around it, but yes, I understand what you mean. If it makes you feel any better, I've had similar thoughts before. And I'm not alone in that line of thinkin'. But where I can't agree with you is that while Isaac was my son, I never felt like he was mine to give away. From the moment I found out I was pregnant with him, I had this feeling, way deep down, that he was on loan to me. He was God's child. I was just takin' care of him until he grew into his own. It wasn't for me to decide who he should marry. It wasn't about what I wanted, what made me comfortable, or this prized possession that I wanted to keep to myself and away from the white folks. So yes, the thoughts have been there. But they were rooted in history and not specifically about Isaac and Lovedy."

"That was really a hard question to ask, and I know I was clumsy with it. I really appreciate both your patience and your candor," I said.

"You don't have to be afraid to ask me anything. I can see your heart. I know you're comin' from a good place. And who knows, we just might learn somethin' from each other." She tilted her head to the side and smiled at me graciously.

"Well, I've certainly learned so much from you, but only because you've been so open and honest. And the journals, I don't know how to thank you for trusting me with them, for being generous with something that is so private. If I have any questions, would it be ok if I call you?"

"That would be just fine with me. You can call me anytime, even if you don't have any questions," she flashed that dimpled smile at me and then scooted to the edge of her giant chair. She lifted her arms upward and outward, inviting me into her world of love and compassion.

It took me a couple of trips to carry the journals to the Jeep. They were leather bound and very thick with the history of this woman I had grown to love in such a short time. As much as I was shocked that she gave me access to them, I secretly couldn't wait to start reading. I wanted to hear the many voices of Clara. How she sounded when she was twenty, thirty, and in all the other decades of her life.

I surprised Lovedy with a beautiful flower arrangement from "The Doghouse." It was a small gesture to thank her for her hospitality, but I wanted her to know how much I appreciated it. When David saw it, he asked, "You went to the Doghouse for flowers?"

"Yes. Is that ok?" I asked, afraid I had done something wrong.

David started laughing and said, "Its fine. I love Rita Anne, but I make it a point to never buy flowers for Lovedy from her shop."

"Ok. Fill me in here. What's going on?"

"What I didn't tell you about Rita Anne," Lovedy said, "is why she calls her shop "The Doghouse." She calls it that because she thinks any time a man buys flowers or chocolates, he's done somethin' wrong. David bought me flowers from her once and it wasn't thirty seconds after he left her shop that she called me and wanted to know what he did to piss me off. Now he buys them from the florist across town. But she was onto something. Like I said before, her business has done very well."

"I can imagine. I thought it was kind of genius when I walked in and saw that she was not only a florist but a chocolatier and a barista."

"Yes, and she is the most discreet person I know. I've tried to get all the dirt about the couples in our town, but she won't tell me a damn thing," she pouted playfully.

They continued to tell me funny stories about Rita while we feasted on wild salmon, roasted potatoes, and asparagus. She also made my favorite dessert, lemon layer cake with buttercream frosting. It was simply divine, and I told her so. But as I helped her clear the table, I had another surprise for her. "Hey, Lovedy?"

"Hey, Farrah."

"I thought I might take another approach this evening with our dialogue. Would it be ok if I included David? I want to talk about how the two of you met."

"Well, that sounds like fun. I'll let him do most of the talkin'."

David just laughed. And so did I because we both knew that was an outright lie.

"What's so funny?" She said, pretending not to know.

"Nothing, nothing at all," I smiled as we all retreated to the living room.

"So, David. How did the two of you meet?" I asked, once we were all comfortable and settled.

"We met in a grocery store. I had seen her in there several times before but that one time I was behind her in the express lane. The limit was ten items and she had sixteen. I couldn't let her get away with that."

"What did you do?"

"I started countin' to ten out loud. Then I said, 'oops' and started to count again."

I looked at Lovedy for confirmation.

"Yes. Yes he did," she said with an annoyed headshake. "And all it did was piss me off."

"But it got your attention, didn't it?" David said with a sly smile.

"I suppose it did, but I wasn't very nice to you," Lovedy said.

"She wasn't nice," David said while he shook his head. "Wasn't nice at all."

"What did she say?" I was almost afraid to ask.

"She looked at me and said that she was glad to know I could count but that I didn't need to show off by counting all the way to ten. And then she asked me if I wanted a cookie or a gold star. I thought, wow. She's pretty *and* scrappy. I need to ask her out."

"So, you did?" I asked.

"Well, not right away. I knew I would see her again eventually and I'm a patient man. I knew I had to ask her out the right way if I wanted her to take me seriously."

"So what did you do?"

"I kept looking for her in the grocery store every time I'd go in there. Finally, I saw her. I got behind her in the express lane again and what do you know, this criminal had more than 10 items again. So, I started counting again but that time I went all the way to seventeen."

Lovedy piped in with a laugh, "Can you believe that?"

"She didn't even look at me," David continued. "She just watched her seventeen items move down the conveyor belt and completely ignored me. So, I started counting louder and then she turned and looked at me with her eyes all squinty and asked me if I was really trying to make a scene about her having too many items in the express lane. I told her that I bombed so bad last time, I figured this time I had to count all of them. I told her I had to impress her with something or how else would I ever get a woman as beautiful as she was to go out with me?"

Lovedy couldn't help herself. "Is that not the corniest story you've ever heard? But I tell you what, he made me laugh and that was a good start."

"Did he ask you out then?" I asked.

"Nope. As soon as the cashier rang me up, I went flyin' out of there. I wasn't gonna give him the chance. He needed to work harder at it than giving me that countin' nonsense."

"I hadn't planned on asking her out then, anyway," David said.

"He's lying. Look at his face," Lovedy said as she pointed to David.

David was smiling as he put his arm around Lovedy. "Alright, Alright. Yes, she got away from me that time. And it was a while before I saw her again. I thought I missed my chance but then one day, there she was in the parking lot. She was putting her groceries in the trunk as I was pulling up. So, I pulled my car right up next to her and got out to help her, and then she asked me if I was stalking her."

"What did you say?"

"I told her that I probably was, a little bit. I missed my chance the last time I saw her, and I didn't want to miss it again."

"And what did she say?"

Lovedy interrupted again, "I asked him what he thought he missed out on?"

David finished with a line I'll never forget. "I told her that I saw her items in the express lane and I suspected that she was a pretty good cook. I didn't want to miss the chance to ask her to make me some supper."

"You did not!" I couldn't believe it.

"I did. And as soon as it came out of my mouth, I just knew I had struck out a third time."

"And did you?"

"It turns out I didn't. She just stood there and looked at me for a minute. Then she said that she didn't know me, so I was not invited over to her house. But if I wanted to take her out to supper, that would be ok with her. We went out that night and we've been eating supper together ever since."

"What made you finally say yes, Lovedy?"

"He made me laugh. And he had kind eyes and a nice car."

"How long did you date before you were married?" I asked.

Lovedy looked at David and smiled. And then she sighed, "I had been on my own for so long and I was happy. I was workin' and enjoyin' my time alone. When I wanted company, I'd spend time with my sisters and their families, or I would go on a vacation with friends. I also had many hobbies that kept me busy. Then along came David and he messed all of that up. It was about a year after we started datin', we were sittin' on that bench by the big magnolia talkin' about the price of gasoline. Out of nowhere, he asked me if I would marry him. I told him no, that I didn't feel the need to get married. He had his house, I had mine. We loved each other and we enjoyed doin' things together. It was perfect. Why mess it up with a piece of paper and a list of unreasonable expectations that could never be met?"

I looked at David. "But you didn't take no for an answer?"

"Hell no, I didn't. I asked her again every day for four hundred and sixty-two days."

"But if she made it clear that she didn't want to get married, why did you continue to try?" I asked, a little annoyed.

"Well, I sure wanted to marry her. We had discussions, you know, about things that had happened in her life," he was sitting there with his arm around Lovedy, but he was looking down and fiddling with the hem of his shirt. "She had been through so much... I... I just wanted to take care of her. Not just when we were out on dates or running errands or fixin' something around her house. I wanted to take care of her all the time. I wanted her to know that she was loved every day."

He was still looking down and I could feel his emotion in the slight quiver of his voice. It put a lump in my throat as I thought of Clara's words. *A field of unconditional love is where we grow to be our best selves.*

Lovedy patted his leg. "And that's what he said the last time he proposed. I couldn't refuse that offer and frankly I was tired of him asking. So, I said yes."

TWENTY-THREE
APRIL 2022

Spring was in full bragging mode as I headed home the next morning. I decided to get off the highway and take the back roads. I whizzed by the fields and farms lined by blooming Bradford Pear trees. The sky was a cobalt blue, and the occasional cloud would float by without a whim or care in the world. The top of my Jeep was down, and the music was up. I felt relaxed, free, and ready to get to work.

As soon as I arrived back at the house, I ate some lunch with Gabe. We took the dogs for a walk, and I told him about my visits with Clara, Lovedy and David. I also told him about the research I had done on possible therapists that could help me get rid of Eris. He didn't say anything. Instead, he put his arm around me, pulled me in close and let out a big sigh. That was his way of saying 'good job'. And I knew he was relieved that I was taking steps towards a resolution.

That afternoon and for the rest of the week, I tackled the box of Clara's journals. I put them on the table in chronological order. The first journal entry was just after she had married Jeremiah. The last one took place just after her sister, Evie, passed away. I took copious notes, photographs and even read some pages aloud, recording as I moved slowly and carefully through the ebbs and flows of Clara's life.

On occasion, a new character would appear in her journal that I didn't recognize. I would call Ms. Clara and she would tell me the life history of each new person that appeared in her journals. It wasn't lost on me how well Clara knew her family and friends, how invested she was in their lives. I thought about my own family and friends and how differently we interact with each other compared to prior generations. I thought about how families break away from each other these days, moving cross country and even across the globe. The art of connecting has changed so much. Conversations occur via email and text and life events are celebrated via social media. We do a decent job communicating the good things that happen to us, but how often do we talk about the hard stuff and how our experiences change our lives or how they make us feel? It made me wonder how well we really know each other at all.

I immediately called Corrina and asked her to meet me for lunch that Saturday.

For the rest of that week I was heads down, reading, listening, writing, and making notes on things I needed to follow up on. Thanks to Clara's journals I had a pretty detailed history already lined up for her and only had a few remaining questions. I needed to focus more on finishing Lovedy's story. I was extremely interested in when and how Lovedy reconciled with her parents, especially her father.

I worked almost all day, every day. Gabe was a good sport, bringing me food and reminding me every hour or so to get up and stretch. I found I preferred to work late into the night. It was in the quiet and stillness of the night that I was able to work quickly and with more clarity. Before I knew it, the week had flown by, Saturday morning had arrived, and I left to see my friend.

We ordered our usual boozy sweet teas and sat out on the back patio of the café again. It felt strange but there were things I wanted to talk to her about that I needed to record. So, I gave my friend, the one I had a million prior conversations with, the same commitment I gave to Lovedy and Clara. She agreed and then I jumped on her about August. "So, did you call him?"

"I did. We talked for about an hour."

"And?" I leaned forward in anticipation.

"And, it was nice."

"Nice? That's what you've got for me? It was nice?"

"I'm still processing all of it. There are so many memories there, most of which are not good. It is a lot to get through. My story isn't anything like Lovedy's. It's way different." She looked at my phone, then gave me a look that was a question without having to use any words. And I knew what she wanted.

"Do you want me to turn it off?"

"Yes. This part is just for you."

I turned off the phone recorder and gave her my full attention. I listened with an open heart as my friend shared her experience with me. The events, the emotions, the impact that it had on her life. She cried when she was sad. She swore at the parts that made her angry. Her story wasn't dressed up for an audience. It was bare and raw. She laid it all out there for me to see. I held her hand when I felt like she needed it. And I backed off when I felt she needed that too. When she finished, I moved my chair closer to hers and put my arm around her. We sat there for a while, our heads leaning against each other.

I knew early on in my friendship with Corrina that she had given a child up for adoption when she was seventeen, but I never knew the circumstances behind it. I thought I knew everything about her. I guess everyone has their secrets, even my best friend who I'd known for twenty-eight years.

"You can turn it back on now," she said. So, I did.

"I'm so sorry that happened to you," I said, now knowing what else to say. "And I'm so angry too. I'm so angry that he did that to you."

Corrina put her hand on mine. "I went to therapy for so long and finally found a way forward. But this thing with August, it has turned me upside down. He didn't do anything wrong. He's not to blame. And I don't want to keep him from getting the closure that he needs. But I don't know if I want to have a relationship with him. It is hard because it was a horrible situation that I don't like thinking about. And yet when I think about what that kind of rejection would do to him, it makes me feel like a terrible person."

"You could never be a terrible person, Corr. Sometimes, life asks too much of us. And I think it's ok to say no if that's what you need to do for yourself. But who am I to give you advice? I'm your best friend, but this is way above my paygrade. Maybe you should go back to therapy and talk to a professional who can help you navigate through it all. It's a lot. It's way more than I ever imagined. And I'm sorry for pushing you all those times to call him. I should have respected you and trusted that you knew best."

"It's ok. I've already made the call. My appointment is next week."

"I love the way you just take care of that shit. No dragging it out, no postponing. If you have a problem, you take steps to resolve it. You're a better person than I am, Corr. I admit it."

She laughed, "Farrah. You still haven't made your appointment, have you?"

"I'm working on it. I'll do it next week. Promise." And I meant it.

"Good. I called Clara the other day. She told me all about your visits. She also told me she gave her journals to you?" She said, lifting her eyebrows.

"She did. It was surprising to me, too. But what a gift those journals have been. Had she told me the highlights of her life from her perspective today, it would have been a much different story. Reading her journal entries that spanned decades of her life, I saw her change and evolve over time."

"How so? What do you mean?"

"Her interests, her worries, and fears, they changed as time passed. That was clear just in the simple matter of what she chose to write about. And what she didn't."

"What did she write about when she was young?"

"At first, it was a lot about adjusting to married life. She was young and really wanted to be a loving and supportive spouse for Jeremiah. Then Evie got married and started having baby after baby. She was self-admittedly envious of how easily Evie became pregnant. When Evie became pregnant with her fourth child she said, 'Evie is pregnant with a baby she doesn't even want, and I can't seem to get pregnant at all.' Once she became pregnant, she filled up almost an entire journal with how much the baby was growing, when she first felt it kick, baby clothes that Evie had given her, blankets that she had knitted. She was so happy to have a baby with Jeremiah. She said she knew she was destined to be a mother.

And then Isaac was born and that filled up *several* journals. She wrote about every milestone he passed when he was a baby and all through grade school. Smiling, crawling, walking, talking, his grades, even how much he was growing. She also wrote down her prayers a lot during that time. She prayed for her family constantly, especially Evie."

"What did she say about Evie?"

"She didn't say it outright, but I suspect there were some domestic issues."

"Really? Are you sure?" Corrina asked, clearly concerned.

"Well, I can't say for *sure*, but she wrote down many prayers asking God to give Evie strength and patience. At first, I thought it was just the size of her family, having all those children. That would be stressful on *anyone*. But then she wrote an entry about a time she took Isaac over to Evie's house for Sunday dinner. She made the comment 'I don't know how she puts up with him. She's a better person than I am.' And then she wrote down a bible verse."

"Which bible verse?" She demanded.

"I don't remember. I think it said Luke something or another. I googled it. It was about loving your enemies and doing good for people that hate you. Which personally, I think is a very tall order."

"Yeah, I see what you mean, now. Did you ask her about it?"

"No, but I plan on it." I said.

We stood up from the table and continued talking as we walked out of the café and found a spot to sit on the big rock next to the lake.

"I'm assuming she wrote about Isaac's death?" Corrina asked

"Oh, yes. She was angry for a long time. By the way, your sweet grandmother has quite a mouth on her." I let my mouth drop open for dramatic effect.

Corrina gasped, "Noooooo…not Clara! I've never once heard her swear!"

"Yes, indeed! She made me promise not to put any of her 'cuss words' in my book. Her anger was part of the grieving process, and she seemed to linger in that stage for a long time. Her prayers were different too. They were feisty, challenging and daring. I imagined her shaking her fist up to heaven." I pulled up the notes I took on my phone to find an example. "At one point, she wrote, 'I've spent my entire life telling people that you're a loving God and now you've taken my only son away from me. If you want me to accept this, you're going to have to help me understand it. It is cruel for you to require me to accept something I don't understand. And I don't want to believe that you're a cruel God. That would make a liar out of you and of me."

Corrina was staring off at the lake again when she finally responded, "I hope I get a chance to read them some day. I've only ever seen her as my grandmother and well, sort of a mother. I don't know any other sides of her. I think sometimes we forget our grandparents and parents are human beings. They go through and feel all the things that come with the human experience. They are just so good at hiding it. Why do you think they do that? Hide things from their children and loved ones?"

"Again, not my area of expertise but I would imagine that parents deal with things that kids just shouldn't be dealing with at their age. Right?"

"I suppose so. Judge and I have a different take on that, though. It's not that we burdened our girls with adult stuff but when either of us were angry or sad, we shared those emotions with our kids. I think it helps for kids to see their parents being human and working through things like disappointment and anger. It reassures them that even though things might not feel happy right now, it will get better."

"What about August, though. You never told them about your pregnancy."

"That's *my* story," she snapped as she whipped her had back towards me. "It happened way before they were born, before Judge and I were married. That was a different time, a different life. That is mine and mine, alone. It's all different."

As she was speaking, a flash of a memory popped into my mind. I was little, maybe five or six. I was in bed and woke up to the sound of someone crying. I got up and stepped out into the hallway. My parents' bedroom door was closed but I could hear my mother in there. My father came upstairs and saw me standing there with my ear to the door. I asked him why she was crying. He told me not to worry, she had just watched a sad movie on TV. And then he tucked me back into bed.

And then I remembered the moon on that night when Gabe and I were driving back from the restaurant. *It made me think about people, even about myself, and how we can so easily ignore things that we know are there but cannot see with our eyes.*

TWENTY-FOUR
2002-2019

ONE OF THE MANY BOOKS I READ DURING THE COVID QUARANTINE WAS A self-help book about love and marriage. The author suggested that a couple should never begin the journey of marriage without first creating a map, agreeing on where they want to go and how they will get there.

Looking back, I've often wished that Gabe and I had created a map, or at least talked about what we wanted our journey to look like. But we were responsible, educated adults who were in love. We trusted each other, believing that we could figure it out along the way. So, what could possibly go wrong?

Gabe and I were married in the fall of 2002. I'm not Catholic like Gabe and his entire family, but I was willing to still get married in a church. I was not, however, willing to convert to Catholicism, so off to the courthouse we went. My dad, Corrina and Judge stood beside us as we promised a lifetime of love to each other and then we all went to the local neighborhood café for chicken and waffles. Needless to say, my relationship with my in-laws was doomed from the start.

Gabe and I didn't live together before we were married, so the first year wasn't exactly an easy one. We both had our routines and were used to doing what we wanted to do, when we wanted to do it. Meals, time alone or with friends, workout routines, hours spent at work, even TV programming all became issues between two adults who were used to thriving on autonomy.

"Compromise" became an evil word that was thrown about during heated discussions. *"Mature adults know how to compromise."*

"If you really loved me, you would be willing to compromise."

"You're not a team player, if you're not willing to compromise."

I began to *loathe* that word. It became the politically correct way of saying, "I want my way and you're not willing to give in to what I want."

It wasn't all bad, though. Roller coasters have inclines and declines but also have adrenaline-inducing thrills, laughter and excitement. And we had plenty of that as well.

Between our jobs and chores and the responsibilities of adulting together, we spent a lot of time between the sheets, took exotic vacations and created memories that we would learn to lean into when times were tough.

About six years into our marriage, it seemed we had finally found our flow. We were well into our thirties, had a network of good people surrounding us and financial stability. We purchased our first home together in downtown Lexington—a charming, early twentieth century bungalow with nine-foot ceilings, three bedrooms, two baths, a detached garage and a sweet little oasis in the backyard. We spent the better part of that year working on the house. We stripped the floors, applied a fresh coat of paint to every room, installed new cabinetry and light fixtures, and replaced the old appliances with shiny new ones. It was hard labor that we both fully committed to in between the hours when we were working and trying to find some precious sleep. In the end, our vision became a reality, and our home became a haven.

During the summer evenings, Gabe would whip up some magic on the grill while we sipped cold beers under miniature lantern lights that hung across the deck. On the weekends, we'd invite our friends over, play darts in the garage or have a dance party outside.

In the fall, our maple trees boasted bright yellows, reds and oranges, we decorated the house with spider webs and pumpkins, drank cold ciders with our neighbors and jumped up with delight every time a trick-or-treater rang the doorbell.

The winters were for ordering takeout, cuddling on the L-shaped couch, watching movies by the fireplace, taking walks in the snow and celebrating the holidays.

One weekend, each season, Corrina would drop her little girls off to spend the weekend with their Aunt Fairy and Uncle Gabe so she and Judge could get away together. We were the godparents of those sweet little angels, and we held nothing back during their visits with unlimited candy, trips to amusement parks, staying up way too late, eating sugary cereal while watching cartoons on Saturday mornings, and sleeping in tents outside after we watched scary movies that their parents would never have allowed.

It was one of those muggy summer nights and the girls had fallen asleep under the sparkling lights we hung inside their tent. Gabe and I were just outside the tent, under the stars, enjoying the peace and quiet after a full day of activities.

"Farrah?" He whispered quietly.

"Yes?"

"I want to make a family with you."

"We are a family, Gabe. You, me, our friends, those little girls sleeping in the tent. We may not have children, but we definitely have a family."

"You *know* what I mean, Farrah. I want to have a baby with you."

"Gabe, I told you in the very beginning of our relationship, I don't want to have children of my own. That hasn't changed," I whispered back softly.

It was dark, but I could still see him by the glow of the twinkly lights coming through the tent. I hated hurting him like this, but it was not something I was willing to negotiate.

"Farrah," he turned his head towards me and softened his eyes, "I have given up so much for you, for us. I barely see my family because you are uncomfortable around them. I don't go to church anymore because you won't go with me. We rarely hang out with my friends because they are too brash for you. It just seems like I am the only one who is making compromises in this marriage." *And there goes that word again.*

"Oh but Gabe, I *did* make a compromise. A *huge* one, actually." It was my fallback; what I threw in his face every time he backed me into a corner.

"Oh? And what was that, Farrah? No, let me guess!" He stood up, towering over me. "You never really wanted to get married? Right? Is that it?"

"You and I both know that is rhetorical question," I tried to say it as nicely as I could, but it still sounded mean coming out of my mouth.

He just stood there, quietly, staring at me in the dark. And then he let out a big sigh. "Are you going to sleep out here with the girls?"

"Yes, of course. Aren't you?"

"No," he shook his head. "I think I'm going to head on inside. I'll see you in the morning. Duerme bien, Farrah."

"Gabe..." I stood up. "Gabe..."

He didn't answer.

I watched him walk into the house and then crawled inside the tent, snuggled up with the girls and fell asleep with the smell of their freshly shampooed hair drifting through the air.

And just as nature's landscape changed with each season, so did our marriage.

In 2009, we both celebrated wins in our careers. Gabe was promoted to detective in violent crimes, and I was promoted to vice-president of client relations. It gave our marriage a much-needed boost and we were on top of the world until we realized that with success, often times, comes tremendous sacrifice.

Before Gabe was promoted, he was patrolling the streets and had a tough but consistent schedule. He worked twelve-hour days on a two-week rotating cycle. He worked Monday and Tuesday, had Wednesday and Thursday off, and then worked the weekend. The following week would be the opposite. It wasn't ideal but between his schedule and mine, we figured out how to make it work.

Once he was promoted, everything changed. He went into the office every day from eight o'clock to four-thirty, usually to do interviews and paperwork. But the majority of violent crimes seemed to occur in the evening and at night. Uninterrupted sleep became a luxury he was rarely afforded, and when his supervisor woke him up in the middle of the night, that meant I was awoken too.

Dinners and holidays were constantly interrupted and his commitment to serving his community and closing his case load meant that he wasn't really excited about going on vacations or even going away for long weekends anymore. His violent crime unit covered horrendous cases, such as homicide, rape, kidnapping, suicide and assaults. His caseload not only changed our lives, but it changed my husband. And not in a good way.

I was always interested in his career. Where my typical workday made for boring conversation about conference calls, spreadsheets and sales reports, Gabe always had plenty of interesting stories. He saw a part of society that most of us don't see at all, the dark twisty deeds done in dark corners, the stuff most of us only see in the movies. We were never one of those couples who ran out of things to talk about, and he was always the storyteller at our dinner parties with friends. Though his stories were sometimes dark, they were often funny and surreal. We were all intrigued about the life he lived and the things he witnessed from day to day, and we hung on every word.

When Gabe was promoted to detective in the violent-crimes unit, his stories changed. They became even darker and more sinister. Late in the evenings, he would pour over images on his computer, reviewing the smallest details of images that no human should have to see.

His affect began to change. The happy, funny, outgoing Gabe that everyone knew and loved turned cynical, quiet and broody. His caseload followed him everywhere, hanging like a heavy cloud above his head. He could no longer fully enjoy the things we used to experience together. His mind was always elsewhere.

One day in the fall of 2013, he called me in the middle of the workday. While that used to be the norm when we first met, it was a rarity since he became a detective and I was traveling so much for sales meetings. We were both so busy, some days we wouldn't talk or see each other at all.

"Hola, mi hermosa esposa."

"Hi. You ok?"

"Yeah, I'm ok. I'm just calling to let you know I've been assigned to a double homicide."

"A double?"

"Yeah, pretty gruesome. Some drugged-out drifter murdered a woman and her husband in their home. It hasn't hit the news yet, but it should be coming out soon. The suspect was captured down in Florida already, so I'm hitching a ride on an agency helicopter to go down there and interview him."

"Gabe, you were just called out last night. You haven't been to sleep in twenty-four hours. Can't someone else do it?"

"No, it's my case, Farrah. And besides, we're short-handed right now in our unit. I *have* to do it."

"When will you be home?"

"I'm not sure. Hopefully it won't take too long, and I'll be back later tonight."

Gabe collapsed into bed at three o'clock the next morning. He was shivering uncontrollably due to exhaustion and sleep deprivation. I rolled over next to him, on my side, and slid his arm around me. I laid my head on his chest and swung my leg across his body, pressing into him for warmth. I rubbed his tummy lightly around and around in circles until the shivering subsided and his breathing became deep and rhythmic. It was the first time I slept in his arms in over a year.

I woke up about three hours later and quietly unwound myself from his sleepy embrace. I reached over and turned my alarm off so that it wouldn't wake him and then I settled back into his arms. I wanted him to sleep for as long as his body needed, even if it meant I was late for work.

Lying there in the dim light of the early morning, I had an epiphany. Things *had* to change. While Gabe's position as a detective was admirable and necessary to sustain a civil society, I wasn't convinced that it was the right position for him. And it certainly wasn't good for our marriage.

In addition to the constant mental, physical and emotional stress he was under, I always struggled with the anxiety that comes with being a spouse of a law enforcement officer. Eris was unrelenting, reminding me every time he left the house that there was a chance he wouldn't come home.

Every night he was awoken by a phone call from his sergeant, I would never be able to go back to sleep. I would get up with him, pull out his shirt, tie, pants and Kevlar vest. I would unlock the gun safe, leaving it open for him to arm himself before heading out the door. Then I would go into the living room and turn on the TV and watch the shopping channel until the morning light began to peek between the blinds.

There were so many days I would show up to work with bags under my eyes and a mind that was convinced I would lose my husband to some violent criminal who was determined not to go to prison. In my nightmares and daymares, it was always the same video reel. Gabe was chasing a suspected murderer. The murderer climbed on top of a roof, looked down and saw my husband running on the street, and then took him out by shooting a .223 round into his skull.

I imagined over and over the scenario in which his sergeant would come to the house and knock on the door to tell me that I was a widow.

Like my own funeral, Eris also planned the funeral of my husband at the sanctuary of the biggest church in Lexington, filled with flags and blue uniforms, shiny badges, and twenty dollars bills stuffed into my sweaty palms as the grievers passed by to express their quiet, tearful condolences.

While I wanted to be a supportive wife, the stress and constant worry about his safety drove my behavior. Some days I was clingy, love-bombing him with praise and affection. On other days, I was distant, trying to create space between myself and the mental video reel that was feeling more and more prophetic.

He finally woke up around noon. I decided to stay home from work that day, so we could talk. Admittedly, it probably wasn't the best timing. He was still physically tired and mentally exhausted. Instead of just giving him time to recuperate, I demanded that we talk about it. I demanded change. I wanted him to give up his role as detective, take a desk job, a supervisor job or even go back on patrol, anything but what he was doing.

"Farrah," he said quietly as he leaned back on the sofa, "my job is difficult, and it is stressful, but I *know* this is what I'm supposed to be doing. I'm sorry that my job worries you, but I'm not going to give it up. I can't, because I love what I do." And that was the end of the conversation.

Life went on and in 2016, Gabe was promoted to master detective. Around the same time, I was promoted to Chief Sales Officer and began reporting directly to the CEO. And while we were each excelling in our own careers, our marriage was dying from gross negligence. We had no one to blame but ourselves.

TWENTY-FIVE
MAY 2022

It was pouring rain, and the wind was whipping my umbrella all around. I had a hard time holding onto it so by the time I made it into the office, I was soaked. Water was dripping from my hair and down my face. My clothes were soggy and cold. I walked straight through the empty waiting area into the restroom and soaked up as much water as I could with paper towels. My skin started to itch, and I was as uncomfortable on the outside as I was on the inside. I thought about leaving and rescheduling but just as I was about to head for the door, she stepped outside of her office and said my name.

"Farrah?"

"Yes. Hi."

"Hello. I'm Dr. Walker. Come on in and have a seat."

Her office was light and bright and smelled like chamomile and fresh oranges. There was an entire wall of books on one side and the sitting area was in the middle of the room. I sat down on the alabaster colored sofa, hoping my damp jeans weren't bleeding blue onto the fabric.

There was a small stack of gardening magazines on a side table along with a box of tissues that I hoped I wouldn't need. She sat down across from me and began writing on her digital tablet. She looked up, smiling, and thanked me for filling out the forms prior to our consultation. Everything about her was stylish, yet simple and easy with a modern flair. She wore designer jeans with a button-down, collared white shirt under a black blazer. Her hair was short and natural with grey around her temples. She wore small gold hoops and a simple band on her left hand. I liked her immediately.

I intentionally picked a therapist that was female and older than me. Someone that not only brought their education to the table, but also their wisdom and expertise that comes from time and practice.

I had filled out a Q&A prior to my arrival that described my desired goals as it relates to therapy. We spent the next forty-five minutes talking about what brought me there, and why I had made the decision to see a therapist. She patiently answered the questions that I had for her about her experience and what approach she would use to help resolve my issues. I learned a bit about cognitive-behavioral therapy. I was all about the behavioral part as I was eager to learn new ways to manage my anxiety that could help me in the here and now. I wasn't exactly excited about the cognitive part. I didn't see how diving into my past would help, but I wasn't the expert.

She was calm, confident, relatable and she really listened to me. She didn't rush me when I was looking for my words. I enjoyed talking with her and that was the last box I needed to check before agreeing to meet with her on a regular basis. We settled on ten sessions and agreed to re-evaluate from there.

By the time I left, the rain had stopped, and the sun was peeking out from behind the clouds that hung around after the storm. I felt hopeful that I was on the right track and wished that I had done this years ago.

I sat in the car and sent Corrina a text that said, '*I did it. Just finished my consultation. Set for ten sessions.*'

She responded, '*Good girl. I know that wasn't easy. Proud of you.*'

I was proud of myself too. I don't know if it was the consultation or the sun that was shining down like a warm hug, but I felt invigorated, empowered.

I stopped by the grocery store on the way home and bought a chicken, some green beans and sweet potatoes. I was determined to make my husband a delicious meal as a way of saying thank you for putting up with my fanciful dreams of writing a book. I could think of nothing better to cook than Lovedy's favorite meal.

I had a few hours before I had to start dinner, so I made a call.

"Hi, Ms. Clara. This is Farrah. How are you doing today?"

"I'm feelin' better. Not as tired as I have been lately. God is good, He surely is."

"I'm so glad to hear that." I told her about my visit with Corrina and asked if it would be ok if she read her journals after I was finished with them."

"Oh yes. That would be fine with me. I'm goin' to leave them for her anyway after I've passed on, so might as well give them to her now. I been tryin' to get rid of all the things I have that she wouldn't want. I don't want to leave her with a big job of cleaning out my apartment.

Besides, I won't be packin' anything for my next trip. I plan on travelin' light," she chuckled again, and I knew why she was laughing. My initial reaction was to laugh because she was laughing but then it felt weird to giggle with her about the impending death that she seemed to be looking forward to so much. I had no idea how to respond, so I just giggled too and kept it moving.

"I read the many prayers you wrote in your journals, and I noticed how often you prayed for Evie. In one entry, you wrote a bible verse reference, I think it was from the book of Luke. Those verses talk about loving your enemies and doing good to those who hate you. Do you recall that time?"

"Yes, I sure do."

"Can you tell me more about what was going on?"

"Well, you know that Evie had five children and that's a lot of mouths to feed. Her husband, Zeek, was under a lot of pressure to provide for the family. They went through some tough times and he wasn't kind to her during those years."

"Was there physical abuse involved?"

"No, I don't believe so. She never said anything to me about that and I didn't see any evidence of it. He just wasn't kind to her. He was always puttin' her down, complainin' because the house wasn't clean enough. Let me tell you, my sister was always cleanin', cookin', and runnin' around after those kids and watchin' other folks' kids so they could go to work. She was exhausted most of the time. But no matter how badly he treated her, she would just love him back with all her heart."

"That's not an easy thing to do. I certainly wouldn't be able to do it," I said defiantly.

"Me neither, honey. The way I heard him speak to her, it took everything in me not to take a skillet to his skull. But she was a better Christian than me. Her faith ran deeper. She had a joy inside that no one could take away. And as little as they had, she was always givin' to people. I remember one time she was watchin' her neighbor's kids. When it was time for them to leave, she saw one of the little boys had somethin' hidden under his shirt. When she asked him to show her what it was, he shook his head no and said he didn't have anything under his shirt. She told him, 'C'mon, It's ok. You can show me. I won't be mad.' He just hung his little head and let the two potatoes drop out that he had stolen from her bin. She kept her promise. She didn't say anything about him stealin' what little food they had. She just went over to that bin and gave him two more potatoes. But that was Evie's way."

"She sounds like a saint."

"She was the closest to being a saint that I had ever known, that's for sure."

"Was it always like that with her husband? Or did things get better?"

"It did get better, especially when those kids moved out of the house. It was like Evie and Zeek found each other again. I think it was all because of her though. She saw through him during those hard times. She understood him and never gave up on him. They had some happy times in their later years. He even took her on a vacation to see the ocean."

"I saw the postcard from her in your journals. I remember how she wrote about the enormity and beauty of the ocean, how she was in awe of it."

"Yes, that trip was one of the highlights of her life. She was so excited."

"Who passed away first? Evie or Zeek?"

"My sweet Evie passed away first. Zeek was heartbroken when she fell ill. But he took care of her the same way she had taken care of him and those kids all those years. I kept goin' over there, takin' them meals and such. I would offer to sit with her to give him a break, but he wasn't havin' it. He wasn't in the best of health either, but he didn't want to leave her side. Zeek didn't last but a couple of months after she was gone. I don't think he knew how to exist without her."

"My husband and I have talked about that several times," I said. "I think I should go first because Gabe would do fine without me. I don't know that I could do it without him."

"I didn't think I could go on after Jeremiah passed either but somehow the good Lord helped me find my way. I thank Him every day for bringing Corrina into my life. She's been such a gift to me."

"I feel the same way about her. She has a light that never seems to burn out. It isn't a light that casts shadows on everyone else. It's the kind of light that brightens up the world for anyone that is near her. I'm so glad she had you, too. She said she found herself through her relationship with you. That when she met you, it felt like she finally found her way home."

"I can understand why she would say that. I'm sure you've talked to her about her childhood, right?" Clara asked.

I nodded. "Yes, I have talked to her about it."

"Then I'm sure you know the environment and the circumstances. Did you ever ask her how she felt about it?"

"I don't think I ever did." And I wondered, at that moment, why I never had.

"Well, I think you should do that. You would probably learn a lot more about your dear friend."

"That's good advice, Ms. Clara. I'll be sure to have that conversation with Corrina soon. We're taking a road trip next month to see Charlotte and will have plenty of time to talk in the car. I'm really looking forward to it."

"Yes, she told me about it the last time she called. She's really looking forward to spendin' that time with you. You've been a good friend to her, and I just want to say thank you for that, Farrah." And because she touched my heart, the lump in my throat showed up and my eyes started to sting. I told Clara I had to run and get dinner started.

"Alright, honey. Thank you so much for callin'. I hope to hear from you again soon."

TWENTY-SIX
MAY 2022

I STAYED BUSY THE FOLLOWING TWO WEEKS AND PUT IN A LOT OF TIME writing, but I also started working on a new hobby that Gabe was thrilled about. Turns out I did like to cook. It wasn't about the art of creating new dishes. I mean, I wasn't *that* good. But I took a tip from Lovedy, and it worked. When I approached cooking from a different angle, I found it more interesting. Providing nourishment for Gabe and even myself was an act of love and I was into it. I even started experimenting with food presentation. I started doing things like horizontal meat cuts, decorating the plates with edible garnishes, and playing with contrasting colors. I learned to stop trying to fill up the plate with food groups that were separated from each other. Instead, I started building height onto the plate using different textures. Unlike the many hobbies I had tackled before, this was different. I wasn't doing it to prove anything to myself or anyone else. I did it simply because I grew to love it.

I also kept my commitment to stick with my therapy appointments. To be honest, it wasn't always easy. There was always something to do that felt more important, especially the writing. I wasn't sure why I felt pressure to get it done. It was not like anyone was making demands on me. There was not a deadline to meet. No one was going to be upset if I slowed down. I brought it up at one of my appointments and Dr. Walker talked me through it. I was still adjusting to a new life that was not as structured or demanding as my entire career had been. And yet we agreed it wouldn't hurt to create a project plan for the book. That would allow me to schedule writing time that was at a reasonable pace and allow time for other things that were important in my life.

During my last lunch with Corrina, we made plans for our road trip to see Charlotte who had moved to New York some years ago. We could have flown but a road trip sounded so much more fun. The plan was that I would drive north to Corrina's, and then we would drive to New York together.

I started worrying because I had planned to finish Clara and Lovedy's parts of the story before I began Corrina and Charlotte's. And while I was almost finished with Clara's part, I still had quite a bit to do on Lovedy's story. I restructured my plan and scheduled a few late-night writing sessions while we would be visiting with Charlotte. There was also one more important thing that I needed to finish before we took our trip together.

Corrina and I had a long history of playing pranks on each other. At some point, it became a competition and we never stopped trying to one-up each other. I knew she would have some good tricks up her sleeve, and I assumed she would pack in as many as she could on this trip. I was supposed to arrive at her house on Friday, so I took some time off from writing and used that time for the epic planning that would be required to beat her at her own game.

Friday morning, I sprung out of bed. I couldn't wait to see my girl and get out of town with her. I had already packed so I took a quick shower and had breakfast outside on the deck with Gabe. He carried my luggage out to the Jeep and gave me a kiss. As he brushed my hair out of my eyes, he said, "Listen, Farrah. I know how you and Corrina are when you two are together. Be careful, for me. Stay focused on the road. And please call occasionally, so I know you're alive and well."

I promised I would, then hopped in the Jeep and backed out of the driveway.

It was warm outside, so I put the top down and turned up the music. I sped down the same back roads that I had driven month after month to see my friend at the café. This time, I passed the dam and kept driving north towards her home in central Kentucky.

I arrived in record time and bounded up the stairs, hoping she was ready. Judge answered the door, gave me a kiss on the cheek and led me into the living room.

Vassy, Corrina's oldest daughter leaped off the sofa and tackled me with a huge hug. "Aunt Fairy! It's so good to see you!"

And then Lauren, Corrina's youngest daughter ran into the room from the back bedroom. "Aunt Fairy! Yay!" Once again, I was tackled by another long-legged beauty. I was always so happy to see Corrina's girls. I was in the delivery room when they were born, and I've always loved them like they were my own. They nicknamed me Fairy when they were little ones because I would always bring them gifts. The name just stuck, and I've been their Fairy ever since. But wow, where had the time gone? It was so hard to believe that they were grown up now, both students at UK. "What are you girls doing home from school?"

Vassy rolled her eyes and said, "Mama made us come home to go out to dinner with her before y'all left for your trip. You know how she is with the guilt trips!"

"I do know, honey. Guilt trips are just one of her many talents. Well, I'm glad she made you come home. It has made my day being able to see both of you! I want a picture of the three of us! Judge, will you take it?" I handed him my phone and then took my shoes off. I stood on the couch, so I wouldn't look like a toddler standing next to those towering beauties. I stood in between them on my makeshift step-stool, as they put their faces next to mine and wrapped their arms around me.

I sat down on the sofa and looked at the photo. Vassy looked just like her mama. She was all legs, with the same warm skin and the dimples that had been handed down through the generations. Lauren was just as tall as Vassy but had her dad's muscular build. She was on the rowing team at school and if she wasn't studying, she was at the gym.

Corrina appeared, looking beautiful and relaxed in her joggers and gym tee. "Let's hit the road, Fairy," she demanded and started moonwalking across the wood floors towards the front door.

I drove the three hours to her house; she drove the first leg of the six-hour drive to Pittsburgh, where we would stop to spend the night and spend half of Saturday before heading to New York City.

We had a couple of rules for our road trips that we had decided on together over the years. The first one, and most important, was that the driver had control over the music. Corrina wasted no time with the first prank. She made me listen to *death metal* the entire time she was driving my Jeep and drove me crazy in the process. I've always hated death metal music and she knew it. It was more like torture than a prank, but I gave her the point.

Regardless of the screeching and screaming coming from the speakers, I still wanted to talk with her about her life in a different way than we ever had before. I knew better than to push her about August, so just like with Lovedy and Clara, I started at the beginning.

"Corrina, I'm turning on my recorder. Now, I know we've had many conversations about your childhood, but they've happened sporadically over the last twenty-eight years. And I'm sorry to say, I don't think I ever asked you how you felt about it. I want you to start with your earliest childhood memory."

"Oh gosh, let me think. There are two specific memories that I have from when I was three or four years old. The first one is a time when my parents had to send me and Sarah to another couple's house to stay for a month. Dad had to go to Boston for surgery to reconstruct his hip and Mom went with him. I remember staring out of a big picture window, watching them drive away. I don't remember the names of the couple we stayed with, but they went to our church. We'll just call them Bob and Mary. Anyway, they had three teenagers and while Bob and Mary were kind to us, my memory is that they weren't kind to their own kids."

"Why do you say that?"

"I remember the way Mary used to talk to them. It seemed like she was always yelling. I remember riding with them in the car. It was nighttime and we were going down a dark road. We passed a building with weird lights on it and the oldest teenage girl said something about the building. The other two teenagers started laughing but Mary became terribly angry and started to scream at her daughter. When we got to their house, Mary told the girl to go into their bedroom and get the belt. I heard that girl screaming and crying and then Mary came out of the bedroom. I went into the bathroom, got a tissue, and took it into the bedroom for the girl. She picked me up and hugged me so tightly. I also remember her gasping for air because she had been crying so hard, which I now know was acute hyperventilation."

"Geez, Corr. That is a horrible memory."

"I'm sure it's worse for that poor girl."

"What is your other early memory?"

"When my parents told Sarah and me that we were adopted."

"How old were you?"

"I think I was about four years old."

"Why do you think your parents told you so young?" I couldn't imagine dealing with that life-altering information at such a young age.

"I've thought about that many times over the years. You'll have to confirm this with Charlotte, but I'm pretty sure it was because we belonged to a very tight-knit community. They didn't want us to find out from anyone else. My sister was six years old at the time and in school. Imagine if some other kid would have told her she was adopted!"

"Yeah, that wouldn't have been good. How well do you remember it?"

"I remember a lot about it, actually. I remember leaning against the cushion of the sofa. It was a floral mid-century gauche sofa, rough and scratchy. It had hard, glossy wooden armrests and pilling on the fabric. I remember twirling those little balls of fiber between my fingers until they broke loose and then I started building a little mountain with them. Sarah was sitting on the other end of the couch, her ankles barely reaching past the end of the cushion. I remember thinking she was mad. She balled her little hands into miniature fists and didn't say a word. She just kept staring at our parents with her mouth hanging open."

"Do you remember what they said?"

"Not the exact words. I remember them talking about how they chose us and stuff like that. There were a few points that were clear in my incredibly young mind. They were not my real parents, I didn't belong there, and I needed to find my real mother. And so, with my four years of human experience, I began my search. I was sure that she was walking around nearby, looking for me too. We just needed to find each other."

"Wow, Corrina. Lovedy told me a story about staying at your parents' house when she was pregnant with you. She talked about sitting on that same couch with your sister and playing with those bobbles of fabric between her fingers too."

"Really? That's wild." She turned her head towards me for a moment, eyes wide with surprise at the similarities of even the smallest things.

"It sure is. Do you remember how you were feeling? Were you sad or scared?"

"I just remember feeling like somehow, I got lost. But at the same time, it made sense to me. They all looked alike with their fair skin, light eyes, and straight hair. I looked *quite different*, and I was aware of it at a very young age. "

"How did that sense of not belonging play out in your childhood? Was it a constant thing?"

"No, not constant. I would forget about it sometimes but there were persistent reminders. Most of my childhood was confined to my home, our church, and the Christian school I attended that was attached to the church. My childhood took place in a ridiculously small world. But inevitably, when we would go out in public to eat or go shopping, some socially inept person would say something to me about my height or my curly hair or my 'tan' skin. They would even have the balls to ask my mother where I got those traits."

"People are idiots."

"Yeah, I don't get that about people either. Like those that say 'wow, you're really tall!' To whom are they speaking? Are they trying to remind me in case I forgot? What is the point of comments like that?"

"No clue. Did the kids in your little world treat you better than the adults?"

"Everyone knew I was adopted, but the kids didn't seem to make a big deal out of that. They just made fun of me because I was tall and skinny, mostly."

"Did they ever talk about your skin color?"

"There were some comments by the kids when I was younger, but they seemed like innocent observations. You have to remember that I was the only person of color in our church and school, which just added to the sense that I was lost and didn't belong there. I had the feeling that people felt sorry for me as a child. Like, look at this poor little mixed girl whose parents didn't want her. Maybe that was my own feelings that I was projecting onto everyone else but that was how I thought people saw me."

"You were a biracial, adopted child who grew up in the south. Did you ever witness any racism? Towards you or anyone else?"

"Towards me? Not overtly. I did hear racial epitaphs used quite often. Not that anyone was using derogatory terms against a specific person, but I heard it used as part of their common language."

"Give me some context, there, Corrina."

"It was stupid things…you know that word I'm talking about. Don't make me say it, Farrah."

"That's *repulsive*. How did that make you feel? Do you remember?"

"I remember feeling confused by it. I knew it wasn't right but there was no one around to explain it to me. I figured it out as I grew up, though." And then she gasped, "Wait, I do remember a mother of one of my friends doing something weird."

"What was it? What did she do?"

"Whenever I would go over to her house to play with her daughter, she would always wash whatever I touched right after I used it."

"What? What do you mean?"

"If I drank water out of a glass, she would immediately take it off the table and wash it. I remember one time I stayed the night over there with a bunch of girls for a slumber party. Every time I used her restroom, she would clean the entire thing after I was done."

"Did she do the same thing when the other girls used the restroom?"

"No. Just me. I remember after the second or third time she did it, I gave her daughter a look. She shrugged her shoulders and mouthed 'I'm sorry' to me. But I was young and naïve. My feelings were hurt because her mother thought I was dirty. I didn't understand that her mother thought I was dirty *because* I was black."

"Geez Corr. I would say that is pretty damn overt." I threw up my hands and shook my head in disgust.

"Yeah, I guess so," Corrina quietly said. "Gosh, I haven't thought of that woman in years. I hope she got her heart right."

"And I hope she died in a fiery car crash," I snapped, while raising my hand in defiance.

Corrina gasped, "Farrah, you can't say that! Ignorance isn't a crime that should be punishable by *death*!"

"I meant what I said, and I said what I meant. No one should be *that* ignorant. But anyway, tell me about your relationship with Sarah." It infuriated me that someone would treat my friend that way. I just wanted to move on.

"Sarah and I were vastly different, but we had, and still have, a remarkably close relationship. Obviously, we didn't look anything alike, but we also had very different personalities. I was outgoing, always trying to make people laugh. I wasn't one to dwell exceedingly long on things that disappointed me or made me sad. But Sarah was quiet, sensitive and took on the role of my protector. She didn't like adults or kids mistreating me in any way. Once she took offense at someone's unjust behavior, she would hold a grudge *forever*. She was my comforter too. When my feelings were hurt or I got into trouble, she would always let me sleep with her. She would scratch my back or play with the curls in my hair until I fell asleep. She was my best friend and the only person in my childhood that I really trusted."

"What kind of things were you doing that got you into trouble?"

"It was usually because I was talking when I shouldn't have been."

"Like during class?"

"Yes, I was *always* talking in class. I was very bored at that school. And I was always either talking or laughing in church. That got me into some *big* trouble. But that was mostly my sister's fault."

"The sensitive, quiet one? It was her fault?" I teased.

"Yes. She may have been quiet, but she was mischievous and an instigator. She knew I would do anything to make her laugh. And because I was the one triggering the laughter, I'm the one that got punished."

"Like physical punishment?"

"Oh yes. It was a popular thing back then. I'll never understand it." When she shook her head, she looked *just like Clara*.

"Lovedy told me it was based on the biblical principle of 'spare the rod, spoil the child'. Was it the same at your church and school?"

"In the seventies and eighties, corporal punishment was used in schools all over the country. But yes, I'm sorry to say, our church and school believed that verse in the literal sense."

"How often did you go to church?"

"Every Sunday morning, Sunday night, Wednesday night and chapel every day at school. If revival was happening, we were at church every night for a week."

"Revival? Did you go to tents for that?"

"No, Farrah. No tents for us. There would be a popular guest speaker that would come to our church and preach every night for a week. They usually had a music group that would travel with them too."

"Why did they call it revival? What does that even mean?"

"I know you didn't grow up in church, but haven't you ever attended as an adult? How can you not know what 'revival' means?"

"I know what the *word* revival means. I just don't understand it in the context of church! I'll have you know that I *have* attended church as an adult. I've been to several funerals. I've attended countless church weddings, including yours. And as a matter of fact, one time before I met you, I even went to Easter Mass with this hot guy that would only date believers."

"You lied about being a believer so he would go out with you?"

"Yes. He was *that hot*."

"So what happened?"

"Well, all I heard him say was that he only dated believers. When he invited me to go to church with him, I figured I could pull it off. I mean, how hard could it be, right? What I didn't know was that he only dated *Catholic* believers. The kneeling and standing I could follow pretty easily, but when the congregation started saying all those responses and prayers and I tried to fake it by mumbling my way through it, he knew something was up. At one point, he looked over at me and watched me faking my way through the prayers. He made a weird face, you know, with one nostril hiked up. Sad to say, I never saw him again after that Sunday."

"I can't imagine why, Farrah," she shook her head and rolled her eyes at me.

"Cut the sarcasm and explain revival to me, already!"

"Ok. I would describe revival in a church setting as a refreshening of the spirit. We went to church so much that we heard the same sermons repeatedly. They brought in those dynamic speakers to liven things up a bit and get people excited about their faith again."

"Gosh, sometimes I think you and Lovedy lived the same life just in different decades."

"I've thought the same before, too. But her parents *did intentionally* find a Christian family that lived in the bible belt. I don't think there was any way to avoid it."

"That's true. Her church seemed very legalistic. Was your church the same way?"

"Oh yes. No pop or rock music and definitely *no dancing*. Women couldn't wear pants or shorts, show cleavage or tummies. No tight clothes. No swimming with boys. They also had a six-inch rule at my school."

"A six-inch rule?"

"Yes. If you were sitting next to a boy, you had to sit six inches apart."

"They would have expelled me immediately."

"Girl, there was all kinds of sex going on at that school. The more they talked about what a transgression it was, the more everyone wanted to do it. The only girl that was actually expelled was the one having sex with the coach."

"Nooooooo."

"Yeeeeesss."

"Did they report it to the police?"

"Nope. They made him apologize to the congregation. Then he left and got a job at another Christian school."

"That is so messed up." I shook my head, not able to comprehend what she was saying.

"I know. I've never gotten my head around that one."

"How did the kids treat you when you got older? Like, in high school?"

"Our school had kindergarten through high school, all in one building. In high school, I had the same kids in my class as I did in kindergarten. Occasionally, we'd get a new student but for the most part, it was the same core group of families in our church and school throughout my time there. I had the same friends until my sophomore year."

"What happened?"

"Well, remember I told you it was a small school. Kids would date and break up all the time just like all kids do in high school. But once you dated a few people, your options became limited. If you wanted to continue dating, eventually, you had to date the friend of someone you already dated. Are you following me?"

"Oh yes. This is getting interesting. Keep going."

"When I was a freshman, there was a boy that used to date one of my close friends. They broke up and he started dating someone else. And then they broke up too. Then he started writing notes to me and passing them to me in the hallway. He was the first boy that had shown interest in me, and I liked it. I started writing back. Then he started calling and we would talk for hours on the phone. He would make cassette tapes for me with love songs on them. You remember all those love songs of the eighties, Lionel Richie, Bryan Adams…"

"Oh, yes. Easily, the best decade for music. But keep going, I'm listening."

"And then one night during church, he passed me a note and asked me to meet him at the school end of the building once the service was over. So, I did."

"And?"

"I walked down the hallway where the lockers were, and all the lights were off. I was feeling my way in the dark. We found our way to each other, and he gave me my first kiss."

"Awww, Corrina. That is so sweet."

"I was so smitten with him, but interracial dating was frowned upon. Everything we did was a secret, which made it even more intoxicating."

"So… you're biracial and there were no other people of color at your church or school…what were you supposed to do?"

"Not date a white boy."

"Oh, c'mon, Corrina. Really?"

"Yes, really. Also, he was a couple of years older than me, and he had a car. On the weekends, he cruised the main drag in our town and eventually made his way down my street, blasting those songs that he recorded on the cassette tapes for me. Charlotte used to fly up the stairs and into my room screaming, 'I know who's doin' that! I know it's him! I'm going to tell his parents!' And then she would ground me from using the telephone."

"So what happened with you two?"

"We ended up getting suspended from school."

"For what?"

"Well, it was Valentine's Day, and I went to school all excited. I remember I put on a red sweater and took him a card that I had made for him. When I arrived at school, I saw him breaking the six-inch rule with a girl by the lockers. I could just tell by the way he was standing so close to her that he was done with me. And a month later, I was called to the principal's office."

"For what?"

"Apparently, he ran his mouth about a time we made out in a storage closet at school."

"Wait, what do you mean by *made out*?"

"Kissing, like teenagers do...*for hours*. Anyway, the principal had me in his office and he was asking me detailed questions about what I did with this boy and how far it went, blah blah blah. I was totally creeped out. He accused me of doing things I absolutely did not do. I remember he had track lighting above his desk, and it was shining in my face. It felt like I was being *interrogated*! They ended up suspending us for two weeks and they gave me classwork to take home. I remember it was the week the Space Shuttle Challenger exploded."

"Did you see it live on TV?"

"I did. It was terrifying."

"Wait a minute. Lovedy told me that Phil and Charlotte didn't believe in having a TV in the home. They must have changed their minds, huh?"

"They did. And let me tell you, once they let that idol into our home, Dad was up late every night *glued* to that TV," she giggled at the irony.

"So, what happened after you were suspended?"

"The summer after our freshman year, that boy started calling me again. At that point, Mom was working outside the home. Sarah was driving and had a job, and I was at home alone. He would stop by, and we would hang out together. What I didn't know was that he was also hanging out with my friend at her house. The condensed version of the story is that I showed up to school on the first day of my sophomore year and no one in my class would speak to me. That went on for the *entire* year."

"You went the *entire* year without any friends?"

"I did. I spent time together with my sister and her friends as much as Mom would allow. But they were older and were doing things I was too young to do. That's the only time in my life I have ever felt depressed. I would dread waking up to face another day at that school and I cried all the time.

"That bullshit is *exactly* why I didn't hang out with girls when I was growing up, Corrina! They are *ruthless*!"

She patted me on the leg, "Don't get all worked up, Farrah. While it was hard when I was going through it, I learned an invaluable lesson along the way about what it means to be a *true* friend and a decent human being. I also started teaching my own girls, at a very young age, the importance of things like inclusion, boundaries, self-respect and integrity so they would learn how to cultivate meaningful, honest relationships with others."

"So how did you move past it?"

"Well, the summer after my sophomore year, I got a part time job where my sister worked and was able to make friends there. Then as the fall was approaching, I begged my parents to let me go to the public school for my junior and senior year. Sarah had graduated and I couldn't stand the thought of going to that private school without her."

"Did they let you?"

"I didn't think there was a chance they would say yes, but they did."

"Did they still make you go to that church?"

"They did. But I had a different attitude about it, by then."

"What do you mean?"

"I had been exposed to the outside world and that changed everything. I made a few good friends at that public school. They were also Christians but not in the legalistic sense. I started going to their youth group activities instead of mine and learned about a God that I never knew."

"Which God is that?"

"The loving one."

"No hellfire and brimstone?"

"Nope. And for the first time, I became friends with black and brown kids. When I say I found a whole new world, I'm not exaggerating."

TWENTY-SEVEN
MAY 2022

Corrina steered the Jeep down the off ramp so we could get out to stretch our legs and switch places. The last three hours flew by as I listened to my closest friend tell me about her childhood and the formative years that shaped and molded her into the person she was to become. At times, I wished that her childhood had been different. Hearing how she felt like she didn't belong in her own home and community broke my heart. But selfishly, I was thankful for whatever path brought her to me.

As I followed the on ramp back to the highway, I continued our conversation.

"So you were a junior at the public school. You made new friends, and it sounds like your life circumstances and environment had improved, right?"

"Yes, greatly."

"You met Lovedy your junior year?"

She smiled. "Yes, I sure did."

"How did that come about?"

"Monica was one of the close friends I had at the public high school. We were hanging out at her house one day and she asked me about my birth parents. I told her the limited information that I had at that time. I knew my birth mother was young and that she was from North Carolina. I also knew that she was white. She asked me if I thought my parents would be open to finding her for me. To be honest, I never considered it. I thought it would be rude in some kind of way and make me appear ungrateful that they adopted me. I had always planned to find her once I was an adult and had moved out on my own. But that planted a seed, and eventually, I worked up the nerve to ask them."

"How did they react?"

"They were very calm and said they would work on it. They warned me not to get my hopes up because they had already looked for Sarah's mother and were unable to find her. But they also said they knew more about my birth mom than Sarah's so the chances were better that they would be able to locate her. They also talked to me about the possibility of my birth mother not wanting to speak with me or meet me. That shook me up a little bit. I had countless daydreams of meeting my birth mother over the course of my childhood and never once did I consider the idea that she might not want to know me."

"Do you remember when they told you that they found her?"

"Oh yes. It didn't take long. I came home from school one day and they were both there, waiting for me in the living room. I knew something was up. They told me they had spoken to her on the phone and that she was open to speaking with me and would write to me soon."

"How exciting was that?"

"I remember just taking a deep breath and releasing all the angst I had held in for so long. I checked that mailbox every day for a week until her letter arrived. I remember sitting on my bed with the door closed and staring at the envelope. She had the most beautiful cursive handwriting, all swirly and loopy. Seeing my name in her handwriting might seem like such a small thing but it was surreal to me. When I opened the envelope, there was a three-page letter and some photos. I must have looked at those pictures twenty times that evening. I wrote her back immediately and included some pictures of myself, mostly those ghastly ones they took at school."

"Were you able to talk on the phone?"

"Eventually. Remember, long distance calls cost money back then. Hearing her voice was dreamlike. She was warm and kind and made me laugh almost immediately. It wasn't awkward at all. From the beginning of our conversation, she felt familiar. I had always dreamt and wondered about her, and then suddenly she was a reality. From the age of four, I had been looking at every tall lady, wondering if she was my mother. I didn't need to keep searching anymore. I had finally found her. She was part of my life."

"Tell me about when you first saw her. Were you nervous?"

"I wasn't nervous, but I was giddy with excitement. She arrived in the afternoon. I was looking out the living room window, waiting for her car to pull up. When I saw her, I just shouted, 'Mom! Mom! She's here!' I flung the door open and stood on the porch. I wanted to run down the sidewalk, but I froze and just watched this tall, lanky, blonde-haired woman walk up the sidewalk towards me. Her face, hair and skin were different, but we had the same body and moved the same way. The feeling of recognizing a part of yourself in someone else for the first time is a tricky thing to explain. I started going down the steps and when I reached her, I wrapped my arms around her. I didn't want to let her go. While Mom and Dad always made me feel at home, this was a different kind of home. One that I never felt before that moment."

"Did you ever call Lovedy and ask her how she felt when she met you?"

"I did. I don't know why I never asked her that before you texted me that day. But listening to her describe all the different emotions she was experiencing when she was walking down our sidewalk towards the house, it really touched my heart. It confirmed for me, all these years later, that I wasn't alone when I was dreaming of her. She was dreaming of me, too."

I quickly turned my head away from my beautiful friend and looked out the window at the passing landscapes, trying to hide my face.

"Farrah! Are you crying again?"

"I can't help it!" I was bawling by this point and snot was dripping onto my lip. I kept my eyes on the road and felt around the inside of the center console for a tissue. I dabbed my face and took a glance in the rearview mirror. I looked like a raccoon, which Corrina did not fail to recognize.

"Seriously, fix yourself. I'm not going to keep talking if you're going to keep crying. If you cry, I'll cry and then…"

And then I saw a tear slip down her cheek, which was the fourth time I had seen her cry in the twenty-eight years I had known her.

"Corrina, seriously. Are you crying? Pull it together."

"Oh, shut up and hand me a tissue."

"I used the last one. Sorry. You're going to have to use your t-shirt."

"Seriously? Not even a napkin or a paper towel?"

"Nope. Nothing."

"Ok, then." And without hesitation, she grabbed the neckline of her t-shirt, pulled it up and wiped her face like a snotty nosed little four-year-old. At which point I opened the console and handed her a tissue.

I pulled onto the next road and asked her to tell me about her weekend with Lovedy.

"I can tell you I didn't want it to end. Mom and Dad let me spend the night with her at a hotel. She brought more pictures with her, which was cool. We went out to get a bite to eat and just talked and talked. We talked about how I wanted to go to nursing school. We talked about the one boyfriend I had and how we got into trouble. I asked her about her parents and sisters. Then I asked her about my biological dad and that's when she told me that he had died. She gave me a picture that she copied from a newspaper clipping. That was pretty wild. Looking at Isaac's face was like looking into a mirror. I had his smile, his dimples, and his eyes."

"How did that feel to learn your biological father was deceased?"

"I don't really know how to explain it. Shock, disappointment, sadness. I was processing so much information at once. I was thrilled just to be with Lovedy, to walk and talk with her, even stand next to her. And yet at the same time the realization that I would never meet my father hit me hard."

"I remember sitting up in my room after she left that weekend. I was rereading her letters and looking at all the pictures. When I saw his picture again, I felt grief and sadness. It was a different kind of grief than losing someone you love. I loved the *idea* of him, the image I had conjured up in my mind of who he was. The grief was more about the realization that I would never know him. I felt like I had been robbed. When I found out how he died, I was angry for a long time. It still makes me angry when I think about it. I still imagine, on occasion, what it would have been like to have known him. To hug him. To be his daughter. It still hits me when I see the bond between fathers and their biological daughters. I'll never know what that feels like."

"Did you see Lovedy again soon after that? How did you both stay connected?"

"We kept in touch mostly through letters. Sarah drove me to see her in North Carolina the summer after my junior year."

"Really? How did that go?"

"It was nice to see her again and the town where she grew up. We met her at Aunt Faith's house. Aunt Patience was there too, with her kids. But I didn't get a chance to meet her parents. I didn't get to meet Hope, either. She had already moved away."

"Which one is Patience?"

"You probably know her as Baby."

"Oh, yes." And then I laughed, remember all the funny stories Lovedy had told me about her.

"How did Sarah handle the whole thing with Lovedy? That must have been hard for her in a way, not being able to find her own biological mother."

"She said she was genuinely happy for me, that it gave her hope that one day the same thing would happen for her too."

"And did it? Did she ever find her biological family?"

"She did, but it wasn't until about three years ago. She did a DNA test and submitted it to one of those website companies that trace lineage. She found matches immediately. Unfortunately, her mother had just passed away the prior year. She did, however, get a whole new family. Her mother had married another man that was not her father and had a bunch of kids. They welcomed her into their family with open arms. She has formed a close relationship with them."

"What about her father? Did she ever find him?"

"Oh yes. That was quite the story. Her father never knew she existed. He and her mother had a one-night stand in their college days, and he never saw or heard from her again after that night. When Sarah found him, he asked her if she would do another DNA test. She agreed, so they did it at the same time at separate locations of the same company. When they confirmed he was her father, he *really became* her father. He wasn't interested in just making the connection, he wanted to be part of her life."

"I'm not crying."

"Liar. Next question?"

"When did you see Lovedy next?" I asked, wiping my face.

"She came up for my high school graduation. We had a little party in the backyard afterwards. I thought it was nice of Mom and Dad to invite her."

"I agree. I have to give Phil and Charlotte some props. From what you've told me, it seems like they managed the complexities of having adopted children pretty well."

"I agree wholeheartedly. It couldn't have been easy for them."

"How were they as parents? Did you have a decent childhood?"

"That's a loaded question. We were a peculiar bunch, our little family of four. We were all so different from each other. Dad was a kind man with a gentle, easy-going personality. He did a lot of work for the church and for missionaries with his printing press. He was devoted to his faith, but he bought the legalism that church was selling, and that part was hard for all of us. Because of that, my childhood was not what you would describe as normal. I grew up with an intense fear of God. That church painted Him as this big angry monster that was waiting to pounce on me and send me to hell if I did anything wrong. Any time I did something that was considered a sin, I was made to feel as if I didn't really love Jesus because I wasn't behaving like Him *all the time*. So, I would pray and beg God to save me from burning in the lake of fire for all eternity. And I did that over and over again."

"I don't know anything about theology, but nothing about that even sounds logical," I shook my head in disbelief.

"It doesn't sound logical because it isn't. If God expected me to be like Jesus all the time, there wouldn't have been any need for the crucifixion."

I squinted in confusion, wanting to know more. "Did you ever have nightmares about it? I remember Lovedy was worried about you growing up in a church like hers. She didn't want you to live in fear."

"Yeah, of course. I used to have nightmares about the rapture all the time. I dreamed that my whole family was taken up to heaven and I was left behind. Imagine what that kind of teaching would do to a kid, even more so to a kid that had already been *abandoned* by her parents. Not to mention, the whole rapture thing made me terrified of trumpets."

"You mean the horn kind of trumpet?"

"Technically, I think a trumpet is a brass wind instrument. But yes, that kind."

"Why are you such a smartass? I was asking because it didn't make any sense to me."

"It didn't make any sense to you because you've completely ignored the book that has been sold more than any other book. *Ever.*"

"Yes. That is true. I have completely ignored that book."

"You should read it sometime. If for no other reason than it will make our conversations easier for me."

"I think that's a very large book, like eight hundred thousand words. Right? Is there an abbreviated version of the bible? I'm not trying to spend a year of my life on one book."

"Yes, there are several."

"For real?"

"For real," she rolled her eyes and shook her head at me.

"So what was the fear of trumpets about?"

"The rapture describes the return of Jesus. It's when all the dead believers rise in the air first and then the ones that are still living follow them and they all go to heaven to live for eternity. The return of Jesus will be announced by the sound of trumpets."

"Oooohhh. I get it. So, when you were little and you heard a trumpet, you thought dead people were going to start busting out of their graves."

"Yes, that's right," she nodded. But she had no idea what was coming.

"Good to know. I think it's time to change the playlist." Louis Armstrong, Chris Botti, Wynton Marsalis, I played all my favorite trumpeters and made her listen to them blow those *horns* all the way to our next stop.

TWENTY-EIGHT
MAY 2022

IT WAS PAST LUNCHTIME, AND WE WERE TIRED OF SNACKING ON GRAPES and popcorn. I asked Corrina to look on her map for the nearest restaurant that served tacos, the kind with soft corn tortillas, marinated meats, cilantro, shredded cabbage, grilled onions, limes, and fresh salsa. She found the perfect place that had outdoor seating. We ordered a variety of tacos, spread them out across the table and shared our lunch under the shade of a big umbrella.

"Being that we're going to see her soon, let's talk about Charlotte. What was she like as a mother when you were young?"

Corrina gave me a genuine smile when she said, "She was a good mom. She took good care of us when we were little. She was a great cook, always kept the house clean. She sewed a lot of our clothes. I didn't think much of it then but now I wish I would have paid attention. I can barely sew a button back onto a shirt.

"What was her personality like?" I asked.

"She was on the quieter side, but she was fun. She was always with us, too. If she went to the print shop with Dad, she would take us with her. She was strict on most things, like how we dressed, the language we used, and how we behaved in public. Manners were important to her. But she was oddly loose on other things."

"Really? Like what?"

"Well, for one thing, she's the reason I'm a really good cheater when I play games."

"What?"

"Yes. One day, she called me down to play a card game with her. She dealt out the hands and I was stunned when I turned my hand over. I started giggling because I had, what I thought, was every good card in the deck and I was about to destroy her. But when the game started, I lost almost immediately. She set the whole thing up to trick me. To this day, I can't play a game without cheating."

"Corrina, I have played so many games with you over the years. Are you telling me you've been cheating all of this time?"

"Well, I can't say for certain that I cheated at *every* single game, but I would say it is safe to say yes."

I was stunned. "All of these years, I thought you were so much more strategic than me. Turns out, I'm just honest. And you're a lying, dirty, low-down *cheater*!"

"I am," she shrugged indifferently. "I can't deny it. But it is so much more fun than just playing board games like they were designed to be played. Who wants to do that?"

"Did you teach your girls to cheat at games?"

"No way, I'm too competitive to lose my edge." Then she continued, "Oh, I have another example of one that I still don't understand."

"Tell me."

"I told you already that I wasn't allowed to wear jeans or shorts or any skirts that were above my knee when I was kid because it wasn't Christian-like. What I didn't tell you is that I *was* allowed to wear scary witch and ghost costumes at Halloween."

We both laughed at that one. "Yeah, because witches and ghosts are so Christian-like?"

"I don't think those rules were really her idea. But she was married to my dad, and they were very committed to a very legalistic church. I think it was more about acceptance and respect than about personal conviction. Remember I told you that we didn't have a TV for the first eight years of my life?"

"Yes, I remember. So, you never watched Sesame Street? Or Schoolhouse Rock?"

"No. And it has always annoyed me when people became nostalgic and sang those songs that I had never heard. At least they would let us listen to a couple of shows on the radio."

"They aired TV shows on the radio in the 1970's?"

"Yes, they did."

"I had no idea. I thought that was a 1930's thing."

"It *was* a 1930's thing and a 1970's thing for people who didn't believe in or couldn't afford a television set. I will tell you that both Sarah and I excelled at reading, and I believe it is because we didn't have a television during those early years. Mom used to read to us all the time. And then when we were older, we read a lot of books and encyclopedias. I didn't learn about all the fairy tales by going to the movies. I learned about them by reading books."

"You weren't allowed to go to the movies?"

"No way. The church thought the devil created Hollywood."

"What about kids' movies? Animated movies?"

"Nope. They believed that if you gave your money to the box office to watch kids' movies, it funded the creation of other movies that were bad."

"Seriously? What about music? You told me you weren't allowed to listen to rock 'n' roll. What kind of music did they allow?"

"Christian, obviously, and classical. Some secular music was ok, as long as it didn't have rhythm to it."

"No booty-shakin' stuff, right?" I did a little dance in the car seat for Corrina's amusement.

"Exactly. But it wasn't only about the rhythm. It was about the lyrics too. I remember one preacher came to our church and he played some records backwards over the speaker. He accused the bands of back masking and said they were lyrics about the devil. I was so scared. I thought demons were going to jump out from underneath the pews, so I brought my legs up off the floor and sat crisscrossed on the pew until it was time to go."

Corrina continued on with her memories of her childhood and the next one made her smile. "She did let us play outside often, which made me happy. We didn't have any other girls on our street, just boys. I grew up riding bikes, making mud pies in the dirt, climbing trees and playing baseball. I always had scabs on my knees and dirt on my clothes."

"I grew up with playing with boys, too. This is one of the many reasons you are my people, Corrina. We're a different breed."

"Yep, and I was a handful, too. One time, I was riding my bike and saw the mail carrier delivering mail to our house. I decided to hitch a ride. I snuck in the mail truck while he was up on our porch. I hid in the back and was giggling as quietly as I could. He was all the way around the block before he found me."

"Corrina! What did he do when he found you?"

"He knew where I lived. It wasn't like I blended in with all the other kids. It wasn't hard to figure out, so he drove me straight home and walked me up to the house."

"You were a bad kid!"

"I was not! I just liked to have fun. Oh, I remember one summer, after playing outside all day, I went into our neighbor's yard and stole all her daffodils and brought home a bouquet for mom. I was so proud of the beautiful flowers I had picked for her. She was laughing so hard when she said, 'Did you get these from Mrs. Samuel's yard?' I told her they were growing in a line up the curb between our yards and they were leaning on our side, so they had to be ours. She made me go over to Mrs. Samuel's house and apologize to that old crabby lady."

I smiled at the thought of little Corrina making a bouquet of flowers for Charlotte. "Even with the stealing, that's kind of sweet. Did Sarah love playing outside like you did?"

"I remember her being out there with me. But she liked being inside more than I did. I would stay outside until Mom yelled for me to come back. I never wanted to go back home."

"Sounds just like Lovedy. She said she always preferred to play outside in the dirt over playing with dolls. Did you ever play with dolls?"

"Oh yes. I loved my dolls. I remember one Christmas, I asked my mom for a boy doll because I wanted my girl doll to get married. She said I couldn't have one, and that it wasn't appropriate. So instead, she gave me an acrobat doll. I took it upstairs with a pair of scissors and cut all her hair off, so she looked like a boy. And my dolls married on my miniature shopping mall escalator. One day, Mom came into my room and gasped in horror when she saw what I had done to the doll. She wanted to know why, so I told her that I wanted my girl doll to marry a boy doll and she wouldn't buy me one, so I made the girl into a boy. She said, 'You can't do that. You can't turn a girl into a boy.' I told her, 'Yes, I can. Watch. And then my dolls got married on the escalator again.'"

I was laughing so hard at the irony. "So, let me get this straight. Charlotte didn't want to buy you a male doll for fear of you doing something inappropriate with the male and female. And so, the girl doll ends up marrying another girl doll with short hair?"

"Yes."

"What did she do?"

"I don't think she knew what to do. She just walked out of the room."

"Did she ever talk to you about sex?"

"Sort of. Well, she told me how babies were made."

"How did that conversation go?"

"She did fine. I was in the third or fourth grade and was blabbing to one of my classmates about how babies are born. Only, I didn't have the right information. My friend told her mother the new and terrifying stuff she had learned from me that day at school. Her mom called my mom. And then mom had to set me straight. She sat me down and explained that my information was not correct and then she gave me a book to read."

"Yeah, I guess a lot of parents do that, even now. I can't imagine it is an easy conversation to have with a kid."

"It's not that hard. I had that talk with both of my girls."

"Well, you're a labor and delivery nurse. I imagine they had already heard you talking a lot about it, right?"

"Yeah, I'm sure they did. But there's much more to that conversation than the science of human reproduction. Personally, I felt the need to break the cycle if you know what I mean. More than the science, I wanted to talk to them about body image, self-respect and how not to have babies before they were ready."

"How did your girls take it?"

"Vassy was into all aspects of it and had tons of questions. Lauren just screamed and covered her ears as she ran out of the room."

"So how was Charlotte as a mother of two teenage girls?"

"I think that's where she struggled a bit. I think she was comfortable when we were young children because she had total control, and we were dependent on her. But then we grew up, started thinking for ourselves, driving, pushing back, and asking why and she didn't know how to connect with us anymore. Dad's health started failing and mom got a job with the state doing administrative work. Trying to keep their heads above water financially, while keeping tabs on two teenage girls was a lot for her. She was carrying a lot on her shoulders, but I think the task of managing our teenage years did her in."

"What do you mean?"

"You know what? I think we should save that conversation for the way home. I want you to spend time with her first and hear her background and perspective. It will change how you hear the rest of mine."

I agreed with her and appreciated the care she was taking to ensure that I wasn't swayed by her entire story without first spending time with Charlotte.

Corrina looked at the map, said we'd be at our hotel in thirty minutes and then asked me if I wanted her to drive through the city.

"Yes," I said. "I'm sick of driving today." I pulled off into a grocery store parking lot and we switched seats. I would find out later, that's when she slapped a bumper sticker on my poor, innocent, beautiful Jeep. It was a political sticker for a candidate that I despised.

TWENTY-NINE
MAY 2022

We finally arrived at our hotel in downtown Pittsburgh. After checking in and putting our luggage away, we freshened up and went down to the adjoining restaurant to get a bite to eat for dinner. The ambiance was very relaxing. The lights were dim, the candles flickered on the tabletops and a pianist was playing instrumental versions of all the great love songs.

Corrina ordered the seabass, and I decided on the salmon, but it didn't really matter who ordered which dish. Like always, we both split our meals in half and shared with the other. Some people may think that it is a small thing but for people who often have food envy, like Corrina, it keeps them happy. And it keeps me from hearing her whine that my dinner looked better than hers.

We finished our meal and ordered Honey Manhattans for dessert. We sipped our cocktails slowly, enjoying the relaxing atmosphere and the conversation. The server came over and offered us another round. Before I could even think about it, Corrina shook her head and said, "I've got this one."

After the waiter brought our drinks, Corrina gave me a weird look and let out an audible sigh. "I have something to tell you, but I need you to not make a big deal out of it. Don't ask me a bunch of questions because I probably won't have the answers and I'm too relaxed to try and figure them out now. And please, do not start up with your weepy crap."

"That was quite the setup. This better be good."

"I spoke with August again," she held up her hand as if to tell me to wait, "And I know you're wondering who called who."

"Yes?"

"He called me."

I took another sip to keep my mouth busy and let her continue.

"We talked more about his life. He's doing well and it seems like he's happy. This time we moved past the surface pleasantries and got into some deeper discussions about things."

She was talking so slowly, measuring each word. It was driving me crazy, but I stayed calm and just kept nodding like an idiot to keep from reaching across the table and ripping the whole story from her throat.

"He spoke to Derek, his father, and it didn't turn out like he hoped. He said everything was fine, at first. They had spoken on the telephone a couple of times and were making plans to meet each other. But when he asked Derek if it was ok to bring his husband, Derek's tone completely changed. He said some unsavory things to August about his sexual orientation and how he could not condone that type of relationship or allow his family to be around it. After August finished telling me the story, he wanted to know what I thought about it." And then she stopped talking, so I took another sip and waited like I was instructed. Apparently I waited too long.

"Farrah, conversations go two ways. When I pause, you speak. That's how it works."

"But you told me not to ask any questions. I'm sitting over here, buzzed off my ass because I've been taking a sip every time I wanted to say something," I slurred.

"You can ask questions but if I say I don't know, that's what it means."

"*You can ask questions but if I say I don't know, that's what it means*" I mocked her like a six year old and then asked her how she felt about August.

"I thought a few different things. I told him that I was happy he had found love in his life. I think that was the most important thing he needed to hear. Then I thought what an absolute asshole his father is, but I didn't say that to him. And then I thought, it's all up to me. I have to do this for him."

"Do what for whom?"

"I have to let August into my life. He's had too much rejection already. I'm not going to add to the pile and make it worse for him. I'm just going to have to get past my own stuff about his father and bury the hatchet. For August's sake."

"Can you do that?"

"I'll find a way. Somehow."

"Did you tell August the things about his father that you told me at the café?"

"No. And I never will."

We finished our cocktails and headed up to our separate rooms. Corrina wanted to share a room, but she snores like a buzzsaw so that was a firm no from me. We said good night and I called Gabe to let him know we had made it to the hotel. Then I grabbed my laptop, laid on the bed and started writing.

The next thing I knew someone was banging on my hotel room door. I woke up, disoriented. The lamp was still on, and my laptop had fallen off the side of the bed. I walked over to the window and opened the curtains. I was surprised to see it was still dark outside. I walked softly to the door and looked through the peephole, but I couldn't see anyone.

I was spooked, and I wondered if Corrina heard the banging too. I went over to the adjoining door and opened my side. I didn't want to wake her up if she was still sleeping but if she was awake, I wanted to talk to her. So, I whispered her name. "Corrina... Corrina. Are you awake?"

"Yes, I'm awake," she opened the door on her side.

"Did you hear that banging?" I asked.

"Yes, I heard it. I think our whole floor heard it."

"It sounded like they were banging on my door!"

"That's what it sounded like to me, too. Probably just had the wrong room. Are you spooked?"

"Yes, totally."

"Want to sleep in my room?"

"Your snoring is worse than the banging."

"Whatever. Enjoy your nightmares." And then she shut the door in my face.

I put my face up next to her door and hissed, "You are so rude!"

I looked at the clock. It was 2:30am and I was wide awake, so I picked my laptop up off the floor, flopped back down on my bed and continued writing. I must have dozed off because the banging startled me out of my sleep again, which pissed me off. I stomped over to the door and looked through the peephole but once again, there was no one there. Then I heard the banging again and it was even louder. It was coming from the adjoining door, so I opened my side. Corrina's side was already open, but she wasn't there. I took a step forward, thinking maybe she was in the bathroom. I took another step forward and turned my head and saw that the bathroom light was on. As I slowly turned the corner, she jumped out in front of me with a white mask on and screamed my name, "Farrah!"

I let out an involuntary, bloodcurdling scream and stomped my legs in anger. "Corrina! Were you the one that was banging on my door the first time too?"

"Yes."

"What is wrong with you!?"

Before she could answer, the phone by the bedside started ringing. It was the front desk making sure everything was ok. They had received a complaint from another guest about the noise coming from Corrina's room. I stood there and listened to her lie her ass off about it being a scary movie on TV. And then she promised to turn the volume down.

"Well, played, Corrina. Well, played. But you'd better sleep with one eye open for the rest of the trip." Then I slammed my side of the door shut and listened to her laughing as I crawled back into bed.

We planned to do a few touristy things in the city before heading to New York, so we met downstairs for an early breakfast. We talked about what we wanted to do that day over coffee and oatmeal, fruit, and scrambled eggs. Fate handed me a freebie when Corrina said she needed to use the restroom. When she came back and took another spoonful of her oatmeal, she met a six-legged rubbery friend with antennae sticking up between the oats. She didn't scream, but bolted straight up and her chair fell backwards, which caught the attention of our fellow early risers.

"Corrina, what's the matter? What's wrong?"

"There's a *roach* in my oatmeal," she whispered.

"Eat it. It's protein. It's good for you." I smirked.

She tilted her head and gave me the stink eye, "Did you put that in my bowl? I should have known."

"Well, you didn't. Now we're even."

We checked out of the hotel and headed straight for The Strip District. It was a beautiful morning to walk along the streets and check out the local shops. There were charming boutiques and countless ethnic and produce markets. We bought chocolates and coffee beans to take to Charlotte and some snacks to keep us sated for the remaining hours of our trip to New York.

Next, we visited The Andy Warhol Museum. We started on the top floor and worked our way down, learning about his life and appreciating his artwork. While I was somewhat familiar with his Pop Art, I didn't know much about his life. I wished we could have stayed longer but we had to get on the road. And after a quick bite in the museum café, we were on our way to see Charlotte.

It was my turn at the wheel, and I turned on my 1980's playlist. We sang along, at the top of our lungs, to the music of our teen age years. And even though Corrina wasn't supposed to be listening to secular music in the eighties, the rebel knew every word to every song. New Edition, Lionel Richie, The Whispers, Run-D.M.C., she knew them all and we did nothing but sing the three hours that it took to drive from Pittsburgh to Harrisburg. Then we stopped off for gas, to stretch our legs and switch places again.

Corrina hopped in the driver's seat and turned on her movie soundtrack playlist. We bopped to the soundtrack from *Grease*, wailed at "Glory" from the movie *Selma* and got all misty-eyed over "Count on Me" from *Waiting to Exhale*. But it was time to get back to the conversation. So, I turned down the tunes and turned on my recorder.

"I know we're not going to talk about August's father or the circumstances that led to your pregnancy, but would it be ok to talk about being pregnant?"

"What do you want to know?"

"You were a senior in high school. Right?"

"Yes."

"And the pregnancy was a surprise, correct?"

"No. I planned to get pregnant my senior year in high school. Isn't that every girl's dream?"

"What is wrong with you, Corrina? Do you have any answers that are not dripping with sarcasm?"

"Not for you," she quipped with a smile.

I gave her the finger and then continued with my next question, "Did you ever consider having an abortion?"

"I did. And while I believe it is a deeply personal and difficult choice for a woman to make, it wasn't the right choice for me. Even considering the circumstances behind it, it just wasn't an option in my heart and mind."

"Would it be ok for me to ask you why not?"

"Sure. I don't mind. For me, the answer to that is pretty simple. While my childhood wasn't perfect, I'm glad I was given a chance at life. I wanted to do the same thing for my baby."

"Ok. I respect that. Did you tell anyone about the circumstances?"

"No, I didn't. I didn't tell my parents, the staff at the school or anyone at the church. I told no one."

"Why?"

"That's easy. I knew that no one would believe me."

"How did the kids at your school treat you?"

"They talked and whispered about it. They speculated, but no one was unkind to me. I just kept leaning on my friends to help me get through it. They stuck by me through the whole thing, thankfully."

"What about the people at church?"

"Oh, they kicked me out. Said I couldn't go there anymore."

"Wait...*what*? Are you serious?"

"Well, sort of. They said if I went forward in front of the congregation and confessed my sin, that they would forgive me. But I refused. It didn't matter if I told them the truth, I knew my reputation was ruined since I was suspended my freshman year for making out with that boy. Those people would never have believed me."

"What about Phil and Charlotte? Did they continue to go there?"

"No. They stopped attending that church and started going to another one just like it in the next town. More props for Mom and Dad. They were truly kind to me, even when I wouldn't talk with them about it. When I told them I wasn't going to keep the baby, they offered to help facilitate the adoption. I knew what that meant and I couldn't bear the idea of my baby growing up in the same situation that I did. I wanted my baby to go to a family that looked like him and would encourage him to spread his wings instead of clipping them. I told them they could help me, but we had to do it my way. And they agreed. I handpicked August's family. They aren't white, and they don't go to the same kind of church that Lovedy and I grew up in. Another dangerous cycle broken."

"Did you go with Phil and Charlotte to their new church?"

"No. I went to the church with my friends from school. They embraced me. Their youth pastor's wife stopped me one night after youth group and asked if she could talk to me. All she did was ask me how I was doing, how I was feeling and then she asked if I needed any help. She wanted to make sure that I was getting medical care. No judgment, no condemnation. She didn't ask for an apology, and she didn't offer forgiveness."

"Did you contact Lovedy when all of this was going on?"

"I did. I wrote her a letter and told her. She wrote back almost immediately."

"What did she say?"

"She was empathetic and kind and then there was this thing she kept writing over and over."

"What was that?"

"She kept saying, 'You will be ok. Everything will be ok.'"

THIRTY
MAY 2022

We finally made it to Charlotte's place that evening in the Bed-Stuy neighborhood of Brooklyn. She was so happy to see us and immediately introduced me to her husband, Michael, who she had married in the fall of 1998. Michael gave us a hug and a big smile and then retreated to the kitchen to finish preparing dinner. Meanwhile, Charlotte took us to our rooms and gave me a tour of their three-story home.

Originally built in 1899 as a two-family home, they had converted it to a single-family residential wonder. The renovation was meticulous, and they kept much of the character and authenticity of a bygone era. Corrina and I were staying on the ground floor which had two bedrooms, a full bath and direct access to the backyard where I found a charming outdoor sitting area. The parlor floor's living and kitchen area was open and airy with lofty ceilings and large bay windows. The primary bedroom and a fourth bedroom along with another full bathroom took up the third floor.

I watched Charlotte, who was seventy-three years old, moving up and down the stairwells of that three-story house like a boss. She appeared to be in great shape. She was petite, like me, with a cute pixie cut. Her eyes were azure, like the color of the sky on a cloudless day and they sparkled like they had stories to tell. I couldn't wait to hear them.

We sat down to a feast of yellowfin tuna steaks with a ginger-honey-soy sauce, rice, and a side of colorful roasted vegetables. After dinner, we went down to the first floor and sipped on cups of coffee punch as we sat under the festive star-shaped lights that were strung above the outdoor patio. The evening air was cool, and we were all full and relaxed.

I watched as Corrina talked and laughed with Charlotte and Michael and admired the closeness I saw there. It didn't escape me that although Corrina may have felt out of place growing up, she had an army of special people who loved and cared for her. I leaned my head back against the headrest and continued to watch them with a smile on my face. I was happy for my sweet friend.

After refusing our offers to help, Michael left us after a brief time to clean up the kitchen. As I sat there with these two women under the night sky, I thought about how little I really knew about Charlotte. I met her for the first time at Corrina's wedding, then I saw her a few times when she came to visit Corrina's girls, but I couldn't recall ever learning much about her. She was usually on the quieter side. Not in a snobbish kind of way, but one in which she was usually listening to others, rather than talking. I knew Corrina had told her why we were coming but I wasn't sure if she told her about recording the conversations. Just when I was about to bring it up, Corrina did it for me.

"Mom, do you remember me telling you that Farrah was going to record our conversations while we are here?"

Charlotte smiled and nodded, "Yes, I remember. I'm still ok with it."

I smiled back at her. "Thank you so much, Charlotte. Being able to record has helped me immensely. I would never be able to remember all of the details. And if you want to keep any parts of your story to yourself, that's perfectly fine, too. I don't want you to feel like you have to tell me things that are deeply personal or you don't really want to share. I also want to remind you that I will protect your identity, so you don't need to worry about that."

She smiled again. "Well, that helps because I do have a story to tell, and it is deeply personal. To be honest, I hope you do publish this work. I think it may help people who have had to face challenges and difficulties in their lives."

I liked where she was going with this, so I asked her to tell me more.

She gazed at Corrina for a few moments, then turned back to me. "Well, sometimes when life is hard, it can feel like it will always be that way. When a person is truly in despair, it is difficult to imagine that life will get any better. But the sun always rises again and offers us a new day, a new chance to experience something different. It awakens us in the morning and offers us hope. There were many days I was in despair, and I just want people to know that they should never surrender their hope for a better life." Her beautiful blues were brimming as she looked back at Corrina.

Her words touched my heart. I had a lump in my throat and my eyes started burning. I had imagined that having these conversations with Charlotte would be more difficult than having them with Lovedy and Clara. They were so talkative and outgoing. I never imagined that sweet, quiet Charlotte would give me the same generous gift of candidness. Corrina quickly snapped me out of my moment of gratitude.

"Mom, I should warn you that Farrah cries at the drop of a hat. In fact, she's getting ready to do it now. It's kind of a new thing. She didn't used to be this way. It's alarming sometimes. If you find it weird, just walk away."

I shot Corrina the bird on the side of my coffee cup so Charlotte couldn't see. Thank goodness Charlotte took to my defense. "Corrina Lane, be kind. You're no different. You have emotions like the rest of us. Some of us just wear ours on the outside for everyone to see."

I had a question for Charlotte. "Was Corrina always so mean? Was she like this as a child?"

She shook her head and laughed. "No, definitely not. She was always funny and adventurous and sometimes could be defiant, but I never knew her to be unkind. Or maybe, she was, and she kept that side hidden from me because she knew there would be big trouble."

Corrina quickly came to her own defense. "There wasn't any hiding…about that anyway. I've always been a kind person. I just like to give Farrah a hard time. It's fun."

"Fun for whom?" I asked.

"Me. It's always fun for me," Corrina said with no hesitation, before tossing her balled up cocktail napkin my way.

Charlotte was watching us with a smile on her face and said, "I always enjoyed watching you two girls together. You seem to really enjoy one another."

"Most of the time we do," I said with a wink at Corrina. Then I turned my attention back to Charlotte. "So, what are our plans for tomorrow? Are we staying here to talk? Or would you like to go somewhere?"

"I thought we could get up and have breakfast here. Michael makes the most fabulous blueberry pancakes. Then I want to take you girls on a field trip. We'll have plenty of time to talk while also doing something fun. How does that sound?"

"That sounds great!" I said and was genuinely excited.

"Good," Charlotte said. "I'm going to head upstairs now. You girls help yourselves to anything you need in the kitchen. Michael and I are early risers, we like to do yoga in the mornings. We'll meet you back here for breakfast. Make sure you wear comfortable walking shoes tomorrow."

I thanked her for the wonderful dinner and watched as Corrina stood up to kiss her mother goodnight.

Corrina and I waited about fifteen minutes before we ran upstairs to make another drink. Then we went right back outside and talked and laughed until almost midnight. We were both excited about our field trip as we headed back inside to get ready for bed.

Corrina called the bathroom first, as always. While I waited, I went to my bedroom to unpack. When I heard her leave the bathroom, I went in to take a quick shower. It had been a full day, and the steam helped my muscles and mind to relax. I dried off, moisturized, and put on my orange Volunteers pajamas. I took my hair down from a high bun and put it in a low loose braid around the side of my neck. Then I brushed and flossed and put on the latest facial products that promised to make me look twenty years younger. I grabbed my clothes and toiletry bag and knelt down on the floor to look under the door for Corrina's feet. "I see your feet, dumbass," I whispered loudly to her.

"Damn it," she said before she walked down the hall to her bedroom and closed the door.

Laughing, I slipped out of the bathroom quickly and ran through the dark hallway to my bedroom. I made sure to lock the door as I was still on high alert, waiting for Corrina's next prank. Thanks to her, I didn't get a good night's sleep the night before and I wasn't about to let her get away with it again. I took a look around the room for potential hazards she may have left lying around while I was in the shower. I knew there was no way she would let the opportunity slip by, but I couldn't find a thing. I put my stuff away, turned down the bed and flipped the light off before sliding underneath the covers. Almost immediately, the curtains of my mind began closing and I could feel myself drifting away. Again, I dreamed of climbing huge magnolias, and running through fields of flowers under the milky light of a full moon.

"Fairy."

I thought I heard someone call my name, but I didn't want to wake up. I ignored it and went right back to sleep.

Then I heard someone singing an annoying song about the sun shining. "Aargghh," I groaned and stretched and then found another comfortable place on the pillow. I listened but didn't hear anything else and drifted back off to sleep.

"Fairy, Fairy, you're so hairy. Time to wake up and eat some dairy."

There was no mistaking that she was in my room. "It better be morning," I said with my eyes still closed. "If you're in this room when I open my eyes, I'm going to beat you until you're shorter than I am."

"Hairy Fairy, you're so scary."

"That's it!" I shot up to a sitting position and opened my eyes. I looked at the clock. It was definitely morning, but there was no one in my room. I got on all fours and looked down around the sides and end of the bed. She wasn't there and I was very confused. I didn't understand how she was doing that. It sounded like the voice was coming from inside my room.

I was afraid to put my feet on the floor, thinking she was under the bed. But that wasn't possible because the door was still locked. I sat on the edge of the bed with my feet still up and then propelled myself off onto the side. As soon as my feet hit the floor I heard her giggling, from inside my room. I moved further away from the bed and knelt down to look underneath it. That's when I saw it, the walkie-talkie that she must have hidden under there when I was taking a shower.

I stayed there, kneeling on the floor, thinking about what to do next. I quietly stood up and tip-toed to the door. I put my ear up next to it to see if I could hear anything. I couldn't hear her, but I knew she was there. I had to use the restroom so badly, but I was afraid to open the door. "Screw it," I thought. Let her scare me, I don't care. I *had* to get into that bathroom.

I unlocked the door slowly, put my hand around the knob and yanked it open as fast as I could while yelling her name, "Corrina!" But she wasn't there. So, I darted down the hall to the restroom, slammed the door and turned on the light. I sat down on the toilet and let out a sigh as my bladder found relief from holding those two cocktails all night. And just as I reached for the toilet paper, the shower curtain flew open, and she screamed "Fairy!" while wearing one of those white scary masks from the horror movies. I screamed, in terror, and she laughed so hard she had to sit down in the tub. I finished my business, washed my hands, turned off the light and slammed the door shut behind me. I could hear her laughing as I climbed the stairs where I was greeted by the heavenly scent of warm blueberries and pancake batter cooking on the skillet.

THIRTY-ONE
MAY 2022

After finishing our breakfast and getting ready for the day, we headed out with Charlotte towards Fulton Street to catch the subway at the Kingston-Throop Avs station. Charlotte's stride was no joke and with Corrina's long legs, I was practically running to keep up with both of them. I sat next to Charlotte so we could chat during our thirty-six-minute ride to our destination. It was a good thing I brought a small notebook and pen. It was loud in the subway, and I wasn't sure that I would have been able to capture everything in the audio recording. I turned on my recorder anyway and was ready to take notes. Corrina sat behind us and leaned forward so she could hear our discussion. Nosy, just like her grandmother.

"Charlotte, I'm so excited to learn more about your life. Will you start at the beginning for me and tell me when and where you were born?"

"I was born in 1948 in Little Rock, Arkansas. My mother, Helen, didn't like to stay in one place or with one husband for very long. My father was her first husband. She was married to him for two years. They had me right away and then my first sister, Marilyn, was born a year later.

When mother was ready to leave my dad, she called my grandmother and aunt to come and get us and then they all decided we were moving to California. Mother found another husband there and had my second sister, Elaine. It wasn't long before she became bored there too. She sold most of our belongings, called my grandmother and aunt and we all moved to Ohio."

"How many times did your mother get married?"

"I can remember the names of *seven* husbands. I know there were at least two more."

"Wow. That's amazing. And I imagine that was a difficult upbringing. Do you think your mother loved you and your sisters?"

"Oh yes, I believe she loved us. It wasn't the conventional love that you would think of when you think of a mother, though, but she loved us. She was a beautiful woman. Stunning, really. She looked like one of those old Hollywood movie stars. She always dressed like she was going somewhere special. Dress, hat, full makeup, the works. Men flocked to her like bees to nectar. But with each new husband, she either became bored with him or his infatuation faded in the light of her mental illness and substance abuse."

"It sounds like you and your sisters were close in age. How was she able to care for three children that were so young and cope with mental illness at the same time?"

"I don't think she did, really. My grandmother always lived with us when Mother didn't have a husband around. When Mother would marry, Grandmother would move out and go live with my aunt until Mother was ready to leave again. I remember Grandmother taking care of us most of the time. When I look back, she was more like my mother than my grandmother. Children should be seen, and Grandmother was the one who saw me in my younger years."

"What do you mean by *seen*?"

"Noticed, heard and loved."

"Can you give an example of a time your grandmother made you feel seen and loved?"

"One year, I told Grandmother that I didn't want a doll for

Christmas because I was a big girl. I knew she was going to buy me one because that is what she bought us every year. On Christmas morning, my sisters unwrapped their dolls, and they were beautiful. I was disappointed that I didn't get one, but how could I say anything? I had told her not to buy me one. But she saw the look on my face and took me out the next day to buy me a doll. When we were walking down the street, a photographer snapped our picture. We were in our coats and had our scarves tied under our chin. The photographer handed her a card so she could pick up the developed photo. I still have that photo."

"What a sweet memory," I said. "Any more examples you would like to share?"

"Another time, when I was about twelve years old, I saw a cardboard music box with a ballerina in it. I thought it was the most beautiful thing I had ever seen. That following Christmas, Grandmother ended up buying me a black wooden music box with a Japanese garden painting on it. It plays the song "Smoke Gets in Your Eyes" by The Platters. I also still have that music box. It is one of my favorite things that I own to this day."

Just then, Corrina interjected and prompted Charlotte to tell me the story about the angel.

That surprised me. "Angel? You have a story about an angel, Charlotte?"

"I can't say for sure but that's how I remember it," she said with a convincing smile. "We were living in a small house in Ohio. I was three or four years old. I don't think Mother was married at the time because Grandmother was there. One night, Mother tucked me and Marilyn into bed in the back bedroom. There was a gas sconce on the wall that she turned on as a nightlight. The window was open because it was a sweltering summer night.

I just remember a man with a very calm voice telling me I needed to wake up. I didn't want to because I was so sleepy, but he kept saying, 'Charlotte, you need to wake up now. Wake up, Charlotte. Open your eyes.' So, I did and that's when I saw the room was on fire. The curtains had been flowing around because of the breeze from the window and they caught fire from the lamp. I started pulling my sister down and away from the fire towards the end of the bed and I was screaming the whole time. Mother and Grandmother came running in and put the fire out with blankets."

"Oh my goodness. That must have been terrifying. I know you were young, but do you remember if the voice you heard was one that you recognized?"

"No, I didn't recognize it. But I wasn't scared of it. It felt very peaceful. I know you don't believe in God or angels or any of that stuff, but it was very real to me."

"Well, whatever it was, I'm glad it woke you up and you were able to get help."

"Yes. And I'm glad Mother wasn't too intoxicated to help us. She usually drank or took pills every night to help her fall asleep. And once she was asleep, it was almost impossible to wake her."

"Sounds like you had some good luck on all sides that night."

Charlotte smiled at me, "You may not believe in angels, but I don't believe in luck. So there, we're even."

I continued pressing on. "I love how you took care of your sister and pulled her away from the fire. Did you always take on the role of caretaker as the oldest sister?"

"Oh, yes. I basically became their mother. After we moved around Ohio for a couple of years and away from a couple of her husbands, Mother met the man that I thought of as my father. His name was Warren. Shortly after they were married, we moved to New York and all five of us stayed in an apartment with his mother for about a month. She was a strange lady. She was afraid of everything. I was happy when we moved out of her place and into our own two-bedroom apartment."

"Two bedrooms? So, you shared a bed with your two sisters?"

"Yes, but I didn't mind. I was always worried about them. If I wasn't watching them, then no one would be watching them. I liked them sleeping in the bed with me. It felt safer that way."

"So, what was it about Warren that made you think of him as your father compared to all the other husbands?"

"Well, she was married to him longer than any of the other ones. We were in New York with him for over six years. Not only did he adopt us, but he would do nice things for us."

"What kinds of things did he do with you, there?"

"Well, he loved art and would take us to all the museums. I saw the Mona Lisa at the MET. I remember we waited in line for about thirty minutes. Once we were in front of the painting, I remember feeling surprised at its size. Most people think it is big, but it isn't. I remember another time he took me to a bookstore because there was an artist that was doing a book-signing. It was Salvador Dali."

"Wow! That's impressive!"

"Yes. I didn't realize how famous he was at the time but looking back now, it was quite incredible. Even though we didn't have much money, he also did little things for us that made us feel special. He took us to Coney Island, we walked around, and he bought us hotdogs. We played that game where they have to guess your age. I was so small for my age, they would always guess it wrong, and I would win a prize.

Another time, he told us he was going to take us somewhere special, and to get our coats because it was cold outside. We rode the subway to a fancy hotel and went to the indoor swimming pool. We were really confused and told him that we didn't have swimsuits. He said, 'this place has swimsuits for you!' We were so happy. We swam all afternoon!

I remember another time, he took us to China Town for the Chinese New Year. I was in the seventh grade, so I was about twelve years old. The streets were full of people. They had a big parade with dragons and dancers. There were so many bright colors and fireworks. They threw candy out to all the kids. I'll never forget that day. It was so fun.

And while Mother and Warren didn't have much money, Warren's father had a lot of it and lived in the Bahamas. One time we all went to meet him in Washington D.C. He was incredibly good to us during that visit. We were walking down the street and Elaine saw a dollar bill on the ground. She picked it up and said, 'Look! I found a dollar bill!' Warren's father told us to keep looking because there might be more. There were dollar bills everywhere! He kept walking around, dropping them for us to find.

He put us up in a fancy hotel with adjoining rooms. We went to a Japanese restaurant and sat on pillows while we were eating. Elaine wanted lobster and he let her order it and showed her how to eat the tail. We were so amazed that we could order anything we wanted. He took us to the museums too. He was a genuinely nice man."

"It sounds like it! Do you remember any other stories of growing up in New York City?"

A frown crept across Charlotte's face as she continued, "It was also around that time in New York City that my little sister, Elaine, got on the back of a bike with a boy. He was going to take her down the road and I waited on the steps for her to come back. The boy came back without my sister, so I asked him about her. He said she was coming, so I waited but she didn't come back. I went to look for her. She had fallen off the bike and was lying on the sidewalk. She had a big knot on the side of her head and was very confused. I told her to sit down, and I went to get Mother. When we got back to my sister, Mother just looked at her and said, 'I don't know what to do.' So, I picked my sister up and carried her five blocks to the hospital. She had a concussion, and they kept her overnight. Mother wasn't happy because we had very little money and she didn't know how to pay for it."

"Did you often have to make decisions for your mother?"

She nodded her head, "All the time."

"How old were you when your mother and Warren split up?"

"I was a sophomore in high school. It was just after JFK was shot. Warren found himself a girlfriend and left us."

I felt the pain for that young teenage girl, "That must have hurt a lot, thinking that after six years your life had finally settled down only to have it ripped out from underneath you. Do you remember how you felt?"

"I do. I was disappointed, but not surprised. I always knew our years in New York would come to an end, it was just a matter of when. I do remember the night he left, I went through the apartment and threw out all the liquor. Mother was good at hiding it. I found it under the bed, rolled up in towels and hidden in the back of closets. That night I slept with her because I was scared to leave her alone. The next day when she realized Warren wasn't coming back, she did the same thing she'd always done—she called my aunt and grandmother. They drove through the night and all the next day and helped us pack up the apartment. Mother made me leave my dog tied to a post out on the sidewalk. His name was Skipper. I was so worried about him, I ran to my friend's house and begged her to take care of him."

"Did she agree to take care of the dog?"

"Thankfully, yes. I don't know if her mother agreed but I want to believe that she took him in and took care of him. When we left, Mother said I had to drive. She said she couldn't see well enough because of her histoplasmosis and Grandmother couldn't drive either. The problem was, I had never driven a car before. She said it was easy and told me which pedal was used for going and which pedal was used for stopping. To make things worse, there was a trailer hitched to the car. But I figured it out, eventually. My aunt and grandmother followed behind us in their car all the way to Kansas City, Missouri. At one point, I had to drive through a narrow tunnel. I told Mother I didn't think I could do it with the trailer."

"What did she do?"

"She just said I had to figure it out. After banging the trailer against the tunnel wall a few times, I finally did. I remember on that trip, my mother and aunt had a little scam going on."

"A scam? What kind of scam?"

"It was a rather good one. Before we would pull into a filling station, my aunt and mother would trade cars. My aunt would make me move to the front passenger's seat, and she would drive the car to the front of the filling station. She would tell the clerk that she was fleeing alone with her children and didn't have any money. Then she would give him Warren's credit card and ask him to charge it for a tire and give her the cash. They bought so many tires on that trip that we never got. They really ripped Warren off."

"Did he ever file charges?"

"No, nothing ever happened. Once we arrived in Kansas City, my aunt got a job and we all moved into a small apartment. With a new school, new books, and new people, I found myself starting all over again. My junior year, we moved four times all over Missouri. We would move to an apartment and stay until the landlord evicted us for not paying the rent. Then we went on to the next place. My senior year, I was blessed enough to stay in one school the entire year."

"Did you ever tell your mother how you felt about moving so much?"

"None of us ever said a word. We didn't want to upset her and be the reason that she drank or took more pills."

"What did you do when you graduated? Did you continue to live with your mother and sisters?"

"Once I graduated, I moved back to Kansas City with one of my girlfriends from high school. I was happy to be on my own and doing very well. But then one day, Mother just showed up out of nowhere.

She was really upset and started crying, saying she couldn't raise the two girls by herself. I told my roommate I was going to have to leave. I rented a three-bedroom trailer and Mother and my two sisters moved in with me. I got a job working at the federal reserve bank as a courier in the mailroom. I helped my sisters get set up in their new school. I started thinking everything was going to be ok. Then a couple of things happened that made me really upset."

"What happened?"

"Well, one thing is that I was missing Warren. I wanted to talk to him, so I called the operator in New York City and got his number. I called him and we spoke for quite a while. I told him I wanted to see him, so he sent me a ticket. But Mother saw it and traded it in for cash. Then not long after that, she got really mad at me because I bought a gallon of milk for my sisters."

"Why would she get angry about that?"

"I always craved milk, but Mom would never let us drink it. She thought children should only have powdered milk. The real milk, she said, was for her coffee. We had a big fight about it, and she left."

"Where did she go?"

"She moved back into the apartment with my aunt and grandmother."

"So you were back to working and taking care of your sisters by yourself?"

"Yes. But then she wanted the girls back and Marilyn was adamant that she was not going to go back and live with Mother again. I wasn't sure what to do about it. I was having problems with Marilyn because all she wanted to do was run off with the boys. I told her that she needed to focus on school, but she wouldn't listen. I was working and couldn't keep an eye on her. She wasn't doing her chores or keeping up with her homework. It got so bad that I called my aunt and grandmother and told them that we wouldn't be living in the trailer anymore. I dropped my sisters off at their apartment and found another place to live."

"Where did you go?"

"I moved into a women's dormitory that was run by nuns. The women who lived there were either single or had husbands that were in the Vietnam war. I had my own bedroom but had to share a bathroom with the other tenants. I found a job at another bank, and I started making it on my own."

"That had to feel good, to settle down, finally."

"It did feel good. I finally felt as if I had some control over my life. And I started to make friends, too. I met a girl who lived in the dormitory. Her name was Melinda, and her husband was in the war. She was really outgoing and fun to be around. We spent a lot of time talking and became really good friends. We didn't have much money to do things, but she made everything fun. Even little things like going to the grocery store together to get snacks was fun with her. She was always laughing and making me laugh too. I had never met anyone like her."

"Were you dating?"

"Not really. I had a couple of boyfriends in high school but nothing that ever lasted or felt serious. It was hard moving around so much. As soon as I made friends or met a boy I liked, we moved again."

"That must have been really hard on you."

"It was. One day, in 1967, Melinda told me she wanted to introduce me to someone. She and her husband were friends with a guy named Phil. We went to a park and got on a boat and Melinda pushed me in front, so I had to sit next to him. He asked me out and I said yes. He was the first guy that really kissed me. We weren't dating long before he asked me to marry him. I was so naïve. I felt like if I kissed him, I *had* to marry him. He genuinely loved me and that was such a gift to me."

"Did you love him too?"

She turned around and looked at Corrina and then back at me as if she wasn't sure she should answer that question aloud. She looked nervous as she fiddled with a tissue in her hands. "That is a question that isn't easy to answer. I feel bad for saying this, but while I didn't love him the same way he loved me, I did care for him. But I felt obligated to return his love and affection. Well, obligated isn't quite the right word. He was offering everything that I always wanted but never really had in my life. I didn't answer him right away. I thought about it for a few days. And when I thought about saying no, that felt like a foolish decision. So, I said yes. We were married in 1968."

"What kinds of things was he offering you?"

"Simple things that most people probably take for granted. He was kind and responsible. He was sober and stable. He was a Christian, which was different for me. I felt like his faith provided him with a moral compass and he would be less likely to get mixed up in the kinds of things I had seen my parents do. I wanted a family someday and he seemed like the kind of man that would be a good father. I should never have married him, but I did. And I really tried..."

Her words faded away as she looked back at Corrina again and then down at her tissue. And just in time, the subway came to a stop at Eighty-First Street.

We exited and began our fifteen-minute walk to the Fifth Avenue entrance of the Metropolitan Museum of Art. I was so excited when I found out where we were going. I had been to New York City once before but didn't make it to the MET and I could hardly contain myself.

THIRTY-TWO
MAY 2022

With over one and a half million objects, artifacts and works of art, we could have spent days in that museum. We skipped the guided tour and walked about in wonder and fascination. Charlotte had been there so many times and was an excellent tour guide for novices like me and Corrina.

We spent a few hours trying to focus on the highlights. We marveled at the classics from ancient Egypt, paintings, and sculptures from almost all of the European master artists and an extensive collection of American works. We took in as much as we could until hunger called us away.

We left the museum and walked a couple of blocks to a quaint Italian eatery where we sat outside and feasted on Zuppa Del Giorno soup and salads decorated with Kumato tomatoes, mozzarella, fresh basil and Castelvetrano olives. I continued the conversation with Charlotte as we lingered there and indulged in plum tarts and Macchiatos for dessert.

"What role did religion play in your life up until the point you met Phil?"

"Not a big one, really. Mother always kind of believed in God but participated only as much as whatever husband she had at the time. When we were in New York and she was married to Warren, we went to an Episcopalian church. Warren did not believe in God and would mention it quite often to us girls. He didn't understand how a God could care about anyone with everything that was going on in the world. But he came to the church when they baptized me. Looking back, I see the irony."

"What irony?"

"That the only father figure I had that loved me didn't believe in my heavenly Father."

"So when did religion become a personal thing for you, beyond what you were exposed to as a child?"

"I started seeking a personal relationship with God when I'd see signs on the highway with John 3:16 on a big board. I would read it and wonder what that was about.

One time, when I was about fourteen or fifteen years old, I was watching a movie about St. Bernadette who saw the angel of God and what it did to her life. I prayed, knowing I was not a saint but asked God to connect with me and show me that He was real. In the mid-sixties, after I had moved out on my own, I joined a Baptist Church. I told Mother that I had found God and that she needed to find Him too."

"And did she?"

"She did. And it changed her life. She was still in Missouri and fell in love with a single pastor of a small church. They were married for forty-two years until the day she died. She still dealt with mental illness, but her husband took diligent care of her and made sure she got the medical help that she needed. Those were good years for her. I'm really happy that she found peace."

"What about your sisters? What happened to them?"

"Elaine stayed in Missouri near Mother and Grandmother. She got married and had four children. She was always an upbeat, happy person. Always positive, no matter what was going on in her life. That never changed. She's still the same even now. She has five grandchildren who live near her. She's had a good life. I see her every couple of years, and it always makes me happy to see her so happy."

"What about Marilyn?"

"Marilyn's story has been quite different. She's been in and out of hospitals her entire life. So often, mental illness and substance abuse go hand in hand. Unfortunately, Marilyn has suffered from both. There were times when she would get out of a treatment center and do well for a while but then she would stop taking her medications and spiral again. She reminded me so much of Mother. Beautiful, just like her, but tormented by mental anguish, also just like her."

"I'm so sorry to hear that, Charlotte. Is she still in Missouri?"

"I think so. I'm not sure. She left a treatment center some months ago and we haven't been able to find her."

"When was the last time you spoke with her?"

"I talked to her when she was in that last treatment center before she disappeared. She was dealing with severe paranoia. She thought the government was trying to kill her."

"It has to be hard to watch your sister go through something like that."

"It is hard. The guilt is the worst. I've given her money over the years, but she just used it on drugs, so I stopped. My sister and I tried to focus on getting her the care that she needed, but she never stuck with it. And now she's out there and I have no idea how to find her."

Corrina leaned over and rubbed Charlotte's arm. "They will find her, Mom. Try not to worry." Then she gave me a look that told me I needed to move on.

"Let's switch gears here and talk about race. You knew that Corrina was not going to be white before you adopted her, correct?"

"Yes, we knew."

"What were your thoughts around that?"

"Honestly, I don't think I had any thoughts about it. I just wanted another baby and a sibling for Sarah, which some people might think is a good thing. But through my conversations with Corrina, I learned that race *does* matter, and it should be considered when adopting a child. I should have done a better job finding ways to expose her to a world that was bigger than the one we lived in."

"You grew up in a time of real conflict around race. What was your exposure to people of different races and cultural backgrounds when you were growing up?"

"We lived in various places all over the country and usually around big cities, where there was more diversity. While I don't remember having that many friends as a young girl, I did make friends in New York. One of my closest friends was a black girl. I met her playing handball against one of the apartment buildings. She would invite me over to her house. They were so nice to me, and I was so curious about their family."

"What were you curious about?"

"Her mom and dad were still married, and I could tell they still loved each other. Her family seemed so close. They were always laughing and kidding around with each other. Everyone in her family just seemed happy. It was so unlike my own home.

I had another friend in New York that was Jewish. I remember she had dark hair and dark eyes. She was quiet like me, but we became fast friends. After school one day, this gang of girls surrounded me on the way home from school and told me if I ever talked to that Jewish girl again, they were going to beat me up."

"Did you stop being friends with her?"

"I wrote her a letter and told her what happened. I told her it was ok if we wrote to each other like pen pals but that we couldn't be seen together. I told her that I was willing to get beat up for our friendship but that my mother couldn't afford to take me to the hospital."

I paid the tab, and we headed out to walk back to Eighty-First Street to catch the subway back to Bed-Stuy. As we walked down the streets of New York City, I tried to imagine Charlotte as a little girl, growing up there and finding her way in life amidst the chaos. As I looked at her now, it was hard to believe that she had such a difficult beginning. It was good to see her living a life of intention. I found it to be very inspiring.

We made our way down the blocks and through the crowds of people in a hurry to get wherever they were going. Corrina was making fun of me the whole way, saying everyone could tell I was a tourist because I kept looking up, but I couldn't help it. I was enthralled with the city. It was bustling, very much alive and had a mysterious energy to it. And yet it made me feel a bit invisible and very small. It was a very different vibe than where Gabe and I had built our life together.

I sat beside Charlotte on the subway with Corrina sitting behind us, again. Every once in a while, I would see Corrina reach up and give Charlotte a comforting rub or pat on the shoulder. Some were touches of encouragement and others were gestures of comfort. Whatever Corrina thought Charlotte needed, she gave it without hesitation.

I pulled out my recorder and notepad again and got right to it. "Charlotte, let's move ahead to after you married Phil. What prompted the two of you to move to Virginia?"

"His father was in the printing business and taught Phil everything he knew. Phil had been working with his father but had an opportunity to take over a business in Virginia. That's why we moved. He used up every penny he had saved to buy that business and got a loan from his father for the rest. We lived in a small trailer at first. We knew that Phil was unable to have children due to a birth defect, and we wanted to have a family right away. So, our church helped us get in touch with a Christian home for pregnant girls and we got on the waiting list. It took about a year before they called us. I'll never forget, it was on Halloween night. I thought it was a joke. Sarah was five days old when we got her."

"Did you ever meet her mother?"

"No. We never saw her."

"Where did you get her?"

"She was born in Georgia. We drove down and stayed with some friends of Phil's parents while we were going through the legal process of signing all of the papers. It was pretty easy. She was a beautiful baby and so quiet. She hardly ever cried."

"And then two years later, you adopted Corrina?"

"Yes, that process was not as easy. We knew we wanted to adopt another baby, but we had to move out of the trailer because it was too small. We purchased a house from the sweetest lady. She was elderly and was moving in with her children. She sold us that house for a very reasonable price and even included some furniture and appliances. It was a charming red brick cape built in 1948. It had three bedrooms and one bath, a huge attic and a detached garage. It was the biggest house I had ever lived in.

As soon as we settled in, we contacted the same girls' home and put our name on the list to adopt. It wasn't long before they called us, but as it turned out, Corrina's adoption would be different. They were over capacity and asked if we could provide housing for the pregnant teenager until she had the baby. We agreed. We went down to Georgia and picked her up and took her to our house."

"Do you remember that trip? Do you remember what you were thinking?"

"I was nervous, and I felt really bad for her. Being away from her family and moving in with strangers who were going to be the parents of her child, that had to be hard for her. And she was young —seventeen, I think, and was just entering her third trimester. I put Sarah in the back with her, so she wouldn't feel lonely. She didn't say much the whole way back to Virginia. When we got to the house, I got out of the car and looked at her through the window. I remember she was looking at our house and she was smiling. I imagined she felt relief to see we had a decent place to raise her baby."

"How was it living with her?"

"I won't lie, it felt strange sometimes. I could tell she was somewhat of a rebel. She didn't seem happy about some things and didn't hide it very well."

"What do you think she was unhappy about?"

"We didn't have a television and wouldn't allow her to use the telephone. We didn't allow her to listen to secular music on the radio either. We made her go to church with us. You know, things like that. At one point while she was living with us, my grandmother died, and I had to leave to attend her funeral. She wasn't happy about that, either."

"Did you form a relationship with her of any kind? Friendship? Or anything like that?"

"Not really. I don't think she was open to that and to be honest, I don't think we were either. She was really good with Sarah, though. Sometimes, when we went with our church friends to visit the sick or elderly, we would leave her home with Sarah. I think she liked having some time away from us. And Sarah became attached to her. She would ask for her first thing when she woke up in the morning."

"Do you remember when Lovedy went into labor?"

"Oh, yes. It was the middle of the night. She woke up in a lot of pain. Phil took her to the hospital, and I stayed back with Sarah, figuring Lovedy would be in labor for a while. A friend took me to the hospital the next morning."

"What did you think when you first saw Corrina?"

"She was the cutest baby. And a big baby! She was over nine pounds! Sarah was only six pounds and was petite even as a toddler. They were so different. But I remember thinking I was glad she was a girl. I knew how to take care of girls and I was glad Sarah would have a little sister."

"How was it when you took her home?"

"I was extremely nervous with that adoption. I don't remember this happening when we got Sarah but when we got Corrina, there was a one-year revocation period. And from day one, I could tell Lovedy did not want to give up her baby. I was terrified she would come back and take her. We also had to put a notification in the paper where the father lived, in case he wanted the baby. I remember when we got home I put Corrina in her crib, and she was crying. I left her in there for an hour before I picked her up. I was afraid to form an attachment with her only to have it broken, like so many attachments in my life. It was an extremely hard first year for me. Social services kept showing up at the house to make sure she was doing well in our care. I remember when the one-year mark had passed, a heavy weight was lifted. I could finally be her mother without fear that she would be taken away."

I turned around and smiled at Corrina before I asked Charlotte the next question. "How was Corrina as a baby? I imagine she was very loud and strong willed. Am I right?"

Charlotte laughed and said, "You are correct. That girl was always hungry. She would finish a bottle and cry for another one. And the minute she learned to walk, I was always chasing her and pulling her off of furniture she shouldn't have been climbing on. She was fearless and incredibly determined. And then when she learned to speak, we couldn't get her to be quiet. *Ever.* She always had something to say. She was a handful, but she was a fun baby and toddler. She liked to laugh. Everything made her giggle. She would laugh at a bird, a cow on the side of the road, anything and everything. I would go into the nursery to get her in the morning, and she would be lying in her crib, looking at the ceiling and laughing."

"Do you remember telling her that she was adopted?"

"I do remember. We decided to tell them when they were young. We lived in a very tight-knit community and were heavily involved with our church. All of the parents knew that our babies were adopted, and we didn't want anyone else to tell them but us. Once Sarah started school, we knew we had to talk to them."

"Do you remember how they reacted?"

"We tried to present it in a positive way. We explained that we were not able to have children of our own and so we wanted to find babies who didn't have a home. We told them that we chose them, that they were very special to us. It is hard to know how much children comprehend. Sarah was older and I think she was sad, which is to be expected. She had to lose a family to gain one and she was old enough to understand that her mother had given her away. She asked us why her mother didn't want her. That was tough."

"What did you tell her?"

"We told her the truth. That her mother was in college and didn't have enough money to take care of her. And that she didn't have a husband to help her."

"How did you know that?"

"The staff at the girl's home told us."

"Do you remember how Corrina reacted?"

Charlotte turned around and smiled at Corrina before looking back at me. "She was incredibly young. I remember she was leaning against the couch and kept walking around. I don't even know that she was listening."

Corrina placed her hand on Charlotte's shoulder. It lingered there as she said, "I remember, Mom. I was listening."

THIRTY-THREE
MAY 2022

We wrapped up our conversation as the subway stopped at the Kingston-Throop Avs station. We exited the subway and walked up to the street where we met the shining sun again. It was a beautiful day. I was not only enjoying the weather but the company, as well. We walked the few blocks to Charlotte's house and found Michael in the kitchen mixing together a marinade for dinner that night.

"Do you always cook?" I asked him.

"I try to. Charlotte spent so many years cooking for her family, so I figure it is nice to do it for her, in return. Besides, I really enjoy it. It has always been a hobby of mine."

Charlotte walked behind him, gave him a quick hug, and whispered, "Thank you."

It was a small gesture, but it didn't go unnoticed. He smiled as he continued to whisk the marinade, and then he said, "I made some margaritas in the machine. And I put out the glasses for you ladies."

Corrina and I about knocked each other over as we grabbed a glass and raced to the dispenser. As the machine poured the frosty mixture into my glass, I had a feeling it was going to be a fun evening.

Michael told us dinner would be ready in about two hours, so we agreed to head downstairs to sit out on the patio. Before we left, Michael poured us a pitcher to take with us which put a smile on both of our faces. We invited Charlotte to go outside with us, but she said she was going to stay upstairs and would join us in a bit.

We found seats next to each other on the outdoor sofa and placed the pitcher on the table in front of us. Corrina leaned her head on my shoulder, let out a sigh and I intuitively knew where it was coming from.

"I know you were listening," I said. "Did you ever try to talk to her about it?"

"No. Charlotte and I have never very been good at talking about our feelings with each other. In fact, some of the things she told you, I had never heard before."

"Like what?"

"Like the stories about her seeing the Mona Lisa and meeting Salvador Dali. I didn't know any of those things that Warren did with her and my aunts when they were young. I guess it is good that you're doing this novel. It's a weird thing to say but I feel like I'm getting to know her better."

"Did she ever ask you how you felt about being adopted? Did she ever have that conversation with you?"

"Not that I can remember. But I wasn't shy about how I felt, especially when I was angry at her. I threw it in her face a couple of times."

"What do you mean?"

"I remember one time, I had gotten into trouble for something. After my punishment, I was really upset, not only because it hurt but because I didn't think it was fair. I was crying and told her that I wanted my real mom because she wouldn't have hurt me that way."

I gasped. "Oh, Corrina. What did she do?"

"She just stood there and looked at me. I remember she looked sad, but I don't think she really knew what to say. She just walked out of the room. What I really wanted was to feel loved but all I felt was lonely."

I put my arm around my friend and pulled her closer to me. I wasn't ready to tell her yet, but I knew how she felt. While we sat there in silence, drinking our margaritas, I remembered when my therapist told me that it is difficult to worry and be grateful at the same time, so I thought about what I could be grateful for in that moment. I was thankful for those people who had come into the landscape of my life, grew roots there and never left. And I was thankful that I was able to do that for Corrina, too.

A few minutes later, Charlotte joined us. She put some tortilla chips and salsa on the table and then sat down across from us in the chaise lounge chair. She stretched her legs out and crossed her ankles. She looked happy and comfortable as she said, "I have a surprise tonight for you girls. I think you're really going to like it."

Corrina sat up, excited. "C'mon, Mom. Tell me! What is the surprise?"

"Nope," she said as she shook her head. "I'm not going to tell you. But you won't have to wait long. You'll find out after dinner."

I had a question burning on my mind since we arrived and figured now would be as good a time as any to ask Charlotte. "Is it true that you taught Corrina to cheat at boardgames and card games?"

Charlotte threw her head back and let out a hearty laugh. "Yes. I'm ashamed to say it is true."

"Do you know that she's beaten me at every game we've ever played and didn't bother to tell me that she cheated until we were on our way to see you? Unbelievable!" I shook my head in disbelief while Charlotte and Corrina continued to get a good laugh about it.

After Charlotte finished laughing at my misfortune, she said, "I will say, by the time she was in fifth grade or so, she had mastered the craft of cheating at games. I had a tough time catching her. She was fiercely competitive at everything she did."

I tousled Corrina's enviable thick and coily mane. "You must be so proud."

"You know better than to mess with my hair. Keep your miniature hands to yourself, woman," she barked as she elbowed me in the ribs.

"Speaking of hair, Charlotte, how did you learn to take care of Corrina's?"

"Oh, that's a *great* question. We didn't have internet back then and I'm sure Corrina has told you, there weren't any other people of color in our immediate circle. I have to give all the credit to a woman name Shirley. She was a nurse at the pediatrician's office and every time I took the girls, Shirley was in our exam room, checking on Corrina. I wasn't offended. I was grateful. If it weren't for her, I wouldn't have known that I was supposed to do anything differently. She patiently explained that maintaining Corrina's natural oils were important for her hair and taught me all the steps from washing to detangling."

Corrina said, "I agree wholeheartedly. Shirley was an angel. She worked at that pediatric office the whole time I was growing up. She was one of those people who seemed really happy to see me. She would always clap her hands and smile really big when I walked into the office. I always felt really happy to see her too. I will never forget her."

I could imagine little Corrina waddling into that office like she owned it. The thought made me smile, but I wanted to jump ahead to her teenage years. So, I asked Charlotte, "How was it being the mother of two teenage girls? I can imagine that is not an easy time for any mother."

"Those were definitely not easy years for me. My entire life, I had girls to take care of and when they grew up and didn't need me as much, I felt invisible. To be honest, I didn't really want them to grow up. They were much easier to care for when they were dependent on me. I found it hard to relate to them during their teenage years, too. I'm sure all of the rules we had in the house didn't help. We were *so strict* on them. We didn't allow them to do many of the things that teenagers like to do. I'm sure she has told you all of that."

"Yes," I answered while giving Corrina a knowing look.

Charlotte continued, "During their teenage years, Phil started having problems with his kidneys. They put him on dialysis when Corrina was a sophomore in high school. I had to run Phil to the medical center three times per week and we were there for at least three hours each time. Sarah was driving by then, thank goodness, and she was able to drive herself and Corrina to school. Phil ended up selling the printing business, but the money was dwindling fast. Our insurance wasn't great, so I had to get a job with better coverage. I ended up getting a position with the state's benefits office. We were able to get him a ride to the medical center with a volunteer organization. They would come and pick him up in a van and then drop him off back home. He was always so exhausted after those treatments. He would sleep it off and then feel better the next day. But then the following day, he would have to do it all over again. It was hard on him and a tough time for our whole family."

To my surprise, Corrina started laughing. Charlotte and I both looked at her, wondering what prompted it. Finally, she told us.

"I remember Dad sleeping all those mornings when I was leaving for school my junior year. I'm ashamed to say, I took full advantage of it."

"Please do tell us, Corrina, how you took advantage of your sick father," I demanded.

"Well, some mornings I didn't want to go straight to school. I had study hall first period and so did one of my friends. So, I would go into Dad's room and get him to sign a piece of paper excusing me for being late. Then I would ask him for some money. He was half asleep, so he would just say yes and then drift off again. He always had wads of twenties in a money clip on his dresser. So, I would help myself and take my friend out to breakfast."

I popped her on the leg, "Corrina! You were so bad!"

"That *was* bad. I was a teenager, though. What do you expect? My girls stole money from my purse all the time. Only, you can't scam a scammer, so I caught them most of the time."

Charlotte just laid back in her chair and laughed at Corrina. She almost seemed proud of her.

I was a bit nervous about the next question I had for Charlotte, but I just dove right into it. "Speaking of the teenage years, do you remember when Corrina told you she was pregnant?"

Before she could answer, Corrina stood up and excused herself to the restroom. I ignored the interesting timing of her exit.

Charlotte's face turned serious as she responded, "I do."

"Do you remember your reaction?"

"I was stunned. She was in her senior year of high school. Phil was sleeping, exhausted from his treatment. The girls and I had just finished eating dinner. Sarah was cleaning up the kitchen and Corrina asked if she could talk to me about something. We went into the living room and sat down. She was very calm. Her face was like stone, expressionless. And she just said, 'I'm pregnant.'

At first, I had no words. I think the first thing I said was 'But how?' And in Corrina's way, she just looked at me and said, 'I think you know *how*, Mom.'

I asked her who the father was, but she refused to tell me. She just said I didn't know him, and he was older than her. She said the father didn't want anything to do with her pregnancy or the child and she wanted to start looking for a family to adopt her baby. She had obviously thought about everything and had a plan. As she was talking to me, it struck me how strong and determined she was behaving. I was falling apart, there on the sofa, and my teenage daughter was holding it all together."

"When did you tell Phil?"

"I let him sleep. I knew he would be feeling better the next day, so I waited until the next morning."

"How did he react?"

"He was heartbroken. He kept focusing on where we went wrong with her and how we could have allowed her to get into that situation. While she was at school and I was at work that day, he made some calls to get information about a Christian adoption agency near us. Then we sat down with her that evening and told her what we had learned and how it would work. We were just honestly trying to help her, but she already had in her mind what she wanted for her child. She said she did want our help, but it had to be on her terms."

I smiled at the thought of her standing her ground and telling Phil and Charlotte how the whole thing was going to go down. "That sounds a lot like our Corrina."

"It was a challenging situation, but I was proud of the way she handled herself during her pregnancy. She continued to do really well in school, and she stayed committed to getting the medical care that she needed. She never complained about all of the appointments and medical tests. She was sure she didn't want to keep the baby, but she did everything she could to make sure that her child had a healthy start in life. Even when she went into labor, I never heard her cry or complain. She went into that hospital with grit and determination and did what she had to do."

"Did you ever think about keeping the baby for her?"

"I did think about it. The thought of having another baby to love made me want to do it, but we had so much going on at that time. Phil was so sick, and I was having some issues of my own. It just wouldn't have worked."

"What kind of issues were you having? Do you mind sharing?"

"No, and this is getting to the part that I mentioned in the beginning when we first started talking. I didn't know it at that time, but I was suffering from depression. I thought that when I was having problems wanting to get up in the morning, it was because I was tired. But I *always* felt tired, and I was weeping all the time. I wasn't just sad; it was more like a deep sorrow that took up my whole being. I didn't know what was going on, but I knew something wasn't right. I kept trying to ignore it because I had so many other responsibilities at that time."

Corrina had returned to the sofa at that point and shared her perspective. "Sarah and I knew something was going on with her. She looked sad all the time. She rarely smiled and always went to bed early. It wasn't until after I graduated and had the baby that I knew something serious was going on with her."

At that moment, Michael popped his head out of the door to let us know that dinner would be ready in fifteen minutes. As we stood up to go inside, Corrina asked Charlotte a question I was not expecting.

"Hey, Mom. Are you ok if we talk about the gun?"

Charlotte reached out and touched Corrina's arm. "Yes, honey. Those aren't happy memories for any of us, but if it will help someone else, I'm ok with talking about it."

THIRTY-FOUR
MAY 2022

We sat down to another delicious meal of braised apple-marinated short ribs, baked sweet potatoes and a cucumber and zucchini salad. I asked Michael about his career as an antitrust attorney. He talked about the work he did, primarily in New York City and D.C. I learned that is how he and Charlotte met. They had a mutual friend who lived in Northern Virginia, who set Charlotte and Michael up on a blind date. They dated long distance for a year before they married, and Charlotte moved to New York to live with Michael.

Corrina and I insisted on cleaning up after dinner and we shooed Michael and Charlotte away to relax in the living room that shared the open space with the kitchen and dining area. We were just about finished when the doorbell rang. Charlotte and Phil were reading the paper so Corrina told them she would answer the door.

I was wiping down the countertops when I heard a loud scream, followed by laughter. I walked around the corner to take a peek at what was going on and there I saw Corrina, with her arms wrapped around Sarah. Charlotte and Phil had bought a plane ticket for Sarah so she could spend the rest of the weekend with us. Because of the virus, it had been two years since Corrina and Sarah had seen each other. I couldn't stop the watery mist from blurring my vision as I thought about how thoughtful of a gift it was for Charlotte to give to her daughters.

Michael took Sarah's luggage upstairs while we raided the liquor cabinet. We settled on a delicious concoction of citrus and orange vodkas, limoncello and heavy cream and poured them into stemless martini glasses.

With Sarah's arrival, I didn't think it was appropriate to go back to the heavy conversation we were having before dinner, so we stayed on the parlor floor and visited with Sarah, catching up on her life, career and family. I watched Corrina and Sarah and marveled at how different they were and yet so similar. Even though they had different personalities, they had the same laugh, the same mannerisms. They spoke a silent language with their eyes, sharing a long, intricate history that was theirs, and theirs alone. I tried to imagine them as little girls growing up together, and I silently thanked the universe for giving each of them the gift of the other.

After we visited for a while, Sarah suggested that we all play a game that involved multiple decks of cards, marbles and a giant octagon-shaped board. We had to play as teams, so Charlotte and I teamed up against Sarah and Corrina at the dining room table. Michael stayed in the living area and went back to reading his paper. But he gave me a fair warning when he said, "Both of them are major cheaters. Pay close attention. If you catch those girls cheating, you can penalize them."

"Oh, we'll catch them, alright," Charlotte said as she rubbed her hands together. "I know all of their tricks."

It was a complicated game, and they had a list of house rules that made it even more entertaining. It took me a few minutes to catch on but once I did, Charlotte and I were on a roll and taking the lead.

The game was long and before I knew it, we were all two martinis in, and the competition became even more intense. They pulled ahead and then we would take the lead again. It kept going back and forth like that for quite a while.

Before I knew it, we had lost our edge, and within another ten minutes, Sarah and Corrina had slaughtered us. They started celebrating their win with high fives and laughs and comments about Charlotte and I being losers. I had to give it to them. They came back hard, and we didn't catch them cheating.

But Charlotte knew better, "Wait a second, here, both of you girls stand up right now!"

I had no idea what was going on, but they started giggling as they stood up from their chairs.

"Now, stand back against the wall," Charlotte demanded as she stood up from her own chair. She walked around to their side of the table, looked down at their chairs and started laughing. "I knew it! Wow!"

"What's going on?" I asked, having no idea.

Charlotte kept laughing and said, "Come around here and look at these big cheats. Look what they did!"

I walked around and couldn't believe my eyes. There were cards on both of their seats that they had hidden underneath their legs. There were cards on the floor, even tucked into their socks. There were cards everywhere.

"Wow. That is impressive," I said. I had to compliment them on their skills. I had no idea how they did that right in front of us. That wasn't just cheating. That was some major magician, slight-of-hand, mind trick stuff.

I looked over at Michael, who was smiling behind his newspaper. Without even looking at me, he said, "I told you. Didn't I tell you?"

"Yes, you told me," I said, still in disbelief.

The girls continued to celebrate their win as we picked up the pieces of the game and cleaned up after our little martini party. It was a fun evening, and while I thoroughly enjoyed the time spent with them, I had this weird feeling that kept nagging at me. I didn't know what it was, but I suddenly felt the need to talk to Gabe. It was getting late anyway, so I said good night and left the girls on the parlor level to continue their visit with Michael and Charlotte. I went downstairs, took a shower, and then climbed into bed. I called Gabe and he picked up on the first ring.

"There's my beautiful wife," he said. "I miss you. You having fun?"

"I am. Corrina and I have been having a great time."

I filled him in about their beautiful home, our field trip to the MET, Sarah's surprise visit, the delicious meals we had and the lying, cheating game we played.

"Sounds like fun but..what's that weird tone in your voice?"

"I'm not sure. I've been feeling weird this evening. Don't get me wrong, I've been having a wonderful time. It's just been this feeling in my gut that I can't shake. I just don't know what it is about."

"When did it start? What were you doing?"

"I guess it started after Sarah arrived and we were all visiting in the living room. I was watching them as they interacted with each other. I felt happy but sad at the same time."

He cleared his throat before he asked, "Do you think it could be jealousy?"

"Maybe. It was more like I was missing out on something of my own. You were an only child, like me. Did you ever wish you had brothers or sisters?"

"Sure, I did but you've asked me about this before, remember? We had a large, extended family. I didn't live with my cousins, but we were so close, they felt like my brothers and sisters most of the time."

"Yeah...that makes sense."

Gabe continued talking about his cousins and the things they used to do growing up together. I could hear him, but I had floated away and was lost in my own thoughts.

"Farrah, are you there? Are you ok?" He asked. "Did you hear what I just said?"

"No. I'm sorry, Gabe. I just got distracted. I'm also very tired. Ok with you if I say goodnight?"

"Sure babe. Get a good night's sleep. Call me tomorrow?"

"Yes, I promise."

We hung up and I slipped under the covers and into my dreams.

I set my alarm for an early time. I wasn't about to let Corrina get the best of me like she had yesterday morning. I hit the snooze button a few times and then headed down the hallway to the bathroom. I finished my morning routine and went to my bedroom to get dressed for the day. But not before I ground some white pepper into Corrina's toothbrush. She should have known better than to leave her toiletry bag in the bathroom. *What a rookie.*

It sounded like everyone was still asleep, so I grabbed my laptop and headed upstairs to do a little bit of writing before the day started.

Michael was already up and handed me a cup of coffee and a "good morning" as I passed by him. I thanked him for the coffee and sat down at the dining room table. I put my earbuds in and went back to my last conversation with Clara. That sweet voice was a good start to the day. I made a note to call her soon, just to see how she was doing.

I was deep into my work when I saw some commotion out of the corner of my eye. Sarah, Corrina, and Charlotte were up and scurrying around the kitchen. Michael had laid out a spread of pastries, Greek vanilla yogurt, granola and fruit for breakfast and they were gathering around the island to eat together. As Corrina sat down, she looked back towards me, and motioned like she was brushing her teeth. Then she pulled a bird out of her pocket, and mouthed "Good morning, bitch."

Laughing, I closed my laptop, poured myself a second cup of coffee and joined the family at the island for breakfast.

Since it was another beautiful day, Charlotte suggested we take a walk and enjoy Fulton Park and then eat lunch at a nearby Cuban café, known for their delicious Cuban sandwiches, empanadas and guava crumb cake. It sounded like a great plan, and I was looking forward to another fun day. Sarah and Corrina went downstairs to get dressed so I took the opportunity to put my earbuds in and finish my work on Clara's story.

Michael opted out of going to the park with us and about thirty minutes later, the girl squad headed out together.

As we moved past the shops, restaurants with outdoor seating and gorgeous trees that towered over the streets, Corrina gave us a walking tour and educated us about the rich history of the neighborhood.

Once we reached the small, triangular park, we saw the statue of Robert Fulton, took pictures of each other by the beautiful ornamental garden and walked among the one-hundred-year-old trees that lined the pathway through the park. Residents were taking full advantage of the cloudless Sunday. Young and old alike were battling it out on the chessboards. Rollerbladers skated past us as well as young families taking their dogs and babies for a walk. A pair of new lovers met for a morning kiss and a stroll by the flowers.

After we walked around for a while, we found a place to sit, rest, and drink some water.

It wasn't me who started the conversation that time, it was Charlotte.

"The reason I wanted to come here to the park to continue our last conversation is that it is a beautiful, relaxing atmosphere. I know these things are not easy to talk about, not only for me but for the girls."

Sarah interjected, "What? What are we talking about? What's going on?"

Corrina filled her in, "I told you about the work that Farrah is doing, remember?"

"Yes, I remember," Sarah answered, hesitantly looking at me.

"Well, last night before dinner, we were talking about Mom's depression. I asked Mom if it was ok if we talked about that summer with the gun."

Sarah looked shocked and looked at Charlotte. "You're ok talking about that, Mom? For real? I mean, you don't have to talk about it if you don't want to."

Charlotte smiled at Sarah and said, "It's ok. I've already told Farrah she can write about it. We've cleared that part up already."

Corrina and Sarah exchanged a glance with each other. I wasn't sure what it meant or what telepathic language they were speaking but they were definitely communicating. I decided to let them hash it out. I wasn't about to force the conversation if any of them thought it wasn't a good idea.

But Charlotte continued on, "I knew there were substantial changes coming that fall. Sarah was planning to move out at the end of the summer and Corrina was going to start nursing school in Kentucky. I was dreading it. As the summer days went by, I fell deeper and deeper into my depression. I didn't feel like there was any reason for me to be there anymore. The girls had their own lives and were barely home and Phil was always sleeping. I still managed to get to work during the day, but the evenings were really hard. I felt invisible, like I no longer mattered. I stopped going to church as much. I would go on Sunday mornings, but I would sit on the back pew and cry the whole time. As soon as the service was over, I would go home to Phil, who was still sleeping. There was a voice inside my head that kept telling me I wasn't worth anything and that I was in the way of everyone else's happiness. Looking back at everything that happened and the history of mental illness in my family, I'm sure it had always been there. Dormant, maybe, but it was always there underneath the surface just looking for a reason to show itself. Taking care of my sisters and then my girls always gave my life purpose and meaning. Once that was all gone, I had no idea who I was and why I needed to be there."

"Is that when you got a gun?"

"Yes. I told myself and Phil that I was getting it for protection. There had been a few burglaries in the neighborhood and Phil was always sleeping so deeply. I knew if anything ever happened, he wouldn't be able to help. That was my reason for purchasing the gun. But once I bought it, I started having a weird affection for it. I started thinking about things I wouldn't have if my mind were healthy. My thoughts turned dark and heavy, and I began taking my new friend for walks through the woods at night."

Corrina stepped into the conversation, "Yes, I remember that. One night that summer, Sarah and I came home from being out with friends. It was late and Mom wasn't there. We woke Dad up and asked where she was, but he didn't know. We didn't know where to look but we got back into Sarah's car and started driving around, trying to find her."

"Did you find her?"

"No. We went back home around two o'clock in the morning and her car was there. She was inside, sleeping in her bed. The next morning, I asked where she went. She said she went for a walk in the woods. I asked her where and she said the woods by the church, which was thirty minutes from our house. I thought it was very strange. That same day, I was putting laundry away and found the gun in Mom's dresser drawer. I was terrified. I ran upstairs and told Sarah about the woods and the gun."

I turned to Sarah and asked, "Do you remember that?"

"I do. I think it was a day or two after that, I was laying in the sun in the backyard. Mom was home, so it must have been the weekend. I was putting more baby oil on, and I heard this loud 'POW!' I freaked out, stood up, ran through the back yard, jumped the chain link fence and crouched down in the alley with my hands over my ears. I stayed there for a few minutes, just shaking. I took my hands off my ears and tried to listen for any noise that would confirm what I knew was true. But I didn't hear anything. So, I walked back to the house and into the back door. Corrina was there, in the laundry room, folding clothes like nothing had happened. I said, 'Tell me you heard that gunshot!' She gave me a look like I was crazy and said, 'Sarah, there was no gunshot. I just slammed the dryer door.' I went back outside and sat down on the back steps. Corrina came out and sat down beside me. I turned to her and said, 'I didn't want to tell you this but there's more.' I got a flashlight from the laundry room and took her upstairs into my room. We went to the back corner, and I removed a section of the wall paneling. I told her to take the flashlight and look back there. She saw what I had found. Behind the walls of my room, Mom had made a bed out of old quilts. There was a flashlight already back there along with a notebook and a pen. Corrina brought out the notebook, I locked my bedroom door and we read the notebook together."

Charlotte was staring off in the distance, wearing the anguish on her face. Even on that beautiful day, the air felt heavy around us. I wanted to stop the conversation there and let Charlotte and her daughters take a break. But Charlotte kept going.

THIRTY-FIVE
MAY 2022

"When the girls were in grade school, we decided to renovate the large attic. There was so much room up there and we thought it would be a wonderful place for the girls to grow up and have their own space to be with their friends, do their homework, and play together. We put a bedroom on each end and the middle had a large open area with a round table and chairs. There was a big game closet and a full bathroom up there. We didn't have tons of money to put into it, so instead of drywall, we put up wood paneling that went from the floor, halfway up to where the coffin-shaped ceiling stopped sloping. I never imagined, when we were doing that renovation, that the space behind those fake walls would become the place where I hid from the reality of my illness."

Corrina and Sarah were talking with their eyes again and then Sarah spoke up and said, "Mom, if it makes you feel any better, Corrina and I had our secret spot in that house too."

Corrina interjected, "Sarah! Don't tell her about that!"

But Sarah started laughing and said, "I can't imagine what the people who eventually bought that house thought when they went up into the little attic space above that middle room."

"Why?" Charlotte asked in mock horror. "What was up there? What were you girls up to?"

"A little bit of everything, Mom," Sarah said. "Basically, everything you wouldn't allow us to do, we did up there in that little attic."

Corrina threw her head back, held her stomach and laughed so hard that the only thing I could hear was her gasping for air.

Charlotte asked her again, "Tell me! Tell me what you did!"

Sarah finally relented, "Well, I won't tell you *everything*, but we had posters of teen heartthrobs taped to the wood beams since you wouldn't let us put them up in our rooms. We also had a stack of clothes that you never would have let us wear out in public. Shorts, jeans, you know, all the sinful stuff. It was our storage space for all of the steamy love letters that our boyfriends wrote to us. We smoked cigarettes and pot up there and I'm fairly sure we had a bottle of cheap grape wine and some candles up there too. It's a wonder we didn't burn the place down."

"You forgot the most important thing, Sarah," Corrina said.

"Shut up, Corrina," Sarah barked with a look of warning.

"Sarah had a *boy* up there, Mom. She snuck him in the back door one evening when you were home. I don't know what she was doing up there with that boy, but it wasn't good. Clearly, she was not a positive influence on me."

Charlotte put her hand over her mouth, in utter shock and horror. "Sarah Anne! I cannot believe you did that!"

Sarah shrugged her shoulders and smiled at her own confession. "Nothing you can do about it now, Mom."

Corrina rubbed her tummy and suggested we head out of the park to get some lunch.

The sun was really warm that day and, every once in a while, a cloud would offer us a reprieve as we walked among the trees and down the blocks to the café. We found a sweet little table outside in the shade and ordered our lunch based on Charlotte's recommendations. While we waited for our food, we sipped on our cold draft beers and Charlotte filled us in about the notebook.

"My mother always wrote poetry. She was actually a published author and I always loved reading her work. It was interesting, even with her mental illness, her poetry was usually upbeat and happy. I started writing poetry when I was about fourteen or fifteen, but it had a very different tone. It was about loneliness, most of the time."

"That summer," Charlotte continued, "before the girls left, I would hide away behind those walls and write for hours, especially on the weekends when I was home, and the girls were usually out. My poems were dark and very morbid, but it was my illness that was spilling out onto that paper. While I never intended for the girls to find it, I'm glad they did. It not only was the catalyst for therapy, but that notebook allowed me to share things with my therapist that I would never have been able to say out loud."

"How was that notebook responsible for your start in therapy?" I asked.

Corrina spoke up this time. "After Sarah and I read that notebook, it was clearer than ever that Mom needed help and we knew that we couldn't wait any longer. We went downstairs into the bedroom, woke Dad up, and talked to him."

"What did he say?"

"He knew something was going on but didn't know the extent of it. He said he would talk to her and would find a therapist for her. He promised us he would take care of it and told us not to worry."

I looked at Charlotte, "And did you start therapy then?"

She nodded and said, "Yes, I sure did. But it took a while before it started doing any good. I started seeing a therapist, but it wasn't really helping much. He suggested that I needed medication, so he sent me to a psychiatrist."

"And did that help you?"

"Yes. He was a Christian, which made me wary at first, but through talking to him, I realized he was a different kind of Christian."

"What does that mean?" I asked with unintended skepticism in my tone.

"Well, he didn't shove theology down my throat and while we did talk about my spiritual life, it was only when I wanted. And the only thing he had to tell me was that God loved me, and he reminded me of that over and over again. He also put me on medication to help me while we worked through the therapy sessions. That psychiatrist addressed all aspects of my experience as a human, and that included the spiritual, emotional, and mental sides. He didn't leave anything out."

"Did the medication help you?"

"It did help me feel a little better, but Phil wasn't happy about it. He thought I should get counseling from the pastor of our church. He had told the pastor that I was in counseling, and they were upset that I was getting treatment from a psychiatrist. They thought my battle was a kind of spiritual warfare and that all I needed was pastoral counseling and prayer, so Phil took me to see the pastor. We were sitting outside of his office and his secretary called us in for our appointment.

When we walked in, there were four pastors there, including the pastor of the church we left after they treated Corrina so badly. I just sat there and listened to what they had to say and then we left. And I stopped going to church for a long time after that. Sometimes on Sunday mornings, I would go and just sit in the parking lot of the church. And while I felt like I should have gone inside, I just couldn't make myself do it."

Our food arrived and we shared our plates with each other as we continued talking.

"Charlotte," I confessed openly, "I just started therapy myself and I know it isn't easy. How long were you in therapy?"

"For three years. It was an uphill battle and the hardest thing I've ever done in my life. I had a lot of issues that I needed to face head on and it was painful to relive all of it. I was also working and taking care of Phil at the same time. To have to wade through the muck of my past at the end of a long workday was incredibly difficult. One night after getting home from a therapy session, I was just exhausted. Physically and mentally, I just felt like I was done. I couldn't do it anymore. I had nothing left inside of me. I was empty. I called my doctor and told him I didn't think I could make it anymore."

"*Make it*...as in..." I couldn't finish the sentence.

"Yes, I didn't want to live anymore," Charlotte quietly clarified.

"Oh my gosh. What did he do?"

"He sent the police to my house, and they forced me to go to a hospital."

"Were you afraid?"

"No, I wasn't afraid. I wasn't feeling anything, really. I just didn't care. But my doctor came to see me, and he would just let me talk about whatever I wanted, and he would mirror back to me everything that I said so I knew I was being heard. I was very thin too. I think I had gotten down to one hundred pounds. My doctor would bring me cookies and we would eat them while he dug deeper and deeper into my soul. We kept digging until everything had been turned up and exposed. It was out there in the open, my secrets, my pain and I couldn't push it down or hide from it any longer."

"How long were you there?"

"I was in that hospital for two weeks. In addition to the session with my doctor, I also had group sessions. I remember sitting in a circle with other people who were in deep despair. Three of them were gay men. Their stories broke my heart. They had diverse backgrounds, but they all had one thing in common; they didn't feel seen or accepted in the world, in their communities, at their jobs or with their families. Contrary to what the church had always taught me, I just wanted to tell them that God saw them, He loved them just the way they were and He would love them for eternity."

I looked around the table at those beautiful women and I thought of all the ways Charlotte's story could have played out. I didn't know if it mattered but I felt the urge to say it out loud, so I did.

"Charlotte, I just want to say that I'm so glad you reached out to your doctor that night. I'm glad you had the courage to save your own life. I'm glad you're sitting at this café after this delicious meal on this beautiful day. I'm so glad you're still with us."

I wasn't trying to make her cry, but she did. Which made me cry. And then Sarah started crying too. But Corrina? She got up and excused herself to the restroom, which made us all laugh.

"Thank you, Farrah," Charlotte said. "To start with a sense of nothingness and build something good out of it, it takes time and a lot of patience. But if you hang on to even a tiny thread of hope and do the work, your life can change for the better. I'm living proof."

Corrina returned from her emotional escape, and we sat around and talked some more about the museums in New York City while we waited for the server to bring the bill.

I looked around at the people sitting at the tables beside us and wondered what they would be doing with the rest of their Sunday. A toddler passed by with her arms up, flying her little airplane self around the tables, saying hello to everyone like it was her job to be the official greeter. Just then, three servers came out with a cake and sparkling candles and started to sing "Happy Birthday." I smiled and looked around, wondering whose birthday was being celebrated on that beautiful Sunday. Imagine my surprise when the server set the cake down in front of me as they all surrounded me, singing and clapping. I was confused and mortified because it wasn't my birthday. Then I looked up and saw Corrina taking pictures of my horrified expression.

We took our time on our walk back to Charlotte's house, meandering in and out of a few shops. We stopped in a quaint little bookstore, and I wandered around, touching, feeling, and smelling the pages of the books. I wondered about the authors of fiction, and non-fiction alike, and how they found the courage to believe that, "There were people out there who would want to read their story."

Corrina read my thoughts as she passed behind me. "It will happen, Fairy, I promise," she said as she tousled the top of my hair.

We stopped in a tea shop, and I picked out a gift set that included a variety of loose-leaf tea pouches and a stainless-steel infuser. I thought it would be a great gift for Clara, considering her obsession with tea. And with the variety of white, green, oolong and florals, she might have been willing to expand her horizons.

We made it back to Charlotte's house late that afternoon. Once again, Michael was starting early preparations for dinner. Charlotte and Sarah went upstairs to their rooms to lie down for a bit while Corrina and I decided to go back downstairs and hang out on the patio together.

Corrina sprawled out on the sofa, and I sat across from her in the chaise-lounge. I think we were both tired of talking, so we just sat there and listened to the best of the eighties that I queued up on my phone. While I didn't fall asleep like Corrina, I enjoyed the quiet and peace of that late afternoon and daydreamed of being a published author one day. I also wondered if I would ever have the courage to tell my own story and if anyone would ever want to read it.

"You can talk to me about Charlotte now, if you want," Corrina said.

"Geez, you scared me," my hand clutched my heart to steady it, "I thought you were asleep. Hold on and let me look at my notes. Oh yes, I asked you in the car how Charlotte managed being the mom of two teenage girls and you asked me to wait until after I had spoken to Charlotte before you shared your perspective."

"Do you understand now why I asked you to do that?"

"Yes, I do. I totally get it."

"Well, to answer your question, I think she did the best that she could with the tools she had been given. I would like to think that is what we all do. We do our best as parents and then our kids do their best and that's how, over time, we evolve as humans."

"I call bullshit."

She scooted up on the couch and countered my challenge. "Why? That was an honest answer."

"That was a vague and generous answer that came from your fifty-year-old perspective that is bathed in hindsight and gallons of grace. Give me the raw version. Tell me the opinions of your fifteen and sixteen-year-old self."

She sat up straight, shooting darts at me with her angry, hazel eyes. I could see I stepped into a sensitive area. I should have backed down, but I didn't.

"Are you looking for more dirt, Farrah? Have we not given you enough? What is it that you want me to tell you? You want me to cry because my birth mother abandoned me, and my earth mother wasn't perfect? Well, you're not going to get that from me. Why don't we talk about *your* mother for a few minutes? Why is it that I've never met her? What's going on there, Farrah?"

I stood up at that point. "Back off, Corrina."

She stood up too, towering over me. "Why, Farrah? Why should I back off? Is the subject of your mother a landmine? Is that why you're all in my family's business? Because you don't want to deal with your own?"

"Why are you getting so defensive?! The whole idea was to write about your story and your mothers' stories. This isn't about me or my family. And I told you, if you didn't want to talk about a particular subject, that you didn't have to do it. We could skip it, edit it out, whatever. But don't come at me all puffed up because I was trying to dig a little deeper! That's not fair!"

She sat back down on the sofa and that one gesture dropped the temperature a few degrees. We both took a breath, but it took a few minutes before we met each other's eyes.

"Ok, Farrah. You're right," Corrina confessed. "You hit a nerve and I reacted harshly. My teenage years were hard, ok? It is a weird time for anyone, I think. I wanted my independence, but I also needed my parents. Those parts are common, natural for a teenager, I think. But everything that was going on with Dad being sick, Mom being depressed, the pressure from the church and the school, it was a lot to handle. I was trying to figure out who I was and especially in my early teens, it was difficult. I looked different than everyone in my family or my church and school. I came from a different place, from different people. I felt displaced. And those were the years I thought about my birth mom the most. I used to daydream a lot about how my life would have been different if I had never been given up for adoption and if my father was still alive. Of course, in my dreams, it was always better. But who knows? Maybe it wouldn't have been. Anyway, to answer your question from my fifteen-year-old perspective, I wasn't happy as a teenager. I thought Mom was *way* too strict. I felt suffocated. I felt like the church and their rules were more important than the health and wellbeing of our family unit. But I look at my life now and everything turned out ok. That's why I give her grace. I can only hope that my girls will do the same for me, one day."

"Well now, I feel like a dirtbag," I hung my head in shame.

"That's because you *are* a dirtbag."

"But you love me, madly," I lifted my head and smiled at my friend.

"Lord knows why," she said as she laid back down and closed her eyes.

"You know, Corrina, you're not as hard as you pretend to be. You act like nothing bothers you, but I see you. I know you. You may not wear your emotions on your sleeve like I do but it doesn't mean I can't see them. I know when you're sad, pissed off and when you're pretending to be happy. I also know when you're elated and joyful. I've paid close attention these last twenty-eight years. You can't fool me, so there's no reason to try. It isn't necessary. I love all of you. The good, the bad and the parts you try so hard to hide."

True to form, she opened her eyes and said, "Mind your damn business, Farrah."

THIRTY-SIX
MAY 2022

WE ENJOYED ANOTHER DELICIOUS MEAL TOGETHER THAT EVENING AND then sat together in the living room on their deep, comfy pit couch. Michael brought in a tray of Irish coffees and sat down with his arm around his wife. There was more that I wanted to discuss with Charlotte but as usual, she beat me to the punch.

"I probably need to fill you in on what happened to Phil."

"Yes. Corrina and I have talked about it briefly, but I don't know a lot of the details."

"He was on dialysis for a few years. It was just after I got out of the hospital that they put him on the transplant list. Sarah had moved out and Corrina was in college. We waited a little over a year and then we got the call in the middle of the night. A young man in North Carolina had been in a motorcycle accident and he was an organ donor. I rushed Phil to the hospital, and they took him into surgery. At first, the transplant worked beautifully but then his body started rejecting the kidney. They had to put him on a drug that suppressed his immune system, and it was an uphill battle from there. Every time he got a cold, he would end up with pneumocystis."

"What is pneumocystis? Is that like pneumonia?"

"It is a type of pneumonia. It's a serious fungal infection of the lungs. Most people who get it have a medical condition like autoimmune disease, AIDS or they take medications that lower the body's ability to fight germs. He had a horrible time with it. He was in and out of the hospital and on and off ventilators. He was exhausted and his quality of life wasn't what he wanted it to be anymore. So, he asked to sign a DNR. He passed away in the hospital on his birthday, in 1994."

"I'm so sorry, Charlotte." *Life is unpredictable and scary*, Eris whispered in my ear. *Be very afraid*.

"Thank you, Farrah. There were so many conflicting emotions that day. We knew when we took him to the hospital that there would be no ventilator. We took him in so they would make him comfortable. We flew Corrina home, and we were all there with him when he passed. We were so relieved that after years of sickness and suffering, he was no longer in pain. But it was surreal that he had left us. He wasn't part of our world, anymore. He wasn't coming home. It was a difficult thing to accept."

Once again, Sarah and Corrina were sharing a private conversation with each other. But their misty eyes gave them away. Sarah grabbed Corrina's hand and said, "He was a good dad. He had his stupid rules, which we hated when we were kids, but he took care of us, and we knew that we were loved. And for that, we will always be grateful."

Then Corrina raised her Irish coffee to the ceiling and said, "Cheers to Dad."

We all raised our glasses with her, and I said a silent thank you to the man who stepped up to be Corrina's father when her own father couldn't be there for her.

Just then, my phone vibrated in my hand. I looked up at Corrina, who was sitting across the couch from me, wondering why she was texting me. I looked at the text, which said, *'Let's go downstairs and do a video call with Clara.'*

I stood up and announced that I should go downstairs and pack.

Corrina and Sarah stood up in agreement and then the three of us went down to my bedroom and sat on my bed. Corrina made a video call and after a few rings, Clara picked up. She was in bed, and we could only see half of her face because she wasn't positioning the phone correctly.

"There's my girl! Where have you been, Corrina?" Clara said with the half of a smile that we could see.

"Hi Nana! We're at Mom's house in New York. I brought Farrah up here so she could interview Mom for the book. Sarah is here, too!"

"When are you going to come and see me again, Evie?"

Corrina paused for a moment and then just continued instead of correcting her, "That's why I'm calling, Nana. I thought maybe we could take a detour and see you and Lovedy on the way back from New York. We're leaving tomorrow, so we should be in your area by Tuesday evening. Would it be ok if we came to visit Wednesday morning?"

"Well, I don't know girl. I'll have to check my calendar. Jesus is comin' to visit me soon," she said with a chuckle.

"Nana! Jesus is going to have to wait. I need a hug and I need to see your face."

"Alright. Just don't wait too long. It's past my bedtime so I'm going to go on to sleep."

"Ok, Nana. I love you and I can't wait to see you."

"I love you too, sweet girl. I'll see you soon."

Corrina looked at me with a puzzled look on her face and said, "I'm sorry for throwing it out there like that without talking to you first. I just feel like I really need to see her soon."

"It's ok with me. You took off work until Friday, right?"

"Yes. I knew we planned on stopping other places on the way back, but I'd rather just drive straight through tomorrow and maybe see her Tuesday, instead of Wednesday. Would that be ok? I know it's a long drive."

"Yes, of course. I've got nothing but time. Let's do it."

"Ok. Then let's get packed, for real. I want to leave as early as possible tomorrow morning."

We packed our suitcases and then went back upstairs and told Michael and Charlotte about our plans to leave early. We knew they would be up to say goodbye in the morning, so we immediately went back downstairs, showered and went straight to bed.

The next morning, Corrina woke me up in a panic. "Farrah, *Farrah, wake up*!"

"I'm awake. What's wrong?" I asked, as I sat up too quickly.

"I just heard a voicemail from Lovedy. She called last night but I didn't have my ringer on. Nana is very sick and doesn't have much time. We have to go. *Now*!"

"Is Lovedy with her?" I was feeling dizzy, and my heart was pounding.

"Yes. She's with her. *Get up*. We *have* to go."

Corrina ran out of my room to get dressed and get her stuff together. I sat there on the bed, trying to make a choice. I could feel Eris in the room, spinning all around me and daring me to stand up. I knew if I rushed and let the panic take over, we would have had another problem on our hands. I stayed there and counted the seconds in my breaths. In, two, three, four. Hold, two, three, four, five, six, seven. Exhale, two, three, four, five, six, seven, eight. I did exactly what Dr. Walker taught me to do. When I felt ready, I stood up slowly and told Eris to go straight to hell.

We got ready in record time and carried our luggage out to the car. We went back inside to say goodbye and explain why we couldn't stay for breakfast.

"I'm so sorry to be rushing out of here," Corrina said as she hugged Michael and Charlotte quickly.

"Don't be silly," Charlotte said. "You have to go. Please drive carefully."

As we were heading out of the door, Michael handed us a bag and two coffees. "There are some muffins, bananas and bottles of water in there."

"You're an angel, Michael," I said as I took the bag from his hand.

Corrina turned around. "Wait. Where is Sarah? Is she still sleeping?"

"Yes, honey. But I'm sure she'll understand," Charlotte said.

Corrina looked at me and said, "Go start the car. I'll be right there." Then I watched as she bounded the stairs two at a time to give her sister a hug.

While I waited for her, I put Clara's address into my navigator. It was six o'clock in the morning. If we drove straight through and stopped three times for fifteen minutes each time, we would arrive at Clara's place before six o'clock in the evening. It was going to be a long day.

As Corrina bounded down the steps towards the car, I closed my eyes and spoke my thoughts aloud. "Clara, I know you're excited to go, but please hold on. Just wait for her." It felt silly. I knew she couldn't hear me, but I said it anyway.

Corrina jumped in the car, and I sped off as she was putting her seatbelt on. We were about an hour ahead of the busiest traffic time, but the streets were still crowded. There were so many turns to get out of the city, it took forty minutes just to get to I-78. Once we hit the highway, I set the Jeep on cruise control and took a breath.

"Food. I need food," I pleaded.

Corrina peeled a banana and handed it to me, then turned her head towards the window.

"You ok?" I asked. I knew the answer but didn't know what else to say besides that dumb question.

"I'm ok," she said. "I just want to see her while she's still alive."

"I know, Corr. I know." I reached over and rubbed her arm. "We'll get there. Just try to relax."

Gabe would have been pissed at how fast I was driving but I wasn't thinking about him. I just wanted to get my friend there as fast as I could. I floored it all the way down I-78 and onto I-81 South.

"I *really* have to pee." Corrina said.

"Crawl in the back and use the solo cup," I told her.

"What? Seriously?"

"Seriously. I'm not stopping until we need gas."

"Ok, then."

There were limbs everywhere. The last time I saw her do something like that, we were twenty-three years old, stuck behind a million cars leaving a parking lot after a concert. "You look like a spider with your arms and legs going in all different directions" I smirked.

"Shut up, Farrah. Don't make me laugh until I get this solo cup situated."

"Don't you dare pee on my seats, Corrina. I'm serious!"

"Ahhhh... ok. We're good," she said.

When she finished, I passed her some hand sanitizer and then she crawled back into the front seat like a giant insect.

We finally stopped for gas in the charming town of Winchester, Virginia. We had no time for touristy stuff. Corrina pumped the gas and dumped her cup while I, contrary to my system of beliefs, went into the gas station to use the restroom. I purchased more bottles of water and two apples and headed back out to the Jeep. Corrina was already in the driver's seat.

"You hungry? Let's eat some fast food," she said.

"You never eat fast food, Corr. Your body wouldn't know what to do with it. It might make you sick."

"I'll be fine," she said as she pulled into a burger joint. We ordered the biggest burgers they had with all the toppings, including bacon and two sides of fries.

We were back on I-81 south in no time, stuffing our faces. "It literally smells like grease in here," Corrina said with a disgusted look on her face. "But it sure tastes good."

We cracked our windows to air out the jeep. I gave up halfway through my lunch, but Corrina kept going, like a champ. She ate every bit of that burger, shoved down all of her fries, and drank two bottles of water.

"I'll give you ten minutes before you start whining that you're going to be sick," I said.

"I'll take that bet. I have an iron stomach. Nothing bothers me." Then she changed the playlist to seventies R&B, and we sang to the Commodores, Smokey Robinson, and Earth, Wind & Fire as we sped through Harrisonburg, Fishersville and Roanoke.

"You've been driving for a while. Want to switch places?" I asked.

"Nah, I'm ok," she said. "Driving keeps me distracted."

"Ok. But you drive like a turtle. We're never going to make it there by six at this speed."

"Yeah, but at least we'll make it there. You know those people that drive faster than everyone else and they weave in and out of lanes all the time?"

"Yes, I hate those people."

"That's you, Farrah. *You* are those people. Those people are you!"

"I do not drive recklessly! I've never even had a speeding ticket!"

"I'm sorry. Remind me how you met your husband again?"

"Well, besides that one. I still can't believe he gave me that ticket."

"I can't either. Especially since you pulled down the front of your sweater to give him a sneak peak of your girls."

"That's a lie! It was buttons! I undid my buttons! But it worked twice before. I have no idea why it didn't work on him."

"He's immune to your wily tricks."

"I know. It's so annoying. Speaking of, I should call him and tell him where we are and what we're doing."

I called Gabe and put him on the speaker. I explained to him what was going on and that I wasn't sure when we'd be back. He asked if I wanted him to drive over to North Carolina to meet us there. I told him not to worry about it and that I would keep him posted as to how things were going with Clara.

A few minutes after the phone call had ended, Corrina said she was tired of driving. We pulled off the road into a gas station, filled up again and switched places. It had been a long day, and we were both tired. I imagined Corrina would be up for a while that night so I said, "You should get some sleep."

"I think I will," she said as she reclined her seat and folded up her arm to use as a pillow.

I turned the music down low and continued to drive, finally crossing into Tennessee. As I drove through Bristol, Piney Flats and Johnson City, I wondered how the next few days would unfold. What did "not much time" really mean? I guess there was no way to know, for any of us, really. Since my fiftieth birthday, I found myself thinking more and more about my own death. Would it be sudden? Would it just feel like going to sleep? Would I die before Gabe? Would it be sudden or long and painful? Did I really want a funeral? Would that really be the end of me? I wondered too if I was the only person who thought about such things.

I followed the twisty turns of I-26 from Johnson City to the Asheville area and called Lovedy to let her know we were close. When we were five minutes from Clara's, I gently nudged my friend awake. "Corr, wake up, honey. We're almost there."

She sat up quickly, looking around as I pulled into the parking lot and asked, "Why are we here instead of the hospital?"

"I spoke to Lovedy while you were sleeping, and I asked her the same question. She said Clara signed a DNR. She's ready to go and they have the medical staff to take of her here."

She rubbed her eyes and said, "Oh, ok. I just had a dream about Nana. We were sitting under a magnolia tree, and she was braiding my hair."

THIRTY-SEVEN
MAY 2022

I parked the car, and we walked up to the front of the building.

"Lovedy told me we should wait here for her to come out," I said, pointing to a bench. We sat down close to one another, in silence, as we waited.

Corrina's leg was bopping up and down. She was anxious and I remember thinking I had never seen her that way. Lovedy came out a brief time after and gave us both a hug. I let her sit down next to Corrina so she could talk with her. "Corrina, honey, I just want you to be prepared…"

"Is she still alive? Please tell me she is…" Corrina pleaded.

"Yes, she is still alive," Lovedy assured her, reaching out to hold her hands. "But she fell asleep, and the medical staff does not think she will wake back up before she passes away."

Corrina laid her head on Lovedy's shoulder and I watched as an ocean of tears crashed over her, pounding with unrelenting waves. My strong, somewhat impervious friend was crumpled in her mother's arms and weeping like a child. I had no words. So I sat down on the ground next to the bench and leaned my head against her leg.

MAY 2022

We stayed there a while, and waited until she was ready to go inside. We walked with her, Lovedy on one side, me on the other through the sliding glass doors of the facility. As we approached Clara's door, I said, "I'm going to give you girls some time with her. Just let me know when it is ok to come inside."

Lovedy winked at me and mouthed, "Thank you" and they went inside together, closing the door. I sat down on the bench in the hallway and wished at that moment that I believed in something bigger than myself, something that I could pray to, something that would hear me and actually do something about it. I didn't want to pray for Clara. I knew this was exactly what she wanted. Had I been a believer, I would have prayed for my friend. I would have prayed for comfort, for grace in the days ahead. I kept thinking about her outside on that bench, how she looked so broken and helpless. I would have prayed to anyone and anything to take her pain away.

I leaned my head back against the wall and waited. After a while I took a walk down the hallway in search of a restroom and a bottle of water. When I returned, Lovedy was sitting on the bench, giving Corrina some time alone with her grandmother. I sat down beside her. "How is she doing?"

"She's gonna be ok, Farrah," she said and put her arm around me. "Grief runs as deep as the well of love from which it is drawn. She loves her grandmother so much. It may take a while, but she's gonna be ok."

"You think it would be ok if I went in there with her?"

"I think that would be fine. You go on inside. I'm gonna sit out here for a while."

I felt nervous as I stood up and approached the door. Before that day, I had never seen anyone actively dying and I didn't know what to expect.

I turned the knob and walked inside, allowing my eyes to adjust to the dim light. I walked through the tiny kitchen and turned left towards Clara's bedroom. The door was opened.

Clara was lying in the bed with the covers tucked under her arms.

Corrina was sitting on the chair by her bedside, leaning forward with her hand resting on Clara. The lamp on the nightstand glowed in the darkness of the room, illuminating the side of Clara's face. She looked at peace. Her face was relaxed as she took sporadic, shallow breaths. There was music playing from the CD player on the dresser. I leaned against the inside of the door frame and listened to Patti Labelle singing a song about walking around in heaven.

I don't know how to explain what I saw there, in that room. It certainly was not what I expected. I thought I would be scared, but all I felt was peace. There was so much love, it was palpable. I could feel it all around them. So much so, that I didn't want to disrupt what was happening. So, I turned around and went back out into the hallway to sit with Lovedy again.

About forty-five minutes later, Corrina emerged. Her face was blotchy and swollen but she managed a smile and said, "You won the bet, Farrah. I lost my lunch in Nana's bathroom and now I'm starving. Is the café still open?"

"Yes, it is open until eight," Lovedy said. "How does a salad sound to you? Or maybe a chicken salad sandwich?"

"A salad sounds great." Corrina said.

"What about you, Farrah? You hungry?" Lovedy asked.

"The sandwich sounds good to me."

"Ok. I'll be right back." Lovedy said as she headed down the hallway.

"Come in with me," Corrina said.

"Are you sure?"

"Yes, I'm sure. I need my friend."

We went back into Clara's apartment. Corrina grabbed another chair and put it on the other side of the bed, so I could sit with her.

"You never asked me about the first time I met Clara," Corrina said in a soft whisper.

"I was saving that conversation for our trip back from New York. When the tides turned, I didn't feel it was appropriate to ask you about it on the way here."

"It's ok," Corrina said with a gentle smile. "I want to talk about it. It is one of the best memories of my life."

I smiled back at my beautiful friend. "I'm listening." I didn't have my recorder on, but I knew I would never forget that conversation.

"I was driving to school for my freshman year at UK. Dad was sick and Mom wasn't doing well, so it was just me. I left a few days early and took a detour so I could spend some time with Lovedy before the semester started. She's the one that introduced me to Clara. It was a total surprise. She told me we were going out for lunch. She drove me to a neighborhood right outside of Asheville. I was really confused when she parked the car in front of a small bungalow. As I was getting out of the car, I saw a tiny woman walking towards me with her arms out. I looked at Lovedy and I knew immediately who she was. She barely came up to my shoulder, so I bent over, and she hugged me for the longest time. She invited us inside and fed us lunch. Jeremiah was there, too. He was quiet but kept smiling at me the whole time. She told me all about my father and gave me a stack of pictures. She kept staring at my face and saying, 'I just can't believe how much you look like Isaac.'

I told her, 'I do look like him, but I think I look more like you.' And then she said, 'Yes, you're such a beautiful girl.'"

We both giggled quietly at Clara's sense of humor before Corrina continued.

"She is tiny in stature but has the biggest heart of anyone that I've ever known. She wrote me letters the entire time I was in school and always told me how proud she was of me. She would encourage me and share scriptures about God's promises in her letters. She would send me money. Not much, but five dollars here, ten dollars there. She would send me pictures of her classes at the high school and tell me how much she loved being a teacher. I looked in my mailbox every day, just waiting for the next letter from her. Meeting Clara changed the trajectory of my life. She opened my world. I finally felt like I knew who I was, where I came from. Over time, she introduced me to her sister, Evie, and all of her children and all of a sudden, I had this huge family.

I will never forget the first time I went to church with all of them. People worship God in all diverse kinds of ways, but I felt right at home in their church. The music pierced my soul, and the sermons moved my spirit. As I'm looking at her now, I know she's getting ready to leave me and all I can think of is how grateful I am. I'm grateful that she was my Nana. I'm so thankful that I met her when I did and for all those years I had with her. I'm so thankful that she loved me. I'm a better person because I knew her."

"I hope she can hear you," was all I could say.

"Trust me, she's listenin' to every word you say," said Lovedy as she poked her head inside the bedroom. "Dinner's here."

We sat at Clara's small dinette and looked through her photo albums and talked as we ate our dinner. I cleared the table while Lovedy and Corrina continued to share their memories of Clara.

"Lovedy, did you get to talk to her before she fell asleep?" Corrinna asked.

"Yes, honey. She was very tired, but we talked quite a bit."

"What did you talk about?"

"Mostly what happens, next. I know she has a will, and she documented her wishes for her funeral. She wants specific music at her service. She also talked about how she wanted her ashes spread over Jeremiah and Isaac's graves. And Farrah?"

"Yes?" I turned around quickly to see how I could possibly have anything to do with Clara's dying wishes.

"She wants you to speak at her home going celebration."

"*Me*? Why me?" That didn't make sense to me at all.

"She said you read all of her thoughts and her prayers in her journals, and you know everything there is to know about her. She said you could speak from her heart."

Clara's words, her thoughts, prayers, cries, flowed through my mind like a river. I knew what she meant but I was still stunned and anxious. "I don't think I'm the person who should be doing that.

Maybe Corrina? Or one of her nieces or nephews? Or maybe even you, Lovedy. But certainly not me."

"You don't have to decide right now. It will be a couple of weeks before the memorial service happens. You have time to think about it."

I focused my attention on wiping down the countertop. Not that it was dirty, but I needed something to do besides think about the conversation that just happened.

Corrina spoke up, "You don't get to bow out of this one, Farrah. If my Nana wants you to speak at her service, then that's what you're going to do. You're going to do it for her and for me. There's nothing for you to think about."

I guess I had my marching orders from the two bossiest women I had ever known. Corrina was right. I had to suck it up and do what I needed to do.

"Ok, Corrina. Don't worry about it. I'll do it."

"Damn right, you will," she ordered then went back into Clara's room.

"That's your daughter, Lovedy." I said with a slight shake of my head.

"I know! Ain't she a hoot!" She laughed quietly.

And then I had another thought. "Is Corrina spending the night here?"

"Yes. She wants to stay with Clara. I thought you and I could sleep at my house and then come back first thing in the morning. Would that be alright with you?"

"Yes. As long as Corrina is ok staying here without us, it's ok with me."

"I already talked to her. She's good with it."

"Ok, then. I'm going to go out to the Jeep and bring in her luggage. I should probably leave my vehicle here for her in case she needs it for anything."

"Yes, good idea. Grab my keys out of my purse and just move your luggage into my car."

I went out to the parking lot, moved my luggage, and then grabbed Corrina's things to take inside. I wasn't sure how I felt about leaving Corrina here by herself. What if something happened overnight? I was nervous but decided to trust Lovedy's plan and go with it.

I pulled her luggage down the hallway and went back into the apartment. We sat with Clara for a little while longer until I saw Corrina nodding off.

I stood up and walked over to her and gave her a kiss on the top of the head. "We're leaving, Corr. I'll see you first thing in the morning. If you need anything at all, even just to talk, call me. Don't think about it, just call me."

She looked up at me with her sleepy eyes, nodded her head and held out her hand. I grabbed it and slowly let go as I walked away.

Lovedy hugged her for a while, and then bent over and gave Clara a kiss on her forehead while wishing her goodnight. And then we left that dimly lit room with the music playing, and a granddaughter holding her dying grandmother's hand.

THIRTY-EIGHT
MAY 2022

Lovedy and I didn't talk much on the way back to her house. We were both exhausted. When we arrived, David came out and carried my luggage into the house for me. I took a hot shower, called Gabe, and slipped under the covers. I texted Corr, asking if she was ok. She didn't respond so I assumed she fell asleep. Around three in the morning, my phone rang. It was her.

"Farrah?"

"Yeah, babe. I'm here."

"I think it's going to happen soon. Her breathing is slow. Every time I think it is her last one, she takes another. I'm trying not to fall asleep because I want to be awake when she leaves."

"Do you want me to come and sit with you?"

"No, I'm ok. Will you just keep me awake?"

"Sure, I'm here."

She told me that Judge, Vassy and Lauren would be there tomorrow. I was glad she would have her family with her.

After two hours of talking and drifting off, Lovedy knocked on my door and poked her head inside. "How long have you been awake?"

I showed her three fingers and then pointed to the phone to let her know I was talking to Corrina.

"Did you get some sleep?" She whispered. "We can go now and let Corrina get some rest. I'm sure she's been up all night."

I gave her a thumbs up and told Corrina we would be there soon. I threw on a pair of shorts, a t-shirt, and some sneakers, tossed my hair up in a bun, brushed my teeth and washed my face. It wasn't a pretty sight, but I didn't care. I just wanted to get to my friend as quickly as possible. I also repacked my luggage just in case Clara held on and Corrina wanted me to stay the next night with her.

Lovedy was ready and waiting for me when I went out into the kitchen. We hopped back into her car and headed back towards Clara's place, stopping at a coffee shop on the way. It was early so we avoided traffic and arrived less than an hour later.

Corrina was in the same spot we left her, sitting in the chair beside her grandmother's bed with their hands intertwined. The music was still playing, and the lamp was still casting its angelic glow on the side of Clara's sweet face.

Lovedy handed Corrina some water and told her to go lay down on the sofa.

"That's a loveseat," she whispered. "What am I supposed to do with these legs you gave me? Fold them up in threes?"

"Ya big, nasty, spider," I said before I could stop it from coming out of my mouth.

Corrina snorted, then I snorted, and Lovedy started in, too.

"Just lay down beside your Nana, then," Lovedy suggested.

"Good idea," she said with a half-smile. She slowly and gently laid down on her side, facing her grandmother. Lovedy closed the door more than halfway, leaving it ajar in case Corrina called out for us.

I stepped into the kitchen and made a pot of tea. I thought about the tea basket I had purchased for Clara in Brooklyn, and it sat heavy on my heart that I would never be able to give it to her.

Lovedy and I sipped our tea and talked awhile about my visit with Michael, Charlotte and Sarah.

The sun was high in the sky when Corrina came out of the bedroom. "She's still with us. Would one of you go and sit with her while I take a quick shower?"

"Farrah, you go sit with Clara and I'll go grab Corrina some breakfast." Lovedy said.

"Ok, sure."

I went into the bedroom and sat down on the chair. I saw what Corrina was talking about. Clara's breathing was different, slower, shallower. I found myself holding my own breath as I waited for her next one to arrive. I didn't know if she could hear me, but I talked to her, anyway. I thanked her for sharing her journals, her tea, and her precious life with me. I told her how much Corrina loved her. I told her how much I wished I would have had a mother or grandmother in my life that was just like her. I told her that she didn't need to worry about Corrina. I would take good care of her.

Around noon, Judge, Vassy and Lauren arrived. I stepped out of the room to let Corrina and her family be together with their Nana.

As I walked into the living room area, Lovedy was resting on the love seat, with her head back and her eyes closed.

I took a seat in Clara's giant recliner and leaned back, rubbing my fingers on the blanket that lay over the armrest. I sat in her chair for some time, gazing out of the window. I imagined Clara sitting there, watching TV, or the birds chirping from trees that dotted the beautiful landscape. I imagined her talking to Corrina on the telephone or reading her bible.

That thought made me look at the coffee table. The bible was still there, on top of some magazines. I stood up for a moment, took it off the table and sat back down, placing it on my lap. The leather cover was faded and worn, and I could barely make out the faded gold ink that read "Holy Bible" on the front. I opened the cover and there I saw a dedication page. It said, "To: Clara Jane Carter, From: Jeremiah Eugene Carter." The dedication was dated August 1, 1951, their wedding day. There was a bookmark made of red ribbon that peaked out from the bottom of the book. When I pulled on it, the pages lifted, and the book opened. Several rows of words had been highlighted with a pink marker. The words said, "We have come to know and believe in the love God has for us. God is love, and whoever remains in love remains in God and God in him." I wondered if that was the last verse she read before she laid down and fell asleep. I read it again.

"She's gone," Corrina said softly.

I looked up from the words on the page to see Corrina standing in the doorway of Clara's room. I placed the book back on the table, walked over to my friend, and pulled her into my arms. There were no words to say to her that wouldn't feel empty, so I just held her until she let go.

"Farrah, you have to write the eulogy and you have to finish the book," she whispered quietly into my ear. "I want the world to know my beautiful Nana. I want them to know she was here and the difference she made in my life and the lives of everyone else who knew her."

"I will. I promise."

Judge and the girls came out of the room, and I went in to pay my last respects. I walked up to the bed and looked at Clara's face. She looked so peaceful. Her tiny body was lying there in front of me, so still and quiet. The vibrance, the intelligence and kindness, the strength and essence of that precious woman was gone. I touched her hand and whispered, "Have a great trip, Ms. Clara. I'll miss you. Say hello to Jeremiah and Isaac for me."

I sat with the family for a while and then decided it was time to leave. Out of respect, I didn't feel that I should stay for the removal of her body, so I hugged everyone goodbye and left to go home. As I started walking down the hallway, I heard Lovedy quietly call my name. I turned around and saw that the staff had put a yellow and white crocheted angel above Clara's door.

"Do you want to stay at my house for the night? I'd hate to see you make that drive this evening."

"That's so sweet of you, but no. I'm anxious to get home to Gabe and the dogs. It's not even four hours away. I'll be fine."

"Ok," she said as she kept walking towards me. "My car is unlocked. You can just grab your luggage." She gave me another hug and whispered "Thank you for being such a good friend to Corrina. I love you."

I don't know why I cried. It wasn't the first time Lovedy had said that to me. I guess it was the last couple of days and everything that was going on. It was an emotional time, and I was feeling every bit of it.

I promised I would send her a text when I arrived safely. I walked outside, pulled my bags out of Lovedy's trunk and went to throw them in the backseat of my Jeep. And then I remembered I had given my keys to Corrina the night before. I left my luggage standing by the Jeep and walked back inside. As I started down the hallway, I saw a man taking Clara out on a stretcher. Lovedy, Corrina, Judge and the girls were lined up in the hallway, watching her leave through the back door.

Corrina looked over and saw me standing there. "Oh, Farrah." she said as she slid down to the floor. At a loss for words, I slid down beside her, both of us content in our silence.

She rested her head on my shoulder then, "You forgot your keys, didn't you?"

"Yes. Yes, indeed." I confessed.

"Dumbass."

"I'm going to let you get away with that one."

"Go home, my friend. I'm ok. I'll call you later."

"I'm not leaving until you get off the floor."

"Why? I'm comfortable."

"Well, I've been sitting crisscross-applesauce, and my knees are stuck. I need help getting up."

"Aunt Fairy, I'll help you," Vassy volunteered as she pulled me to a standing position.

"You've always been my favorite, Vass," I said, giving her a big squeeze. "You're sweet, unlike your mama."

I went back into Clara's apartment, rummaged through Corrina's purse, and found my keys. Back in the hallway, I waved goodbye to everyone again and blew a kiss to Corrina. She was still sitting on the floor, hugging her legs with her forehead resting on her knees.

Part of me wanted to stay with her. She was my friend, and I felt a deep sense of responsibility to make sure that she was going to be ok. But she had her husband there, her girls and Lovedy. I knew there was so much love there to lift her up and support her. My emotional tank was running on empty. And while it felt a bit selfish, I was feeling the need to seek out comfort for myself. I desperately wanted to be in my husband's arms.

I called him on the way home and told him the whole story. I wanted to get it out, then and there, and not wait until I got home.

The sun was setting into the mountain's sky as I took the ramp onto I-40 westbound. I had my playlists and podcasts to keep me company, but my mind kept wandering to the events of the last few days. I had only known Clara a short while, but she had made a deep and lasting impression on me. I loved her even before I met her. I loved her because she loved my friend, so completely and unconditionally. Clara gave from her heart, openly and without reservation or fear. Her life was never about what others did for her but how she could give of herself to others. I thought about what I would say at her service that would even come close to representing the remarkable human being that she was during her time on this earth.

As I drove up the mountain, it was my turn to speak into the recorder. Before I turned it on, I spoke aloud to Clara and said, "Help me to see your heart. Help me to find a way to share it with those who are missing you so that they will be comforted in their grief." And then I talked about Clara, into my recorder, all the way home.

THIRTY-NINE
MAY 2022

I slept late the next morning. My body, mind and heart were worn out. The aroma of coffee floated underneath the door, into our bedroom and gently woke me up. I laid there for a bit and thought about what I would do that day. I had a mental list of things to do around the house and also had an appointment scheduled with Dr. Walker. And while I really wanted to stay home with Gabe and the dogs, I also wanted to talk with her about all that had happened. I sat up slowly and opened my eyes. And there he was, standing in the doorway with a cup in his hand.

"Buenos dias, hermosa," he said.

"Morning. Come and sit next to me," I said, shifting over to the middle of the bed.

He handed me the coffee and sat down gently on the edge of the mattress.

"How's my girl this morning?" He asked with a smile.

"I'm tired, but I'm good. I have an appointment at noon with Dr. Walker, but other than that, I just want to hang out with you and spend time with the dogs. I've been gone so much lately, they've probably disowned me by now."

"Hey, they aren't the only ones that have missed you, lady."

"I know. I've missed you too," I said, as I reached over to grab his hand.

"Eggs? Oatmeal?" He asked.

"Oatmeal, with bananas and brown sugar, please."

"You got it. It will be ready when you get out of the bathroom."

I took a hot shower, and as I stood under the water, I felt the tension that was gripping my body. My neck was stiff, my shoulders were high and rigid, and my lower back was throbbing. I breathed in deeply and held it, then slowly exhaled as I dropped my shoulders. I surveyed every muscle in my body, just as Dr. Walker had taught me. With every breath, I released all the things I had collected and bottled up over the last week. I imagined them leaving my body through the bottoms of my feet and circling down the drain.

I put on my robe, twisted my hair up in a towel, and walked out to the kitchen to eat breakfast. We sat at the island together with the dogs at our feet and talked about Gabe's research that he had done on ways we could give back. He had some pretty interesting ideas and I loved that he had obviously put a lot of time and effort into it while I was gone. I was excited that we were going to do something good together. And whether we decided to travel across the globe or help families in our own community, it didn't really matter to me. The universe had been so generous to us, and I couldn't believe it was meant to be kept all to ourselves.

After breakfast, I checked my messages. Corrina left one to tell me that Clara's service would be on Saturday of the following week. Right then and there, I made up my mind that the novel would have to wait until after the service. I had more important things to write over the next eight days.

Gabe and I took the dogs for a long walk. The day was warm and bright, and it felt so good to be back home with my little family. We talked about my therapy appointment that day, and I told him that I was looking forward to seeing Dr. Walker. It had been a week since I saw her last, and there were some specific things I wanted to talk to her about, questions I was hoping she could answer.

"What kind of things?" He asked.

"Let me talk to her about it first, then maybe I'll tell you."

He stopped walking and turned to me. "Farrah, I am in total support of you getting help with your anxiety. You know that, right?"

"Yes, of course. Your encouragement was what pushed me to do it."

"Yes. I just..I don't know. I guess that I miss talking to you. It seems like now that you are talking to her, you don't talk to me about the hard stuff anymore. Maybe it's because you've been gone, and we really haven't had the opportunity to connect a lot lately. I don't know… I just want to make sure you're ok with me. We're ok, right?"

"Yes, Gabe. I'm ok. We're ok. I get what you're saying and I'm not trying to leave you out, but this anxiety didn't come out of nowhere. Dr. Walker gave me some guidance on how to manage stress and anxiety in the present, but we are also working through some things that are at the root of it. That part, I'm just not ready to talk about it with anyone else. Not yet. Even you. I'm still trying to understand it, myself."

"Oh," he said quietly as he looked down at the ground and rolled some pebbles around with the bottom of his shoe. "Is it serious?"

"Like I said, I don't quite understand all of it myself, but what are you worried about?"

"I'm worried about a lot of things. I'm worried that someone in your past hurt you. I'm worried about what that will do to you now. I'm worried that you'll be different when you get through all of this therapy. I'm worried our relationship will change."

"I may be different when I'm done with therapy, but I really think it may be in a good way. Change doesn't necessarily have to be a dreadful thing, you know."

"I know, I know," he sighed. "You're right. I guess I just have to trust the process. It's hard for a man like me to stand off and not be involved. Especially when it comes to the woman that I love. If you have a problem, I want to be there to fix it for you. That's my job."

"Not in this case, Gabe. It isn't your job at all. It's mine. I've had this anxiety issue for many years, and I just tried to ignore it. It's my job to dig it up and address the reason why it has been part of my life. The only thing I need from you is your love and support. Would that be ok? For now?"

"Whatever you need, I'll give it to you. You know that."

He held my hand, and we walked quietly back to the house. We released the dogs from their leashes, and I went inside to get a bottle of water. Before I stepped back out into the garage to leave, I turned to Gabe and said, "You mean everything to me. Just because I'm working on myself doesn't mean that I feel differently about you. Ok?"

He smiled. "Ok. I'm good. We're good."

"Promise?"

"Promise."

I wanted Gabe to feel comfortable with the work I was doing with Dr. Walker. But I noticed, as I drove to my appointment, that I was now worried about him and our relationship. Half of me resented him for that but I also recognized that I wasn't single. I was married and it wasn't just all about me. I remembered when he would have a horrible day at work or was tormented about a life that was lost, it affected me too. We were in this together, for better or worse and I had to find a way to communicate with him while also respecting the boundaries I had set for myself.

The only word I could think of to describe my appointment with Dr. Walker was *productive*. It wasn't fun. It was *work*.

I told her about a few of the challenging moments during my trip. The first one was the feelings I had on the couch when I was watching Sarah and Corrina together. I told her that I couldn't shake the feeling that I had missed something in my childhood. And even today, I still felt like something in my life was absent. I told her about the panic that had set in the morning when Corrina woke me up because of Clara's failing health. I also told her about when Lovedy told me that she loved me and how it made me feel sad. I wasn't expecting the questions that Dr. Walker asked me that day. They made me think about things I had never considered. I was also not prepared for the homework she gave me. Part of me wanted to push back and tell her it wasn't necessary, that we didn't need to involve my parents. She left it up to me but strongly encouraged me to do the work.

I left feeling nervous but more determined than ever to kick Eris' ass. I was also a bit frustrated. It seemed the more I saw Dr. Walker, the more the well of problems deepened and the magical cure for what was ailing me moved further away. Nevertheless, I had no intention of giving up.

I stopped to get some takeout for lunch on the way home. Gabe and I sat out on the deck and munched on our chicken sandwiches and fruit salad. In keeping with my commitment to communicate better, I told him what I could at the moment. "Dr. Walker wants me to talk to my parents."

"About what?"

"About my childhood."

"Wow. How do you feel about that?"

"I think I'm ok talking with Dad, but calling Mom is not an option I will even consider. I think I'm going to keep it casual and call him today. There's no point in waiting. I have some questions for him and I'm going to try to work them into the conversation."

"It sounds like you have a plan. You're good at getting information from people and besides, your dad's a good guy. I'm sure it will go fine."

"Speaking of getting information from people, remember those journals that Clara gave to me?"

"Yes?"

"She told Lovedy before she died that she wants me to speak at her homegoing celebration. I have an idea of what I want to say, but I need to type it all out, so I won't stumble all over myself."

"You're a great speaker, Farrah. I heard you lead presentations during all of those conference calls when you were working from home during Covid. You're a boss."

"This is different, though. That was business. This is real life. Real death. It's emotional. Not just for me but for the people who will be there, grieving the loss of someone they loved. I just want to be prepared."

"There's a reason she wanted you to speak. She trusted you. If you're doubting yourself, trust that Clara knew what she was doing," he reached over and squeezed my hand.

"Gabe, I would love to have you there with me. Will you go with me?"

"Yes, of course. I'll be there."

"Good," I smiled, and we stood up to go back inside.

I decided to tackle my list of things to do around the house. I started with giving the girls a bath. I don't know what they got into while I was gone but they both smelled like a dumpster. I cleaned the bathrooms, the floors, and checked my email. I was going to wait until after dinner to call my dad but then decided it was better to do it right then.

I always had a good relationship with my dad. He was a cheerleader kind of parent, always there for me and always a positive influence. He believed I could conquer the whole world if that was what I wanted to do. And in his eyes, even after all of my stupid mistakes and bad relationships, I could do no wrong. His voice always brought a smile to my face.

"Hello!"

"Hi Daddy."

"Sunshine! How's my girl?"

"I'm good. I've missed you."

We talked for a while. He caught me up on his latest golf game and the murder mystery he just finished. I filled him in about the book I was trying to write. Then I asked him about a vacation that he and I took during the summer after second grade. That opened the door for me to ask why Mom didn't go with us. His answer raised many more questions for me. He gave me the answers as best as he could. When I told him about the therapy sessions and the anxiety and panic, something changed. He stopped waiting for me to ask specific questions and just freely gave me some information that he knew would help me. To be honest, I was stunned. When I asked him why he never told me, he said that he and Mom decided not to because they thought it would cause me unnecessary pain. He admitted that it probably wasn't the best decision, and he apologized over and over.

We talked for over an hour. It was an emotional conversation on both ends. I was unrelenting with my questions and my need for details. He filled in the blanks for me, the spaces in my life that I never understood. I ended the conversation with him on good terms and with a much deeper understanding about my relationship with my mother.

"Are you going to tell Mom that we spoke about this?" I asked.

"Oh, I don't know. I don't talk to her much these days. I think it would be better for her if I didn't, don't you?"

"I agree. And Dad? Thanks for telling me, I know it wasn't easy."

"Are you ok, Sunshine?"

"I'll be ok. Don't worry about me. I'm just glad that I know."

"I'm proud of you for starting therapy and taking care of yourself. That makes this ol' man incredibly happy. I love you, Sunshine."

"Love you too, Daddy."

I went into the bedroom and sat down on the edge of the bed. I was in shock and didn't even know what to think or how to feel about the information he had given to me. About that time, Gabe walked in and over to the side of the bed. His arms were crossed, and he didn't look happy. "I wasn't listening intentionally, but you were walking all over the house while you were on the phone. Did I hear you right? You had a twin?!"

"Yes. She was my identical twin. Her name was Tarrah. She was what they call a sunset baby. It makes sense to me, now."

"What makes sense?"

"Why Daddy calls me Sunshine and why I've always carried around this sense of loneliness with me like a heavy backpack. Why Mom was always crying and never wanted to hold me. Why everything good that I did was never good enough for her. She blames me, Gabe. She blames me for Tarrah's death."

"You know that's not logical, Farrah. How could you be responsible for your twin's death? That doesn't make any sense."

"I know it doesn't make sense, Gabe. But it doesn't matter. It's what my mother believed all of my life. The impact on her life was very real. It was also very real to me."

"How are you feeling about it now?"

"I feel a lot of different things. Shock and anger, mostly. Guess I'll be scheduling more sessions with Dr. Walker."

"Deceased twin or not, Farrah, the way your mother treated you was inexcusable. And her behavior was about her, not you. Don't ever forget that."

"My mind knows it, but I'm afraid my heart will never be able to forget it."

"Maybe you should write about it, and then burn it," he said angrily.

"I've spent my whole life trying *not* to think about how she treated me. I've never told anyone but you. I've never even told Corrina."

"It's your story. Keep it to yourself or tell the entire world. Either way, I'm here for you. And you'll get through this, I promise."

FORTY
JUNE 2022

GABE AND I PLANNED TO ARRIVE IN NORTH CAROLINA THE THURSDAY before the service. I wanted to be there early to help Corrina and Clara's family with the arrangements and anything else that needed to be done. I had a lot to do over the next few days.

As busy as I was, random images and thoughts continued to appear in my mind like lightning bolts. They came and left in bits and pieces.

Growing up, I always thought my childhood was normal. Looking back, I wouldn't have known anything different. I didn't have anything to which I could have compared it. The memories were coming so fast and furious, it made it hard to concentrate on the tasks I needed to finish before we left town.

As a coping mechanism, I started a journal. Each time an image, conversation or event flashed inside my mind, I wrote it down. I didn't want to forget, and I thought it would help to free my mind to focus on the things I had to get done. But as soon as I wrote one down, the next one would show up. It was as if someone opened a dam inside my brain and the reservoir of memories was released all at once.

JUNE 2022

By Monday evening, I had an entire journal full of childhood recollections. I marched into Dr. Walker's office on Tuesday afternoon with a purpose, slammed it on the table and asked, "What is that?"

"Well, I don't have x-ray vision, so you're going to have to tell me," she said calmly.

"I may need two hours today. Is that a thing? Am I allowed to have two hours? I definitely need two hours," I demanded as I collapsed on her sofa.

"No, Farrah. That is not a thing. I have back-to-back appointments today. Why don't you start by telling me what is going on? Has something traumatic happened since last Thursday?"

"I did what you told me to do. I called my father. And my mind, which used to feel like a tightly wound ball of yarn, now feels like a plate of spaghetti. I'm all over the place. I'm losing it. I'm sure of it."

"Tell me about the conversation with your father. And then we'll talk about what is in that journal."

I told her everything. The twin thing and all the things Daddy told me about my mother and her behavior towards me. I told her all of the things that I couldn't even say out loud to Gabe. And then I told her about the journal.

"I know this may not feel like progress to you, Farrah, but I need you to trust me when I say this is what they call a breakthrough. This discovery is the first step towards healing for you. I know you were hesitant about talking to your parents. I'm really pleased that you took that step forward for yourself." Then she looked at her watch.

"See why I said that we need two hours?" I complained.

She smiled at me, "I do, Farrah. But you're going to have to continue to trust the process," she pulled out her tablet to look at her calendar and then asked me what I had going on over the next few days.

"I'm leaving Thursday, with Gabe, to go to North Carolina.

Clara's funeral is on Saturday, and she asked that I speak at her celebration."

"How do you feel about that?"

"I'm a little nervous, but I want to do what she asked of me. She was so open and honest with me about her life, I feel like I owe it to her." It was then that I noticed Dr. Walker was looking at my leg which was bouncing up and down, ratting me out.

"Farrah, obligation is not an appropriate response to a gift. Gratitude is preferred, but only if it is authentic. If you're going to do this, do it because you genuinely want to do it. Ok?"

"I want to do it. I think she was an incredible human being. I was moved and inspired by her strength, perseverance, and especially her kindness. Yes, I want to do it."

"Now *that* sounds like a valid reason. Unfortunately, our time is up, but I will see you on Tuesday and we'll talk about your journaling."

"Ok. That one is full," I said as I pointed to my leather bound book of disparate thoughts and feelings lying on her coffee table. "Do I leave that here for you to read? Or do I take it with me?"

"Whatever you want to do is fine with me."

"I'll leave it here for you to read. I'm sure I'll fill another one before I see you on Tuesday."

I called Corrina on the way home to see how she was doing. She had gone back to Kentucky for a few days to get things organized at home before returning back to North Carolina for the service. She sounded good, considering everything that had happened. I didn't tell her about my conversation with Daddy. I wasn't ready and it wasn't the appropriate time for it. My friend was going through a tough time, and I wanted to be there for her. My stuff could wait for a lakeside lunch when our lives returned to something that resembled normalcy. I asked her about accommodations the following weekend.

She told me that she and her family were going to stay at Lovedy's house and recommended a nearby hotel for Gabe and myself. I told her we would be in town Thursday evening and that we would meet her at Lovedy's house on Friday morning.

"Hey, Farrah?" Corrina said just as we were about to hang up.

"Yeah?"

"Thanks for the road trip and being there for me. I don't believe in coincidences. God's timing is impeccable. I wouldn't have been able to get through it without you by side."

"You're welcome, my friend."

"And Farrah?"

"Yeah?"

"I won. I won the prank contest. I'm the queen of pranks. You shall bow to me the next time I see you." And then she hung up in my face.

Wednesday was spent packing up the dogs and taking them to the local dog hotel, doing laundry, a little house cleaning and packing our suitcases for the trip. We ordered a veggie pizza and a salad for dinner, then we sat out on the deck with a couple of cold beers and watched the sun disappear into the night sky. I went to bed early, content with everything I had accomplished that day. There was only one thing to do the next morning.

After a hot shower and breakfast with Gabe, I opened my recorder app on my phone and my laptop. Before I began, I did a web search for the root of the word *eulogy*. The Greek root was *ue* (good) and *logos* (speech). Basically, my job was to write an encomium. I knew offering words of praise for Clara wouldn't be hard, so I went right to work and was done by lunch time.

We ate leftover pizza for lunch and then headed out on the road to go see my longtime friend and celebrate the life of a new one that I had recently lost. I had done so much driving over the past couple of months, so it was nice to let Gabe take the wheel. I was able to put my head back and relax. I had made a playlist of all the music Clara loved and closed my eyes while I listened to all of her favorite gospel songs. It was a calming vibe and fit perfectly with the beautiful drive to North Carolina.

We arrived in town around five o'clock. I asked Gabe to stop by "The Doghouse" so I could order flowers for the service. I also wanted to order an arrangement to be delivered to Lovedy's house. Gabe went in with me so he could stretch his legs. The little brass bells tinkled as we opened the door to the aroma of fresh flowers and luxurious chocolates.

"Farrah Acosta! How are you doin', darlin'?"

"Hi Rita! I'm doing well. How are you?"

"I'm busier than an anteater at a church picnic!"

I shook my head and laughed, then introduced her to Gabe. "Rita, this is my husband."

"Hi Rita, I'm Gabe" he said as he waved to her and flashed his perfect smile.

"Good Lord. I'm gonna need to come 'round there and get a closer look," she wiped her hands on her apron and walked around to the front of the counter. She sized him up and then said, "God was good to you, son. Yes, indeed. Incredibly good to you."

Gabe blushed and thanked Rita for the bold compliment.

"Rita," I said, "I want to order some flowers for Clara's service and another arrangement to be delivered to Corrina. She's staying at Lovedy's house. I know you can handle the local delivery but is the service too far for you to drive?"

"I'm goin' to the service, honey. I wanna be there for Lovedy and Corrina. It won't be a problem. Just tell me what you want, and I'll take care of it."

I tried to explain to Rita what I wanted to order for the service. I wanted a beautiful, vibrant standing spray of flowers that reminded me of Clara. Rita created a true work of art, a gorgeous, lively arrangement with yellow roses, blue hydrangeas, lavender, peach delphiniums, and red daisies.

For Corrina's arrangement, I knew exactly what to order. A wild and unruly arrangement of purple lilacs, purple sweet pea, purple clematis and purple scabiosa. My girl loved everything purple, and I wanted her to know that I loved her and everything and everyone she loved.

With that errand finished, Gabe and I took it easy the rest of the evening. We had dinner at a quaint little mountain bistro and picked up a bottle of wine to share back at the hotel. We sat outside on the balcony, enjoying the wine and the cool evening mountain air together.

The next morning, we got up with nothing on our agenda but to go to Lovedy's house and help in any way that we could. We headed downstairs to the hotel restaurant for an early continental breakfast. I had a muffin, banana, and a glass of water with my coffee. Gabe ate like it was his last meal. He devoured pancakes, waffles, sausage, bacon, scrambled eggs, oatmeal, fruit and three pieces of toast.

"Honestly, Gabe. Where do you put all of that food?"

"I run, so I can eat."

"And I don't eat, so I don't have to run."

"Besides, these hotels act like continental breakfasts are free. They aren't free. We paid for it in the ridiculous price of the room. So, I'm going to eat my share, damn it," he said with syrup dripping down his chin like a toddler.

"And everyone else's share too, apparently," I said, handing him a napkin. "Wrap it up, Acosta. I told Corrina we'd be there by nine and we still have to stop by the grocery store on the way."

"What are we getting at the grocery store?"

"I don't know yet."

"Then why are we going?"

"I'll call Corrina on the way and let you know."

"I'm confused. We're going to the grocery store, but you don't know what we need to buy?"

"That's right," I nodded. "Everyone always needs something from the grocery store. I just have to find out what she needs."

He shook his head at me and smiled. "And what if she doesn't answer the phone?"

"Then we'll buy wine and ice. Everyone needs wine and ice when a large group is gathered together at someone's house."

"Girls are weird."

"I'm ok with weird."

He was right. She didn't answer the phone. We went to the grocery store and bought the best bottle I could find in the wine and beer aisle and two bags of ice.

We arrived at Lovedy's house right on time. I knocked on the door but just heard a loud "Come in!"

The door was unlocked, so we walked in and found the whole family in the kitchen, huddled around the island, eating breakfast together. Multiple conversations were going on at the same time. It was loud and lively, and for a moment, I felt like we were crashing their eight o'clock pancake party. A sliver of envy flickered in my heart, threatening to disrupt the primary focus of why I was there. I shooed it away as everyone took turns hugging us and welcoming us into the kitchen and into their hearts.

Judge and Gabe immediately took off with David to slobber over his car collection in the massive garage. Because the ladies knew what was really important, we stayed in the kitchen to gossip with Vassy and Lauren about everything that happened at school, who they were dating and what their plans were for the summer.

"Mornin' August!" Lovedy said, out of nowhere.

"Morning everyone!" And there he was, Corrina's gorgeous son, walking into the kitchen in his tight white T-shirt and gym shorts, muscles straining to be noticed through the threads of the fabric, the morning sun picking up the golden flecks in his green eyes. His skin was hairless and dewy and reflected the light on his perfectly smooth, dark amber skin.

I picked up my phone to text Corrina. *'Holy Moses. You made that beautiful creature?!'*

'I did. Isn't he magnificent?' She texted back from across the island.

'I cannot be held responsible for my thoughts about your son.'

'He's gay. He has nothing for you.' She said, with a scowling emoji.

'I don't care. He's not gay in the thoughts I'm having at the moment,' I messaged back with a happy emoji that had hearts for eyes.

'Stop, or I'm going to read your texts to everyone at dinner.' And then she slammed the phone down on the island.

"Mom," Lauren said, "Were you and Aunt Fairy just texting each other?"

"I don't know. Were we texting, Fairy?" She looked at me with a dare in her eyes.

"I think we were just texting at the same time, Lauren." I lied.

"You going to show me later, Mom?" She asked.

"Yep. I sure will," Corrina said as she smiled at me.

"So what's the plan for today? How can I help?" I asked, trying desperately to change the subject.

"Well," Lovedy graciously answered, "we told Clara's family that we would bring some chairs and other things over to her niece's house for the repast. You could help transport some of the stuff in your Jeep and follow us there. It's about thirty minutes away."

"Sure thing. Are we getting the guys to help?"

"We can help load," August volunteered.

I turned around and saw August there with his arm around his husband, Miles, who had just entered the kitchen. He was every bit as beautiful as August. I had to text Corrina again.

'It has to be some kind of crime to have so much beauty in one relationship.'

'I'm not talking about this anymore,' she snapped back.

'You're no fun.'

'We're preparing for my grandmother's funeral. You want fun?'

'Are you shaming me? Is that shame you're throwing at me?'
'If the shoe fits your miniature toddler-sized foot, wear it.'

"Now I know you're texting each other!" Lauren exclaimed. "That's rude! It's like whispering! You two should know better!"

Corrina waited about two seconds and then quickly ratted me out. "Your Aunt Fairy thinks August and Miles are a gorgeous couple. She's been going on and on about it."

"Really, Corrina?" I snapped.

"Ok, folks," Lovedy said as she stepped in between us. "Let's load up the vehicles. August and Miles, you guys can grab the folding chairs in the garage. Vassy and Lauren, help me take out the trays of food that I have in the outside fridge. Corrina and Farrah, the paper products are already bagged up in the pantry. Once we get all of that loaded up, we should be ready to go."

We all did as we were told, and then we were on our way. August and Miles stayed back with the guys, Corrina rode with me, and her girls rode with Lovedy.

"So, now that we're alone, Corrina, how are you really doing?" I asked.

"I'm ok, I guess. It's weird though because although I miss her physical presence, now that she's gone, I feel her with me all the time. I don't know if that makes any sense, but I'm relishing the memories of her. Is there a phase of grief that's all about gratitude? Because that's what I've been feeling all week. I'm just so thankful God allowed us to connect, that she became a central part of my life. Honestly, I don't know what I would have done without her."

"That makes perfect sense to me. Oh, I made a playlist of her favorite music. You'll be happy to know that I listened to it all the way here. I don't know what any of the words really mean, but it's really pretty. Here, I'll turn it on for you."

She just shook her head and laughed at me, then she sang those gospel songs at the top of her lungs all the way to Clara's niece's house. We dropped off the chairs, food and paper products and spent a bit of time with three of Evie's daughters who were at the house.

JUNE 2022

From the looks of things, they were expecting a very large crowd. I was looking forward to the repast and talking to the people who loved Clara during the many chapters of her precious life.

We said our goodbyes and promised to go back to the house after the service. On the way home, Lovedy rode with me, and the girls rode with Corrina in the other car.

"How is your book comin' along, Farrah?" Lovedy asked.

"I haven't worked on it much lately. With everything that happened, I kind of put it on hold. I have most of the content recorded. I just need to finish writing it. There is one remaining piece that I need to talk to you about. Would you mind if I asked you now?"

"I know what you're going to ask me."

"You do?"

"I do. You want to know how I reconciled with my parents."

"Yes, how did you know?"

"Forgiveness is the most important part of any life story. It is inevitable that we will all be hurt or disappointed by those that we love and count on the most. We're all faulty, imperfect human beings and most of us are doing the best we can. When we make mistakes, we learn and evolve and become better people. That's the hope, anyway."

"So what made you finally forgive your parents?"

"I'm the nurse in the family, so I did what daughters do as they were aging. I took care of them. I ran them to all of their doctors' appointments and helped them make decisions about their medical care. I built a house right next door to them, so I was making their meals, handling their complaints, making sure they took their medications. And then eventually, Daddy's heart failed. He entered end-of-life care at home. We had nurses coming in to help but I stayed with them every day and night until he passed. It was a few days before his final breath that he confessed to me that he was wrong in how he treated Isaac and Jeremiah and even me. He said he gave in to the pressures of the town for his own financial security. He was afraid of what would happen to the dairy farm and our livelihood if he took a stand against white supremacy. It was the only time I had ever seen my Daddy cry. He kept begging me to forgive him."

"And did you? Forgive him?"

"Of course I did. I wished it had happened years ago, but I believe he died with peace in his heart. Mama passed just a few months later. She had her bedside confessions too. She was sorry for not being a stronger woman, for not standing up against Daddy's nonsense. Then she started saying some funny stuff."

"Like what?"

"She was talkin' about eatin' pancakes at a theme park with some of her girlfriends that had already passed on before her. She started having conversations with them about sewing patterns and how she played the piano better than Louisa and how much cuter the new pastor was compared to the last one. My mama was gossipin' until she died. And I was laughing so hard, it was a few minutes before I realized she was gone."

I didn't want to laugh out loud. Lovedy was talking about her deceased mother, and it would have been inappropriate. I held it in as long as I could. Thank goodness she started laughing, so I could laugh with her.

There was one more thing I wanted to tell her as I took a left onto her street. "Lovedy, I wanted to say thanks to you, personally, for sharing your story with me. I've been going through some stuff of my own lately. I'm not sure how everything is going to turn out, but you've been such an inspiration to me, along with Clara and Corrina. The way you've lived your life with intention and purpose and continued to carry on in the face of everything that happened to you and around you...I just..I just want to say thank you. It gives me hope that I can get past my own stuff. Thank you, Lovedy. Thank you so much."

"I'm glad to hear that, Farrah…" And then she paused for a few moments, as we sat in her driveway. She looked at me, like she was looking *through* me and then quietly said, "And if you only remember one thing I've ever told you, just remember that you're not alone. You're never alone." Then she reached over and squeezed my hand, the way a friend does, or a mother does when they see an unspoken need in the heart of someone else.

Lovedy grabbed her things and went back into the house.

I sat in my Jeep and cried.

FORTY-ONE
JUNE 2022

IT WAS A BIG DAY AND NO MATTER HOW IT TURNED OUT, I INTENDED TO give it my best. I owed Clara at least that much. I showered and went to the first floor of the hotel to eat a small breakfast with Gabe, then went back to our room to get ready. I put on the vintage Chanel skirt-suit I bought for the occasion. I wore simple stud earrings, a pendant necklace and put my hair back in a chignon at the nape of my neck. I pinned a matching fascinator to the right side of my head and slipped into my strappy pumps. A little waterproof mascara and a muted peach lipstick and I was ready. I took a step back and had a little talk with the girl in the mirror, "Keep it together. You can do this."

It was the perfect Saturday morning, and the air was graciously cool on my face. I could hear the leaves rustling in the breeze as we walked inside.

The usher gave us a program and walked us to the front of the sanctuary so we could view Clara's body and pay our last respects. Gabe took my hand as we walked down the aisle and approached the casket. Clara looked so beautiful, wearing a navy-blue dress with a cream lace collar, pearl earrings, her hair perfectly in place. She looked so at peace and in that moment, I hoped she was right. I

JUNE 2022

hoped she was on a permanent vacation for eternity with her Jeremiah, her Isaac and her Heavenly Father, all of whom she loved so very much.

I kissed my fingers and touched the side of the casket briefly, "Goodbye Ms. Clara. I feel so lucky to have known you."

Gabe took my hand as we walked across the front row, expressing our love and condolences to Clara's family. When I reached Corrina, we wrapped our arms around each other and held on for a while.

"I love you, my friend." I whispered in her ear.

"You're rockin' that suit, girl," she whispered back. "Remember, breathe in, hold, breathe out. I love you too," she gave me another squeeze before letting go.

We found our seats reserved in the second row behind the family. I looked at my surroundings and marveled at the beauty and history of that extraordinary place. I thought about the many stories it could tell and the secrets it knew that were now buried with its owners up on the grassy hill. The ceiling was soaring with beams that stretched from one end to the other. The furniture was beautifully crafted and there were flowers everywhere. Mums, roses, dahlias, even yellow sunflowers. There was a band playing lively music while we waited for everyone to pay their last respects and find their seats.

When it was time, the music stopped, and the room grew quiet. Then an enormous video screen was lowered against the wall at the back of the stage. Clara's beautiful face appeared. She was looking upward with a huge smile and those same dimples she gave to her baby boy all those years ago. As we watched photos and videos of her life fading in and out, Mahalia Jackson's "Take My Hand Precious Lord" started playing. Her vibrato floated out over the room, light and fluttery like the wings of a baby bird taking flight.

The pastor stood up and led the congregation in a prayer. I bowed my head with the rest as I listened to him thanking God for the blessing of Clara and for her steadfast faith. The crowd murmured "yes" and "amen" as the pastor continued in prayer. Then the choir stood up and sang "Bye and Bye." The whole congregation stood and joined in with them, clapping and raising their hands.

Music was a big part of the service and in between songs, Clara's nieces, nephews, and friends would take to the stage to talk to the congregation about how much they loved her. We listened to story after story about how she had impacted, inspired, and encouraged everyone that had crossed her path.

The pastor and other family members shared scriptures, but it was Corrina who stood and shared her grandmother's favorite passage, from the book of Isaiah. *"But those who hope in the Lord will renew their strength; they will fly up on wings like eagles; they will run and not be tired; they will walk and not be weary."*

Eventually, the pastor called my name. Gabe squeezed my hand as I stood and took a step out into the aisle.

As I ascended the stairs and turned to stand behind the pulpit, it tugged on my heart to see Corrina and her family sitting there together with Lovedy and David. I briefly thought about those lovely women and how they were so closely intertwined with the beautiful life we were celebrating that day. I looked across the sanctuary at the sea of faces. People were sitting shoulder to shoulder in the pews. I realized there wasn't an empty seat as I saw multitudes of people standing on the sides and in the back of the church. Clara packed the house, and it made me smile to think about all the love in the room. It was all for her.

I glanced at her tiny body lying in the open casket below me and then I took a deep breath in, held it for a moment and released it with all the anxiety I had been holding in my chest. I cleared my throat, lowered the microphone, and began.

"Good morning. My name is Farrah Langford-Acosta. I want to thank you for allowing me to speak this morning as we celebrate Clara's life together. I met Clara just a few short months ago. I had the opportunity to spend quite a bit of time just talking with her about her life, her achievements and the family, friends, and students that she loved so very much. I'm not exactly sure why she asked me to speak about her life at her homegoing, but in the time I spent with her, I quickly learned that if Clara asked me to do something, I should just do it and not ask any questions. So, here we are." The audience laughed quietly in agreement with slight shakes and nods of their heads.

"Clara Rose Carter was born on April 6, 1933. It was Easter Sunday when Joseph and Shirley Carter welcomed their first baby girl into the world. A year later, her baby sister, Evelyn, was born and their family was complete. Clara and "Evie" were the best of friends and did everything together. Growing up, they shared so many things. Their bed, their hopes and dreams, their secrets and their love for reading. Both Clara and Evie read the Bible in its entirety several times before they each turned ten years of age. It is no wonder she had memorized so many passages in her lifetime or as she would say, 'hid them in her heart.'

Clara and Jeremiah Carter, her loving husband, had known each other since birth. They were teenagers when Jeremiah asked for Clara's hand in marriage. Their love did not run in shallow streams. It was not one of convenience or obligation. Their commitment to honor and cherish one another was deep, wide, and ever-present as they navigated through the turbulent, winding river that was set before them. They were each other's life raft in the most difficult times, pulling one another up to safety when weariness would overcome them. Their mutual, persistent faith in a loving God was the foundation on which they built their life together.

On March 18, 1953, Isaac Eugene Carter was born. Clara often spoke of how happy Isaac was as a child. And oh, how Isaac loved his mother. In letters from Vietnam to loved ones at home, Isaac once described his mother as an angelic warrior, loving and fierce, the queen of his heart. And when he considered the vastness of space and time, he felt like the luckiest person on earth to have Clara Carter as his Mama.

The tragic and unjust death of a beloved son would be enough to crush anyone's spirit and Clara was no exception. Her strength, her enormous heart, even her abiding faith was no match for the grief that would rain down on her and Jeremiah on the days after they lost Isaac. It was a heavy and very cruel anguish that, on some days, would not even allow her to lift her head. And even in the midst of her intense rage at a God that failed to protect her only son, she never stopped believing. Her only solace was that she would see her beautiful Isaac again one day.

In 1982, at the age of forty-nine, Clara earned a bachelor's degree in history and her mother's dream became a reality. Clara taught at the local high school for sixteen years until she retired in 1998. She once described teaching as the hardest and most rewarding work she had ever done. She said it wasn't just about educating her students. It was seeing and listening to the students, watching their hearts expand and their minds grow as they were evolving into what would become our nation's future. And her students, many of which I'm sure are here today, loved Mrs. Carter. To those of you who were thoughtful enough to write a letter to Ms. Clara, you should know she kept it in a box for the rest of her days. The box had a label on the front that said, "My kids."

And then one day in the spring of 1988, Clara met her granddaughter, Corrina Lane Bannerman. Clara described that moment as the sweetest surprise of her life. And she described her relationship with Corrina as oxygen, breathing life back into her weary soul. It was an immediate and intense bond, built from history and bloodlines and most importantly, unconditional love.

On June 6, 1992, Clara's beloved Jeremiah very abruptly left this earth and went to his heavenly home. Once again, Clara was thrown into the depths of grief and despair. In a letter to her sister, Evie, she described her grief as a jealous rage. Her anger was rooted in the reality that she was left here while her husband and son were together in heaven.

After Jeremiah passed away, Clara sold their home and moved into a small apartment. She invested the earnings from the sale of their house to start the Isaac Eugene Carter Scholarship fund. To date, that investment has provided financial aid in the form of partial scholarships to nine minority, widowed mothers seeking to further their education.

Clara loved this church and she thought of it as her spiritual home. She once told me that the fellowship and support that she experienced in this place was her saving grace ever since she was a small child. She could not have imagined a life without it and without all of you, her spiritual brothers and sisters.

In closing and with Clara's permission, I would like to share a passage from one of her journals. The setting was in September of 2018. She has just returned from celebrating the home going of her baby sister, Evie. And I quote:

'As I sat there looking at my baby sister sleeping so peacefully, I was filled with so many emotions. I missed her already, but I also felt joy. She was no longer suffering. There was no more pain. No more tears. After such a prolonged battle, she was finally resting in the arms of Jesus. These days, I think a lot about this long life that I have lived, and I know that soon, it will be my turn. There has been so much joy, so much sorrow and sometimes those experiences have happened all at once.

Life is so sacred, such a precious gift. So many folks have expectations that life should always feel happy, that this experience is only meant to be joyous and yet looking back it was during the hardest times that I learned my greatest lessons. The more my faith was challenged, the deeper and stronger its roots grew into the ground.

So many people focus on what they can take from this life instead of what they can give. They fight each other, they push back and push against, always vying to be first in line, to have the best, to have the most, to take what didn't belong to them in the first place. It breaks my heart that folks believe *things* will make them happy. The pursuit of happiness shouldn't be a pursuit at all, for everything any one of us ever needed has always been there, right in front of us.

I wish people could see that despite our geographical locations, our cultural differences, even the sins of our fathers, every single human on the planet was created in the image of a loving God. We are all the same and He has given us everything we need to live together, in peace and harmony. I daydream about a world where people have a heart for serving others and being kind to one another. Where the collective wellbeing of our planet and all its inhabitants becomes more important to each of us than ourselves. I daydream about a world where people are more like my sweet sister, Evie. Always doing good, even for those who hated her.

With every day that passes I am one step closer to finally going home. I can feel it drawing near and my heart is full of anticipation. For I know what waits for me on the other side. What is there is the same as what was meant for here. And in the end, it is the only thing that matters. From the beginning, the instructions were so easy, simple and profound and yet this one piece of infinite wisdom has been sadly ignored by a world that has become lost unto itself. *Love one another.'"*

I'd never seen a food spread like the one at Clara's repast. Every comfort food you can imagine was laid out on the enormous family dinner table. Mac and cheese, casseroles, pull-apart rolls, salads, baked ziti, chicken, deviled eggs, meatballs, funeral potatoes, coffee, sweet tea and every dessert you could imagine. There were chairs in every corner of the dining room and living room. The place was bustling, with lively chatter, music, dancing, and children playing. Pictures of Clara with her family and friends were scattered about and the video that was played in the sanctuary was showing on the television in the family room. It was truly a celebration. Clara would have loved every minute of it.

Lovedy and David, Corrina, Judge and their girls, even Rita and her husband were there. At one point, Rita tried to force her way into

JUNE 2022

the kitchen but was quickly booted out by Evie's daughters. She saw us laughing but didn't think it was very funny.

"What are y'all laughin' at? I was just tryin' to help!"

"Really, Rita?" Lovedy scolded. "This isn't The Doghouse. You're not the boss, here. Just park your butt in a chair and have some more meatloaf and potato salad."

"Your butt could use a little more meat and potatoes, Love. Have you tried that baked spaghetti? It's so good. I'm goin' back for seconds. Come with me!" She demanded, grabbing Lovedy's arm.

"Alright, alright," Lovedy relented, and they both walked back to the table, arm in arm.

David, Judge and Gabe were off in the corner, talking about cars and Lauren and Vassey were dancing with Evie's grandchildren. I looked around for Corrina but couldn't find her anywhere. I walked outside, around the house and found her sitting on the steps of the back porch.

"Hey, Corr. What are you doing out here?"

"Just enjoying the fresh air and watching the kids run around. Come and sit." She moved over and patted the step. I squatted down and took a seat beside her.

"How are you feeling about all of this?" I asked.

"They say funerals aren't for the dead. They're for the living. That's never been truer than it has been today. Clara's gone, she's with Jeremiah and Isaac and we're all here, without her. The food, the music, the memories, it's all for us. Not only to celebrate her life, but to remind us that life goes on. But it feels different, like the earth has shifted on its axis. The world doesn't look as beautiful, it doesn't feel as kind. I can only hope that another little Clara is running around somewhere, full of love, patience, and compassion."

"I only knew her for a few months, and I feel that too." I sighed.

"Your fascinator is crooked. Fix yourself," She smirked as she pulled it down even further.

"We were having a moment, here. Why do you always have to ruin it?" I laughed as I jabbed her in the side with my elbow.

"It lightens the mood. It helps my weary heart. Seriously, let me fix you. You look ridiculous." She laughed as she adjusted the pins holding it in place.

"I loved seeing all of the people at Clara's service," I said. "You know, I've often thought about my own funeral and wondered if anyone, besides you and Gabe, would show up."

"Vassy and Lauren would probably come too. But that's it. No one else. There, that looks much better," she smiled with approval.

"After getting to know Clara, and seeing all the people who loved her, I'm thinking I should have been a kinder person in my first fifty years." I sighed again.

"We could all be kinder, Farrah. That's something I've had to work on in my own life. I get so busy with work, family, chores, and everything else that comes with being an adult. Sometimes I forget about the small but significant things that can make someone's day a little brighter. A smile, opening a door, a simple compliment, those things matter... They make a difference."

"Yeah, but if we were both really nice people, would we even be friends?"

"Probably not. It was your brashness and your sarcasm that I found to be so charming that day I met you in the café at the hospital. I knew instantly that we would be friends."

"Really? Not me. I thought about it, but you were so freakishly tall, all I could see was a lifetime of awkward pictures. But you kept showing up to lunch and paying for it, so how could I refuse?"

"And my first thought was that your mother should have given you some growth hormones. When I stood behind you in the café line that day, I thought, 'I wonder why this kid is skipping school.'"

I smacked her on the thigh, "You always have to one-up me, don't you!"

We sat there on the steps at her grandmother's repast, reliving the stories of our friendship and laughing together. Corrina was right. The world felt different without Clara, but there was hope for the future and maybe, just maybe, Evie and Clara passed on their love and compassion to Corrina's girls or to one of Evie's great-grandchildren who were running around in the backyard, playing, and laughing in front of us. Maybe, just maybe, there would be other Claras in the world to make it a more beautiful and kinder place one day.

FORTY-TWO
2020

The holiday season prior to Covid was a lonely one. Gabe was called out to a homicide on Christmas Eve and didn't return home until late in the evening on Christmas Day. I celebrated at Corrina's house, determined to enjoy my time with my best friend and her family, regardless of my own circumstances. As usual, I overdid it and showed up with my car packed to the gills with gifts and stockings, a huge ham and every kind of pie you could imagine.

The new year was no different. Judge and Corrina invited us to go out to dinner with them and then over to their house to drink champagne and watch the ball drop.

We had just been seated at the restaurant when Gabe's phone started ringing with another homicide that required his attention. As he stood up from the table, he apologized over and over to all of us. Judge stood up with him, patted him on the shoulder and said, "No problem, man. You be safe out there."

Gabe bent down to kiss me goodbye, and I gave him a very cold cheek, closing my eyes to keep the tears from flowing. I was resentful and angry because his job had become more important than our life together.

As I sat at the table across from Judge and Corrina, fiddling with my food and drinking too much wine, I thought the only thing worse than being alone was being in a relationship and *still* feeling lonely.

Not being in any condition to drive, Judge and Corrina took me to their house. We drank champagne together and watched the ball drop at midnight. I borrowed a t-shirt and shorts from Vassy, curled up in the corner of Corrina's massive couch and fell asleep.

I woke up early to the sounds and smells of breakfast in the kitchen. The girls were up and the whole family was bustling about, making eggs and pancakes, pouring juice and coffee and talking about their hopes and expectations of what the new year would bring.

I snuck into the bathroom and put my A-line black dress on that I had worn the night before. I washed my face and scrubbed away the black streaks of makeup that had found their way down my cheeks. I brushed my teeth with my finger and pulled my hair back in a knot. I slipped into my five-inch spool heels and sat on the toilet to tie the straps. And then I went back into the kitchen and asked for a ride back to my car.

"Why don't you sit for a minute and have a bite to eat?" Corrina made it sound more like a question than a demand, but I knew by the tone in her voice that I didn't really have a choice in the matter.

"I don't really feel like eating," which wasn't a lie. I was hungover and nauseous, and I just wanted to get home.

"Sit," she ordered as she pointed to a barstool behind the island. "I'll make you a rebound shake."

I sat down as instructed and watched as she pulled out the blender and mixed mangos, bananas, avocados, spinach, ginger and coconut water. She poured it into a tall glass and popped a straw into it before handing it to me from across the kitchen island. "Drink up, sister," she winked at me.

I sipped my shake while I listened to Vassy and Lauren talk with

Judge about their plans for the day. They were going to a flag football game later that morning at the nearby park before returning home to watch the bowl games on TV.

Corrina was staying home to begin preparing her traditional New Years feast of black-eyed peas and greens with ham hocks, and her delicious warm cornbread. On any other day, I would have hung around and harassed her while she was cooking but all I wanted to do was go home, take a shower and crawl under the covers.

It was noon by the time I made it home. I immediately jumped in the shower and tried to scrub away the scent of alcohol that seemed to permeate from my skin and hair. I brushed, rinsed and flossed my teeth. I moisturized my entire body with sesame oil. I carefully layered a leave-in conditioner in between the strands of my wavy hair. I put on one of Gabe's huge undershirts and crawled under the covers. But sleep wouldn't come.

I turned on the TV in the bedroom and put an old movie on that I knew by heart. I turned the volume down low and closed my eyes and watched it by memory, behind my eyelids. I tried everything to avoid the thoughts and chatter in my brain. *It's New Year's Day and you're all by yourself. Why does your husband care more about his job than he does about you? Your marriage is circling the drain, girl, and you'd better do something about it. Do you even want to be married anymore? Is it worth the heartache and the loneliness? If this is all there is, maybe being alone is actually better. Maybe you should leave before he leaves you. Maybe he just doesn't love you anymore. Is it possible he is seeing someone else? Maybe you should check his emails and text messages.*

And then, in an instant, I bounded out of bed and walked towards one of the spare rooms that was also our home office. I stood in the doorway, staring at his computer. Never once, in our relationship, had I looked at his phone, checked his emails, or rummaged through his files. It never even crossed my mind. With all of the stress and anxiety I had experienced in my lifetime, Gabe's faithfulness to me and our relationship had never been a question or cause for concern.

Until now.

My heart was pounding as I sat in front of his computer. Once I opened his email, there was no going back. I contemplated walking away. What was the point of this? Would I find something? Or would I feel foolish when I found out nothing was there? I would never be able to forget this moment when I violated his privacy. Was it worth it?

And then my finger clicked the cursor on the email icon and the decision was made. His email inbox was open, in front of me and it was a mess. At least ten thousand emails, mostly marketing emails about cars, some fantasy football emails, others were about products for law enforcement officers and members of the military. I scrolled at quickly as I could. More emails about healthcare, workout routines, and dogs that were available for adoption. And then I saw it.

Her name was Christina. The email was titled, '*How are you?*' It was *unread*.

My hand was trembling as the cursor hovered over the email. My brain started thinking steps ahead like I was in a chess match. If I read it, I would have to delete it, and then I would have to delete it again from the digital trash bin. *Open it*, Eris said. *Open it now*. And then my trembling hand did what I did not want it to do.

I read the email, then I read it again. It was warm and friendly. It was personal and familiar, but it didn't have the tone of a lover. It sounded like an email from an old friend. What didn't sit right with me was that I had never heard of this person. Who was she? Who was she to my husband? And why hadn't he said anything about her?

I was never one tell my husband that he couldn't have female friends. Neither one of us had ever felt threatened by friendships with the opposite sex. And who was I to say anything? Most of my friends for my entire life had been boys and men and Gabe never challenged me on it.

But this felt different. Rather than scroll through the rest of the ten thousand emails, I decided that what I really wanted to know, I could find in the "sent" folder. I wanted to see what he had written *to her*.

It was more of the same friendly banter, warmth and compassion. It was obvious he cared about this woman, but the context seemed to be just friendship. He asked about her children. He showed empathy because her back had been hurting. He suggested she take a warm bath with Epsom salts. He gave her suggestions on movies to watch and talked about new songs that he heard on the radio.

I continued looking but found nothing new, or anything incriminating. And yet, it didn't feel right. Nothing was solved, I had more questions than answers. I was frustrated.

I closed his email and put his computer in sleep mode like I found it. I put the mouse in the exact same position on the mouse pad and then made sure the office chair was pressed up against the desk. I walked backwards out of the room, making sure I didn't leave any evidence at the scene of the violation of trust.

I cruised by the kitchen to get a glass of water before returning to the bedroom. Then I crawled back under the covers and laid there, looking at the ceiling, thinking about what I was going to do with this new information about my husband's friend. I decided there was nothing that I *could* do. I found no evidence of infidelity, physical or emotional, but Eris seemed to disagree with me. She played out a million scenarios in my mind. *What if they weren't just old friends? What if they just met and things were just heating up? Was he lonely too? Was he looking for something that I wasn't giving him? Was I too hard on him? Was I too set in my ways? Did I not care enough about his needs? Was my lifelong determination to protect my heart going to be the downfall of my marriage?*

I tried to sleep, but the thoughts kept circling around and around in my mind.

2020

The new year brought us Covid. And Covid brought in a whole new level of anxiety and stress. By March, our entire company began working from home, which brought a whole new set of challenges in how we would balance the needs of our employees and clients and still keep our business afloat.

Gabe, being an essential employee, was out and about in public settings every day. He was religious about wearing a mask and sanitizing his hands but so much was unknown. Each time he would come home from work, he would strip down in the laundry room and immediately put his clothes in the washing machine or seal them in a bag to take to the dry cleaners. Then he would shower and brush his teeth, rinsing his mouth multiple times with mouthwash to flush out the germs.

I, on the other hand, didn't leave the house at all. Anything we needed I had delivered. Groceries and household goods would be left on our front porch. I became friends with our regular shopper through muffled conversations we shared on either side of my front door.

I became very close with my neighbors during that quarantine period. There were many evenings when we would have a "happy hour," with the residents pulling their portable chairs to the end of the driveways doing virtual "cheers" and yelling stories across the street.

I missed my Daddy, Corrina, Judge and the girls. We made video calls almost every day, but it wasn't the same. Corrina, like Gabe, was an essential employee. She would call me, exhausted at the end of a double shift at the hospital, crying from the death and despair that was coming at her in wave after wave.

I handled the pandemic the only way I knew how. I created spreadsheets and started tracking infection and death rates, state by state. It was maddening but I was obsessed with the data and the trends. And for all of the sadness and stress and anxiety that came with the pandemic, there was a silver lining, at least in my house. It was the year that Gabe and I found each other again.

With the quarantine in effect, crime went way down, and my husband began working a normal number of hours per week. He was sleeping through the night again and I would find him smiling in the mornings. He started acting like his charming, loving, funny self again.

Not being able to travel to visit clients or go into the office every day or spend time with my friends or visit my father, Gabe became my everything. And in the midst of the madness, we began to laugh together again. Our affection for each other blossomed like a flower in the middle of a dark, dense forest. It was beautiful and very unexpected. The positive changes we experienced could have been forced by the pandemic, but it didn't matter to us. We were focused on teamwork and survival and for a time, we were able to set aside our issues and just love each other.

It was during the pandemic that Gabe first brought up the idea of moving. At first, I thought he was crazy. I had no intention of leaving my father and all of my friends in Lexington. It just didn't make any sense. But as time wore on and the pandemic continued, any sense of normalcy began to feel like a thing of the past. I was beginning to doubt that my work life would every return to normal or that I wouldn't be afraid of infecting my dad every time I stopped by to see him.

We began taking little trips on the weekends, staying in vacation rentals all over the southeastern United States. By the time we made a decision, we knew almost every town in the Carolinas, Georgia and Tennessee.

It was Tennessee that took our breath away. We found a sweet little town with the most breathtaking views and decided to make it our new home.

And once again, we had a new project to bond us together and keep us focused on the future. Gabe retired and we threw a massive

2020

party, inviting all of our friends to celebrate my hero. And that's when we told all of them that we were on to our next adventure. That's also when I started second-guessing our decision.

We put our house on the market and it sold for top dollar in about two weeks. The next thing I knew, we were packing up our life and my mind was filled with regret. But with every question and every tear, I reminded myself of all the sacrifices Gabe had made for me. And I decided that no matter how much I wanted to stay, I had to do this for him, for us.

I finally compromised, and it was either a selfless act or the biggest lie I had ever told.

FORTY-THREE
JUNE 2023

"Go forth, Christian soul, from this world in the name of God the almighty Father, who created you, in the name of Jesus Christ, Son of the living God, who suffered for you, in the name of the Holy Spirit, who was poured out upon you, go forth, faithful Christian. May you live in peace this day, may your home be with God in Zion, with Mary, the Virgin Mother of God, with Joseph and all the Angels and Saints."

I watched from the sofa, as the priest prayed over my mother. I couldn't relate to the prayer and didn't understand the meaning or significance of everything he was saying but what I felt was the finality, the end of my mother drawing even closer. His voice was quiet and peaceful and there, alone on the couch, my whole being unraveled under the weight of his words.

I just turned fifty-three years old and while I knew my parents wouldn't live forever, I wasn't ready for this to be happening now. There was so much more to do, more conversations that needed to be had. I wanted to ask her about my twin sister, and if she truly blamed me for her death. I wanted to know if that was the reason she was so distant and critical during my childhood, why I wasn't enough to make her happy. Did she ever really love Dad? Did she ever really love me? So many questions, to which I would never have the answers. It wasn't like I didn't have an opportunity over the years to ask her. I just put it off, always thinking I would have more time, a better time.

The priest finished praying for my mother and offered to pray with me. I shook my head in refusal but thanked him for offering.

As he was leaving, Seth came into the room and said, "Farrah, you have a visitor."

I stood and wiped my face with my hands just as Jake walked into the room.

I was surprised to see him. We hadn't really spent much time together. A few times when I stayed at the bungalow, he came over to check on me or to fix something in the house that wasn't working properly. One evening, he brought over some cold beers, and we sat on the front porch and talked about my mother's illness.

I stood there frozen, not sure what to say.

He took two hesitant steps towards me, "Hi..uh..I don't know really why I'm here. I… uh… just didn't want you to be alone."

I was alone, so very alone. I was desperate and stricken with grief. Those were my reasons for falling into his arms and staying there, in his embrace, for a long time in front of my dying mother. At least that is what I told myself.

He picked up a bag that he had placed on the floor and put it on top of the overbed table. "I brought you some food. I'm guessing you haven't had a meal since you arrived."

"That's very thoughtful of you, Jake. Thanks for the fruit basket and the note, too. You've been so kind to me through this whole ordeal." I found myself looking into his eyes. They were the same color as the ocean and just as intimidating in a way that made me feel shy. The waves of his salt and pepper hair barely touched the back of his shirt collar. His legs were smooth and tan extending out from the bottom of his khaki shorts.

"Let me go grab a couple of water bottles. I'll be right back," his leather flip flops were clacking as he walked away, leaving the room smelling of his woodsy, musky cologne.

When he returned, we sat down and shared some grilled chicken, pasta and salad as my mother continued with her sporadic, short breaths.

It was awkward and it felt wrong in a way. He was just trying to be kind, but part of me wanted him to leave. The other part of me didn't want to be alone.

My phone started buzzing from deep inside my oversized bag. I stuck my arm in and felt around until I found it, glad to be busy doing something else besides sitting in awkward silence with my handsome stranger-friend, listening to my mother's lungs searching for air.

I missed the call and then realized I had four missed calls—two from Gabe, one from Corrina and one from Lovedy.

Jake stood up, started collecting the trash from our dinner and then generously said, "I better get going. Uh… if you need anything, don't hesitate to reach out. I'm just around the corner."

"Yes, um… Thank you again for everything," I said, trying not to look in his eyes.

"Sure. Take care, Farrah," he waved as he took two steps backwards before turning around and walking out the door, flip-flops still clacking.

I called Gabe first, but he didn't answer. I left him a voicemail and gave him an update on my mother. I called Corrina and Lovedy too but neither of them answered either, which annoyed me.

The room was quiet again as I laid down on the sofa and tried to rest. My body wanted to sleep but my mind wanted to stay awake for her. And then my phone buzzed again.

"Hi Daddy," I whispered.

"Hi Sunshine. How are you doing?"

"I'm ok. I'm with Mom, just laying down on the sofa."

"How is she?"

"She's getting close. It won't be long, now."

"I'm sorry I can't be there with you, honey. Is Gabe there?"

"No. He's back home, taking care of Ouizer and Truvy. I told him not to come yet and that I would call him after I got settled in and updated on her condition."

"So, you're there by yourself?" He asked, with concern in his voice.

"I'm ok, Daddy" I lied. "Don't worry about me."

"I'll always worry about you. That's my job."

"Hey, Daddy?"

"Yes?"

"I know I haven't told you this enough over the years..but thank you for loving me. You've been a great father..I just wanted you to know that."

"You've made it easy, Sunshine. Being your dad has been the best part of my life."

"I love you."

"Love you too, so much. Take care of yourself and keep me updated."

"I will. Bye, Daddy."

"Bye, Sunshine."

I sat outside on the little patio, watching as the sun dipped down over the water. The remaining light scattered about in bursts of luminous pinks, purples and yellows as it clung to the aerosols and particles floating in the air. It was still humid, but as I laid my head back on the chair, a gentle breeze brought some relief and cooled the beads of sweat that had collected on my forehead and chest. I closed my eyes and practiced my breathing exercises. In, two, three, four. Hold, two, three, four, five, six, seven. Exhale, two, three, four, five, six, seven, eight. And there, on the back patio of my mother's room at the Crystal Waters Hospice Center, I fell asleep with the sun.

"Farrah!" I heard her calling my name again, somewhere deep in the recesses of my mind. Still half asleep, I went inside to check on her.

"Mom? Do you need me?" I sat in the chair by the bedside. *Please open your eyes and tell me that you need me, that you've always needed me,* I thought to myself.

She took a shallow breath as I took her hand. And I waited there, for the next breath that never came. There was no noise, no jolts or gasps—just silence, as her essence vanished from this earth. My mother was gone and as I continued to hold her hand, all I felt was that chasm, now so infinite, between myself and this deceased woman that gave me life.

I stayed there for a few moments, in the silence, reflecting on the memories that began bombarding my brain, crashing down on me like the waves just outside the door. The way she would always moisturize her hands after washing them, the way she hummed when making my breakfast. What was that song? Oh yes, it was "The Long and Winding Road" by the Beatles. I remembered how she would always keep the dining room table set as if we were expecting guests that rarely arrived. I could still smell the expensive perfume that Daddy bought her and recalled how she would only wear it on special occasions. Every year on their anniversary and Christmas Eve, our entire house smelled like magnolias and bergamot oranges.

I wasn't sure what the rules were about how long one was supposed to stay with the deceased body, so I stayed until I just couldn't do it any longer.

I stepped out into the hallway and kept my head down until I reached the lobby, looking for a nurse, for anyone that could help me with the next part.

Once I crossed the tile onto the wood floor, I looked up and immediately stopped walking. There, in the doorway, stood my husband and Corrina.

They both walked towards me and wrapped their arms around me at the same time, suffocating me with their affection.

"Seriously, you two" I muffled my words into their chests, "I can't breathe. I need air."

"How are you? Have you eaten? How's your mom?" Gabe peppered me with questions.

"I'm ok. Yes, I've eaten. Mom is gone, as of about an hour ago." I looked down at the floor, not wanting to look him in the eye for some reason.

"Lo siento mucho. Ven aqui, hermosa," he pulled me into his arms again. I was rigid in his embrace, at first, afraid to release all that was bottled inside my heart. But standing there in the lobby, in my husband's arms, I remembered what Faith said to Lovedy. *When grief knocks at your door, invite it in. Surrender to it, feel all of it.*

So that's what I did. I held onto him tightly as I heard the groans and anguish rushing out of my body. My mother was gone. She was no more.

It was late at night when the coroner finally arrived. Stupid thoughts kept invading my brain as I watched him pick up my mother's body and place her in the bag. *Please don't drop her. She can't breathe if you zip it up. Please make sure she is really dead before you incinerate her.* It didn't make any sense. None of it made it any sense.

Once she was gone, Gabe and Corrina took me back to the bungalow. I invited Corrina to stay in the extra bedroom and immediately went to take a shower. As the water ran down my body, I looked at my hands, my arms, my skin, and veins. I was alive and it felt strange, as if I were aware, for the first time, of every living cell in my being. I thought of my mother when she was my age, living it up in Ybor City with her family and friends, without her daughter and husband. And now, just twenty years later, she was gone. Life was fleeting and the thought of my own mortality washed over me.

FORTY-FOUR
JUNE 2023

THE NEXT MORNING, CORRINA WENT OUT TO THE GROCERY STORE AND brought back everything anyone could possibly want for breakfast. I wandered out of the bedroom with puffy eyes and a stuffy nose and was greeted by a feast spread out on the dining room table. Pancakes, bacon, sausage, eggs, blueberry muffins, sliced fruit from the basket, Greek yogurt, granola, orange juice and freshly brewed coffee.

"I know you probably haven't eaten a decent meal since you got here. I don't know if you want to eat but I'm famished," she exclaimed while popping grapes into her mouth.

"You are your mother's daughter," I mumbled as I sat down next to Gabe and rubbed my eyes, not quite ready for the day to begin.

"Buenos dias, hermosa," Gabe said as he poured a cup of coffee and set it down in front of me, kissing me on the top of my head.

"Mmmm..." Corrina moaned. "If you were my husband, I'd make you speak Spanish all the time."

Gabe and I just looked at her, neither one of us smiling.

"That wasn't funny? I was the only one that thought it was funny?" She asked.

We just shook our heads.

JUNE 2023

"Sorry. Too soon, I guess."

"I should have Mom's ashes back in seven to ten days," I told them while I continued to rub my eyes. "I want to have a small, informal service for her by the water. She didn't express any wishes except that her remains be spread in the ocean. Today, I want to go by her niece's house and let them know that she passed. I'll stop by the office at her retirement community and let them know as well. I don't know if anyone will want to come to pay their respects…I guess we'll see."

"Do you want some company?" Corrina asked.

"Sure, that would be nice."

Gabe looked at me, reading my face. "You want some girl time?"

I nodded. "Would that be ok?"

He reached over and grabbed my hand. "Whatever you need, mi amor."

The brims of my eyes began to burn, his kindness touching my battered heart.

Corrina and I left the bungalow just before noon. It was another hot and muggy day, and the storm clouds were already gathering in the distance.

I headed down Coronado Drive towards the roundabout and turned right onto SR 60. Driving across the bridge, I looked out onto the water and thought how beautiful it was and for a brief moment, understood why my mother loved it there.

"Its so pretty, here," Corrina commented, reading my mind.

"I was just thinking the same thing. I can't tolerate the heat, but the scenery is gorgeous."

"Hey, who is Jake?"

"What?" I was confused and surprised by her question. "How do you know about Jake?"

"I don't. I just saw the card by the fruit basket this morning…"

"Oh...umm...Jake is the guy that owns the bungalow. We've gotten to know each other a little bit since I've been staying there so often."

"Seems like a really nice guy. What's his story?"

"I don't know, really. He doesn't talk about himself much."

"I see," she paused and then, "How old is he?"

"I don't know that either. I'd guess he's in his early fifties, around our age."

"Married?"

"I don't know."

"Does he wear a ring?"

"I haven't noticed." *Or did I?* "Geez Corrina. What's with all the questions about Jake?" I asked, wanting to get off the topic that was making me nervous and uncomfortable.

"Just making some conversation, Farrah. Some guy sent a fruit basket to my best friend who was staying at a bungalow in a strange town by herself, grieving the imminent loss of her mother. I want to know who he is, and that you're safe."

"I'm safe, Corrina. Jake is a nice guy. He came around a few times to fix some things at the bungalow and one evening, a couple of months ago, he stopped by with some cold beers and we chatted about Mom's illness."

"Ok, that's all then?"

"Yes, that's all. Oh, and yesterday evening, he showed up at the hospice center and brought me dinner."

"That was nice of him. How did he know you were there?"

"Because when I'm on Clearwater beach, I'm either at the bungalow or at the Hospice Center. It's not like I'm out strolling by the water, watching the seagulls, and taking in the sunsets, Corrina. I haven't been coming down here on vacation."

"Sorry," she muttered.

"It's fine. I have so many friends that are guys and you've never asked me this many questions about *them*. Why is it different with this one?"

JUNE 2023

"I don't know. Probably because you're away from home, in a vulnerable state. I feel worried for some reason."

"Corrina, I'm fine. It's all good, I promise. I'm an adult and I'm comfortable around men. If a woman owned the bungalow and was sending me a fruit basket and bringing me dinner, I would ask for your advice." I leaned over and patted her on the leg. "Thanks for worrying about me, though. You're a good friend."

Hoping to avoid the need for anymore conversation about Jake, I turned the music up as we crossed the ten-mile Courtney Campbell Causeway that connects Clearwater to Tampa. I took the exit for I-275 N and hopped on I-4 for a brief moment before arriving in the Ybor City Historic District.

"You hungry? We could stop for a bite to eat before we get to my cousin's house," I offered.

"I can always eat," Corrina agreed. "But are *you* hungry? Or are you just procrastinating?"

I smiled at my friend who knew me so well. "Yeah, I feel the need to sit and relax for a bit," I admitted. "I don't have a relationship with my cousins. They are family, but Mom and I were estranged for so many years. We just started talking again about a year before she got sick again. And while I barely knew my Aunt Maria, I've never had the opportunity to meet her children. This could be very weird."

"Let's go procrastinate over some food, then."

We popped into a Cuban café on the 7th Avenue corridor and munched on Cuban sandwiches and Yuka fries, while sipping on refreshing, cool mojitos.

"So, what's your plan," Corrina probed, "Do you have a plan? What are you going to say when you meet them?"

"Hi, I'm Farrah, Mercedes' daughter. She's died yesterday."

"Farrah..."

"I'm just kidding. I don't know exactly what I'm going to say. I don't have a plan, which usually fills me with anxiety. But I'm so emotionally spent, I think I'm simply good with winging it. Besides, I have you here to fill in any awkward silences."

"I've got your back, Farrah. It will all work out. Are you ready to go?"

"Yes, I think so…"

We pulled up to a row of houses built in the early twentieth century. My cousin's house was painted a cheery yellow with terracotta-stained stairs ascending to a large, covered porch. There were white rockers on the porch that hosted views of the little rock garden full of pink and magenta Bougainvillea.

I knocked gently on the red front door and wiped my sweaty palms on the sides of my shorts. Twenty seconds went by before I heard footsteps. I glanced at Corrina, "Here we go, my friend."

A woman opened the door, and I could have sworn it was my Aunt Maria, twenty-some years ago. She was the perfect likeness to her.

"Hola, can I help you?"

"Hi. I'm Farrah. I'm Mercedes' daughter. I'm looking for Nora. Is she home?"

"You are Mercedes' daughter?" Her face broke out in a huge smile.

"Yes, I am."

She didn't say anything else. Instead, she stepped out on the porch, wrapped her arms around me and immediately started to cry.

I hugged her back and turned my head to the left where Corrina was standing, "Help me" I mouthed.

She shrugged her shoulders, not knowing what to do or how to save me.

The woman took a step back then introduced herself, "I am Nora!" she exclaimed as she patted her chest with her hand. "Maria's daughter! It is so good to finally meet you!"

She embraced me again, still crying, shoulders shaking.

I patted her back, trying to comfort her in some awkward way while ignoring the kink in my neck from her tight squeeze. "It is so nice to meet you, as well."

"Come in! Come in!" She stepped to the side and waved her arm into the living area.

"Thank you, Nora. Uh..this is my friend, Corrina."

Nora caught Corrina off guard as she instantly stepped towards her and wrapped her arms about her waist. The height difference was a good twelve inches, and I couldn't help but laugh seeing Nora's face buried in my friend's chest.

"You are very beautiful and very tall!" Nora laughed with me, obviously a little embarrassed by the close and intimate contact.

We sat in Nora's living room and talked for hours over mint tea and shortbread cookies. I told her about my mother's passing and she gave me yet another heartfelt embrace.

She filled me in on the years my mother had spent in Tampa Bay, how she lived with her parents until they died and then moved in with Maria.

The sisters started a catering business and eventually opened a café in West Tampa. She talked about how much my mother loved to sing and how they would go to dinner and karaoke every year on her birthday.

When Maria passed away unexpectedly in 2017, Nora said my mother was heartbroken but eventually became like Nora's mother. She said her sister, Elise, felt the same way about her. She went on and on about how loving my mother was towards both of them, how she cooked for them and always threw the best birthday bashes for their families. She talked about how the children always loved to sleep over at Tia Mercedes' house. *Doted?* I thought to myself. *When did my mother ever dote on anyone?* And then I imagined her brushing her great-niece' hair away from her face while she was tucking her into bed saying, "Buenas noches, cumpleañera. Dulces sueños."

I learned so much that I didn't know about my own mother, and it was odd, at times, listening to Nora talk about this woman that sounded so much like a stranger. But what struck me the most was the love and adoration that Nora obviously felt for her. I smiled as she reflected on the memories of her beloved aunt but inside my heart was breaking because I never knew this wonderful woman she described—the one that had a catering business and loved to sing karaoke.

Nora and I exchanged phone numbers and I promised to call her when I decided on a date for the beachside service. She walked us outside and hugged us both again before Corrina and I hopped in the four-wheel furnace to drive back to Clearwater.

The retirement community was a maintenance-free mobile home park with lush landscaping, soaring palm trees, two swimming pools, shuffleboard, and tennis courts. My mother had been renting one of the homes there before she moved into the hospice center. As we drove slowly through the community, I thought about Clara when I visited her in the assisted living facility and wondered if my mother loved this community as much as Clara loved hers.

"Wow, this is pretty nice," Corrina commented. "I wouldn't mind living in a place like this when I retire."

"It's too hot, Corrina. We're not moving here!" I insisted.

"Oh, you're going to live with me when I retire?" She laughed at my assumption.

"No... Well maybe. But you're not going to live in Florida while I stay in Tennessee, that's for sure. It's too far."

I parked in a visitor's spot in front of the community center, and we walked inside, thankful for the air conditioning that dried the sweat from our bodies after the short trek down the sidewalk.

There was yacht music coming out of the walls, and the place was decorated in an ocean theme. Large pink and blue starfish clung to a wide net that hung on the wall above the oversized leather couches.

A young woman looked up from her desk and smiled, "Have a seat, and help yourself to some water or cookies. There are also some booklets on the coffee table that explain all that our community has to offer. Take a look and I'll be with you in just a moment."

Corrina leaned over and whispered out of the side of her mouth, "I wonder if she thinks we want a tour or something. We don't look old enough to be living here, do we? This is a sixty-five and over community, Farrah. "

"Maybe she thinks we're looking for our parents or something" I whispered back, ventriloquist style.

"Hello," the young woman said as she walked towards us. "I'm Katie. How can I help you today? Are you interested in a tour?"

I stood to my feet and introduced myself, "Hi Katie. I'm Farrah and this is my friend, Corrina. My mother was a tenant in this community. Her name is Mercedes Langford." *Was I supposed to use past tense or present tense,* I thought to myself. Her death and my pain were so very fresh.

"Oh, yes. I know your mother. How is she doing?" Her young brow was crumpled in concern as she waited for my answer.

"That's why I stopped by," I didn't want to say the words again. It sounded strange coming out of my mouth, "To let you know that she passed away yesterday. I plan to have a small, informal service on the beach in about ten days or so. I thought maybe she might have some friends here that would want to come by and pay their respects? I wasn't sure…"

"Of course, yes," she reached out and touched my arm, "I'm so sorry for your loss. Your mother was always truly kind to me."

"Thank you," was all I could think of to say.

"I'll be sure to send out a communication to let our residents know about her passing. Would you like to give me a call when you have scheduled the service?"

"Yes, I will do that," I nodded, wondering again who this lady was that was so kind to her.

I took her number and we left to return to the bungalow. As I crossed the bridge towards Clearwater Beach, I felt resentment bubbling up from my gut. I didn't understand why my mother was so distant and critical of me but yet so kind and fun and loving towards everyone else. It was a huge disconnect, that chasm that I had always felt with her.

"Why the big sigh?" Farrah jerked me out of the rabbit hole I was mentally traveling down.

"I don't want to talk about it. I just want to get home and take a nap."

"Ok. I'm here for whatever, whenever. You know that."

"Yes, I know."

As soon I walked into the bungalow, I gave Gabe a hug and mumbled, "I'm so tired, I'm going to take a nap," and began walking towards the bedroom.

"Hey, wait a second," he grabbed my hand and gave it a slight tug, pulling me gently back towards him, "Can you talk for just a few minutes? I'd like to know how it went with your cousin. Did everything go ok?"

I could tell he needed time with me, but I just didn't feel like I had anything to give.

"It went fine. I met my cousin, Nora. She looked just like Aunt Maria and was extremely kind to me. You'll meet her at the service, I'm sure. I really need to go lay down now. Ok?"

I was irritated that I had to coax my husband into giving me what I needed. Time alone, I just needed some time by myself. Why couldn't he see that?

"Ok, I'll come lay down with you in a few minutes."

But I don't want you to lay down with me. I want you to leave me alone so I can grieve my mother's death in private, away from you and the rest of the world. I should have said it aloud, but I didn't have the energy or courage to tell him how I really felt and what I truly needed.

"Ok," I conceded.

I walked into the bedroom, collapsed on the bed, pulled the

covers back over my head and wept. When the anguish finally subsided, I laid there, just listening to the hum of the air-conditioning unit outside of the window, and counting the seconds in my breaths, until I fell asleep.

"Farrah," he whispered.

I felt him moving the hair that had fallen across my face. He began tucking it behind my ear as he continued to whisper my name.

I was annoyed. I had *just fallen asleep*. Why was he trying to wake me up?

"Farrah, you have a visitor."

Without opening my eyes, I mumbled, "Can you tell whoever it is, that I'm sleeping and to come back later?" *Who could it be*, I wondered to myself, still half asleep. *Who knows I'm here?*

"Sure, mi amor." Even his voice was irritating me.

He left, I'm guessing to do what I asked him to do, but I was awake at that point. I heard Corrina talking and two male voices coming from the front of the house. Curious, I got out of bed and went to the bathroom, brushed my teeth, and tied my hair in a messy bun at the nape of my neck. I stared in the mirror for a moment, marveling at how I seemed to have aged overnight. Under-eye bags were raging beneath my red-streaked eyes, my skin was dry and ashy. *Who cares*, I thought. *I'm mourning, not trying to win a beauty contest.*

I walked into the dining area and was surprised to see Jake sitting at the table, talking with Corrina and Gabe. I hesitated for a moment, wanting to run back into the bathroom to fix myself. Corrina and Gabe had already seen me at my worst, but I wasn't prepared for Jake to see me in the raw. And I'm not sure why I even cared.

"Hi Jake," I said, pretending like I was comfortable with the situation in front of me.

"Hi Farrah. I'm sorry to wake you. I just stopped by to see how you are doing."

"I'm doing ok. Thank you."

"Corrina told me about your mother. I'm so sorry to hear about her passing."

"Thank you." I realized I was awkwardly standing in the middle of the room and found a seat next to Corrina at the table.

"Jake is going to join us for dinner," Corrina announced, "I thought you'd prefer to stay in for dinner tonight and Jake knows the best pizza place in town that will deliver. Sound good?"

"Sure, that's fine," I gave her a look that only she would know. That kind of look that says, *what is happening here?*

"I picked up some wine yesterday when I went to the grocery store. Would anyone else like some?" Corrina offered.

"Yes," we all three answered simultaneously and with a little too much gusto.

"There's a wine bottle opener in the second drawer to the left. Here, I'll help you," Jake stood up and walked into the kitchen with Corrina. Meanwhile, I was ignoring Gabe's obvious stares. I didn't have the energy to answer the million and one questions that were certain to come my way.

FORTY-FIVE
JUNE 2023

About a week after my mother passed away, I went by the crematorium to pick up her ashes. They handed the remains of my mother to me in a cardboard box. I took the box, returned to my Jeep, and sat there for a few minutes with my thoughts about all that happened since she left us.

Corrina left the morning after our dinner with Jake because she needed to return to work, and Gabe left because we got into a huge argument that night after Jake left and I needed space.

I needed space from Gabe. I needed space to grieve. And I needed time to heal.

I realized that night that I would not be able to do what I needed to do with my husband around. I know he loves me, and I know that I love him, but his needs are different in life and in relationships. *We are vastly different human beings.* And while that worked for more than twenty years, it wasn't working for me now. And to be honest, while he is the same, steady, constant rock that he has always been, I'm the one who has changed.

When I retired from my corporate career, in hopes of following a

JUNE 2023

dream and discovering true meaning in my life, I found something that I didn't expect.

Without the demands from my job, my thoughts became stripped down. My mind was bare, my heart was raw, and I had the time to contemplate things like values and priorities. I spent time in therapy and learned when and how they originated. I was able to challenge my own system of beliefs and look at life and the world from a new and unfamiliar perspective. I was able to unravel my views about my own value from those of my mother's. Her life was not my life. Her experiences were not my experiences. Her opinions of me did not define me.

I continued seeing Dr. Walker for quite some time after Clara's funeral. It took many sessions to walk back on more than fifty years of building my belief system. It wasn't an easy thing to do, and we left no stone unturned. I explored my childhood relationships with adults and children, my apprehension about friendships with woman, my comfort with male friendships and also why I let my relationships only go so far. We examined my marriage from the first day and reasons behind my behaviors and decisions. We stripped down the iron dome I had built around my heart and exposed every secret I spent a lifetime trying to hide.

I spent so many years trying to control everything around me, but I wasn't really protecting anything or reducing the risk of being hurt, physically, mentally, or emotionally. I was just missing opportunities to experience joy and love and even friendships.

Spending time with Charlotte, Lovedy and Clara also helped me to see life in a different way. Even with all of the sorrow and tragedy each of those women experienced, they still put their hearts out there. And while they couldn't change the past, they somehow knew that joy would come in the morning. Maybe not the next morning but eventually, each one of them found a way to coexist with their incredible losses and embrace the good things that life still had in store for them.

MIXED

As I sat in the parking lot of the crematorium, thinking about my next steps, I picked up my cellphone and called Jake to ask him if he wanted to meet me for dinner and drinks. We met at a local beachside pub and ate grouper sandwiches and fries covered in ketchup and washed them down with draft beers in icy mugs.

It wasn't a date, at least that wasn't my true intention. I just liked the guy.

I liked his quiet, unassuming way and how he was kind and thoughtful without any expectations of reciprocity.

Over dinner I learned that, like me, he was a former corporate executive. After his divorce in his late forties, he decided to do something different with his life. He never had kids, and with nothing to hold him back, he moved to Florida, bought a few investment properties, and decided that living a quiet life on the water was what he really wanted for himself. And oh, how I admired his courage.

I told him about my book and how close I was to finishing it. I explained how long it took to find a publisher, how I had been going rounds with the editor, and that I had about a few weeks' worth of updates to do before I could submit my final work. I rambled about the road trip that I took with Corrina to see Charlotte and the time I spent with Lovedy and Clara. He listened quietly, with a smile that showed up every once in a while. I noticed the corners of his eyes would crinkle when he was amused by my storytelling.

There was something about him that made me feel hopeful and at peace. Some people drained my energy just by their mere presence, but not Jake. I always felt refreshed and renewed after seeing him. I didn't know what that meant, I'm not even sure I cared. All I knew is that I wanted him in my life.

We finished our meal and walked back slowly towards the bungalow, talking about insignificant things like the weather and all of the pets we've had in our lifetimes. It made me miss Ouizer and Truvy.

He walked me to the door, and we said goodnight after a quick, harmless hug.

But something shifted inside of me when I stepped inside and closed the door. I smelled his cologne on my cheek and my shoulder and all I wanted to do was open the door again and call his name. I wanted him to come inside and let me sit in the safety and peace of him, again.

We met two more times for dinner and drinks that week and then the day came for my mother's service.

Gabe arrived the night before the service. I picked him up at the airport and we drove back to the bungalow, making small conversation, trying not to rock the boat. We had spoken a couple of times on the phone but mainly about household issues and coordination of travel and care for the dogs. We were both aware that something was changing in our relationship but both of us were afraid to articulate it, as if saying it aloud would make it a reality that we couldn't ignore.

We went into the bungalow, and I reheated some leftovers and poured us both a glass of wine. We watched a little TV together and then I retreated to the bathroom to get ready for bed.

Freshly showered, I stepped into the bedroom, wearing boxers and a T-shirt, my wet hair up in a towel. I saw Gabe sitting on the edge of the bed, his face in his hands.

"Gabe? Are you ok?"

"I just miss you, mi amor. I just miss you."

When he kissed me, I felt his hunger and his pain and I knew that my behavior, the changes that were happening in my life, were hurting him. But I also knew that the plans we had been making to travel, to make a difference in our community together and any desire to patch the growing holes in the fabric of our relationship would have to wait.

I didn't want to be the cause for his suffering. He did nothing to deserve it and the truth was, I still loved him very much. But I had more work to do, some additional repairs that needed to be made in my own heart and life.

But before I made my demands of space and time that I so desperately wanted, I surrendered and, from an empty well, gave my husband what he needed that night.

The next morning, Corrina and Judge arrived at the bungalow. The four of us spent the early afternoon together walking on the pier, strolling on the beach, and picking up seashells. Corrina and I left the guys at a bar while we wandered in and out of the shops looking at T-shirts and beach bags and every knick-knack a tourist could want to remind them of their wonderful vacation on Clearwater Beach. But it only reminded me that vacation wasn't the reason I was there. In only a few hours, I would say goodbye to my mother, toss her remains into the ocean breeze and let it carry her across the water, just like she wanted.

We grew tired of the shops, walked across to the waterside and found seats at a Cabana bar that sold fruity drinks with paper umbrellas in them.

"Wow, we have to be careful with these," Corrina warned as she sipped on her slushy rum punch. "We don't want to show up to your mother's service all liquored up."

"Yeah, I don't think that would go over well," I agreed.

"Are you and Gabe ok?" *Nosy, just like her grandmother.*

"I was wondering when you were going to ask that question. I'm surprised it took you this long, Corrina." I avoided eye contact with her and continue stirring my drink with the straw.

"Wanna talk about it?"

JUNE 2023

"There's really not much to say. We've taken a wrong turn somewhere and we're struggling to find our way back. It's more me than him. He's the same, loving person I've always known. I still love him, I just...I'm dealing with a lot right now and I need space."

"Do yourself a favor, Farrah."

"What's that?"

"While I understand your need for space, remember that not only have you been navigating through major life changes the past two years, but your mother just passed away. Don't make any major decisions right now. Don't risk causing irreparable damage to the beautiful life you have built with him because you're *dealing with a lot*. You may not like the hand that life has dealt you recently but don't blame Gabe for that. It isn't his fault. He's not the reason you feel unhappy right now."

"What you're saying makes perfect sense and yet I can't stop thinking about taking some time for myself. I've actually thought about staying here for a while longer after the service this afternoon."

"Really? So, Gabe goes home to Tennessee, and you stay here in Florida? For how long, Farrah?"

"I'm not sure. At least for a week or two. I thought it would be a lovely place to finish the work on my book. I could relax and think, take walks on the beach, watch the sunsets, and just breathe again without worrying about anyone else."

"Hmmm...I thought you hated the heat, here?"

"I do but there's something about this place that makes me feel closer to Mom. And I've been thinking that while I'm here, maybe Nora and her family would be open to spending some time with me. I would really like to get to know them better.

"Are you ever going to tell me about your relationship with your mom? I've always wondered why you never really talked about her."

"Yeah, I wanted to talk to you that day at Charlotte's when we got into that little argument, but it just didn't seem like the right time."

"We've been friends for over thirty years, Farrah, and have had countless conversations about my childhood and my birth mom and earth mom. Why haven't you ever wanted to talk about *your* mom?"

"I don't know. I had a good childhood, Corrina. I didn't go through stuff like you and Lovedy and Charlotte did. My parents took diligent care of me and never tried to physically hurt me. I was safe and secure and had a good education and exposure to activities that made my life as a child pretty well rounded. I didn't really feel like I had a right to complain. There are so many children out there that are abandoned, neglected, and abused. My stuff just feels trivial in comparison."

"Your stuff matters, Farrah. It obviously matters to you, and it definitely matters to me. *You* matter to me," she reached out and put her hand on top of mine. "Are you crying again?"

"My mother just died. I'm allowed, Corrina."

"True, I'll give you a pass on this one," as she handed me a napkin.

We sat at the Cabana bar, ordered another round of umbrella drinks, and I filled Corrina in on my relationship with my mother. The emotional distance, the criticism, the loneliness, how unhappy she was all of those years in Lexington with me and Daddy. And then I told her about Tarrah.

I cried a lot, mostly because the story I told Corrina was my story and it was so broken, never to be altered or repaired. It was locked into my past forever and though Mom and I started talking just before her illness, we never got down to the business of reconciliation. There would be no more opportunities to tell her how I felt, and how much I always needed her. I wouldn't be able to just sit and gab with her and get to know the woman I wished I would have known all of those years. Accepting that reality felt like an impossible thing to do.

JUNE 2023

We rented about a dozen chairs and a small table and found a spot on the beach away from the crowds. We put light refreshments and bottled waters on the table for people to enjoy as they arrived.

The sun was setting over the horizon and the water rushed forward, tickling our feet as each person took their turn sharing their memories of my mother, their sister, their friend. I tried my best to stay present, to take in all the wonderful things they said about her, to make their memories a part of my own story.

As Nora was speaking, I looked around at the thirty or so guests that came to pay their respects to the memory of my mother. And just to the edge of the crowd, off in the distance, I saw his salt and pepper hair being tossed around in the breeze. He was sitting down in the sand with his arms resting on his bent knees. He knew better than to join us, but still offered his support, quietly, and with the space that I needed.

After the sun disappeared, Nora passed around small notecards and pens to everyone. We each wrote a message to Mom, tucked it inside a paper lantern and sent it floating up to the sky. Gabe stood behind me, his arms wrapped around me as we both watched the thirty lanterns sailing above the ocean, dotting the horizon with twinkling lights and messages of love.

After the last light had disappeared into the night sky, everyone gathered around as I took the bag of ashes out of the cardboard box and poured the remains of my mother onto the sand. We watched in silence as the water rushed up to meet her and carry her back out to the sea.

It was a beautiful service, but unlike Clara's repast, I didn't invite everyone to come back to the bungalow for food and fellowship. It seemed right to end it there in that moment.

I met Nora's sister, Elisa, their children, and grandchildren and they invited me to attend a birthday party for Elisa the following week. I smiled and accepted the invite, realizing how good it felt to make plans with my mother's family...*my family*.

After everyone had left, Corrina and I took a walk and left Judge and Gabe to fold up the chairs and table and gather the remnants of my mother's goodbye party.

As Corrina and I walked along the water's edge, she grabbed my hand and held it.

"It was a beautiful service, Farrah. I think your mother would have loved it."

"I think she would have too. The only thing that was missing was karaoke, and I'm thinking maybe that is something we can continue to do each year on her birthday to remember her."

"I like that idea, Farrah. She would like it too. But there's one thing I really need to know…" Her voice trailed off as we continued to walk along the beach, holding hands, with the moonlight shining down, creating a corridor that reached from the horizon to the sand.

"What's that?"

"I want to know what you wrote in your message to her," she stopped walking and turned towards me, the moonlight casting a halo around her head.

"Corrina, I swear, you are the *nosiest person*. You're just like grandmother! That's confidential information and I'm not telling you," I started walking back towards the spot where we celebrated the life of my mother.

"Oh c'mon, Farrah," she shouted over the noise of the waves crashing at our feet.

"Fine, I'll tell you. But I don't want to ever hear about it again. Promise?"

"I promise." She caught up with me and walked by my side again.

"Well, you know I don't believe in the afterlife," I held my hands up to the sky.

"Yes, Farrah. I'm aware," she pointed her finger at me, "but you still wrote a message to her and sent it to the heavens in a floating lantern."

"Yes, indeed. I did that," I giggled at the irony of it all.

"So, what did it say?" She continued to press me.

JUNE 2023

"It said simply, '*I know you did the best you could. I'll always need you, Mom.*'" I stopped walking and turned my head towards the ocean. I couldn't believe she was gone, forever.

We took a couple more steps in silence and then I heard it. The sniffle gave her away.

"Corrina! Are *you* crying?" I looked at the face of my beautiful friend and saw a tear glistening on her cheek under the light of the pale moon.

"*Shut up*," she waved me away with her hand, "My *agnostic* friend sent off a paper lantern to the heavens with a message for her mother. What do you *expect* me to do?"

"Hey, did I not tell you to never mention that again? *You promised!*"

"That was before you mocked me for crying."

I decided to flip the question on her. "So, are you going to tell me what *you* wrote in the message to my mother?"

"No, that is *also* confidential information and I will not tell you," she stuck her nose up in the air.

"Oh, c'mon, Corrina...let it out. Tell me, you know you want to…"

"Fine. I told her what I knew to be true in my heart."

"And what is that, my friend?" I asked as I grabbed her hand again and we continued walking back.

"I told her that I would always take care of you."

I didn't say anything, I just squeezed her hand to say thank you for her love and for being the constant in my life.

"And then I told her not to worry and I promised her that you will be ok. *Everything will be ok.*"

ABOUT THE AUTHOR

Beka J. Perez enjoys a quiet life, living in the mountains of the Southeastern United States. She is an avid nature-lover and kayaker, a novice painter and photographer, but her real passion is spending quality time with her husband and two dogs.

www.ingramcontent.com/pod-product-compliance
Lightning Source LLC
Jackson TN
JSHW020754040425
81982JS00003B/7